EMERLAND
The Return of The Dark Lord

SIMAR BENZ

Publisher:
Australian Self Publishing Group, Pty. Ltd.
PO Box 159, Calwell, ACT 2905, Australia.
Phone: 61-(0) 2 6291-2904
http://australianselfpublishinggroup.com

A catalogue record for this book is available from the National Library of Australia

National Library of Australia Prepublication Data Service

Author: Simar Benz

Title: **EMERLAND – The Return of the Dark Lord**

ISBN: 978-1-923449-72-5 (print)
ISBN: 978-1-923449-73-2 (ePub2)

Contents

1. The Hollow Star

"From the roots of ruin shall a crown arise,
And in her blood, the war returns.
One must fall for all to stand."
                    — Whispers of the Graveyard Runes

In the First Dawn, ere yet the stars were set in their courses by the hands of the High Ones, and while the rivers still bore the laughter of the moon upon their silvered tides, there fell upon the world a darkness unforeseen—a great war between the Eldar and the Shadow that walked uncloaked. This was **the war of The Hollow Star**, waged in that hallowed realm where magic was not learned but born—a land of deep enchantment, where the very waters were woven with spellcraft, and the hills whispered in tongues long lost. And that land, fairest and most perilous of all under heaven, was called Emerland.

None now living recall the first stirrings of the Shadow, nor can any loremaster name the hour of its birth. Some say it was born of envy—a bitter spark in the heart of the void, where no light dared wander—a longing to unmake all that was bright and fair. Others claim the Shadow had ever been: lurking beyond the veil of time, unseen and waiting, a silent watcher bound by no name, no law, no mercy. When at last it moved, it fell not with noise, but with stillness—a great and smothering silence—across Emerland, that land of green-gold glades, skyborn crystal, and rivers that remembered the stars.

The Elves, eldest of the earthborn, named it only in whispers—*the Nameless Fear*—for it bore neither form nor voice, only the endless hunger of a thing that had never known the light. So terrible was its presence that even Death, the pale shepherd of souls, turned its gaze and passed it by.

Yet the Elves did not flee.

With blades forged in the fires of the morning stars and voices tuned to the deep harmonies of the world's making, they stood. Their songs summoned storm and flame; their courage sang louder than their sorrow.

Seasons turned. Forests burned and bloomed anew. Blood fell, and light returned.

And at last—though the cost was deep and bitter—they prevailed.

The skies rang with the music of Elven joy—high and clear as the stars themselves. Crystal torches bloomed like fireflowers along the soaring spires of Emerland, casting prismatic light upon marble streets and moonlit gardens. Laughter rolled down from the mountaintops, wild and golden, and songs wove through the night like silver threads embroidered into the fabric of darkness. Joy flowed freely—unbound, unburdened—for the Elves believed, with hearts tender from long sorrow, that peace had truly come.

They danced beneath the stars as if the wounds of the world had finally healed. Hope burned bright in every soul.

But peace, like starlight at dawn, is fleeting.

In the midst of their revelry, a hush fell—vast and absolute, deeper than silence itself. Time seemed to falter. And then, from the high vault of heaven, there descended a light unlike any ever known—not the gold of sun, nor the red of fire, but something older, purer, and unnameable. It drifted like falling grace, settling gently upon the earth where shadow once reigned.

And in that breathless stillness, a voice rang out—not heard by ear, but felt in the marrow of all things.

The voice of the Gods had returned.

"Thou hast prevailed in this strife," intoned the Gods, their voices vast as creation, mournful as the deep.

"But be not deceived. Evil dieth not—it sleepeth.

It slumbers in silence and watches the turning of the world,

gathering wisdom in the hollows of forgotten time."

Then the Elves, radiant and unbowed, raised their voices in defiance. Their song rang like steel drawn in moonlight, and even the winds stilled to listen.

"Then we shall rise anew!" they cried.

"If darkness dares return, we shall stand against it—

and we shall prevail, as we did before!"

But the Gods answered not with praise nor hope. No warmth stirred in their gaze. No blessing fell from the sky.

Only silence—deep, ancient, and terrible.

Their eyes, older than the stars, turned upon the Elves with a sorrow that shook the heavens.

And their words came like thunder wrapped in stillness:

"If the dark returns, that doom shall not be thine to meet.

And shouldst thou rise unbidden, thou shalt fall—and with thee, all the light thou hast kept alive."

A hush fell—not of peace, but of dread.

Cold as winter in the bones of the earth, it stole across the gathered hosts.

Even the starlight seemed to dim.

And the Elves, for the first time in all the ages of the world, were silent. It was a bitter stillness, but they did not argue. The will of the Gods had been spoken, and they bowed to it—not in shame, but in solemn acceptance of a fate no longer theirs to shape.

"Then who shall bear the burden of such doom, if not we?" asked the Elves, astonished, for none among the mortal or immortal kindred did they deem greater than themselves.

And then, from the farthest reaches of the heavens—beyond sun and storm, beyond time and telling—the answer came.

Not in flame, nor thunder, but in prophecy:

A whisper written in the bones of the world,

Foretelling one yet unborn,

Whose coming would turn the tide.

> **"When creeping shadow wakes once more, and ancient malice stirs anew,**
> **Then shall the Starborn rise—child of the fae, blood-bound to fair Emerland.**
> **If fire within be kindled bright, and steadfast hearts endure the storm,**
> **Then shall the light prevail, and hope not fade.**
> **But if the Starborn falters, if the flame is lost,**
> **Then night shall fall eternal,**
> **And Emerland's last hope be swallowed by the dark."**

Even the mightiest of the Eldar could not still the trembling within their immortal hearts. Though their hands bore the weight of victory, their spirits carried the shadow of what had been unleashed. In silence and sorrow, they laid the cursed dead to rest— not in hallowed glades or sunlit tombs, but in a hidden necropolis, veiled in grief and sealed with runes older than stone, older even than the first-born stars. The earth there turned black with mourning, and none dared speak the names of the fallen.

What fragments remained—splintered enchantments, blighted relics, bones steeped in ruin—were cast from the realm of grace into a forsaken quarter of the world. And there, the dark did not sleep. It clawed at root and rock, poisoned wind and water, until the land itself twisted in agony. Thus, was born the *Forbidden Forest*, a weeping wilderness where no birds sang, and the trees whispered madness.

At the forest's heart stood a monument to ruin—the *Fortress of Dread*. Empty of life, hollow of soul, it stood like a wound upon the world, its towers echoing with the cries of lost minds. No starlight touched its stones. No mercy lingered in its halls.

But the Elves, though weary, had not yet surrendered all to despair.

To shield what beauty remained, they gathered the last untouched embers of the world's first light—pure, untainted, eternal. With this radiance, they shaped a sacred lake: a mirror to the heavens, glowing softly in defiance of the dark. So clear were its waters that the stars themselves would halt in their paths to gaze into their own reflection. And when one looked upon its surface, the lake did not show the face— but the soul.

Thus was born the *Lake of Wonders*.

And beyond its luminous shores, shielded by light, watered by ancient grace, the land of *Emerland* bloomed—unspoiled, unbroken, unmarred.

And so, the ages turned.

The moons waned and waxed like breaths of the divine. The stars traced their eternal courses across the firmament, bearing silent witness to a world that remembered in whispers. The Elves remained—ageless, undying, guardians of memory—and the great war lived on only in their songs, sung beneath starlit boughs.

Yet once in a thousand winters, when even the wind dared not stir, and the ancient trees stood in breathless stillness, a hush would fall across the glades.

Then, in voices barely more than wind on water, they would speak the old words:

Of the child not yet born.

Of the flame yet to awaken.

Of the Starborn—

the last hope,

and the first light of the end.

2. The Stars Turning

In the fair and fading realm of **Emerland**, where woods whispered secrets and rivers sang like memory, time moved not in hours, but in songs. Beneath the ageless gaze of the immortal Elves, life unfolded like a dream unbroken—soft, golden, eternal.

Once, a prophecy had stirred beneath starlit skies, spoken in hush and firelight. But now, even that ancient promise had drifted into legend, like mist dissolving at dawn.

Then came a day stitched by fate.

Eight Elves rode out beneath the green cathedral of the forest, laughter rising with the wind. The trees swayed in rhythm, their leaves murmuring in welcome. The hunt had begun, drawn by the spectral roar of a lion not seen, only heard—calling them ever deeper, toward the edge of all they knew. Toward the Lake of Wonders.

But as the sun sank and shadows thickened, the roar faded into silence. They turned to leave—and there it stood.

A tomb, ancient and forgotten, emerged beside the crumbled bones of the **Fortress of Dread**, as though the world itself had exhaled a memory. It had always been there, and yet never seen.

A chill crept through the trees.

This was no resting place.

It was a warning.

They returned to the castle beneath moonlight, the silver gates yawning open as if they too remembered what the day had unearthed. In the stillness of the night, the Elven King bent over weathered tomes. The old pages trembled as he turned them, voices of prophecy whispering from the ink of centuries.

And there he saw it.

The **curse of concealment**, cast long ago over the cemetery where the Nameless Fear lay buried, had begun to fray. The veil was lifting. The lock was weakening.

And with a sorrow that stretched through time, the King understood:

The war to come would not be theirs to fight.

So it was that the Elves, keepers of light and lore, chose at last to leave the mortal world.

But before they vanished into the stars, one final task remained—

To crown a ruler.

Thus was set the quest in motion—a noble pilgrimage to seek a worthy heir, a lord to govern the Emerland and its folk, and to preserve the light, the very light of Emerland itself.

From the deep wells of magic, where time and memory entwine like roots beneath the earth, three names rose—carried on the sighing breath of fate itself: **Hematite**, and **Kanopus**.
Baba Yaba, the hunter.

Baba Yaba - A man Shaped by seasons, not merely counted but weathered—his face etched with lines that told of loss, of love, of battles both seen and unseen. His eyes, steady as the northern star, bore the quiet ache of a wife long passed into the realm of shadows. Yet in the golden hush of twilight, he found light still—in the untamed joy of his sister, **Baba Yaga**, whose laughter could chase away dusk itself.

At his side stood **Alexandrite**, Baba Yaba's Son, standing tall on the brink of manhood. Sixteen winters behind him, and countless paths ahead, the boy's spirit flickered with promise— bright, untamed, untested.

Beside him, too, walked **Morganite**—a boy Not of Baba Yaba's blood, but chosen all the same. Orphaned young, and marked by quiet strength, Morganite carried sorrow like a blade honed to resilience.

Far to the east, where the trees grew thick and kind and the rivers curled like ribbons of song, lived a gentler power.

The **White Witches**—keepers of healing and harmony—made their home in the soft folds of the Emerland woods. Among them rose **Hematite**, serene and steady, the matron of magic spun not for conquest, but for care.

She walked with the trees, listened to the soil, brewed spells with herbs and hope. Her sanctuary, a weathered coffeehouse nestled at the woodland's edge, smelled of roasted bark and morning rain—welcoming all who wandered weary through the forest paths.

Her hands healed, her words soothed, and beneath her calm lay an ancient knowing—quiet, enduring, and deep as the roots of Emerland itself.

Though her name rose with the others, Hematite bore no hunger for power. Her heart leaned not toward thrones, but toward the rhythm of leaves and the warmth of shared tea.

But not all magic whispered.

In the shadowed south, where the light of Emerland dimmed beneath darker boughs, stirred the third name: **Kanopus**.

A master of the twilight arts, he walked the borderlands between spirit and madness. His magic moved like smoke through a broken mirror—beautiful, fractured, dangerous.

The witches who followed him did so not out of fear, but reverence. He did not command them; he simply *was*.

Kanopus lived with his beloved wife **Zelda**, and nearby, her brother **McVellian**, whose deeds would soon stain the tapestry of fate.

For McVellian, reckless with forbidden spells, had broken the sacred edicts of the Elves—using dark enchantments to torment the innocent. Word of his cruelty spread like wildfire, from **Morganite** to **Alexandrite**, to **Baba Yaga**, and at last to **Baba Yaba**.

The Elves, swift in justice, cast McVellian into exile—banished beyond the known realm.

Zelda wept bitterly, blaming the hunters who bore the tale. Vengeance curled in her heart like smoke, but **Kanopus** remained silent. He spoke neither in defense nor denial.

His thoughts were his own, veiled and deep. He watched. He waited.

And the Elves, seeing in him the strength to master darkness without succumbing to it, marked him too as a candidate for the crown.

Kanopus did not speak of destiny. He did not dream aloud. But inside him, something turned like a wheel long buried—slow, inevitable.

He believed.

His time would come.

No spirit, no spell, not even the wind that whispered through the elder trees, could trace the path McVellian had taken—none, save one.

Her name was **Jabba Doom Gabbro**—a witch of cursed fate and haunted fortune, who dwelled in a weather-worn hut at the forest's edge, too close to the brooding maw of the Forbidden Forest. No other place would have her.

With her lived her silent son, his three wild-eyed daughters, and her peculiar brother **Toxico T**, who spent his days brewing and sipping toxic tea potions that filled the hut with fumes and folly. Even the Gabbro hut had its guardian: a stubborn rooster that strutted about with pomp, as if master of the yard, though the children only called him "the Cluck."

The Gabbro household was a knot of smoke and spells, strange herbs, stranger laughter, and even stranger children. Jabba, though spoken of in wary tones, survived by trade—bartering chores for coin, secrets for supper, or broom-work for scraps of forbidden magic.

She did odd tasks for **Obsidian Swish**, the shadow-weaver and quiet companion to Kanopus's court. In return, she gleaned whispers of ancient spells and half-forgotten truths—things better left unearthed.

One dusky evening, as the light spilled like blood over the Lake of Wonders, Jabba saw something move between the trees—gaunt, flickering, barely a man.

It was **McVellian**—alive, wandering the heart of the Forbidden.

The news reopened wounds long scarred.

Zelda said little. But her sorrow curled quiet and deep.

When the tale reached Kanopus, his voice held no tremor.

"Zelda's brother is but torment for torment," he said, waving his hand like brushing aside ash. "If the tale is true, he is the tormentor of the Forbidden, not its prey."

And so, Jabba, who had seen what no wind could find, returned to her hut beneath twisted trees—laughing softly to herself, a sound that echoed like prophecy half-remembered.

Yet the Elves, seeing Kanopus's restraint, his unshaken judgment, and his command of darkness without succumbing to it, deemed him worthy of the sacred crown. And Kanopus, long patient, felt the weight of fate begin to shift.

He did not smile, but deep within, he believed:
The time had come. His time.

The call to the castle came not by trumpet or scroll, but by the soft toll of silver chimes, rung only thrice in a millennium. The sky dimmed that day, not from cloud, but from anticipation.

Hematite arrived first—graceful, still, her gaze turned inward. She stood before the gathered Elves, her words soft but resolute.

"I have no thirst for the throne," she said. "Power is not my path."

With a quiet nod, her name was removed from the list.

Then came **Baba Yaba**, wrapped in the quiet dignity of years. At his side stood **Alexandrite**, his son, and **Morganite**, his ward—each walking with the humility of those who have known both loss and wonder. Baba Yaba's eyes held the weight of memory, but his step did not falter.

And at last came **Kanopus**, solemn as nightfall. Shadows gathered at his back like loyal hounds, and beside him, **Zelda**, cloaked in silence. She said nothing. She barely did, and only to spit fire.

In the shadows beyond the torchlit hall, half-hidden beneath her threadbare shawl, stood Jabba Doom Gabbro. Tears glistened in the hollows of her cheeks—not from grief alone, but from a longing too strange to name. She wept for her doom, for a crown she knew was never meant for her brow. And then—she laughed. A brittle, breathless laugh that rose and fell like a cracked bell, startling even herself. The absurdity of hope—how it still clung to her, ragged and cruel—was a jest too cruel not to laugh at.

Across the hall, in the space reserved for guests of shadowed esteem, stood Obsidian Swish. Cloaked in onyx robes that shimmered like oil on midnight water, she did not weep. She watched. She waited. Her gaze did not seek the crown, but what lay beyond it—unfettered power, the release of darkness bound too long. She did not dream of glory. She dreamed of freedom—freedom for shadow, for ruin, for the old doom that once whispered beneath the roots of the world.

Jabba wept for what might never be.

Obsidian Swish burned for what must.

The Hall of Choosing waited in reverent hush, lit by moon-fire and memory. At its heart stood the **Elven King**, ageless and tall, his silver robes trailing like mist.

In his hands, upon a velvet cloth woven from starlight, rested the **Crown of Emerland**.

He looked upon the two contenders with the gravity of centuries. Then, slowly, he lifted the crown—its golden arcs inscribed with the runes of the first tongue, its centerstone flickering with a light not born of flame.

He stepped first toward **Kanopus**.

The Elven King held the crown above him, but paused. The magic within the relic stirred—faint, resistant. The air itself grew colder.

Kanopus did not blink.

Then the King turned.

He moved toward **Baba Yaba**, and this time the crown seemed to warm in his hands, as if recognizing something ancient, kindred. Slowly, with great care, he placed the crown upon Baba Yaba's brow.

The moment it touched him, the hall filled with quiet radiance—no flare, no thunder. Just a soft gleam, like stars breathing. The crown had accepted him. And the realm had found its guardian.

In that stillness, **Baba Yaba became king**—not of command, but of keeping. A bearer of sorrow and wisdom, crowned by grace, not might.

Around him, treasures from the old world shimmered to life—maps drawn in forgotten ink, jewels that hummed with memory, winds from places no foot had touched. Gifts not of conquest, but of understanding.

And in the hush that followed, Kanopus stood still.

His face betrayed nothing—serene, composed, carved in shadow and dusk. But behind his eyes stirred something wordless.

Not jealousy.

Not regret.

But promise—coiled and patient, like a serpent beneath stone.

He bowed when the moment called for grace. He smiled when courtesy required it.

But deep within him, a fire waited.

Because crowns are worn…

Until they are not.

Across the hall, Zelda watched him—watched as his silence rippled with pain only she could name.

She had slept for so long—more myth than woman, her fire banked in frost.

Yet now, the ache in Kanopus's eyes struck a chord in her marrow, a truth long whispered by her brother McVellian had spoken in veiled riddles and half-dreams.

"Something ancient sleeps beneath the bones of the world," he had once whispered. "And someone must wake what dreams too long."

Zelda had long awaited the awakening.

But she could not be the first to act—someone else had to bear the weight.

Her brother, McVellian, had dared.

He had reached into forbidden shadows, wielded spells the Elves had long since banished.

And for that, he was exiled—not because he failed, but because he crossed a line no soul was meant to.

That exile had carved hollows in Zelda's heart, stolen her peace, and left her in a waking sleep.

Watching Kanopus—so still, yet aching behind eyes that once held stars—Zelda felt the ice within her crack.

The silence shattered.

The fire returned.

And in its light, she made her choice:

She would finish what her brother began.

From the far edge of the hall, Jabba Doom Gabbro slipped away—unnoticed, as always.

The crowd feared her doom, and so none dared speak. But Jabba did not walk alone.

Beside her waddled a bedraggled rooster, feathers puffed and eyes fierce—her only friend in a world too wary for her kind.

He had no name once, only a shrill cluck and an attitude.

Until one moon-drenched morning, she understood him.

And he, her.

"Jabba the Cluck," she had named him with a wheeze of laughter.

And as they vanished into the forest's edge, she whispered to him softly—not sorrow, but plans. Somewhere beyond the trees, the wind listened

Obsidian Swish remained behind.

She said nothing.

Her gaze was fixed on Kanopus—not with affection, but calculation.

Would he move? Would he rise?

He gave no sign. He never did.

He believed in stillness before the storm.

But Obsidian burned.

To her, it was a bitter jest that hunters—those without magic—now sat atop thrones while she, a weaver of shadow, bowed.

She hated them.

And she did not forget.

McVellian had failed. He had tried and been cast down.

"She would not fail. She would perfect what he had begun. And when she struck, the world would know the sound of fire reclaiming its name."

There among the gathered hosts stood the well-wishers of the Emerland Crown—beings born of sky, soil, flame, and root. **Bulwark**, the half-bird, half-man guardian, shimmered beside his two sons, whose wings bore the same spell of flesh and feather. And over them towered **Rock the Hawk,** high sovereign of the boundless winds.

With wings vast as legends and feathers glinting like forged bronze, he circled once above the throne.

"To you, Baba Yaba," he cried, voice like thunder made of wind, "I give my winged blessing. May your reign rise higher than storm."

Then, with a cry that split the sky, he soared aloft—upward through cloud and light—returning to his roost upon the tallest tree in the world, where the heavens bowed to his watch.

So was the crown passed—not through conquest, but through grace. The air held its breath. A hush, vast and weightless, settled over the land.

But beneath that silence, destiny stirred.

For the Elves had yet one final truth to speak—one last thread to weave before vanishing into the starlight forever.

They came forward then, cloaked in sorrow and solemn joy, their silver eyes bearing the weight of uncounted years. The moment was neither farewell nor farewell's sorrow, but a gift. Not of blade nor banner, but of prophecy—woven from memory, starlight, and the marrow of fate.

From the heart of the gathering, the Elven King stepped forth—tall and ageless, crowned in moonlight and silence. His presence drew stillness like gravity; even the wind bent to listen.

And when he spoke, his voice moved through the air like wind through hollow stone, echoing deep into the bones of those who stood before him.

"Take heed, Baba Yaba," he said, his gaze fixed not only on the man, but on the ages that would follow him. "The throne you claim will not yield to your touch without trial. It demands not just lineage, but soul."

He raised his hand, and for a moment, the wind stilled—as if the world itself listened.

"The soul of the future ruler is more than breath and blood— it is the flame that binds Emerland's destiny. Should an enemy grasp it—through spell, curse, or deceit—the heir becomes a hollow vessel. A breathing shadow. A prince in name, but bound in chains of sorrow and silent torment."

The Elves behind him bowed their heads. The trees seemed to do the same.

"You have but eight days," the Elven King continued, "to reclaim the stolen soul, should such fate come to pass. On the ninth, it will belong wholly to the captor—twisted to their will, fed by their malice. And with it, the crown. And with the crown... dominion over all."

He stepped back, his cloak sweeping across the marble like falling dusk.

"Guard the soul well, Baba Yaba. For it is not just the child who will suffer if it is lost. It is Emerland."

Then, the Elven King raised his hand, and the air seemed to hush.

"I leave behind two visions—threads of fate destined for a child not yet risen. Star-touched, this child shall carry the burden of change. "These are not dreams," the Elven King said, his voice like wind through ancient boughs. "They are **living threads of fate**, spun from the loom of what may yet be. The chosen one will not merely see them—they will *step into them*, as one steps into rain or fire. In that place, they will live as if it were real. They will bleed. They will fear. They may love. And yet, when they return, the memory may drift like mist—half-forgotten, half-felt, echoing only in the soul."

"Two visions. One life. Three chances in all," said the Elven King, his voice low with gravity.

"But heed this well—should the child falter within a vision, should the hourglass remain unturned, that life will be lost. Their thread will unravel, severed from the tapestry of the world."

He paused, the fire of ancient stars flickering in his eyes.

"Even the fireborn," he murmured, "must not walk alone... nor forget what came before."

Baba Yaba bowed—deep, solemn, as one receiving a burden too sacred for words. Yet behind his calm, a flicker of unease stirred. He sensed truths left unspoken, veiled beneath the Elves' parting gaze like secrets lost in moonlit mist.

Still, he stood tall. Seasoned by years of loss and wonder, tempered by the long hunt of life. He trusted in his son Alexandrite's quiet strength, in the goodness that had guarded Emerland since the world was young. And he believed—heart and soul—that no storm could rise his kin could not weather.

The Elven King, who once bore prophecy like a blade across his soul, looked not as ruler now, but as brother. In silence, he removed from his neck the **Pentacle**—a relic born before time had breath, when the first war shattered the sky and stars wept silver fire.

Legends spoke of its power: that when wielded by one chosen by fate—not the strongest, but the **truest**—it could change the tide of destiny itself. Its fivefold arms bore the markings of Gods now lost, and within its heart shimmered a light that had never gone out—a flame untouched by shadow.

Many had held it. Few had ever **wielded** it.

For the Pentacle does not burn for the bold. It burns for the steadfast.

With reverent hands, the King placed it into **Alexandrite's** waiting palms. The young man stood still—not proven, not yet tested—but steady. A hush fell over all gathered, like the breath before a storm.

The **crown** had chosen **Baba Yaba**.

But the **Pentacle** had chosen **another**.

And as the light of the Elves began to fade, the King offered no command—only a farewell wrapped in prophecy.

A final vow.

A quiet warning.

And as the stars turned, a new thread spun—flame-bound and waiting.

3. The Unborn Flame

In the fullness of years, Alexandrite grew into a man both noble and just—brave of heart, measured in mind, beloved by the people. When his sixteenth winter passed, Baba Yaba and Baba Yaga deemed the time ripe to seek for him a bride—a princess who would one day ascend beside him as queen. So began their quest, spanning the wide lands of Emerland and beyond, from one kingdom to the next. And yet, Alexandrite turned away from every hand offered. Not from cruelty nor pride, but as though some unseen veil had fallen over his soul, forbidding love. His refusals, gentle though they were, troubled Baba Yaga deeply. For it was held a dark omen when an heir of light found no heart to match his own.

With the weight of unspoken dread upon her brow, Baba Yaga climbed the ancient stair to the tower where the oldest tomes lay, their bindings worn by time and breath. There she lit a single flame, the kindling of memory, and drew forth a book bound in silver leaves. With trembling hands she opened it, and the pages turned as if blown by a breath not her own.

She uncovered no clear prophecy, but found instead warnings—cryptic and veiled—of a crown that tests the soul of its bearer, a throne that devours the weak-willed, and a fire that shall burn only for those born of both lineage and loss. The words stirred something within her, a sense of unraveling threads, yet the pattern remained just beyond her grasp.

In the shadowed hours of Twilight, Baba Yaga opened up to Baba Yaba and Baba Yaba confided his deep anxieties unto Kanopus, whom he still named his steadfast friend. And Kanopus, who had remained ever at the hunter's side since the crowning, listened well—his quiet counsel masking a deeper intent. For in friendship, he had learned much, and in loyalty, he had glimpsed the hunter's heart—not to cherish it, but to know where it might one day break.

"I fear something stirs," Baba Yaba admitted as they stood upon the high balcony, watching the pale stars gather in the sky. "Alexandrite refuses them all. It is not pride, nor whim. I have hunted long enough to know the scent of foreboding. His heart is bound to something yet unseen."

Kanopus, clad in a robe the color of storm clouds, kept his gaze fixed on the horizon. "Then perhaps fate has other designs," he murmured.

"I have dreamed of thrones crumbling," Baba Yaba continued, his voice hoarse with worry. "And of fires that burn too brightly, consuming all."

Kanopus inclined his head. "Then perhaps, old friend, you are right to worry. But dreams are only smoke, and not yet fire."

Yet within Kanopus's breast, something coiled—a tight and terrible thought that the crown might yet pass to another if he did not act. He left the balcony in silence, but his mind churned. That silence wasn't peace—it was the hush before a storm still gathering.

When he relayed the tidings to his wife, Zelda, she did not turn from the window.

She stood where moonlight stitched silver through her hair, her silence deeper than shadow.

Only after a long moment did she speak—softly, like a charm spoken through sleep:

"So the counsel my brother McVellian whispered to me in the dark... was not without truth."

Kanopus did not answer. He had heard enough shadows in his time to know when one should be left alone.

He believed—perhaps foolishly—that Zelda's grief had driven her to chase ghosts, to seek her fallen brother through the haunted margins of memory.

But he did not know.

She was not seeking McVellian.

She was seeking **what he sought.**

The curse beneath the world. The one spoken of only in the oldest tongues, in spells that stung the air when uttered. The one that did not sleep—it waited.

Since the crowning of the hunter, something had unraveled in Zelda.

Her dreams grew long and labyrinthine, her gaze turned inward, as though she listened to a language that no longer belonged to mortals.

She wandered the edge of forbidden texts, breathed the air of ruined altars, and spoke aloud in tongues not heard since the world was young.

But she told Kanopus nothing.

He, bound by laws older than oaths, would never consent to awaken the One who sleeps.

The Lord of the Forbidden Realms.

The Shadow That Devours.

The Nameless Fear.

His name was never spoken—because it was not meant to be known.

Kanopus believed in time. In fate. In the turning of the stars.

He believed the Dark One would rise **only** when the hour was ripe.

But Zelda—

She no longer believed in waiting.

She no longer believed in mercy.

To her, the time was not "someday."

It was now.

Or never.

Yet somewhere beneath her resolve, a flicker—a memory of warmth, of simpler days—tried to rise. But she buried it.

And somewhere in the deep folds of the night, something ancient stirred— drawn not by ritual, but by **will.**

That eve, Zelda stepped through the moonlit archway at the edge of their lands,

her cloak trailing behind like a Wraith's sigh.

She crossed the threshold into the Forbidden Forest—not with fear, but with resolve as ancient as the stars.

The trees did not resist her.

Whether they welcomed her, or simply consumed her, none could say.

No birds stirred.

No wind breathed.

Only silence.

And her.

In the days that followed, tales took root like vines in shadowed corners.

Jabba Doom Gabbro—witch of strange doom and stranger wit—claimed to have seen her.

"She moved like sorrow dreaming," Jabba muttered through tooth and tea,

"Her hands already weaving spells the forest remembered…"

Some said it was grief.

Others, fate.

But all who heard the tale agreed:

Zelda had crossed into something old,
and the forest would never be the same.

And Kanopus—oh, Kanopus—retreated behind the iron doors of his cold, high citadel.

None saw him smile. None heard him weep. The grief he bore for Zelda was the same he once carried for McVellian— silent, proud, and sealed behind stone.

But silence speaks to those who listen. In its stillness, Obsidian Swish stirred.

Once a sorceress cloaked in civility, she now felt the veil lifting—

a hush before the storm, a crack in the order of things.

She had heard the whispers:

that Zelda sought to wake something whose slumber had once shaken the stars—

a being whose dreams disturbed even the Elves into flight.

She did not know its name, but she would learn it—and wield it, whatever the cost.

And that was enough.

With Kanopus cloistered, the air itself seemed to loosen—
as if the ancient laws of light, so long unchallenged, had begun
to bend.

The fire in her chest—the fire that once flickered—now roared.
Hatred for hunters.

A hunger for power.

A promise of darkness, unbound.

She stood in her chamber of shadow and spell-smoke,
the silence thick with memory and menace.

"First the Elves denied us," she whispered,
"and now even the hunter-king bows to light."

She raised her hand to the mirror, saw not her face, but the
shape of what might be.

Her voice dropped lower, colder, truer.

"So be it."

By candle's final flicker, she read from an ancient tome buried
beneath a cairn of dust and chain. It fell open of its own will.
She expected words, but instead came visions—flickers of the
ancient war—The Hollow Star, the Elves rejoicing beneath the
silver boughs.

Then, silence.

And then, voices—neither from the book nor from the room—
but from beyond.

*"When shadows lengthen and ancient malice awakens anew,
the Starborn shall arise—scion of the fae, bound in blood to fair
Emerland.*

*If the fire within kindles and steadfast hearts endure, then
may light still triumph.*

But should the Starborn stumble, and their soul be lost...

*Then within eight days, the darkness shall devour all, and
Emerland's final hope be swallowed by night."*

Obsidian Swish froze. Her heart thundered like hooves on hollow ground. Somewhere far away, a window shattered. A dog wailed. The fire died.

Her lips curled. "So... they will bring forth a savior?"

She needed no more.

With the flick of her wrist and a breath like ash, Obsidian Swish began to chant. Her eyes rolled back. Her voice became wind, her shadow long as death. Beneath a blood moon, she carved sigils into the earth. And when her spell was complete, the veil between the realms closed—not with a slam, but a whisper that sealed the fate of the fae.

No fair folk could now pass into Emerland. The forest fell silent. Their laughter vanished. Their songs, once bright in the wind, were gone. What followed was a stillness like none had known—as if the soul of the woods had been stilled.

And in the depths of Emerland Palace, Baba Yaga awoke gasping—the same words burning on her tongue. She spoke them aloud once, then again, until she shivered. Everything she had read now became clear.

"The Starborn..." she whispered, "is not yet born. That is why Alexandrite turns from love. His heart seeks one not yet among mortals... but of faerie blood."

In that hour, the fate of Emerland began to shift.

With dawn's first breath, Baba Yaga told Baba Yaba and Alexandrite all that had been revealed. A faint ember of hope stirred in the old king's chest—for the Elves had spoken of such trials. Still, he knew the path forward would be perilous.

But even as they spoke, Morganite, guardian of the Emerland Woods, burst into their chambers, eyes wide with dread.

"No birds sing," he said. "No fairies laugh. No music echoes from the groves. The gates to their realm are closed. A spell lies heavy upon the trees. I fear... we are sealed from them."
Baba Yaga's lips tightened. "The darkness stirs already."

They knew: if fairies were sealed away, no Starborn could be born. The fate of Emerland hung by a thread. Without delay, they crowned Alexandrite as King, hoping still that a way would open, that the fairies might return. And as they crowned him, a celebration unfurled.

All of Emerland shimmered in joy. Lanterns strung across tree-tops swayed like stars. Fireworks cascaded in blue and gold. Children danced in the courtyards. Song echoed from mountaintop to riverbend. It was as though the realm tried to hold back the rising dark with laughter.
But no sooner had the last toast been raised then Death arrived.
She came not in shadow, but in silence—a stillness so pure that even joy seemed to hush. Her form wavered like heat above a flame, yet all saw her, all felt her. Where she passed, warmth fled the stone, and even candlelight bent low in mourning.

A hush fell over the great hall, as though even the stones held their breath.

Then, from the farthest shadow, **she stepped forth**—a figure cloaked not in darkness, but in absence. **Death.**

"I come for Baba Yaba," she said, her voice like falling ash, dry and final, the echo of a funeral bell no one had rung.

But the **Immortal Throne** stirred.

Its ancient spells ignited like embers under snow, glowing with the light of ages past. The enchantments woven by Elven hands long gone flared around Baba Yaba—lines of gold across the air. **Death's hand trembled. Her reach, for once, halted.**

Baba Yaba rose. Not swiftly, not with fury, but with the slow, deliberate strength of earth and time. His staff met the floor with a sound like thunder wrapped in resolve.

"There is no place for Death beneath this roof," he said, voice low but unyielding. "Not while light endures."

But in his heart, a shadow coiled. He knew. **Death did not come unbidden.** She had been summoned—drawn by a darkness bold enough to breach the wards of Emerland. Something ancient. Something rising.

Still, for now, **he was strong enough**—strong enough to resist her. And resist her he did.

Death's expression did not change, but her eyes narrowed—twin abysses without end, where stars went to die.

"Then I shall take all," she whispered. "You. Your son. If not today, then tomorrow. If not tomorrow, then soon enough. One by one... until the throne is dust."

And with that, she turned.

She vanished not with rage, but with stillness.

But behind her stillness was **a mind deep and cruel**, and already, it had begun to spin.

Far across Emerland, where the mists never lifted and the trees leaned as if listening, Death walked—her steps soundless, her presence a shiver in the marrow of the land.

She came upon a hut, crooked and sagging into the fog, its chimney coughing smoke like a sigh too tired to rise.

Inside sat **Jabba Doom Gabbro**, hunched and muttering her woes to a rooster that blinked in solemn understanding.

At the door, her silent son stared at nothing, and behind him, his three wild-eyed daughters—**the Doom Sisters**—drew shapes in the dirt with sticks and shards of bone.

At the hearth, **Toxico T**, brother of Jabba, stirred a bubbling pot of foul tea that smelled of regret and ruin.

Death lingered at the threshold.

She watched.

She smiled.

In Jabba's curse, she saw a door—cracked and creaking, waiting to be opened. She did not knock. Not yet. But she marked the place.

She turned from the hut and drifted onward, a shadow through fog.

Across the stones of the **cursed graveyard**, she passed, brushing her hand along forgotten tombs. At one—carved with symbols no tongue dared name—she paused.

With a single finger, she **lifted the lid** and left it ajar.

Then she walked the **battlements of the Fortress of Dread**, long abandoned by light.

And there, one by one, she **opened the forbidden gates**—not with force, but with memory. The walls groaned in reply, ancient iron waking from its long slumber.

Last, she came to the **shadowed heart of the forest**, a place where even wind had forgotten how to breathe.

She stepped into its breathless dark.

The trees whispered.

The ground trembled.

And **deep beneath the world**, wrapped in roots and ruin, **something ancient... something buried... opened its eyes.**

And with its waking—

the world forgot how to sleep.

4. Seeds of Darkness

As Death lifted the lid of the ancient grave, far across Emerland, the crown upon Alexandrite's head slipped—clattered to the marble floor of the great hall as if struck by an invisible blow. He had been King but a single day. Now he stood frozen, the weight of a kingdom suddenly hollow in his hands. Baba Yaba and Baba Yaga masked their dread behind solemn grace, while Morganite stepped forth, voice low and urgent.

"There may still be hope," he said. "A faerie hidden in the deep woods. One who might yet turn the tide."

But Alexandrite said nothing.

He turned from them all, retreated into his chamber, and closed the door.

There, in the hush that followed, a book tumbled from the high shelf. Its cover bore a single title etched in fading gold: *The King Before Darkness.*

He picked it up—though not by will, but by something older, something deeper, that moved his hand.

The pages opened. The tale spoke of a forgotten king who had stood alone against the shadow. He died fighting it. His only daughter was taken—not slain, not lost, but *unmade*—joined to the darkness until even her name faded from memory. His kingdom was devoured by the void. Nothing remained.

Alexandrite closed the book.

He could read no more.

In that moment, he made a silent vow—not of cowardice, but of unbearable sorrow.

He would never father a child.

Even if that child might be the Starborn.

For the thought of losing such a soul—of seeing it consumed by the very darkness he was meant to resist—was more haunting than death itself. He did not know the ancient king. But as he stood beneath the same stars, he *felt* him.

And the pain was his own.

At the same hour the crown clattered to stone and fate wavered in the throne room, Obsidian Swish awoke. Not to morning's hush, but to the croaking din of a thousand crows—perched on her roof, her trees, her windowsills, the very bones of the yard. Black wings stirred the mist. Feathers fluttered like ashes. But she was not afraid. She smiled.

She knew what the birds heralded.

The darkness she had sought through smoke and shadow had found her.

She rose without haste, every motion a dance with dread made welcome. And as she opened the door, it did not creak— it exhaled, like something old returning home. There, lying at her threshold, was a letter—hurled like a curse. No messenger. No breath. Only a scroll sealed in black wax, cracked like dried blood, bearing the sigil none dared summon: the mark of Death.

She knelt.

Unfurled it.

The script inside was inkless, as though etched in frost or memory:

"The seals weaken. The time nears.

The Starborn must never rise."

Obsidian's breath caught, sharp and sweet. This was no whisper of fate—it was the thunder before the storm. A summons from the abyss. A gift. Her smile bloomed like a thorned flower—one not seen since the Elves exiled her blood from the silver glades of wonder.

If the Starborn could be stopped...

The Lord of the Forbidden Realms could rise.

And she—she would be at his side.

At dawn's edge, with the scent of the message still clinging to her hands, Obsidian Swish found Kanopus in the upper halls, veiled in silence since Zelda's vanishing. She came not as ally, nor foe—but as a herald cloaked in fire and breathless promise.

"Do you feel it?" she asked, her voice like coiled smoke, curling in the still air.

"The world turns. But not for you—unless you seize it."

Kanopus did not speak. He looked not at her, but through her—into the waiting dark. He had once believed in fate. In the turning stars. But now... now the hour ripened, and the summons had come.

And he—
He would answer.

That same night, at an hour no star dared shine, Jabba Doom Gabbro's son awoke—gasping from a dream too dark to speak. Sweat clung to his brow like a second skin. And there—on the crooked door—something glittered.

He rose.

Drew the latch.

And found it: a thick, glimmering book bound in snakeskin, its cover breathing slow as sleep, its eyes—yes, eyes—still blinking. The boy snatched it, his hands trembling, his gaze already devouring the promise hidden in its folds.

Jabba stirred, sensing the shift.

She followed—but her son said nothing. He merely sat, and opened the book.

Or perhaps, the book opened him.

Words spilled like venom. Whispers coiled in the air. Whether he read, or listened, or dreamed—none could say.

Jabba turned back toward the door, and there upon the threshold she saw something far worse than a cursed tome.

A trinket.

Small, cruel, impossibly old.

Carved not from bone alone, but from sorrow itself—**the Deathly Chattel.**

A relic whispered of in shadow, feared even by witches. Not made in this world. Not meant to be found. It held but one purpose: to pierce time. Not to glimpse the past—but to walk through it. To enter what once was... and what should have remained forgotten.

Jabba's breath hitched.

She had heard of it, in tales spun by dying tongues. A thing of Death. A tool of endings. That it should appear here—in her hut—was no accident. No mercy. A message.

She knelt, hesitant fingers brushing the carved edge.

"What fool would want to return to sorrow?" she whispered.

From behind, a voice replied:

"Deathly Chattel is the place where lives everyone's past."

It was the rooster—**Jabba the Cluck**—perched solemnly on the rafters, blinking with ancient knowing.

But Jabba had no answer for him.

Her worry for her son pulled her back. She crept toward his door. Knocked once.

No reply.

She knocked again.

Inside, the boy sat unmoving, the book wide open in his lap. Letters swam across the pages like eels beneath water. Spells uncoiled. Promises darker than midnight curved into his heart.

Night after night, he read.

Or it read him.

The air in his room turned cold, brittle. His pupils deepened into wells. He no longer blinked.

And then—on the seventh morning—he closed the book. Rose. And without a word, stepped into the forest. Into the dark.

Behind him came his daughters —the Doom Sisters—barefoot, silent, their eyes lit not with play but purpose. The wind did not stir their hair. The ground made no sound beneath their feet.

When Jabba awoke, the hut was too quiet.

She looked once.

Then again.

And fell to her knees.

Her wail split the dawn like thunder on a clear sky.

"He chases ghosts," she wept. **"But ghosts know how to find the living."**

No spell could bring them back.

No bird dared answer.

That very day, hollow-eyed and shaking, Jabba murmured to the trees that she had seen Kanopus ride by, cloaked in shadows atop his monstrous boar.

"The forest did not resist him," she said. **"It bowed."**

Upon the eve of the morrow, a hush descended upon Emerland—a silence so complete it rang like a bell struck in reverse. It fell, heavy as grief, thick as smoke, curling through the trees and halls alike. No owl stirred. No breeze dared whisper. Even the waters of the Lake of Wonders, ever rippling with secret magic, lay flat as glass—still, watching, waiting.

The stars blinked once.

Then vanished behind a shroud of cloud, as if the sky itself refused to bear witness to what would come.

That same evening, wrapped in twilight's dying breath, Obsidian Swish departed Emerland. She did not flee, nor sneak—but passed through the veils openly, her steps sure, her shadow long. She left the lands of light behind and walked the Forbidden Path, vanishing into the breathless dark.

And there, in a place forgotten by time and feared by the living, they gathered.

Those who had vanished into darkness.

Those whose names were no longer spoken.

They met beneath the crooked boughs of the **Cursed Cemetery**, where no flower had bloomed in a thousand years, and the soil reeked of ash and bone. The wind avoided this place. The trees leaned away.

As the conspirators stepped across the cracked stones, the skies above Emerland began to churn—slow at first, then wild. Clouds spiraled like torn veils. Lightning flashed, but no thunder followed.

The world was shifting.

Something buried had opened its eyes...

And the earth would never be still again.

First came the wind—wild, shrieking, clawing through the trees like a thousand desperate hands. Then came the **storm**, a deluge so fierce it seemed the heavens had been torn open by wrath itself. The rivers swelled. The forest groaned. The soil trembled as if resisting what was about to awaken.

Obsidian Swish stood at the center of the old graveyard, her cloak snapping like a banner of ruin in the wind. Around her stood Kanopus, McVellian - who waited for this day since vanished from Emerland, Jabba's Son, and the three cursed daughters, their eyes wide as glass and twice as hollow.

Above them, thunder cracked like a whip across the sky. Lightning clawed down the hills and set fire to trees that did not burn. A **red moon** bled through the cloudbanks, staining the rain like spilled blood.

Emerland was watching. And weeping. And warning.

Obsidian lifted her arms.

"When shadows creep once more," she shouted above the storm, her voice like flint striking steel,

"and ancient malice stirs anew,

The Starborn shall rise—scion of the fae, bound by blood to fair Emerland.

If the fire within kindles and steadfast hearts endure,

Then light may yet prevail.

But should the Starborn falter, and their soul be lost...

Then within eight days, the darkness shall devour all,

And Emerland's final hope be swallowed by night."

As she spoke, **the ground cracked open** beneath their feet— not wide, but deep. From it wafted the stench of things that should never breathe. The wind turned warm, then cold, then hot again, and the storm above seemed to rage in rhythm with her words.

Kanopus looked skyward, and his jaw clenched.

"We tempt ruin," he said.

"We summon justice," Obsidian replied. "The justice denied to us when the Elves banished our blood."

"But the rite," said McVellian, his voice uneasy, "requires three offerings: a willing soul, flesh and blood of the cursed, and the dagger upon which the Crown once rested…"

Obsidian narrowed her eyes. "The dagger is beyond my reach."

She turned to Kanopus.

"You were never meant to kneel before Alexandrite. The throne calls to you now."

Kanopus said nothing. But the wind seemed to twist around him like a crown. He turned and vanished into the rain.

The moment Kanopus departed, a sudden hush fell across the cemetery—as if even the storm had paused to see what he would do.

But elsewhere, the skies howled louder.

He rode like a curse loosed from its seal, astride his monstrous boar, hooves striking sparks against the sodden earth. The Castle of Emerland rose in the distance, its ancient towers silhouetted against a sky ablaze with lightning. It did not welcome him.

The gates stood shut, but he did not stop.

With a scream of rage and a burst of dark magic long denied its name, **he shattered the iron bars**, sending molten fragments raining across the courtyard. The trees of the Emerald Woods bent away from him. Statues cracked. Windows burst. The very walls **groaned**, as if sensing what had come to claim what was never his.

Within the castle, the dagger still stood—lodged deep within the stone pedestal beneath the Crown. It pulsed faintly, not with light, but with memory.

Kanopus approached it. His steps faltered. The storm outside thundered.

"You do not belong here," whispered a voice in the wind.

"I do," he growled, and seized the hilt.

It burned him. His veins lit like molten wire beneath his skin. His eyes rolled white. The dagger refused him. It fought back—not with steel, but with sorrow. Every lie he had spoken, every envy hidden, every love betrayed pressed down upon his soul like iron chains.

But Kanopus would not let go.

He screamed—not in pain, but in defiance—and summoned the bitter flame that had long smoldered beneath his silence. He remembered Zelda's loss. He remembered every moment Baba Yaba - a hunter sat above him on the throne. He remembered Obsidian's words.

With one final wrench, he tore the dagger free. The dagger was, "Forged to seal the fate of kings, the dagger was not meant for hands like his."

The moment the blade rose, **the Castle shook**. In the catacombs below, the dead stirred. **A bell rang where there had never been one.** Far across the land, a stag fell dead for no reason at all.

Emerland felt it.

And so did the Nameless Fear.

Kanopus staggered, the dagger clutched in trembling hands. He was not whole. Something had left him in that moment—a piece of soul, a spark of breath, or perhaps something even deeper.

His boar waited at the gate. Together, they vanished into the rain. (All within the palace moved as if under a dark enchantment; their eyes unseeing, their souls stilled—none beheld the theft, nor the doom that followed, until knowing came too late.)

At the cursed cemetery, Obsidian Swish stood at the broken tomb unearthed by Death itself.

Kanopus returned—silent, dripping, hollow-eyed. He gave Obisdian Swish the dagger.

And so the rite began.

She drew the blade across his chest. Blood spilled, black in the lightning light. She chanted the old words, older than trees, older than moonlight.

The grave opened. Kanopus fell into it.

And something **rose**.

First a hand. Then a face—familiar, yet ruined. Kanopus's face, but twisted. His eyes were not his own. His voice was thunder swallowed in stone.

"I... am not Kanopus," it said. "I am the storm unborn. I am what your Gods buried. I am..."

A pause. Then a smile that cracked the sky.

But it was not Kanopus who smiled.

It was something older. Something buried.

From the open tomb rose not a man, but a whisper in flesh. The Nameless Fear had awakened—but its form was frail, its essence still bound in the roots of the world. It had no shape to face the waking realm. No voice to shake the mountains. Not yet.

"You woke me too early," it said, its voice ragged, drifting like smoke over broken stone.

Obsidian Swish raised her eyes—perhaps to beg, or perhaps to question—but no words escaped her.

With a motion that tore through the veil of reality, the Nameless Fear **ripped the flesh from her bones**, seizing her soul and memory, and **began to shape itself anew.**

And where Obsidian had stood—there remained only ashes and a name no longer hers.

From her form, it conjured a new vessel—**a woman, cloaked in shadow and thunder, with eyes like molten glass and lips that bled frost**.

"I will walk as her," said the Nameless Fear. "I will speak with her tongue, command with her will."

"And I shall be called... Evil Basalt."

Jabba's son tried to step back—but fate had already closed the door.

The new witch—Basalt—turned upon him, eyes blazing.

"You were only a door," she said coldly, and **split his soul in two**—half hurled into silence, half scattered into winds that carried his name no more.

Then she turned to the three daughters.

Small. Silent. Still clutching each other's hands.

But Basalt saw not children.

She saw potential.

"You will serve—not as slaves, but as my weapons."

She stepped forward and laid her hands upon each one.

To the first, she gave the gift of deception—eyes that could twist the world into lies.

To the second, she gave the gift of fear—her body became a cloak of dread that could choke courage itself.

To the third, she gave not one form, but three—**Wraiths**, silent and watchful, drifting at the edge of thought.

Basalt's hair, long as grief, flowed behind her—and into it, she **wove the daughters' essence**, each lock a shadow-thread, a living spell.

"They shall be my tresses," she murmured. "To be unbound when ruin is needed."

McVellian fell to his knees, pleading for mercy. Evil Basalt only smiled—cold and knowing—as if to promise, *for now.*

Fleeing the wrath he had awakened, McVellian vanished into the corridors of time, surrendering his present to Jabba Doom Gabbro. Thus he became the first man to wield the Deathly Chattel, the first to teach its dreadful craft—and the one who offered Gabbro her first taste of power. For the first time, she felt needed, and from that moment she never looked back.

In her grasp lay two relics of doom—the Deathly Chattel and the Deathly Book.

Evil Basalt, too proud to notice or care, stood as the winds bent to her raised arms. She was power incarnate—and she knew it.

She lifted her arms—and the winds obeyed.

At last, the newly wrought witch turned her steps toward the Lake of Wonders to quench her thirst of ages. The storm parted just enough to let her gaze fall into the black-glass surface.

There, in the reflection, she did not see herself.

She saw **Him**.

The **Nameless Fear**, not in human form but in shadow—**tall as mountains, vast as night, faceless but watching.** Its mouth did not move, yet she heard it speak in her mind:

"You are mine. My shadow. My shape. Walk the world in my name."

Basalt lowered her gaze—and smiled.

"I will burn Emerland to ash," she whispered.

The water darkened. The reeds shriveled. The fish turned belly-up.

Basalt stepped away from the blackened lake, her breath thick with power.

But then—she paused.

There, in the tall grass beyond the shattered tomb, **something stirred**. A rustle. A presence she could not see but somehow **felt watching her**—faint, like a memory not her own.

Her eyes narrowed. The hair on her neck prickled.

"Who dares linger?"

She turned sharply and **hurled the dagger**—the very one stolen from the heart of Emerald Castle—into the dark.

The blade flew swift and silent.

But then—

a cry split the air.

Not of shadow. Not of spy.

But of **Bulwark**—half man, half bird—an enchantment given flesh, who fell saving another.

He had come, silent as mist, to witness the unmaking—and the dagger struck him square in the chest.

He staggered into the open, his wings flaring once as if to lift skyward—

—and then collapsed to the earth, **lifeless**.

The grass was wet with his blood. The wind held its breath.

Basalt's face changed, for a flicker of something passed through her—**surprise, perhaps. Regret? No. Only calculation.**

She stepped over the grass slowly, carefully.

And there, beside Bulwark's still form, lay **his son**, curled like a fallen star, feathers dusted with dew and ash.

Basalt knelt.

She lifted the child gently, almost reverently, and gazed into his trembling eyes.

"You shall not die," she whispered. "You shall be remade."

She raised him high, and the dark clouds churned above as though sealing the vow.

"You are the firstborn of night. Your name shall be **Topaz**, for your eyes glisten like gems steeped in venom. Let the world see beauty in ruin," she said, brushing blood from the boy's feathered brow. "Even the stars may fall in love with darkness." His feathers, once dusk-brown, shimmered faintly now—shot through with veins of gold and coal.

And as she spoke the name, the storm broke loose again, wild and terrible.

Yet not in fury.

But in mourning. And somewhere, far across the sky, a single star dimmed—for innocence had been torn from the earth, and night would remember its name.

Far away, Alexandrite sat with the book still in his lap, unaware that the page had turned itself again.

5. The Quiet Before

Far from the cursed cemetery where dark storms gathered and shadows stirred, beyond the reach of witches, kings, and all who had gathered to awaken evil—there remained a single, sacred corner of Emerland left untouched. It was a quiet clearing, deep within the forgotten woods, where no map reached and no blight dared linger. Here, beneath the hush of ever-blooming trees, lived a girl with eyes like morning stars.

Her name was Diamond, though she did not know why. And though the world beyond had begun to tremble, her days still passed like pages in a story not yet told.

She lived in a small moss-covered cottage with two guardians: Morganite, the quiet steward whose hands knew the language of plants and stars, and Onyx, the gruff old creature with eyes like burnt stone and a heart that thundered with silent affection.

Of her parents, Diamond knew only what Master Steward had chosen to share.

"Your father entrusted me with your care," he had once told her. Of her mother, he revealed only that she was of the fair folk. "Such beings are seldom seen by mortal eyes," he would say gently, "not in this realm of earth."

Diamond's thoughts would sometimes drift toward the mystery of her parents. She felt their absence as a quiet ache, yet not a wound—for Master Steward had raised her with a love and tenderness so deep that she never truly yearned for more. In him, she had known the heart of both mother and father.

Peace and quietude were her companions, amidst the humble home she called her own, the green fields that stretched far and wide, the sweet songs of birds on the breeze, the steadfast trees that stood like ancient sentinels, the blossoms that adorned the earth with color and scent, the lively creatures that roamed free, and beyond all, her beloved little Onyx, the treasure of her days.

Diamond was content within the opulence of her hall, spending countless hours each day amidst its grandeur. Ever clad in garments reminiscent of fairy-kind, she reveled in the thought that she hailed from an enchanted realm where such beings dwelt. Oftentimes, she would gaze into the depths of her looking-glass, beholding her reflection with great affection. Great was her delight in adorning her ears with Master Steward's masterful creations—some wrought from gleaming metal, others delicate adornments fashioned from petals of flowers.

At the break of dawn, she would rise to the sounds of stirring birds, preparing water for morning tea for herself and Master Steward. Then she would feed Onyx, then would scatter feed for birds on their homestead, later on would tend to the flowers in the garden. She brought warmth to the home with her presence, greeting the sentinel trees and the rising sun with radiant smiles. This cherished routine marked the beginning of her day. Afterwards, she stayed indoors, devoting her time to maintaining the house and preparing meals. She often conversed with Onyx, her dark-furred dog, and frequently watched Master Steward as he labored under the open sky.

Yet, over time, Morganite came to see that Diamond had created a secluded world for herself, a sanctuary she had no desire to leave, so he tried to ask Diamond to venture the lands beyond their home.

"Diamond, my dear child, might you grace the market stalls with your presence this day?" he would inquire softly.

"But Master Steward," she would protest, "Onyx and I are deep in our game."

"Why not have Onyx to accompany you to the shops?" Morganite would suggest wisely.

"Onyx is too scared to go anywhere, Master Steward," Diamond would reply, conveying the deep understanding that further words would be as leaves scattered by the wind.

"Onyx," Diamond would muse aloud, her voice a gentle whisper like the wind through ancient trees, "Master Steward spends his days beneath this roof or toiling in the farms, from the first light of dawn until the shadows of dusk, always speaking of his yearning for us to tread the bustling marketplaces. These errands weigh heavily upon my spirit. Why, oh why, must we venture to the shops at all? Could we not find the sustenance we seek woven within the tapestry of our own dreams?" With earnest solemnity, Onyx would nod, his agreement as steadfast as the stars in the night sky.

Though Morganite harbored concern over Diamond's behavior, he never imposed his will upon her, preferring instead to lose himself in his own world and thoughts. In his study, filled with ancient tomes and scrolls, or while tending the fertile soil of his land, he seldom spoke. Yet, when he did, his words were deep and enigmatic, carrying wisdom such as, "What you believe to be true, my child, may seem strange and foreign to others," or, "Truth often hides itself in unseen veils," and, "Our two mortal eyes cannot see all that exists." Such utterances rarely made sense to Diamond. Words of power held little sway over her, nor did she see in Onyx's eyes anything but the same bewilderment. In this mutual understanding, Diamond found reassurance about the soundness of her mind, and Onyx, with a solemn nod, echoed this sentiment.

Yet as the seasons wove their ancient spell, a shadow crept into Morganite's heart. No longer did he lose himself in the realms of his books with the same fervor; his once powerful words fell silent, and he lingered less in the fields that needed his tending. More troubling still, his eyes seemed drawn to the horizon, where the sky's familiar blue gave way to a dreadful crimson, mirroring the dread that gnawed at his soul.

Diamond, innocent of the world but not without sense, felt the changes in Master Steward and the weight of air gone strange. Trouble stirred in her heart. The once fertile farm now lay desolate, its crops smitten by blight, and the tranquility that once blessed their land unraveled. Thus did their lives darken, and the days grew heavy with dread.

A few more days passed, and a profound unease began to settle over the household. For many days, Master Steward had wrestled with illness and a troubling, elusive discomfort. Diamond, her voice edged with doubt, finally asked, "Please tell me Master Steward, what troubles us?"

Morganite, as if he had been waiting for this question for days, let his thoughts wander to memories untold and stories he had never shared with Diamond. Often, silence seemed the safest refuge, for words could cast shadows on the hopeful days yet to come. Yet he knew she must be prepared for the trials that lay ahead. Struggling within, he decided to reveal bits of his past, hoping these tales would strengthen Diamond for the unknown journey before her.

"Diamond," he started, with a voice that seemed to carry the weight of many past seasons, "you have lived in these lands all your life, safe and apart from the world. But the years go by, and there is a truth I must share with you."

He spoke with a voice heavy with ancient wisdom, "In another realm, there is a young man living in the darkness with a witch once doomed, the destiny meant for you, as you now tread the path meant for him."

Diamond struggled to grasp his words, her brow furrowed in deep consternation. "A young man living my destiny?" she inquired, confusion clouding her gaze.

"Verily," the steward replied. "A young man, Amethyst he is called, bears your fate because your father chose to shield you. Though I have cherished every moment we shared, that young man is my son. As my remaining days dwindle, my heart yearns to see him."

"What do you mean, Master Steward?" Diamond's befuddlement only grew deeper.

"Diamond, thou are a princess—nay, the Princess of Emerland, a realm spun from the very fabric of dreams and joy. Emerland was a land where laughter danced upon the breeze and light bathed the hills, until the shadow of the Evil Witch Basalt crept forth, turning beauty to darkness. King Alexandrite, thy sire, and I did strive to hold at bay her fell power for a season. And then you were born—and so was Amethyst, both of you on the same day, in a place not quite of this world, where old magic still lingers. It was a wonder wrought by magic, a blessing and a beacon of hope for Emerland. Yet thy father, fearing for thy safety should the witch return—for evil never dies—did charge me to bear thee far away, to shield thee from harm. For the witch might lay claim to Emerland only by grasping the soul of the star-born. You are the starborn—offspring of the fae, bearer of Emerland's sacred bloodline. To shield thee, I have brought thee hither, far from that dark fate, whilst the Evil deem Amethyst to be the Starborn and covet his soul—a burden never meant for him to bear."

"Soul?" Diamond cried out, a torrent of emotion flooding her heart.

"Deep within your heart lies a mighty power," Morganite said, his voice heavy with sorrow. "A power so strong that if the dark witch Basalt should grasp it, her strength would grow beyond measure, and Emerland would fall into shadow and despair." He paused, a chill passing through him. "Sometimes, when I hear you sing the song of the 'Place of My Soul,' a great fear takes hold of me. You hold your soul close, yet you do not know that far across this wide world, a cruel witch watches, longing to steal it away, to break it and rule over all, filling the hearts of folk with dread."

"I do not wish to know more," whimpered Diamond, her tears beginning to fall, as if the mere thought of the evil witch ensnaring her soul filled her heart with dread too profound to bear.

Diamond sat in stunned silence, scarcely able to believe the words of Master Steward.

After a brief pause, Morganite spoke again, "Princess of Emerland, heed my counsel and follow my guidance. Should misfortune befall me, seek sanctuary in the woods or any haven you can find. Take Onyx with you. As long as you and Onyx remain safe, the evil witch Basalt cannot grow in power."

Tears streamed down Diamond's cheeks as she clung tightly to Morganite's arm, for it was too much for her to bear.

"You are a princess, my dear... yet even princesses weep. But never forget—you are the Starborn, and the hope of Emerland."

"But you told me to hide," said Diamond.

"I beseech you to hide, for as long as you remain unscathed, Emerland remains unscathed as well, though this understanding may yet elude you." With these words, Morganite cast his gaze across the shadowed hall and beckoned her to follow.

He then drew forth an ancient chest, richly adorned with various treasures, and from its depths retrieved a resplendent pentacle. A silver serpent, artfully entwined around a luminescent star, adorned the talisman with a mystic elegance.

Diamond lifted the Pentacle high, its light catching in her eyes like twin stars waking from sleep. Morganite watched her—not just the movement, but the meaning. Then he looked down at the talisman, as if its shimmer drew memory from the oldest well of time.

"This Pentacle," he murmured, "once belonged to a girl not unlike you. Many ages past, when Emerland first stood against the rising dark—long before Basalt—she took up this very star and rode with the Elves into battle. She was only sixteen, born of wind and river, yet the crown of the land called to her."

His voice lowered, like a hush falling over old stones.

"They say she bore no noble blood. And still, the Pentacle bound itself to her—as flame finds air. Some say it was a gift from her dying father, meant to save her... but he could not. In the end, she was lost to the dark. She became one with it."

Diamond's gaze drifted toward the horizon, as though some part of that tale still lingered there.

"In the final days of the Hollow Star, when all hope had drained from the land," Morganite went on, "she returned to the gates of the Emerald Castle. There, she called down light from the heavens through the Pentacle. They say she stopped the Hollow Star—if only for a breath."

He paused.

"And that breath... was enough.

Enough for the Elves to rise.

Enough for them to win."

His voice trembled now, thinner than before.

"But the breath she gave..." He faltered. "It cost her something. Perhaps something that was never truly hers to give."

He fell silent, unwilling to speak the rest aloud.

But Diamond was no longer listening.

Her fingers traced the edges of the Pentacle, reverent, entranced. The metal pulsed—warm, living, known. A whisper curled through her—old as moonlight, soft as her own breath.

"And you think..." she whispered, barely more than thought, "I'm like her?"

Morganite's smile was gentle, but heavy with sorrow.

"I think the Pentacle chooses," he said. "I think it remembers. And whatever the truth is... it lives in stories. In you."

Then, quietly, he laid his hand over hers.

"Whatever happens, you must carry this light. Not just for yourself... but for all of Emerland. Though it pains me that you must go there yourself. Yet my heart longs more to see my son than to hold to my duty. I am old, and I wish to hold him in my arms before I depart from this world." He then pointed to Onyx, saying, "Keep watch over Onyx well." Turning to Onyx, he said, "Protect Diamond with your life, dear Onyx."

Onyx gave a solemn nod.

"I cannot bear to be without you, Master Steward," Diamond clung to Morganite, her tears cascading down her cheeks.

"I am here still, my dearest," Morganite replied gently. "Remember, you may find solace and refuge within the woods." He chuckled softly, then said with a smile, "Come, we must go about our duties; nightfall approaches."

Thus, Diamond busied herself with the cooking, while Onyx darted in and out of the house, and Morganite set about chopping wood for the morrow.

As the day waned, Diamond sang softly to herself:

A little place full of chaos
things here, things there
I still love it, though, a place for my soul

My sweet little room
full of books, made of dreams
pen here, paper there
that open window, but who cares?

The kitchen has all the food
the jam here, butter there
wood and fire, I cook as I desire
clean the shelves, do all the chores

A green yard to play
dog running, flowers smiling
Dad is reading; I am weeding
a lot of work, to keep it tidy

A little place full of chaos
things here, things there
I still love it, though, a place for my soul

As Diamond's final note lingered in the air, a chill wind swept softly through the open casement, stirring the curtains like the whisper of ancient trees. Beyond, a solitary blackbird peered in, its gaze fixed and unblinking, as if borne of shadowed realms. For a fleeting heartbeat, the very breath of the world seemed stilled, caught in a silent pause. Then, as all things must, the moment waned, and the hearth's flames crackled once more.

From that hour forth, whenever she spoke the word "soul," the warm tide of joy was no more; instead, her thoughts were beset by the dark visage of the Enchantress Basalt, whose shadow haunted her mind like a lingering dusk.

6. Dream, Grief, Dawn

Upon the morrow, when Diamond awoke from her slumber, a heavy weariness clung to her, like the fog that coils over lonely moors at dawn. The warmth of her bed beckoned her to remain wrapped in its fragile comfort, yet a stirring had taken root within her chest—a longing, urgent and quiet, to speak of the strange visions that had haunted her dreams to Master Steward. She rose, pale and slow, as if her very limbs were reluctant to leave that fading world of sleep. With trembling fingers, she brewed a cup of tea, letting the steam rise like spirits from the kettle, one for herself and one for him.

Cradling the tray close, she moved with reverence toward the room where he always slept—where his steady breath had long been her morning's assurance. But when she arrived, a terrible stillness greeted her. His bed lay undisturbed, untouched by sleep or stirring. The world tilted. Her hands loosened, and the cup slipped from her grasp. Porcelain shattered against the floor like broken promises, and her voice broke with it. "Master Steward!" she cried, her words cracking against the silence. No answer came. Only the hush of absence, heavy as grief, filled the room.

She sank to the ground, her heart collapsing inward, and wept until her soul felt hollowed out. There, beside the shards and silence, she poured her sorrow into the ears of her only companion, Onyx. She spoke endlessly—of trivial things, of forgotten tales, of nothing at all—trying to drown the ache inside her chest. But Onyx, faithful though he was, could offer no reply, only the warmth of his presence. When the sun rose once more, Diamond's tears had dried, but the ache remained. The absence of Master Steward was a wound that would not close.

And yet, a quiet resolve began to bloom. She would find him—somehow. Though she knew not where he had gone, nor how to reach him, the pull within her grew stronger. The path ahead was cloaked in shadow, but still... she would follow it.

"What am I to do, Onyx?" Diamond whispered, her voice thin as winter wind. "I know nothing of the world beyond this quiet home. How am I to find him?" Her gaze wandered toward the heavens beyond the windowpane, where stars blinked cold and constant, their ancient glow offering neither comfort nor direction. They watched in silence, unmoved by her sorrow.

Two sleepless nights passed beneath their indifferent gaze, and despair began to coil around her soul like ivy upon a crumbling wall. "What purpose remains for me?" she murmured into the stillness. "If this is life without him... perhaps the end is kinder. If I set you free, Onyx, and cast myself into the well, maybe then I'll find peace."

She lay still, her breath shallow, the thought lingering like a ghost beside her. But as the veil of sleep slipped over her, a dream seized her—vivid and terrible in its clarity.

She saw Master Steward, imprisoned in a cage wrought of iron and shadow, his form curled in silence beneath the watchful eye of a dark figure. A woman, cloaked in midnight and menace, her presence cloaked in whispered legend—Basalt, the witch of nightmare and tale.

"Return to me my powers... my tresses," came Basalt's voice, as cold as stone and as sharp as sorrow. But Master Steward gave no reply.

"Then let the flames take him," she said, turning not to Diamond, but to another—an unseen figure standing just beyond the dream's edge.

Diamond jolted awake with a cry caught in her throat. Her skin was damp with fear, her heart thundering. The dream still clung to her, too vivid to ignore, too cruel to forget. "Master Steward is in danger," she whispered to the shadows. "And I must save him."

She rose to her feet with a strength drawn from desperation. "Onyx, we must go," she declared. "I will not let despair claim me. If I must perish, let it be while trying to bring him back. I know not the road. I know not the rules. But we must try."

And Onyx, eyes dark with quiet loyalty, gave a solemn nod—as if he, too, had seen the dream, and accepted the burden it placed upon them both.

Diamond stood in stillness, the hush of the empty home pressing in like snowfall. Her eyes fell upon the ancient trunk—the same one Master Steward had once opened before her, long ago, when his words were riddles and his smile bore secret weight. A shiver ran down her spine as she approached it.

She knelt before it with reverence and caution, her fingers brushing against the aged wood. Slowly, almost as if afraid it might vanish, she lifted the lid. Inside, she discovered a tome—leather-bound, weatherworn, and steeped in the scent of dust and time.

"Let us peruse its pages, Onyx," she whispered, her voice soft yet certain. Onyx padded to her side and curled in her lap, his head resting upon her knees as she opened the book and began to read aloud.

Hidden from the eyes of the unfaithful lies another world—
One that reveals itself only to those who believe in its beating heart.
Hold faith, and the veil will part.
Beyond that veil lies Emerland, a realm of song and sorrow.
Once ruled by the valorous King Alexandrite, whose spirit blazed bright and true,
Yet age now bends his back, and even kings grow weary.
Behold: the key to Emerland.
But tread with care.
For only those whose hearts burn with hope and courage may pass.

As the final word left her lips, the letters shimmered like starlight—then dissolved into nothingness. In their place lay a simple key, cradled in the hollow of the page.

Diamond stared in awe. "Did you see it too, Onyx?" she asked breathlessly. "The key... we hold it now."

Her voice grew stronger, fiercer. "Though you may question my courage, know this—these past days I have weathered grief alone, and yet I have not crumbled. My heart beats with hope, and I am ready to lay down my life to save him."

She looked down at her companion. "Now tell me, Onyx... do you also possess the bravery and hope that we need?"

And Onyx, eyes full of quiet resolve, gave a solemn nod. No words passed between them—but none were needed.

"I am filled with great enthusiasm," Diamond said, her voice catching fire. "We shall go to Emerland. I shall vanquish the malevolent Witch Basalt and bring Master Steward home. If I must perish, let it be while fighting for light."

She paused, turning the key over in her hand. "But... to what purpose does this key serve?" she murmured. "Its use will reveal itself, I suppose—so long as we carry faith."

And with that, Diamond turned from the only home she had ever known. She and Onyx stepped beyond the threshold, leaving behind the quiet comfort of familiarity and stepping into the unknown. They did not know the path. They did not know the end. But they walked with purpose, and in her pocket, the key to a forgotten realm shimmered faintly—like a sliver of dawn just before the dark breaks.

"I wonder where Master Steward might venture to procure our needs," Diamond mused aloud, her voice soft with fatigue and curiosity. For what felt like hours, they had wandered the wilderness—no markets, no houses, not even a whisper of another soul. The trees thickened, their roots gnarled like ancient hands clutching secrets, and the mist thickened around their ankles like forgotten dreams.

At last, beyond a bend wrapped in ivy and silence, they stumbled upon what seemed a forsaken coffeehouse—oddly whole, oddly still—nestled in the crooked shadow of a massive tree whose trunk could have housed a kingdom.

"No shops are to be found in these parts," said Diamond, casting a glance toward Onyx. "All that lies before us is this decrepit coffeehouse."

The bark of the tree groaned as if in response.

And just then, as her words slipped into the hush of the forest, shimmering letters unfurled across the door—etched in light itself:

"One sees what one believes."

Diamond blinked. Then, slowly, understanding bloomed behind her eyes like dawn after storm. "It is here," she whispered. "We see it because we believe. Henceforth, it stands before us."

She stepped forward and tried the handle. It would not yield. The door remained firm, ancient and unmoved. A flicker of doubt shadowed her expression—but then she remembered the key.

"We can employ the key," she said, and reached for it, her fingers trembling just slightly.

Onyx, ever silent but ever sure, gave a small nod.

Diamond inserted the key. It turned with a satisfying click.

7. The Quiet Beginning

In the blink of a breath, the world tipped.

Colors unraveled like ribbons caught in a storm. The wind twisted sideways, carrying with it the scent of wild flowers, ancient paper, roasted beans—and something stranger still. Was it memory? Was it magic? The forest peeled away as if exhaled by a dream, and suddenly, they stood at the threshold of something impossible: a coffeehouse stitched from wonder, stitched from whimsy, standing whole in the hush between heartbeats.

Every corner bloomed with color: shelves lined with glass jars glowing faintly, lamps that shimmered like fireflies, tables carved from tree stumps and polished so smooth they reflected the candlelight like pools of still water. Strange trinkets—wind-chimes without wind, feathers from birds not seen in this world, teacups that hummed lullabies—danced in the corners of Diamond's vision.

A small crowd lingered, patrons lost in quiet contemplation, their faces unfamiliar, their eyes distant. Diamond studied them carefully. "We have met none save Master Steward and you, my dear Onyx," she whispered. "So perhaps these are but ordinary folk... or perhaps not."

Then from behind the counter emerged a figure—at once commanding and serene.

An old woman.

Her presence was unlike any Diamond had known. Her hair flowed like molten gold, each strand gleaming beneath the café's soft glow, alive with a grace that defied age. Her robes were pale as moonlight, woven of linen so fine they seemed to float around her frame, whispering as she moved. She was not beautiful in the way tales often described queens or maidens—but there was something in her. A warmth. A fire. A kindness that made the air gentler around her.

And in her grasp, a staff—tall and gnarled like a branch of the World Tree itself—stood not as a weapon, but as a beacon. A silent bearer of stories long buried.

"The witch has returned," she muttered, not to Diamond, not to anyone, but to the air itself. "Morganite is held captive."

Diamond froze.

Then came another murmur: "The malevolent Witch Basalt seeks a soul to consume... and until she attains it, her discontent shall endure."

Diamond felt as though the floor beneath her shifted. A shiver moved through her like wind through reeds.

The woman looked up—and locked eyes with her.

That gaze was no ordinary glance. It pierced her like a blade of morning sun through fog. It was not cruel, nor harsh, but **deep**—as though it reached beyond Diamond's name, beyond her skin, into something more ancient than memory.

Diamond stood still, heart thudding.

She did not know this woman.

And yet, she did.

The feeling was undeniable. As though their souls had once touched in some forgotten dream.

Diamond remained there, as one cast adrift upon a vast and soundless sea, her spirit floating in a realm where neither time nor warmth could reach. It was as though her very soul had been pulled from the hearth of her old life and cast into an unfamiliar dream. The world she had known, filled with the soft cadence of Master Steward's voice and the steady comfort of Onyx's breath beside her, seemed to dissolve like mist at sunrise. All that remained were echoes—haunting fragments of a home now veiled in sorrow.

"Home is where your heart resides," Master Steward would often say, his voice like a lullaby. *"And my heart yearns to find him,"* Diamond whispered, the words catching like a prayer in her throat.

Onyx, loyal and constant, responded with a quiet nod, as if his soul, too, was reaching across some unseen chasm in search of the man who had once lit their days with laughter.

As Diamond sat in stillness, her breath shallow and her thoughts a quiet tide, the coffeehouse around her began to stir—unfurling like the petals of a sleeping blossom touched by spring's first light. The walls, once blurred and dreamlike, sharpened with a strange vibrancy. She noticed now that the café was nestled in a clearing ringed with ancient trees, their bark silvered with age and their roots entwined with moss and memory. The walls of the shop were woven from living things—grass and stone, bark and bloom—and every surface hummed with stories older than she could name.

All was quiet but for the low murmur of distant wind, and a single curious window behind the counter—slightly ajar, though sealed fast. It offered no view save for a curtain of silver fog that shifted and danced like ghost-light. Etched upon the window's wooden frame were runes, delicate and curved like vines, telling tales that eyes alone could not comprehend.

The peculiar woman—Hematite—stood behind the counter, her eyes narrowing as she caught Diamond's lingering gaze. For a heartbeat, the light in her expression kindled into something fierce—recognition perhaps—but then, just as swiftly, it dimmed into sorrow.

"Ah," she murmured, her voice like the creak of an ancient tree, "so it is your soul the malevolent Witch Basalt seeks."

Diamond turned, startled. "I beg your pardon," she said softly. "I was only looking out your window. I... I'm not sure where I am today."

Hematite stepped forward, the staff in her hand making no sound upon the ground. "Perchance," she said, her gaze gentle but unyielding, "you have wandered into shadow that you may better find the light. For you, child, have been walking in borrowed footsteps since the moment of your birth. The path you follow now is yours—if you dare to walk it."

Diamond, bewildered, responded softly, "I am sorry, but your words are a mystery to me."

The woman's eyes shimmered with a quiet knowing, and her voice flowed like wind through tall grass. "You must grasp the essence of things swiftly, for time is a fleeting specter. Already, sorrow circles you like a hawk above the moors. Shadows gather behind the veil, and darker forces stir beneath your feet. It is essential that you awaken to this knowledge."

Fear flickered across Diamond's features. Her voice trembled. "Do you walk the path of goodness... or evil?"

The woman did not laugh, nor scorn the question. Instead, her expression softened like dusk over still water. "There are no wholly good or wholly evil folk. In one moment, you may act with kindness, in the next, with cruelty. A single soul may carry both light and shadow within, just as day carries the promise of night. Your essence is your truth—unchanging, like the gem for which you are named."

She reached out with a hand weathered by time, yet graceful as falling snow. "Shine with the brilliance and strength of a diamond. Guard your pain like a jewel, for sorrow unshielded is sorrow exposed—and there are those who would take it from you to use for their own ends."

Diamond's voice fell to a whisper. "But how will I know if someone means to harm me? If I must hide my sorrow... how will I know who to trust?"

"You will not see, child," the woman replied, tapping gently over her heart. "But you will *feel*. Trust the stirring beneath your ribs. The spirit often senses what the mind cannot."

She paused, watching Diamond closely. "King Alexandrite sought to shield you from all this. He feared the weight would crush you. But he did not understand—one cannot escape the Unknown forever. Sooner or later, it finds you. And what then? Without any knowledge, how shall you endure?"

Diamond stared, the name catching her attention like a song half-remembered. "King Alexandrite…"

The woman's tone softened with a thread of fondness. "Yes. And Morganite too. Whenever he came here, I would ask him to bring you, or at least to send word. But he would always shake his head. 'I will not compel her,' he'd say. 'She must come when her heart is ready.'"

Diamond sat up, breath catching. "Master Steward? He's been here? I'm searching for him. Please—do you know where he's gone?"

The woman's gaze drifted toward the misty window, as if seeing a path no one else could glimpse. "He was here. He came with weariness in his bones but fire in his heart. He chose to follow where that fire led."

Her voice grew distant, solemn. "There comes a time in every soul's journey, Diamond, when we feel the stirrings of our deepest longing. A pull so strong it drowns out every other sound. And when that moment comes, nothing frightens us—not even death—for we have felt lifeless for far too long."

Diamond swallowed, not fully understanding, yet wounded all the same. Her eyes found Onyx, seeking comfort in his silent loyalty. He blinked once, gently, as if to say he was listening even when the words grew too heavy.

"Some truths, young one," the woman said at last, "remain shrouded in the mists of mystery until the weft of fate spins them into your experience. It is through trials borne of the heart that wisdom unfurls its wings. And yet, I perceive within you the lineage of nobility and a spirit well-born. In time, all shall be unveiled."

She straightened, her staff tapping softly upon the wooden floor like the ticking of time itself. Then, with a voice that shimmered with both destiny and grace, she asked, "Are you, then, prepared to embark upon the journey to Emerland?"

Diamond hesitated, her breath catching in her throat. "How shall I traverse to this legendary realm?" she asked, eyes wide, filled with awe and uncertainty.

"It lies," said the old woman—Hematite, though Diamond had not yet asked her name—"but in the act of leaping from that very window."

She gestured toward the solitary frame at the back of the coffeehouse—the one veiled in carvings and crowned with mist. A smile, ancient and serene, played upon her lips, as though she had posed this riddle countless times and always knew the answer before it was spoken.

Diamond turned toward the window. The fog behind the glass swirled like breath upon cold glass, dancing to a silent music only her heart could hear. Was it madness to believe? Or madness *not* to?

She looked to Onyx, whose soft eyes mirrored her own uncertainty—but also her quiet courage.

"I must leap," she whispered.

And so, Diamond closed her eyes and clutched Onyx tightly to her chest, her heart a drumbeat of defiance and wonder. She stepped onto the wide stone sill. The world beyond was not visible. Only mist. Only faith.

"I am ready," she whispered—not to anyone, but to herself.

And there she stood, between fear and flight, with her heart quietly prepared to leap.

"I am the keeper of the olden paths," Hematite intoned, her voice like wind winding through catacombs of forgotten time. "Heed me well, child of the woods—for once the path is chosen, it cannot be unwalked."

A faint wind rustled through the café, though no doors had opened. Hematite's gaze did not land on the dog beside Diamond, but in the instant her eyes drifted—she saw. Yet even as the words left her tongue, Hematite faltered. Her gaze drifted—unbidden—past Diamond, past the room... to the shadowed thread of what had not yet come.

She did not mean to see.

But she did. **She saw Evil Basalt, wings black as sorrow, tearing into him. She heard his cry—brief, brave, final. And she saw Diamond fall to her knees, her scream cracking the sky. The pain was not one of grief alone—it was the kind that silences the soul, that unravels fate.** The vision struck Hematite like cold fire. Her lips parted slightly, but no sound came. The wind itself seemed to stop.

In that moment, Hematite made her decision—not to spare Onyx, but to spare Diamond. Or to begin teaching her how to live with loss.

Her staff tapped the wooden floor—a sound soft as snowfall, yet it echoed like thunder in a chapel of ghosts.

"If I grant you this boon," she continued, her eyes not yet on Onyx, "you must render a token of your delight. A gift for the gift. That is the law, ancient and eternal. All paths demand balance. To step forward, you must let go."

When she spoke again, her voice was barely a whisper.

"...I desire him."

Diamond recoiled. "Onyx?"

Hematite met her eyes now, at last. "Yes. He must remain here."

"No," Diamond breathed. "No, take anything else—jewels, stories, time itself. I'll return, I'll find something worthy. Please."

"There is no clock that runs backward," Hematite said softly. "Only forward. And this is the hour. It is now, or never."

Diamond dropped to her knees, wrapping her arms tightly around Onyx. Her tears spilled without shame.

"I need him," she cried. "Onyx is my world."

At her words, Onyx looked up at her—his eyes brimming not with fear, but calm. He gave a solemn nod. Once. Twice.

The old woman's voice sharpened. "You are on a quest to save your realm, Diamond. Be prepared to relinquish all you hold dear. If you cannot let go, then the journey ahead will devour you."

Diamond clenched her jaw, but Onyx nudged her gently. He had accepted what she had not.

Even now, he stood steady while her world trembled.

"Why must it be him?" Diamond choked. "Why this cost?"

But Hematite did not answer. Not with words. Only with silence—the kind that comes after thunder, when the world decides whether to bloom again or break.

Diamond kissed Onyx's forehead. "I promise," she whispered. "I promise I'll return for you."

And Onyx, brave to the end, gave a final nod, his eyes gleaming with the tiniest flicker of joy.

Hematite stepped forward. "Take this," she said, pressing an old parchment into Diamond's trembling hands. "A map. It will lead you through the veil, if your heart stays true."

Diamond clutched it tightly.

Then, without ceremony, Hematite raised her staff—and the window behind her flared with white mist.

"Go now," she commanded. "Leap. Seek what you must. And may you not fail those who still depend on you."

Diamond turned one last time.

"Forgive me," she whispered to Onyx.

And before grief could anchor her again, Hematite thrust open the window—and pushed her through.

The mist swallowed her.

The glass shut.

And in the silence that followed, Onyx sat down beside the crone, ears forward, gaze steady.

Watching.

Waiting.

For the day she'd return.

8. In the Wonders

She fell—not as a stone plummets, nor as a leaf drifts—but as something lost between sky and sorrow.

Diamond tumbled through a corridor of starlight and shadow, her limbs suspended in silence. The air turned to frost upon her skin, and her breath crystallized midair. Around her, the sky shattered into shards of silver and violet, drifting like petals in a cosmic breeze. She reached out—blindly, instinctively—and her fingertips brushed a ribbon of light that pulsed with impossible warmth.

Then—

She landed.

Softly. Not with a thud, but like a sigh touching the earth.

She blinked. Grass. Petals. A sky blooming with lavender clouds. The world around her breathed with color.

"It is magic," she whispered.

"No," came a voice—gentle and strange, as if the wind itself had found words.

"There is no such thing as magic in the way you imagine it. True magic lies not in spectacle, but in your power to transform your longing into reality."

Diamond turned. Before her stood a flower—small, delicate, impossibly alive. Its petals were tinged with silver, and it pulsed faintly with light.

"But mind this," the flower added, voice laced now with warning. "Do not think me defenseless. I may seem frail and rooted, but I will not suffer destruction lightly."

Before Diamond could respond, the earth began to tremble beneath her. A distant, rhythmic thunder swelled—hoofbeats, wild and many, galloping through unseen fields.

"Hide," urged the flower, its voice tightening with urgency. "Quickly, if you wish to keep your life."

There was no time to ask questions. Diamond flung herself into the tall grass, its emerald blades swaying like dancers around her. She held her breath as the tremors grew, rising to a crescendo that seemed to shake the sky.

And then—

From between trees that did not look like trees—twisted into impossible spirals and stitched with threads of gold—a figure emerged.

A rider.

He towered upon his steed like a statue carved of fear and bone, his face shadowed by a helm of thorns, his nose flaring sharply as he sniffed the wind.

"I heard something," he snarled. "A trespasser, perhaps. Something new in the air..."

Diamond pressed deeper into the grass. The flower remained upright, unflinching, glowing faintly.

After a long moment, the rider gave a grunt and turned his mount away. The sound of hooves faded into mist.

Only when silence settled like dust did Diamond rise, heart pounding. "What just happened?" she asked the flower, breathless.

The bloom's glow dimmed slightly, as though sighing. "He passed. That is what happened."

"But who was he?"

"A brute," said the flower, "one who possesses strength of limb, but not of thought. I am bound to this soil. You are not. And yet... you seem unsure of what kind of strength you truly carry."

Diamond said nothing. Her eyes searched the strange sky above, wide with wonder and fear, as if she had stumbled into a story she didn't yet understand.

Then the flower, in a voice tinged with wistful curiosity, asked, "Did Hematite not tell you anything of this place? Of what lies ahead?"

Diamond shook her head. "No," she whispered, her voice barely a breath. "She did not."

"Ah, it seems she believed you capable of discerning it yourself," intoned the flower.

"Am I dead?" Diamond asked, her voice barely rising above the stillness. The world around her was haze and light, unreal and shifting, like a memory remembered wrong.

A dry chuckle came in reply, somewhere between mirth and warning.

"You would have been," said the flower, **"had I not plucked you from the claws of that foul sentinel—the one who serves the dark witch Basalt with a grin like cracked stone."**

Diamond blinked, struggling to make sense of the shapes and the light.

"I do not understand your meaning," she said softly. **"Please... speak clearly."**

The flower tilted its head—mocking or amused, she could not tell.

"At least you *know* that my words carry weight. That's a start. But don't stand here like a faded portrait hung too long in one place. Ask later. Move now."

Diamond hesitated, still caught between realms of sense and nonsense.

"Morganite," the voice continued, sharper now, **"they took him—just days past. He came back here, poor soul, after a long time hiding. Thought he could walk unseen. But the dark sees more than light dares."**

Her breath caught.

"What must I do?"

"Consult your map. It bears more truth than your trembling heart knows how to hold. Find Baba Yaga. She walks the paths no shadow dares cross. She remembers the beginning—and the end."

"Baba Yaga..." Diamond whispered, the name curling in her mouth like a secret. **"Who is she?"**

"Baba Yaga, as I said," the flower repeated, its petals fluttering like lips caught in a breeze. "Seek her out. And listen well—grasp not only what is spoken, but what is left unsaid. The wise speak in riddles, and truths hide between their lines."

Again came the thunder—a clatter of hooves, rising like a storm across the earth, shaking the meadow's quiet heart.

"Go now," whispered the little flower, its voice hushed and trembling. "I cannot feign innocence forever. If they find you here, all is undone."

With haste, Diamond darted to the edge of the meadow, where shadows clung to mossy roots and the trees whispered secrets. In a quiet hollow, she unfurled the map Hematite had given her.

It was beautiful—etched with delicate inked flowers, winding vines, and tiny trees—yet maddeningly useless.

"Oh dear," she murmured, brow furrowed. "She's given me the wrong map. This shows only the very ground beneath me. How on earth am I to find Baba Yaga?"

She turned instinctively, seeking Onyx's steady gaze. But he was not there.

But at the sound of that name—*Baba Yaga*—the map shivered in her hands. Ink bled and swirled. The flowers faded. And slowly, a single winding path emerged, like a spell unfurling. It pointed ever upward.

The path etched upon the page was strange—a narrow alleyway that led nowhere but upward, steep and unyielding, like a staircase carved from sky. No forks. No turns. Only ascent.

"How, in the name of all that is sacred, am I meant to climb this?" she muttered, glancing around as if some invisible hand might offer a ladder. But Onyx was gone.

The map snapped shut on its own, like a scolded book.

"Seek the answer within yourself, you dawdling girl," it hissed.

Diamond blinked. "Excuse me?"

"Wait—don't you dare fold up on me!"

But the map curled tighter. "I will offer guidance," it said with a sniff, "only when you've shown you're worth the climb."

Defeated, Diamond slumped beneath the boughs of a towering tree—its trunk gnarled like the knuckles of a story long forgotten. She closed her eyes and sighed, longing for the riddles

Master Steward once shared... and the stories he never had the chance to tell.

A low hum vibrated through the bark behind her.

"Hmmm... are you new to these parts?" rumbled a voice—deep, slow, and ancient.

Diamond sprang to her feet, eyes wide. "Who said that?"

The tree did not move, but the bark rippled slightly, as if breathing.

"Who am I?" the tree echoed. "No, no, little one. The real question is—who are *you*, to disturb my slumber and sigh beneath my branches?"

"Have you no sense at all?" rustled the voice from above, as leaves shimmered with a slow, sardonic breeze.

"I am the Tall Tree, plainly so. Some truths, child, are like the sky—vast, open, and simple. Yet you twist them into puzzles. What is it you seek, wandering beneath my boughs?" asked the Tall Tree, its bark creaking like old bones shifting.

"I seek the way that climbs," Diamond replied, lifting her eyes toward the canopy. "A path that leads me higher.

"Stubborn as sap in winter," the Tall Tree sighed, "but perhaps not hopeless," its branches trembling with leafy laughter. "To climb, look up—as one would look left to walk west. Not all journeys are paved. Some are vertical."

"But no stair nor ladder reveals itself," Diamond murmured, then added, almost in wonder, "Unless... you mean to be climbed."

"Return when the sun truly wakes," the ancient tree advised, its voice lowering like a hush before dawn.

"But it *is* day..." Diamond began—but the words turned to frost in her mouth as a shadow fell. It swallowed the tree whole, and with it, the warmth of the world. All light vanished, devoured by a silence so thick, even the wind dared not pass.

"How strange..." Diamond whispered. "Should I rest?" Yet no sleep beckoned. And far off, where the darkness thinned, she glimpsed a scatter of lights—glimmering like distant stars spilled across the forest floor. "Perhaps they know the way."

She pressed on, yet the lights slipped farther with each step, like dreams dissolving at dawn. At last, her legs gave way, and she curled upon the petal of an enormous bloom—soft and trembling beneath her weight. There, she surrendered to sleep.

In dream, the world brightened. Birds sang golden songs, beasts leapt through morning's veil. But then—the dream soured. A shadow stepped forward. Basalt. Her voice was silk and steel. "Give me your soul, and I will return him to you."

Diamond reached toward the witch, her soul trembling on the edge of surrender. But before the bargain could be struck, a radiant white light burst from within her—a flare so pure it cast the nightmare away. She fell from the flower like a drop of moonlight, landing breathless on the soft, sunlit grass below.

Morning bloomed around her—birds in jubilant chorus, beasts dancing through dew-kissed glades, the sky blushing with light.

But beauty could not banish hunger.

Within her, a hollow ache pulsed like an unanswered question. She had not eaten for days. And each night, her dreams returned—whispering, clawing, devouring what little strength still clung to her soul. And though the world shimmered with light, she felt herself fading.

For even in paradise, a soul cannot wander long without hope... or hunger.

9. To the Sky

"**A**re you hungry?" came a gentle chirp from above. A small bird—bright-eyed, unafraid—tilted its head with a knowing curiosity.

Diamond replied softly, her eyes still shining from the strange dreams of night. Her hunger was not only of the body—it reached deeper, a longing to make sense of what the night had revealed. The bird, without further ceremony, fluttered down with a tray of wild fruits and golden honey. Steam curled from the morning tea like a beckoning spirit. Diamond sipped it slowly, the warmth spreading through her limbs like courage, and then glanced toward the horizon. "I ought to return to the tall tree," she said at last.

"Nay," came the voice, delicate but firm, "you must not return. You must move forward. That is the way of those who are called."

Diamond blinked, confused. "Forgive me, little sparrow," she said, her tone courteous, "but I have left behind a tree of great height. I was climbing it—it may yet hold the path."

"Nay, nay," the bird chirped, feathers slightly ruffled. "You have already moved onward, and thus, onward you must go. The journey is not a spiral, nor a wheel—it is a thread pulled straight through the fabric of fate. Should you turn back," said the bird, "you will become tangled in yesterday's threads. The forest does not wait. Its roots move, its paths drift. That tall tree you seek—perhaps it has already gone on without you."

Diamond tilted her head, puzzled. "That sounds very much like a riddle," she said. "I am but a newcomer here."

"Aha! And so the newcomer speaks without knowing!" exclaimed the bird with theatrical indignation. "Mark well my name, child—I am not 'little sparrow.' I am *Olivine the Dove*. If ever you meet the actual little sparrow, you may call her so—she still owes me ten sticks, mind you, which *I* saw first and *she* had the nerve to collect!"

Diamond stifled a laugh. She was not sure what amused her more—the grumbling or the formality with which the bird declared her name. Yet she listened with care, for there was strange wisdom in this whimsical creature's words.

"Would you have me accompany you on your way?" asked Olivine the Dove, eyeing her over a folded wing.

"That would be most helpful," Diamond replied sincerely.

"Then you must carry my nest," said Olivine the Dove cheerily. "For I dwell where I roam, and roam where I dwell. Birds do not build homes and then abandon them at whim—unlike men, who build houses and then wander in search of meaning. We carry meaning with us." She laughed—a bright, fluting sound like bells in the wind.

Diamond stared at the nest—small, simple, yet impossibly important. Like her, it held meaning shaped by quiet love.

Diamond took the nest without protest, carefully cradling it in her arms. "From Onyx," she murmured, "I learned to embrace what comes." The thought of her faithful companion tugged at her heart, and for a moment, a quiet ache crept into her chest.

She walked on in silence, unwilling to ask more questions. The answers here—when given—seemed always wrapped in mystery, layered like the petals of a flower that only opened for those who already knew its scent.

Yet Olivine the Dove had spoken true. When they reached the tall tree, it no longer stood as it had. It had shifted, subtly but unmistakably. The climb, once a goal behind her, now rose again ahead—as if the world itself was bending to guide her.

Nestled on a thick, sturdy branch sat the very nest she carried, as though it had always belonged there. Olivine fluttered from Diamond's arms and settled gracefully within it. She sighed contentedly, wings tucked beneath her. "I have always wanted to fly to the sky," she mused aloud.

"But surely," said Diamond, surprised, "you could fly there now."

"I could," said Olivine, nestling deeper into the twigs, "but I will not. I built this place with my own beak and feathers—with patience and love. What would it mean, to abandon it for the sky? One must not always chase the highest perch. Sometimes, it is nobler to stay with what one has shaped."

Diamond slipped off her shoes, cradling them in one hand before casting them aside. Barefoot, she stepped onto the first branch. It trembled gently beneath her weight, as though testing her resolve.

She began to climb.

But the tree did not yield easily. Each branch she grasped betrayed her. As though the tree itself questioned her worth. Her fingers ached. Her breath caught. "I cannot," she whispered—not to Olivine, not to herself, but to the quiet fear in her chest.

"No, you cannot," came a prim, indignant voice just above her. "I do not understand why you insist on climbing in such a chaotic fashion. You are delaying me as well."

Diamond looked up. There, perched upon a limb like a whisper of moonlight, sat Olivine the Dove, her feathers catching the soft glow of the sky. The bird ruffled her wings, clearly unimpressed.

"What am I supposed to do, then?" Diamond called out, bewildered.

"Stay still," Olivine replied with crisp finality. "Do not move."

"Do not move?" Diamond echoed, disbelieving. "How will I ever reach the top if I do not climb?"

"You need not stir to rise," said the dove. "These branches are not merely wood and leaf. They are old, woven with the enchantment of the Hidden Grove. They carry those deemed worthy. If you are meant to ascend, the tree shall lift you."

Diamond blinked. "But I don't understand... I don't know the way."

"You have a map, have you not?" asked Olivine, tilting her head.

Diamond reached instinctively for the scroll, surprised that it had not fallen in her climb.

"I do," she admitted. "But I don't know how to read it. It feels... alive."

"That is because it is," said the dove. "Unfold it. Speak your destination aloud."

Diamond did as told, her fingers trembling as she unrolled the parchment. Its surface shimmered faintly, like moonlight caught on flowing water.

"To visit Baba Yaga," she said aloud, her voice steady now.

The map stirred.

Ink began to bloom like petals across the page, sketching a path of winding vines and rising branches. Tiny symbols unfurled—spirals, stars, and signs of the old tongue. And beside each one, a soft pulse of light, like a heartbeat guiding her way. One spiral shimmered like the star she used to wish upon as a girl, and for a moment, she wondered if fate had been mapping her steps all along.

"Now, inquire as to the manner," instructed Olivine the Dove, her feathers shimmering with the light of the unseen sun.

Diamond hesitated only a moment before whispering the question.

At once, the map stirred in her hands—not with ink or words, but with motion. Lines unfurled like rivers drawn by wind, and images danced upon its surface like ripples in still water. She saw the great tree, vast and ancient, its crown crowned with starlight and its roots deep in forgotten soil. She watched the path reveal itself, not as a command but as a living story. It was not merely shown—it was *shared*.

"I am grateful," Diamond murmured, bowing her head with reverence. "For showing me how to read the way."

Olivine ruffled her wings and tilted her head with a matron's pride. "Then take heed—and care for my nest in my absence," she said, her voice a silken thread woven with strength.

Diamond blinked. "And where do you journey, dear Olivine?" she asked, a trace of wonder dancing beneath her words.

The dove's eyes gleamed with something rare—yearning. "I seek the one who completes the arc of my flight," said Olivine. "When that meeting comes, I shall return."

Her wings rose, scattering feathers like silver petals. She soared into the morning, and became one with the sky.

Diamond's brow furrowed with quiet sorrow. "But... you once told me you never abandon your nest."

"I do not," Olivine replied gently. "But a time comes when the heart must follow its call. I entrust it to you—not as a burden, but as a bond. Watch over it, as I once watched over you. And remember—our wings are made for flight, not for clinging to what has gone. Look forward, Diamond. Always forward."

Her wings lifted once, slowly—then again, as though remembering the rhythm of dreams—and she rose into the sky. Her form rose, a silhouette against the tapestry of clouds, until she was no more than a dream dancing in the breeze.

And so, Diamond stood alone—guardian of the nest, her hand upon the branch, the bough swaying gently beneath her feet as if breathing with the old magic of the forest.

"Step forth from here," murmured the branch—and at its bidding, the tree dissolved into mist, vanishing like breath upon a mirror, until Diamond stood alone in the air, adrift among drifting clouds. Diamond hovered between substance and dream. For a moment, she thought she might fall; the mist coiled around her like a sigh. She hovered, not falling, not flying, but held aloft by longing. The world reshaped itself in answer to her will.

Before her eyes, a wonder took form—a dwelling spun from vapor and light, delicate as lace, majestic as a dream remembered from childhood. Its arches curved like the wings of birds in flight, and its walls shimmered with the softness of starlight.

Diamond's breath caught.

Her gaze swept across the cloud-woven expanse, and there, striding toward her with a grace both ancient and ageless, came a figure cloaked in calm.

An elder—tall, cloaked, serene. As the figure drew near, her voice carried like the hush of snowfall, gentle yet commanding:

"I am Baba Yaga."

10. The Third Trial

"Welcome, dear Diamond," intoned Baba Yaga, her voice deep as a drum in the bones of the world, resonant with an ancient gravitas that echoed through the air like the tolling of a long-forgotten bell.

As Diamond stepped across the threshold, the dwelling unfolded before her like a dream half-remembered. Walls shimmered with the colors of starlight caught in dew. The air pulsed with warmth—not heat, but the warmth of a hearth one had not known they'd missed. Every breath was thick with memory, as though the very air remembered other souls who had passed through long ago.

She turned to Baba Yaga, awe and confusion mingling on her face, her voice trembling like the wing of a bird in the hand of a storm. "Pray tell, where am I?" she asked, seeking the shape of truth in a place that bent the edges of reality.

"Ah," said Baba Yaga, her eyes deep pools of night and moonlight, "you stand in Emerland."

The word itself rang through Diamond like a chord struck on the strings of her soul.

"Emerland," the old woman continued, "a realm both hidden and aching to be found. Perhaps Hematite—the lady of the coffeehouse—whispered it into your bones when you were not listening."

Diamond's brow furrowed. "The lady of the coffee shop—who might she be?"

Her voice carried the eagerness of a child and the weariness of one who has lost much.

"She is a white witch," Baba Yaga said, her voice low and laced with reverence, "a keeper of secrets, one who sees beyond sight and knows more than she dares to speak aloud." The words curled through the air like incense, ancient and intoxicating, carrying with them the weight of stories untold.

With a gentle motion of her hand, Baba Yaga summoned forth new garments—woven from threads that shimmered like moonlight on still water. She guided Diamond toward a velvet-draped sofa, its cushions deep and inviting, as if it had waited a hundred years for her to sit. Then, with a flourish, she conjured a feast—bowls of golden pears, plums the color of dusk, and cakes that steamed with warmth. The table groaned under the abundance, a spell of hospitality laid with care.

Baba Yaga, seated upon a high-backed throne carved with spiraling runes, watched in patient silence. But Diamond only shook her head gently, eyes soft. "I have already broken my fast... with Olivine the Dove."

Baba Yaga's expression flickered—just a moment of surprise, then understanding. "Ah," she said, voice trailing like wind across an old grave, "then you have been well tended."

With a snap of her fingers, the grand table vanished, replaced by a simple tray bearing tea, warm milk, and a plate of soft biscuits dusted with sugar and memory. The air stilled.

Yet something deeper stirred beneath the quiet—a sorrow, unspoken, wrapped in dread. It lingered at the edges of the room like stormlight before rain, casting shadows that dimmed the once-luminous walls.

At last, Baba Yaga spoke again, and her words struck like a bell rung from the bones of the world. "Your coming here was written in starlight long before your first breath, child. Darkness creeps across Emerland like rot through roots. And only one born of the stars may bring its light again."

Her gaze held Diamond fast—ancient, kind, and immovable.

"When shadows lengthen and ancient malice stirs anew," she intoned, "the Starborn shall rise—child of the fae, crowned in blood from Emerland's line. If fire stirs in their soul and steadfast hearts endure, the light may yet triumph. But if the Starborn falters, if their soul is broken or lost... then within eight days, the darkness shall consume all, and Emerland's final hope shall be devoured by night."

The silence that followed was not empty. It pulsed. It breathed.

Diamond stood still, her fingers curled into the fabric of her lap, heart thudding like a distant drum. She felt the weight of prophecy settle over her shoulders like a cloak spun of ice and fire.

"What doom has touched Master Steward?" she whispered, her voice scarcely more than a thread in the hush. "Has he... has he come to you, Baba?"

Baba Yaga's voice darkened with reverence, the weight of memory pressing upon each word. "Morganite stands among the noblest of heroes—the bravest, I dare say, who ever rose to shield Emerland from its doom. Seventeen winters ago, on that cursed eve when all hope seemed lost and darkness crept through every branch and hollow, it was Morganite who dared what none else could. He faced the witch Basalt with no sword but courage, and no shield but love. With heart unyielding, he enticed her, lured her close, and in one final act of defiance, seized her in his grasp. Together, they vanished through the cursed threshold of the Deathly Chattel—a passage of time and torment few ever survive."

She paused. Her eyes, old as mountain stone, held Diamond's gaze. "There in the past, Morganite did what many believed impossible. He stripped her of her power. One by one, he cut the darkness from her tresses—each strand a vessel of ancient sorcery, severed and scattered. For a time, Basalt was no more than shadow without substance. Silence fell across the land."

Baba Yaga's tone grew heavy, her face lined with weariness. "But even silence has its limits. Emerland stayed silent for seventeen years, and then that foul trickster, McVellian, broke her chains. He brought with him the blood of an innocent werewolf—one of our own—offered as a sacrifice to reignite her ancient might. Thus reborn, she rides once more upon her phantom steed, her cloak of shadow spreading like rot through the glades of Emerland, where no dawn ever touches the earth."

"Yet Morganite sensed her rising. His bond to her, forged in pain, had not withered. He longed to protect his son... but alas, the moment he crossed back through the window of fate, she was waiting. Her snare was already set."

"Behold," quoth Baba Yaga, her keen gaze narrowing like the shadowed hollows of the ancient woods, upon Diamond. For a fleeting moment, a glimmer of hope kindled within her eyes, like a star faintly shining through the dusk. Yet before her stood not the valiant warrior of olde tales, but a fragile shade—an echo pale and wan, draped in sorrow as if the very flame of her spirit had been drowned beneath the ceaseless tide of grief, cold and unyielding as the winter sea.

"What fate awaits this beloved land of Emerland..." Baba Yaga whispered, her voice unsteady, like old wood straining under storm. She lifted a chalice to her lips—its waters cool, pure, and trembling as her own hands. Behind its rim, her eyes glistened with tears she dared not let fall.

"Diamond," she intoned, her gaze fixed as if peering through time itself, "within you beats the heart of a champion. When the hour calls and the banner of fate is unfurled, your strength shall rise to meet it. But now... it lies quiet. Sleeping. As though the world has not yet earned your fire."

"What do you mean, Baba Yaga?" Diamond asked, her brow drawn, her voice tinged with confusion. The sorceress's words felt like riddles carved in mist—truths half-seen and swiftly fading.

Baba Yaga began to pace, her long robes sweeping the floor like whispered secrets, echoing with the hush of forgotten ages. "This is not your first dance with the shadow, child. Nor your first crossing into peril. The ground beneath your feet remembers you... though you do not remember it. This path—this war—it is not your beginning. But it may be your end."

"What tale is mine to tell?" Diamond murmured, her voice barely louder than the rustle of leaves beyond the window. The more she learned, the more it slipped through her fingers—like water refusing to be held.

Baba Yaga's voice flowed like mist curling through ancient trees—soft, solemn, heavy with memory. "When you first came into this world, King Alexandrite—your father, burdened with fear—came to me. He begged to see what fate the stars had written for you. My own sight could not pierce so deep... so I turned to the elder Visions of the elves. And they answered. They spoke of the Starborn. Of you. Child of the fae. Bearer of Emerland's crown."

"When first I summoned the vision," Baba Yaga continued, her voice growing heavier, "I clung to hope—that the child of stars would rise, that you would overcome the darkness. But then... your face turned pale. You saw something—something terrible—that none but you could name. A death. A fate so dire, the Eldar warned: to see such an end is to draw it nearer. I was forced to sever the sight before it could take hold.

Still, I tried again. And again, your ruin was revealed. Twice I reached for light... and twice I was shown only shadow."

"This evil is deeper than you can reckon," Baba Yaga said, her voice a hush that trembled with warning, **"and the dark stone of Basalt is but a shadow upon the grander stage. A mightier force stirs beyond sight—hidden from all but you. And in that glimpse, your spirit is cast adrift, like a withered leaf torn from its branch and carried helpless upon the wind."**

A hush fell over the room, heavy with knowing. In the stillness, the truth rang louder than any bell.

"In that solemn hour," Baba Yaga continued, **"King Alexandrite, his heart burdened by love and dread, made the bitter choice: to send you away. Far from the perilous shadows that crept ever closer. Twice already, you had faltered on the path. Twice already, darkness had drawn near. And he**

feared that if it touched you a third time, it would be the end of you—and with it, the final hope of Emerland.”

Diamond lowered her gaze, shame and sorrow swirling within. Her voice cracked like brittle glass.

“How might victory be mine, when twice before I have fallen?”

Baba Yaga stepped nearer, her presence wrapping around Diamond like the hush of snowfall.

“You are the Starborn,” she said, **“the bearer of light destined to banish the shadow that seeks to devour our world. But you must not look only to your pain. To stand against the coming night, you must draw from the deep well of your memories. Not from their sorrow—but their truth.”**

Her staff tapped gently, like a drum summoning remembrance.

“When the dark hour falls again—as it shall—let the trials you have faced before become your guide. Let the fire of what you endured burn away fear. Let your survival be the answer.”

But Diamond’s thoughts strayed elsewhere.

All she could recall were her quiet days beneath the eaves of the cottage, the voice of Master Steward at twilight, the way Onyx curled beside her in sleep. And the ache of that memory overflowed her soul, spilling from her eyes like gentle rain falling on parched soil.

“Ah, my beloved,” quoth Baba Yaga, her voice a gentle murmur, steeped in enchantments older than the moon. “Behold, Emerland lies before you—a land breathing magic with every leaf and stream. Rest now, child of stars, for none may say what the dawn shall bring.”

With a grace born of exhaustion and destiny, Diamond ascended to her chamber. The journey had etched weariness deep into her bones, and the bed—soft, silent, and warm—beckoned her like a cradle of forgotten peace. She lay down without a word. The world dissolved around her, and sleep took her swiftly, drawing her into its tender hush like a leaf drifting down a still stream.

Yet even as slumber wrapped her in its silken veil, something stirred within the folds of dream. Not Baba Yaga's voice. Not her own. But a whisper, low and cold, coiling through the mists like breath upon glass.

A presence.
Watching.
Waiting.

11. Mist And Memory

In the hushed embrace of the ancient castle, where wind whispered like ghosts through stone corridors and time had stitched its tapestry with threads of silence and sorrow, **King Alexandrite stood alone**, as the storm gathered like a judgment overhead.

Beyond the towering windows, the sky was ablaze with fury—**clouds torn open by lightning, rain slashing the earth like a scourge**. Thunder rolled through the heavens like a voice too ancient to name, shaking the stones of Emerland as if they, too, remembered. It was not just a storm—it was memory, returning in sky and wind and wrath.

Seventeen years had passed, and still he waited—**a man tethered not to hope, but to the slow-turning wheel of dread**. His thoughts wandered, unbidden, to the day Diamond was born—**a day he had never spoken of, not even to the wind.**

It had not been a day of joy.

It had been a fracture.

A day when **light and shadow were born side by side**, twin echoes of something older than war.

Diamond had not been expected.

She was a ripple the world had not planned for, a spark that arrived uninvited and unblessed.

And yet she came—**not heralded, but warned against**.

The past rose before his eyes, alive again — as if yesterday had never ended. How could he forget? That same day, Evil Basalt awakened in the world — as though the stars themselves had split open, birthing light and darkness in one cruel breath. Alexandrite had sensed it even then: the balance had tipped, and the story had begun.

He had sat with his head bowed over *The King Before the Darkness*, the cursed book cradled in trembling hands. Its pages had bled with truths too sharp for the living. And as he wept in silence, **Baba Yaba had turned—not toward the future, but into the shadowed corridors of the past.**

For he alone understood: **Basalt's undoing did not lie ahead. It lay behind.**

And so Baba Yaba departed the present and sought the one who might open the gate: **Jabba Doom Gabbro**, who was no longer doomed, for she now held the *Deathly Chattel*—the forbidden relic capable of sending a soul spiraling into the past, not to change, but to **watch, to learn, to remember**.

He stepped into the Chattel's cold embrace beneath a sky howling with fury... and he never returned.

When word reached Morganite that Baba Yaba had stepped into the **Deathly Chattel**, he did not weep.

He **roared**.

Storming from the high chamber, his cloak a tangle of wind and fury, he vanished into the wild with fire in his veins.

"I'll destroy her myself!" he spat, voice cracking like thunder.

But beneath his rage beat a truth too bitter to say aloud:

If Evil Basalt could be slain by might alone, Baba Yaba would have done it himself.

Still, **he could not endure the waiting**.

He chose wrath over wisdom.

And so he disappeared—into the forest, into the storm, into grief too vast to carry in silence.

And in the stillness that followed, **King Alexandrite remained**.

Alone in the wake of ruin.

The hall felt colder now—**each stone heavy with absence, each shadow longer than before**. His crown sat like lead upon his brow, and his breath came thin, like someone walking further and further from the edge of life.

Even Baba Yaga, for all her ancient knowing, could not mend what had broken. She stood beside him, hands folded, mouth quiet. Her power was vast—but some griefs are beyond magic.

Then, through the rent skies of the North, **a cry cut the clouds**—sharp, solemn, and swift as judgment.

Out of the storm came a blur of wind and feathers—**Rock the Hawk**, King of the Sky, streaking across the firmament like fate in flight. He descended through gales and memory, talons tight around something wrapped in cloth and blood and silence.

He landed in a swirl of leaves and lightning.

From his grasp, he offered a child—small, shivering, breathing.

"This one I could save," Rock said, his voice low as thunder before it breaks.

"The child of Bulwark who yet lives. I could not find the other."

Baba Yaga stepped forward. She took the boy into her arms, her face unreadable, her sorrow **tucked deep into the folds of her robes like a forgotten spell**.

She named him **Jade**.

And though her heart ached with losses unnamed, she whispered lullabies into the boy's hair, as if **rocking him might silence the ache of a prophecy unraveling**.

But Alexandrite did not move.

He stared into nothing, into the stillness where futures collapse, where crowns mean nothing and kings are only fathers too late to save what matters.

Until Rock the Hawk turned once more—wings spread, eyes blazing with celestial fire—and with a cry that seemed to shake the very air, **he called the king back to life**.

"A king must not kneel to despair," he cried.

"Rise, Alexandrite. Take the Deathly Chattel. Find your father. And bring him home."

And in **King Alexandrite**, a flame stirred.

Flickering at first. Then rising—slow, relentless—like fire drawn from the marrow of stars.

Far from the throne room steeped in sorrow, in a place where time bent like branches in stormwind, **Jabba Doom Gabbro** stood cloaked in shadow and power. Once cast in pity, once broken by grief—**she had become something else entirely**.

The witch once doomed now wielded the *Deathly Chattel* like a blade forged from midnight and memory, its smoke curling through her fingers like whispers of the dead.

It was her son's final gift—*the Book of Death*—that had taught her what no living soul should know. Secrets written in ash. Rites carved in silence.

And with that knowledge, **she bartered**.

To those who sought the past, she offered visions.

But never freely.

Each glimpse came with a price—**a lock of hair, a cherished memory, the beat of a heart once given in love**.

Always something dear.

Always something lost.

But King Alexandrite did not flinch. His resolve was iron wrapped in flame.

He would pay any price—for his father, for a kingdom unraveling like an old song forgotten by the stars.

He would walk into yesterday—even if it meant surrendering everything that remained of who he was.

In her twilight sanctum, **lit by the cold fire of dying candles**, Jabba Gabbro met him.

Her eyes gleamed not with malice, but with a grief that had folded itself into steel.

"He is bound," she said, voice low as distant thunder. "Baba Yaba walks the corridors of the past.

And the past is a beast that does not let go."

"You will not find him easily. You may not find him at all."

Alexandrite said nothing. But the storm in his gaze spoke for him.

She studied him—a king worn thin by time, but still unbent.

And slowly, like a priestess reading fate from flame, **she named her price**.

"To command the Chattel, you must pay. And the cost, dear king, shall be mine to name."

She stepped forward, her cloak stirring like smoke on a battlefield.

"In exchange for its power, I ask only this:

The first shimmer of joy that touches your heart upon your return from the past...

That, my king, shall be mine."

Her voice did not tremble. It rang with **ancient finality**, like the tolling of a bell that could not be unheard.

And Alexandrite—**noble in sorrow, resolute in love**—did not waver.

What treasure lay beyond his reach that he would not surrender?

What flicker of joy could outweigh the hope of reclaiming the dead?

What moment of gladness could not be burned, if it lit the way for those still lost?

He bowed his head, and the pact was sealed.

Not with ink.

But with silence.

And fire.

So it was that **King Alexandrite**, soul steeled by sacrifice and sorrow, stood before a **timeworn chamber cloaked in dust and hush**.

Its walls held no grandeur—only memory. And upon one faded surface hung **a poster**, brittle with age, its ink a grim sketch of **death's pale hand**, reaching from shadow as if to claim all who dared remember.

Beside him, **Jabba Doom Gabbro** watched in silence, her breath shallow, her gaze distant—as if she, too, stood upon the edge of something sacred.

"Take it," she whispered, her voice neither command nor comfort, but something older—like a spell cast in mourning.

"Grasp what others flee. Hold death, and let it show you where time bleeds."

With quiet courage, **Alexandrite obeyed**.

He reached forth, his fingers trembling not with fear, but with the gravity of longing.

And when his hand met the painted one—**chill and lifeless as stone in moonlight**—the world shuddered.

A storm rose.

Not wind nor rain, but **a maelstrom of color and sound**, swirling around him like starlight caught in a whirlpool. **Songs he had forgotten filled the air—lullabies, laments, old courtly tunes**

twisted by time. Each note pulled at him, lifting, unraveling, undoing.

And then—**in the blink between breath and silence—he was gone**.

He stood now in a place not bound by walls or sky.

A realm shaped of **memory and mist**, **achingly familiar**, yet rearranged by the hand of the past.

The **paths he had once walked now shimmered**, distorted yet sharp, like dreams too long held.

King Alexandrite stood firm amidst the crashing tide of recollection, his heart burning with the need to find **his father—the wise and wandering Baba Yaba**.

He wandered through the corridors of memory, **where ghost-light danced across the faces of the dead**, and the past unfurled around him like a great, sorrowed tapestry.

Each vision rose—a flicker of joy, a burst of grief, a forgotten kiss—and he reached for them as a drowning man reaches for air.

Time fractured. Names echoed. He followed shadows.

Sometimes, he would pause, breathless before a familiar image—hoping, praying, *pleading* for it to be Baba Yaga. But each time, the vision faded like mist before dawn, leaving only the ache of what was not found.

He pressed on.

And then—**his foot caught on a hidden root**, invisible until too late.

He stumbled, falling not into fear, but into fate.

And there before him rose **the One-Wish Tree**—its trunk gnarled with ancient longing, its branches veined with silver and sorrow, leaves trembling as if they remembered every wish ever whispered.

A sentinel of dreams.

A witness to all things hoped, and all things lost.

Alexandrite knelt before it, heart raw and open, unsure if what he had found was an answer... or a beginning.

King Alexandrite stood in reverent silence before the **One-Wish Tree**, his soul hushed beneath the vast hush of its radiance.

Its limbs, wide as the dreams of Gods, reached heavenward, **heavy with blossoms the color of blood kissed by starlight**.

A wind—gentle as breath and wise as time—moved through its boughs, stirring **a shimmer of diamond-lit pollen** that danced like fallen stars caught in twilight's sigh.

All that he carried—the grief, the weariness, the years of longing—**seemed to dissolve**, as if the air itself had whispered a spell of forgetting.

This was no mere tree.

This was the **One Wish Fairy**, veiled in bark and bloom, keeper of dreams never dared aloud, and guardian of the one wish that could alter the weave of fate.

And she, ancient and unbound, felt the stirring in his heart—**a love slow and sovereign, like the first bloom after frost**.

His spirit, scarred but noble, **called to her not with words, but with longing that even silence could not contain**.

Moved by that quiet devotion, by the ache and the awe within him, **she revealed herself**.

Light spilled from the branches.

The blossoms unraveled like secrets.

And there stood she—the **One Wish Fairy**, radiant as moonrise, her laughter like water tumbling over forgotten stones.

Their joy danced together—**like fireflies beneath a midsummer storm**, like two forgotten notes finding harmony again.

It was love born not of flesh, but of soul—a rare, delicate magic, fleeting as snow on spring wind.

But even such magic must answer to time.

As the sands slipped through destiny's unseen glass, the hour came to part.

Yet in that final breath of closeness, the **One Wish Fairy**, moved beyond grief, made her gift.

From the joining of love and miracle, she placed into the king's arms **a child—a daughter gleaming like morning dew upon jeweled grass**, aglow with a light not her own but born of all that had been lost and given.

She gave the king his heart's truest wish, the child of his soul's unspoken yearning.

And then—**with a shimmer like the first snowfall upon ancient stone**, the fairy became again the tree.

Her form melted into bloom and bark, her presence lingering only in scent and shimmer.

Alexandrite, trembling with awe, held the newborn close.

"You are more precious to me than all the treasures of the realm," he whispered, the words rising like a prayer into the branches above.

"Your name shall be **Diamond**—for no light is brighter, no bond more eternal."

But as joy poured into him like fire into an empty lamp, a cold memory stirred.

He remembered the pact with **Jabba Gabbro**.

He remembered the price.

You must give what you hold most dear.

And now—**he knew what that was**.

Not gold. Not crown. Not power.

But this child.

This moment.

This flicker of heaven held in trembling arms.

And though he would not yet say it aloud, a dread whispered through the bloom-stirred air:

To love something so deeply... was to risk losing it.

He lay motionless, entombed in sorrow, as though the very air around him had thickened into shadow. "What have I wrought?" he whispered, and the words fell like broken glass. Salt-flecked tears etched silent rivers down his weathered face—rivers that bore the weight of a soul split at the seams. The parting from his daughter had struck not like a wound, but like a curse. She was the last living thread to the One Wish Fairy, the star-born light fated to rise. And he, the father who had loved and lost in the same breath.

"I cannot give you away," he murmured, barely more than a breath, his gaze resting on Diamond as though she were the last star in a darkening sky.

"Shall I deliver you to Gabbro?" he asked, bitterness curling in his voice. "A woman whose heart is a riddle written in smoke and sealed in ash?"

His purpose—his reason for braving the Deathly Chattel—had all but faded beneath the tide of his grief. He had come seeking Baba Yaba. But the past had taken hold of him, thick and clinging, like a forest grown wild with sorrow. Twilight gathered on the horizon as if the sky itself wept.

And then, like a whisper from fate, Morganite returned. His steps were silent as falling leaves, and in his arms, wrapped in moonlight and linen, lay a child—a boy. He named him Amethyst.

"I sealed Basalt in the Deathly Chattel," Morganite said softly. "Her evil, for now, is bound. And for that courage, a fairy came to me... and gave this." He looked down at the infant, his voice trembling with awe. "What once was dread has now flowered into joy."

King Alexandrite listened, eyes still veiled with sorrow, but a flicker of purpose stirred behind the grief. "I made a vow," he said, voice low and heavy. "I must give my most precious gift to Jabba Gabbro. And now I stand at the edge of the knife."

But even as he spoke, his soul recoiled. A shadow moved within him—regret, slow and serpentine, curling around his ribs.

"No," he said at last, each word a weight falling into place. "Diamond is the Starborn. She must not be delivered to Gabbro. When Basalt rises again—and she shall rise—the world will call for its light. And she alone can answer."

Morganite remained silent, caught in the threads of a fate neither of them could untangle. So it was that King Alexandrite, cloaking anguish with resolve, proclaimed Amethyst as his son before Jabba Gabbro, fulfilling the promise made in desperation. And they returned to the palace, though the shadows followed them—clinging like smoke to skin.

But in the vision of Baba Yaga, Diamond faltered twice. Twice the future had darkened beyond repair. To protect her, Morganite, with a courage cut from starlight, led her away—far from the lands of prophecy and peril, into a realm where sun still touched the earth and the past could not so easily find her.

In the days that followed, sorrow carved its name deeper into King Alexandrite's soul. The guilt—sharp and ceaseless—gnawed at him. He had surrendered Amethyst, an innocent, into the hands of a woman who dealt in riddles and ruin. His nights grew long. The colors of Emerland faded. The once-glorious king walked now in dusk, both within and without, haunted by the shadow of a child not his own... yet named by his hand.

And still the stars watched, silent as stone, waiting for the tale to turn.

12. When Memory Breathes

In the fair realm of Emerland, dawn did not arrive with silence, but with a pulse—**soft as a heartbeat, old as the bones of stars**.

Above the waking world, in a dwelling stitched from **mist and the breath of mountains**, Diamond stirred. Sleep clung to her like the last hush of night, but already her heart beat with a quiet ache—**a yearning wrapped in gold thread, spun from dreams not yet named**.

She hovered between knowing and not knowing—**between the ache of longing and the hush of fate unspoken**.

Desire burned low but bright within her, a lantern in the fog.

The road ahead lay veiled, veined with shadow—its end concealed even from the stars that once whispered her name.

Beneath the endless sky, where the sun spilled gold across the grass like spilled wine, a grand table waited—**dressed in royal linens and the shimmer of enchantment**.

It stood not in a palace, but beneath open air—as if the world itself had paused to feast.

Diamond approached, her breath a hush of hope and nerves.

Her heart beat like wings held still, caught between innocence and what destiny might demand.

The rich, dark perfume of coffee rose to meet her—**warm as memory, deep as a father's lullaby**—and wrapped itself around her like a beloved cloak.

She sipped it slowly, and the tension in her shoulders dissolved, a little.

Before her lay scones, split open like secret tomes, **lavished with golden jam that gleamed like sunfire**, and crowned with clouds of cream soft as snowlit dreams.

Each bite was a quiet joy—a moment of stillness within the tremble of an unraveling world.

And though the morning was kind, something old and unnamed stirred beneath its sweetness.

"Are you prepared, Diamond, to greet thy sire?" Baba Yaga's voice wove through the air as though borne on the breath of ancient woods, heavy with the whispers of olden tales. Inside Diamond, a fleeting shadow of nerves flickered, but she felt the weight of Baba Yaga's words settle upon her like the deep roots of the enchanted forest, holding countless stories within their grasp.

"Hmm," answered Diamond, her brow furrowing in thought.

"Let us journey forth on foot, dear Diamond. In this way, you shall come to know the land of Emerland, and perhaps, within its heart, the memories of the 'Visions' shall awaken."

Thus, Baba Yaga and Diamond departed from the dwelling that floated amidst the clouds.

As they journeyed forth, they beheld the wondrous sights: trees that danced with life, speaking birds that sung melodies of old, and creatures dwelling in cozy abodes nestled within the sturdy

trunks. Emerging from the embrace of the forest, they chanced upon a quaint little city, vibrant with shops and bustling folk. Yet, shadows flickered in the light of their smiles—the hint of worry lay upon their brows, for some establishments were shuttered, and others tended to locks that seemed too soon to be secured.

"Perchance, it is the dread of the dark Basalt," Diamond replied to her own query, her voice tinged with a quiet unease.

In that very instant, her eyes were drawn to a castle unlike any she had ever seen—a colossal marvel that stretched boldly into the sky, its spires reaching out as if to touch the heavens themselves. Wrapped in a grand wall, lavishly adorned and vast, it stood with a commanding presence that rendered all else around it small and insignificant.

She realized how little she truly knew of its boundless expanse. She had believed herself alone in a world often cold and rigid, save for the steady presence of Master Steward and her beloved Onyx. Yet, hidden from her sight, distant hearts beat softly with a tender warmth, quietly treasuring her very being. Lost in this quiet musing, she contemplated the fragile strands of destiny, spun by chance and fate, drawing kindred spirits together along the winding roads of their shared voyages.

"Such is the enchantment of life," Baba Yaga intoned wisely. "It hearkens to love and binds it to our realities, fulfilling hidden yearnings."

They both shared a gentle smile, for Diamond marveled at how Baba Yaga seemed to pierce the veil of her thoughts.

As they stepped into the ancient hall, Diamond found herself enveloped within a chamber rich in wonder and steeped in history. The walls were festooned with splendid portraits of King Alexandrite, noble in countenance, and whimsical illustrations depicting the joyous days of Diamond's youth, alongside Amethyst. These images, woven with enchantment, stirred to life before their eyes, unfolding the tapestry of their shared tale with each graceful motion.

"For what reason does King Alexandrite possess paintings," Diamond asked, her voice barely above a whisper, "when he cannot even behold them?"

Baba Yaga's gaze drifted toward the hanging frame, her eyes half-veiled with memory. A smile touched her lips—**not of amusement, but of knowing**.

"One needeth not the gift of sight," she said, her words slow and reverent, "to behold that which the heart hath long perceived. The images speak—not to the eyes alone, but to the soul. They unfold their tale unto those far from the scene, yet forever bound to it."

Diamond stepped forward, drawn as if by gravity, the dust-speckled light catching in her hair. Her hand hovered just above the glass, where age had fogged the edges, as if time itself had exhaled upon it.

"But this girl," she murmured, her fingertip tracing the outline of a small figure nestled in the painted garden, dappled with sunlight, "she looks like—"

"You," Baba Yaga said gently, finishing the thought as if the memory belonged to her too.

Her voice was the warmth of hearthfire in winter, blooming with the softness of spring after a long and bitter sleep.

"Indeed. You were here. Not in the eye of the painter, perhaps—but in our thoughts. In our hearts."

A moment passed—silent, sacred.

And then Diamond laughed, the sound light and true, **like wind dancing through crystal chimes strung in the boughs of ancient trees**.

They both laughed—not merely with mirth, but with the quiet joy that blooms when memory is no longer lost but called home again. Around them, the air stirred, as if the past itself had exhaled. In that moment, the painting no longer hung silent—it breathed, it shimmered, alive once more, like embers fanned by remembrance. For all stories live anew when shared by those who still remember.

Outside, the weather turned—a slow wind drifting through the open colonnades, heavy with the scent of old rain and the hush of leaves that had heard too many goodbyes. The clouds, once distant, gathered like thoughts unspoken, pressing low over the realm of Emerland, as if even the sky could not hold back its grief.

King Alexandrite emerged from the far end of the great hall, cloaked not in robes but in the weariness of years. He moved like a man long at sea, guided not by sight but by the memory of stars long vanished. His eyes, veiled and gray, seemed not to look upon the present but into the caverns of time. Sorrows swirled around him like mist clinging to a forgotten battlefield.

In his hand, he carried *The King Before the Darkness*—its leather cover worn thin, as if his soul had turned each page a thousand times. He had read the ending long ago. He knew what was written: the death of the king, the fall into shadow, and the daughter lost in darkness.

What he had once believed was allegory had become a slow-dawning truth. And now, with Diamond returned and the tale unfolding before his eyes like a tapestry he could not unweave, he felt as though the book itself were watching him.

He could not bear to read the final lines again. He feared them.

Feared that the end was already written—that he, **an aging king with a crown grown heavy with regrets**, was bound to its ink and helpless to alter it.

So it was that the life within him began to wane... not by death's hand, but by the slow, unrelenting weight of a fate foretold.

Yet even so, upon his lips there lingered the faint echo of a smile—fragile as frost beneath the morning sun, haunted by a fear that never spoke but always listened.

He drew near, each step a whisper through the wind-polished stone, and reached for her—Diamond, his child, his heart's unfinished stanza.

His fingers, weathered by time and loss, reached up to trace her cheek, reverent as if touching something holy.

"Oh, my dearest," he breathed, his voice breaking like twilight through stormclouds, soft, trembling. "Words fail me—for the joy that swells within my heart at your return to this hallowed realm is beyond measure."

In that moment, an inexplicable tether seemed to bind their fates, as if her heart had known his for an age uncounted. Tears, shimmering like the dew upon a morning leaf, gathered in her eyes, and with a voice trembling like the leaves in the wind, she breathed, "Why must I seek my father in an hour so fraught with peril? Why does joy not tread upon this earth unburdened by the weight of sorrow? Why, alas, must happiness and heartache be forever entwined in an unbroken dance?"

King Alexandrite, with a gentle yet heavy heart, rested his hand upon the silken crown of her fair head. "Oh, my cherished Diamond," he spoke, his voice resonating with the weight of ages, "I find myself ever ensnared within the labyrinth of 'whys,' a treacherous maze that offers naught but shadows and riddles. Sweet child of mine, forsake such ponderings and instead, let your spirit dance freely amidst the tapestry of existence, for life oft chooses to weave its mysteries in silence, leaving questions hanging like stars in the night sky, tantalizing yet unreachable. Do not tread my weary path, my precious Diamond, burdened

by the quest for answers; rather, embrace each gift that the morrow bestows upon you, for in acceptance lies the true essence of life's grand adventure."

Diamond felt a strange and unspoken connection to King Alexandrite, a bond far deeper than the one she shared with Master Steward; his words, often cloaked in mystery, flickered through her mind like elusive shadows—strange, distant, yet strangely compelling. Yet within the quiet sanctuary of her heart, she mused, "My love for Master Steward is an endless ocean, vast and free, not confined by the narrow lines of blood or birthright." She held this truth close, wrapped in its warmth, never seeking the harsh edges of doubt or division.

King Alexandrite drew her close, wrapping her in a tender embrace. His voice, soft and full of warmth, whispered, "My beloved child, look upon these images and tell me—do they capture the essence of who you are? You have lived within my heart always, a shining star that lights the darkest night. How I have yearned to watch you grow, to walk life's journey hand in hand with you."

With a profound sigh, King Alexandrite spoke, "You are indeed a child blessed by fortune, my dear one. Words fail me in expressing the depths of my gratitude to Morganite, a true ally who has sheltered you from the relentless perils of this world. I shall spare no effort to safeguard his well-being," he declared, his thoughts intertwined with the heavy burden of crafting a plan to uphold this noble oath.

"I shall set forth on a journey to save Master Steward and return him to the sanctuary of home. To you, I pledge this solemn promise," proclaimed Diamond, as her heart for the first time felt unyielding as timeworn peaks, her loyalty to King Alexandrite eternal as the stars."

"Never chain your soul with vows, my precious one," King Alexandrite urged, his voice thick with the burden of age and sorrow. "Promises are slippery shadows, ready to twist and tear apart the fabric of your life. Remember this truth: let not mere words steer your course, but seek delight in every step you take."

With a heavy heart, he added, "As for your departure, it shall not come to pass. I cannot consent to such a loss; I cannot bear the thought of you slipping from my grasp once more.

Here, within these hallowed halls, you shall remain—for your presence is the last light my weary soul still clings to." And with these poignant words, King Alexandrite withdrew to his chambers, his heart a silent plea, resolute in his decision to keep Diamond nestled safely within the castle.

Baba Yaga followed King Alexandrite, her voice steeped in the hush of ancient wisdom. "Diamond's heart yearns for one thing only: to rescue Morganite. She carries no promise of deliverance for Emerland—yet that does not diminish her path. Though I long for a miracle to save Emerland, you must let her walk this perilous path. Hiding will not shield us. True safety lies in facing the darkness that threatens to consume us."

King Alexandrite's voice trembled with wearied sorrow. "And how shall she stand against Evil Basalt, when even our boldest warriors have fallen? She knows not the depths of her own power. How can a flicker of light withstand a storm that has drowned even the brightest flames?"

"It is her destiny," said Baba Yaga, her eyes reflecting the weight of ages. "She must awaken to it—no one else can walk this path for her."

The king's words dropped like stones. "You've seen her fail twice already. You cannot deny it, Baba Yaga. What if that is all fate has written for her?"

Baba Yaga drew a long breath, as if inhaling centuries. "The Throne of Emerland tests its heir. If she falters again, she may be deemed unworthy—and then, darkness shall rule unchecked.

But hesitation serves no one. We must lend her our strength, not bind her with fear."

King Alexandrite had no answer. He returned to his throne, its grandeur dimmed by the fractures in his soul. And though his crown still gleamed, his heart was shrouded. At the chamber's threshold, Diamond stood in silence, her spirit pulled between love and duty. She had heard enough. There could be no turning back now.

And far above, beyond the castle spires and the weary weight of kings, the dawn pressed on—quiet, steady. It did not call attention to itself, nor break the sky with fire.
But it pulsed.
Soft as a heartbeat.
Certain as a star returning after storm.
And in that pulse, Diamond felt the shape of what she must become—**not a girl caught in prophecy, but a flame yet to rise**.

13. The Disguised Dawn

As dawn unfurled its golden banners across the sky, light poured through the high arched windows of Emerland's palace, gilding the stone walls and casting long shadows across the marble floor. Three sat in silence at a table carved from the heart of an ancient tree: Baba Yaga, wise and eternal; King Alexandrite, cloaked in sorrow; and Diamond—bright-eyed, yet burdened, her soul suspended between longing and the weight of fate.

Their meal lay untouched, as if food had no place where destiny lingered.

Between sips of bitter tea and silence heavy as prophecy, a question hung in the air—unspoken yet undeniable: should soldiers be sent into the haunted expanse of the Forbidden Forest? To march into that ancient dark was not simply a gesture of courage, but a reckoning with history itself. Even Alexandrite, ever steadfast, could not ignore the tremor of dread beneath such a decision.

"Dearest Diamond," said Baba Yaga, her voice a low current in the hush of dawn, "if you choose to set foot upon the shadowed trail, hope shall awaken in the hearts of our people. They will see you not as a child, but as the flame that dares walk into the maw of dread. Even the faint-hearted will find their courage stirred by such a sight. But beware, my Starborn one—this road is wound with peril. Emerland rests not merely upon living soil, but upon the bones of wars long buried, and those bones remember."

She fell briefly silent, as if listening to distant voices only she could hear. Then, with grave weight, she continued, "Amethyst must be saved. The whispers reach me like smoke—Evil Basalt sees in him not only the heir to Emerland, but a vessel for power far deeper. Her ambition is not content with thrones or titles— she desires his soul, and she will strike when Morganite's light wanes and her own strength returns. That hour draws near, too near."

"We must find him," Diamond said, her voice tight with urgency, trembling like a string drawn too far. "If he dies in my place... it will break Master Steward. His heart won't survive such a wound."

"Beneath these darkening skies," intoned Baba Yaga, her voice a hush before thunder, "many deaths lie waiting—some written in prophecy, others hidden deep in the folds of shadow. In war, emotion betrays, and sentiment binds like iron. If you walk this path, Diamond, let it not be to perish in glory. Walk it to make meaning. Walk it to matter."

Their council was broken by the quiet arrival of Jade. No horn heralded him—only the silent footfall of a soul shaped by storms. His wings shimmered faintly in the lamplight, catching threads of starlight and sorrow, moonlight and memory. Diamond turned, breath catching. His beauty was unearthly, like a being half-born of sky and shadow—but it was the calm in his gaze, the stillness of spirit, that held her in awe.

"She has not yet met him," murmured Baba Yaga—not to Diamond, but to the silence that held the world still. Her words floated like embers in the air, meant for time itself.

Then, her voice flared—sharp as a blade drawn beneath lightning.

"Jade was found on the night Basalt rose—when the heavens cracked open with a scream of thunder and the stars themselves recoiled. It was Rock the Hawk who saw him first—torn and trembling, his small body cradled in the roots of the Forbidden Forest, as if the earth had tried to keep him hidden from doom.

We did not find him by chance.

He was woven into the fabric of prophecy—a thread laid down by the unseen hand of fate.

He is the son of Bulwark the Brave Bird.

And Bulwark... had two children.

But when the storm came, and the trees screamed, and blood soaked the boughs—

Rock the Hawk could only save one."

Diamond felt her heart stir—not with fear, nor awe, but with a sudden, sacred kinship. As if this boy, Jade, had lived inside her dreams all along, unnamed but known. Her soul recognized him, like a song long unsung. And Jade, as if hearing that same silent tune, offered her a quiet, knowing smile.

"I will go with her," he said, stepping forward, his voice soft but unshaken. "Though I am young, I am Avion—born of sky and soil. My wings were not shaped for flight alone. They were shaped to guard."

King Alexandrite's breath caught. "Jade... I saved one child at the cost of my soul, and let another fall into shadow. If I lose you too—then I fear I shall lose what remains of me."

But Jade did not falter. "You saved me to soar, not to be hidden. Let me become what I was born to be."

A shadow spilled across the land like ink bleeding over ancient parchment. A thousand black-winged corvids rose as one, erupting from the trees with a furious chorus, their cries slicing through the morning hush like a prophecy spoken far too late. They wheeled above the palace in wide, mournful arcs, their wings casting restless omens that flickered across the white marble below.

Baba Yaga moved to the window. Her weathered hand, trembling only slightly, reached forward—then closed it with a slow, deliberate motion. The latch fell into place with a click that sounded like the seal of a tomb.

"The witch stirs," she said, voice low as thunder beneath the hills. "There is no more time for counsel. If we hesitate now, we fall."

"They must not learn of Diamond," the king whispered, his voice cracked and hollow, thick with fear.

But Baba Yaga did not turn. Her gaze remained fixed on the sky where the shadows circled. "It is already too late," she murmured. "The pieces are in motion. The board is set. Seal the castle."

Jade turned toward Diamond, who stood motionless by the window, her gaze fixed far beyond the glass—as though searching the horizon for truths not yet revealed.

Morning light spilled across her face, tracing her features in a soft, golden silhouette—fragile, luminous, unyielding.

With quiet reverence, Jade reached for her hand.

Diamond did not resist.

She turned, and together they stepped back from the brink.

Then Baba Yaga rose.

She turned to Diamond, her eyes glinting like stars reflected on frozen water. Her voice, when it came, bore the weight of ages—layered with grief, wisdom, and the hush of ancient things.

"Ah, Diamond... Princess of Emerland," she murmured. "Heir to a crown forged in sorrow and starlight...

You now stand upon the knife's edge of choice.

Will you remain—shielding this realm from the rot that spreads in silence?

Or will you descend into the Forbidden Forest, risking all to reclaim Morganite—and to stir fate itself toward mercy?"

With the resolve of a champion tempered by sorrow and silence, Diamond rose. "I will go," she said, her voice a blade honed on grief. "Into the Forbidden Forest—whatever dwells within, I shall face it. I must bring him home."

"So be it," said Baba Yaga, her tone brisk and immutable, like stone carved by centuries of wind.

King Alexandrite stepped forward, protest trembling on his tongue—but she stilled him with a single glance.

"There is no time for sorrow," she said. "No hour left for mourning. The only cure for despair is movement—and even a flawed step forward is better than standing still."

His shoulders slumped, and the fire behind his eyes dimmed. Words failed him. He bowed his head.

With Diamond's fate now cast, King Alexandrite turned at last to Jade. The lines of his face deepened, etched with fear and doubt.

"She must not go alone," he murmured. "But Jade…" He paused, the weight of his own thought halting him. "You are scarcely older than her. You have never ventured beyond the reach of these walls."

"I fear for your life," Alexandrite confessed, his voice low and hoarse—**threaded with the rust of sleepless grief**. "Each day, I carry the weight of saving my daughter while abandoning Amethyst to a land where **even truth forgets its name and time walks backwards**. And you, Jade—you alone have remained. If I were to lose you too…"

His voice cracked—**a fracture in stone**, raw and trembling. A sound born of **love and failure braided together like thorn and vine**.

But Jade did not falter. He stepped forward, **his shadow long beneath the flame-lit chamber**, and when he spoke, his voice rose like **a clarion horn above the ruins of war**—clear, unshaken, fierce.

"I would sooner clasp the hand of death than linger in this gilded tomb, where gold piles like autumn leaves, yet **freedom withers at the root**.

Amethyst fights in a place where light itself cowers—and now Diamond is called by blood and prophecy, her path inked in starlight and sorrow.

Do you call me frail because I bear wings? Or do you doubt the storm that beats within them?

I am not forged of fear—I am fire feathered in bone. I will burn through shadow if I must. I will fall from the sky before I let those I love fall alone."

"Nay, my son," said the king, and his voice trembled like wind through a cracked cathedral. "It is not as you imagine."

A hush fell. His gaze lowered, and for a moment he was not a monarch, but a man worn thin by fear and memory. "The fire I see in you—it is not unknown to me. But my caution is no slight. It is a promise I once carved in silence... to Rock the Hawk, beneath a sky we thought would never break."

The words hovered in the air, heavy as fate, and the silence that followed was thicker still.

King Alexandrite lingered, one breath more—then turned away. Not in anger. Not in shame. But in surrender.

He vanished into the solitude of his chambers, where grief had built its altar, and the walls—mute and ancient—offered him the only company that would not ask him to speak.

"I shall bind myself to whatever price you name," Jade declared. His voice was steady, but beneath it burned the quiet blaze of oath and flame.

Baba Yaga turned—slowly, deliberately. Her eyes, ancient as the stars that sang the world into being, fixed on him with gravity carved from centuries.

"Then listen, child of Emerland," she intoned, her voice low as thunder walking the hills. "You shall walk this path clad not in your name, but in the guise of a woman."

The air shifted. Between Jade and Diamond, a single glance passed—silent, unwavering. No surprise, no retreat—only a mutual recognition of the strangeness they must now embrace. The road ahead shimmered, not with light, but with possibility— and peril.

"A woman's face may yet mislead the eyes of the malevolent," Baba Yaga murmured. "Two wanderers, cloaked in sorrow and shadow, may pass where soldiers would fall. Thus, shall you walk into the Devil's realm and find your brother beneath the shroud.

"If the winds do not turn against us," Baba Yaga continued, her voice threading reverence and warning into one breath, "then both Amethyst and Morganite may yet walk again beneath Emerland's sun."

"At first light, you will cross into the forbidden realm," she said. "When the dark is weakest. As the Devil's gaze sleeps. And if Basalt looks upon you, she will see no threat—only two broken women, drifting like ash through ruin. That is our hope."

She turned to Jade once more, raising a finger etched with runes only death could decipher. "And when the hour reveals itself—when shadow lifts from the path—you must fly. Fly to the hut of Jabba Doom Gabbro. There, speak not in riddles but in truth. Stir the heart of Amethyst. Tell him his name must rise again, and the war waits for him beneath the crown of twilight."

Then Baba Yaga turned to Diamond, and with a reverent breath she opened her palm.

There, resting against her lifeline, lay three slender leaves— emerald green, veined with silver threads that shimmered like starlight trapped in dew. They pulsed faintly with warmth, as though they still remembered the tree from which they had fallen.

"These," she said, voice soft as falling dusk, "are from Ememory—the sacred tree that bears witness to all who pass beneath its dreaming boughs."

She held them higher, as if the air itself should take heed.

"One to flee," she whispered. "One to return."

Her gaze deepened.

"And one to shield you... from what even the stars dare not name."

In the twilight hour, as the vile Witch Basalt departed her Fortress of Dread—a place steeped in silence, sorrow, and the stench of old curses—a sliver of hope pierces the veil. It is brief, barely a breath in the life of the world, but in that fleeting moment the barrier between despair and salvation weakens. Through that seam—thin as the mist that clings to forgotten moors—two souls might pass. If they dared," murmured Baba Yaga more to herself than anyone.

Diamond and Jade stood motionless beneath the deepening sky, their breath shallow, their eyes fixed on the invisible thread of fate now loosening before them. Around them, the wind whispered warnings. The trees bent slightly, as if leaning in to listen. All of Emerland held its breath.

Then Baba Yaga spoke.

Her voice, like earth cracked by age and echo, emerged from the stillness:

"To tread upon forbidden paths without foresight is to summon ruin. Yet when fate unravels the thread, do not forget the pattern that first inspired your steps. In chaos, recall the original weave—and find your way anew."

Her eyes, wise and relentless, turned to Diamond and saw what no mirror could reflect—fear, longing, power not yet awakened.

"Before you dare to rescue Emerland, or Morganite, or any soul you cherish, you must first descend into yourself. For if fear rides beside you unchallenged, you may fall into a chasm where no light lingers—and no return shall ever be granted."

Then, with a gesture elegant and timeless, she summoned the hidden fairies.

They came like wind-borne stars, their wings glimmering with ancient enchantments. Spiraling around the companions, they spun threads of moonlight and memory, wrapping them in garments fit for those who would walk toward legend. Cloth woven from valor. Seams stitched with hope. A mantle of stories yet to be written.

Jade stepped forth, reborn in disguise. A young boy now clad in a woman's form—yet no artifice could dim his radiance. Light paused to study him. Though draped in unfamiliar folds, he shone with the gleam of unspoiled joy. He had not yet tasted deep sorrow, and in that innocence lay a strange power: a promise untouched by fear.

King Alexandrite stood apart, his crown heavy, his spirit bent beneath unseen wounds. Still, he gave his blessing—though it came like ash caught in his throat.

"Go," he said. Then, after a pause, he turned to Jade.

"Seek Gabbro's hut. Find Amethyst. And if peril tightens its grip—return. Do not linger in its jaws."

"I shall return swiftly, Father," Jade answered, his voice clear and brave. He bowed in disguise, then rose in truth—and in that single motion, healed something long wounded between them.

Alexandrite turned to Diamond. The words he spoke were scarcely more than a breath.

"Go well... and come back. I beg you. Return."

Diamond did not weep. She only nodded—solemn, still, and sure.

And so, beneath the twilight sky, clad in borrowed courage and threaded prophecy, Diamond and Jade stepped beyond the final threshold of their safe world.

Into the waiting forest they vanished—

Toward shadow.

Toward sorrow.

Toward the unknown.

14. Silence and Steel

Jade and Diamond had slipped away into the veil of night, their departure hushed, their footsteps hidden from all but the most watchful shadows. They believed none would follow, and yet... the game of evil had already begun.

Deep within the forgotten reaches of the realm, where no stars dared shine and the soil remembered only sorrow, a new name was etched into the ledger of the damned: **Toxico T**, brother to Jabba Doom Gabbro.

He had dwelled long in doom's shadow—too long to forget its taste. But now the tide had shifted, and with it, so had the world. Those who once spat upon his name now turned to him, seeking the very wisdom they once scorned. And Toxico... liked the feeling.

The power of power—it sang to him. And he craved more.

Even Jabba, weary and wise, warned him of the hunger that consumes its bearer.

But he would not listen.

Twisted by solitude, thick with old resentment, Toxico no longer feared the dark.

He welcomed it.

In the shattered mirror of fate, he saw his reflection gleam with ambition—and without regret, he chose his side.

Under the crooked moon and trees that whispered treason, he stood before Basalt—her presence like stormlight bound in flesh. The air trembled between them, dark magic curling in the hollows of their silence. Toxico did not flinch.

For him, the source of power mattered not. Only that it was his.

Together, they sealed their pact—his cunning, her fury, braided into something cruel and everlasting.

Once, she had asked him gently—by her measure of gentleness—to convince Jabba to surrender Amethyst.

"Speak to your sister," Basalt had whispered, voice smooth as shadow poured through silk.

"Tell her it need not end in ruin."

But Jabba had only laughed—low, grim, unshaken.

"Not over my bones," she had said, "nor the dust they'll become."

And she meant it.

Armed now with the **Deathly Chattel** and riddles torn from the pages of the forbidden book, Jabba was no longer the frail, doomed witch the world had once dismissed. She had risen—fire-tempered, sorrow-forged, and wise beyond fear.

And that truth, Toxico dared to share.

"She will never yield," he said, voice low as dusk. "Not to me. Not to you."

Basalt's eyes narrowed, gleaming with fire not her own.

"Then she will break," she hissed.

"Or I will."

Her breath steamed in the cold like smoke from a dying star.

"And if I shatter before reclaiming what is mine—then *he* will rise. The Nameless Fear, the one that watches from the grave of shadows, the one even the Gods have forgotten—he will come."

A pause. The wind held its breath.

"And when he does, it will not be for mercy."

She did not speak his name lightly. None dared. Not even the wind.

Toxico T lingered in silence, draped in the fortress chamber's gloom. As shadow thickened like a second skin, a new presence crossed the threshold—a youth of otherworldly beauty, his wings gleaming like polished topaz. This was Topaz, first servant of Evil, born of Bulwark, the innocent child Basalt had turned into evil at the moment of her becoming. He moved into the doorway with the stillness of a sentinel carved from moonlight. At his arrival, Toxico seemed to dissolve into irrelevance, as though the very chamber had forgotten him. Topaz fixed his gaze upon the witch—not with fear, but with the weight of unshaken resolve—and the air itself fell silent in deference.

"I bring tidings," Topaz declared, his voice a clear chime in the gloom—resonant and precise, like the toll of a temple bell cutting through the hush before a storm.

Basalt lifted her gaze slowly, lounging upon her twisted throne like a serpent coiled in velvet. **"And tell me, are they sweet as morning honey or bitter as a widow's wine?"** Her tone was silk wrapped around steel, each word measured with suspicion veiled in charm.

Topaz's eyes flicked briefly to the side—toward Toxico T—then returned to her with cold intent. **"This news is for your ears alone, my lady. It concerns the soul we hunt."**

Toxico T, who had been loitering near the throne with the smug air of a jester pretending to be a prince, gave a soft grunt and drained the last of his swirling, greenish brew. **"Then I shall retreat into shadows where secrets fester,"** he muttered, smacking his lips. Rising with exaggerated grace, he swept into a bow so shallow it mocked reverence. **"My queen."**

His coat dragged behind him like a fading curse as he vanished into the corridor, though his eyes lingered—too long—on Topaz, betraying more interest than he dared voice.

From the hour of his first memory, Topaz had known only Basalt. It was she who had drawn him from the jaws of storm and shadow—not with tenderness, but with command. He had served her faithfully ever since. His loyalty was forged not from affection, but from debt. And yet, with the arrival of Toxico T, something within Topaz began to tremble.

He mistrusted the newcomer's oiled charm, the easy betrayal that clung to him like a second skin. "How can one who sells his own blood be trusted with ours?" Topaz asked once, his voice low and sharp as flint.

Basalt's reply was colder than iron. "You serve me. He serves with me. That is the difference." Her eyes held no softness. "Never forget who rescued you when all others left you to die."

Silenced, Topaz bowed—not from reverence, but from the weight of a debt he could never repay. Yet even as unease coiled in his chest, he stayed.

And when the doubt grew loud, when the world pressed too close and the silence threatened to crush him, he would look to his wings—vast, golden, and radiant. "I have the best wings," he would whisper, tracing the feathers with quiet pride. "And nothing can make me sad in their presence."

And each time, it was true. For a moment, at least... he smiled.

Basalt had kept Toxico T close not for loyalty, but for usefulness. In her vision, he was the lever—a fool easily swayed, yet well-placed to tempt his sister into surrendering Amethyst. She believed her victory would come not through bloodshed, but persuasion. What Toxico lacked in cunning, he made up for in timing.

Topaz, however, was different. He did not yet grasp the full depth of her design. His heart bore remnants of goodness, flickers of kindness long buried. And yet, he served a purpose shaped for evil.

Once the heavy door groaned shut behind Toxico T, Topaz stepped forward. "There is news," he said quietly, his voice carrying a strange urgency. "A girl has entered Emerland. Her name is Diamond. She searches for Morganite. Calls him Master Steward."

Basalt stilled. "Diamond?" she echoed, tasting the name as if it were foreign and unfinished. "Who is this girl?"

"I do not know," Topaz admitted, his gaze flickering toward the window. "But she walks as if the stars have heard her name. Even the wind stilled when she passed."

Basalt rose slowly, the hem of her dark gown dragging like spilled ink across the stone floor. Her eyes, sharp as obsidian shards, narrowed. "She seeks *Morganite*?" she muttered, more to herself than to Topaz. "Then perhaps... she is his hidden whelp." A twisted smile crept across her face. "Ah, love—the oldest weakness. If he holds her dear, then she shall be the blade to draw out his secrets."

Without hesitation, Basalt extended both arms. From her right shoulder leapt **Corvus the Corvid**, black as coal smoke, and from her left, **Vultur the Vulture**, feathers tattered and stinking of the grave. "Go," she commanded. "Unravel the truth of this Diamond. Watch her. Haunt her steps. If she carries Morganite's blood—or worse, Alexandrite's—bring me every whisper, every clue." With a single beat of their ragged wings, the spies vanished into the gloom.

Across the lands of Emerland the dark-winged spies soared, casting fleeting shadows upon meadow and mountain alike. Their flight was bold, unhidden, a sign of Basalt's growing confidence—or perhaps her disdain for concealment. Wherever they passed, farmers paused mid-plow, mothers drew children close, and shepherds whispered old prayers, for these were no common birds. They were omens, watchers of doom. Their presence declared what words dared not: **the roots of Emerland were rotting**, and its skies no longer belonged to the light.

"This is a most fortuitous turn of fate!" Basalt exclaimed, rising with a glint of triumph burning in her eyes. "We shall ensnare her—this Diamond—and compel Morganite to reveal what he did with my tresses... my powers. My undefeatable powers: the three Wraiths, the Clock of Darkness, and the gift of illusion."

Her voice twisted with venom as she strode toward the shadowed firelight.

"I have never felt so powerless. Even Jabba Doom Gabbro dares to believe she is stronger than I. Amethyst walks freely beneath my gaze, deep within the forest I command. All I need is his soul to quench this thirst—to make me undefeatable."

She paused, lips curling with contempt.

"Morganite will yield. He must yield—if he holds this Diamond dear. If he led her down the Deathly Path, then she must mean something to him. And if her life hangs in the balance, he will give me what I seek."

Her hand came to rest upon Topaz's shoulder, cold and possessive. "Ensure she is brought to me the moment her feet touch the forbidden realm. No delay."

Topaz bowed low, his voice sharp with purpose. "I will not fail."

"See that you don't," she said coldly. "You owe me everything."

As Toxico T turned to leave, a shiver stirred the chamber air. The spies had returned—ragged-winged and silent, their whispers clinging to the walls like cobwebs of shadow. What they brought confirmed what Topaz had already feared: the girl had left Emerland. She moved across the land like starlight—unseen, yet leaving ripples in every heart, stirring awe and dread alike. But she bore a weakness still. Morganite. The girl had walked the long path into Emerland for no crown, no prophecy—only for his life.

"Traitor Morganite cast me into the Deathly Chattel," Basalt hissed, her voice curdled with venom. "Had McVellian not broken the seal, I would still be rotting in that prison of silence."

A flicker passed through her eyes—a vision unbidden. She saw again the moment Morganite cornered her, the struggle, the spell, the terrible plunge into the past. The Chattel was not merely a cage—it was Death's own relic, bound by a single, immutable law: *Death never reclaims what it has given, nor returns what it has taken.*

"That rule," she muttered darkly, "cost me years."

She leaned back, the fire in her gaze burning brighter. "I do not forgive. And I never forget. Morganite shall know what it is to suffer."

Then came her laughter—high and sharp, like shattered glass hurled into darkness, a sound colder than the void itself.

Without delay, Topaz departed—swift as wind, silent as breath—following the trail of Diamond and Jade. They were unaware of the hunter in their midst.

Diamond and Jade had entered the brooding hush of the Emerland Woods, guided by a brittle, age-worn map. Though the true Forbidden Forest still lay ahead, the rot had already crept here—its touch visible in the graying bark, the withered vines, the sickly silence between branches. It was as if Evil Basalt's shadow had begun to stretch its long hand across the land.

From the limbs above, grotesque spiders descended in silence, harbingers of the dread that loomed beyond. When the path beneath them dissolved into moss and swallowed earth, they took shelter beneath a towering tree—its gnarled branches like the outstretched hands of time clawing at the heavens. It stood defiant against the encroaching gloom, an ancient sentinel at the threshold of fate. Beneath its shadow, they paused. The map had marked this place—where destinies diverged and choices take root.

Jade, his heart firm yet shadowed with worry, prepared to head north—toward the strange hut of Jabba Doom Gabbro, perched upon chicken legs, where he hoped Amethyst still lived. Diamond, torn between dread and duty, would turn west—deeper into the cursed lands where Master Steward remained imprisoned under the grip of Evil Basalt. Though their paths now split, their fates remained bound—threads of light drawn taut against the rising storm.

They believed themselves alone. But unseen among the trees, Topaz watched—silent, patient, predatory. His eyes tracked

Diamond's every movement, waiting for the perfect moment to strike. Unlike the sluggish creatures of evil who stirred only when summoned, Topaz hunted with the cold discipline of dawn. He rose early, moved without sound, and missed nothing. And so it was that Baba Yaga's plan faltered—undone by a servant who never slept.

Diamond and Jade lingered at the threshold of the Emerland Woods, where the trees stood like silent judges and the air trembled with secrets. The sky above them had dimmed to a bruised gray, and the wind carried no birdsong—only the breath of something unseen, watching.

Jade glanced sideways, noting the shadow behind Diamond's stillness.

"What troubles you?" he asked softly. "You wear silence like sorrow."

Diamond hesitated, her gaze wandering toward the trees as twilight deepened.

"My thoughts stray to Amethyst," she said softly, her voice laced with a yearning she could not explain. "It's strange—I've never seen him, yet I wonder how he fares. Banished with Gabbro, unaware of who he truly is. Master Steward once said... he walks the path meant for me. Imagine him beside you now, and me, far away—living out his life in Gabbro's care."

The words tumbled out before she could catch them, as if her thoughts had slipped free of her grasp.

"You must quiet your thoughts, Diamond," Jade said gently, sensing the weight of her unease. "There's comfort in not knowing everything. Even I—who remembers so little—have found a strange peace in forgetting. But truth…" He paused. "Truth brings sorrow."

He drew a breath. "Jabba Doom Gabbro is not evil—but she is… unstable. Twisted by grief and bound by old ambitions. She clings to power, and in Amethyst, she sees a future king. A vessel for legacy. She won't let go easily. Not without a fight. So far, evil has kept its distance… but that peace won't last forever."

He turned toward the looming forest, the line of his jaw hardening.

"There's danger ahead, Diamond. But perhaps… there's also truth. Mark this place well. You now stand at the edge of the Forbidden. It does not welcome the tender-hearted or the soul ruled by feeling. Here, grief is a weapon. Regret is bait. Emotions may bind us—but only reason will keep us alive. And it is for survival, not sentiment, that we tread these cursed woods."

The wind seemed to pause. Even the trees leaned in.

Jade placed a steady hand on Diamond's shoulder, trying to shield her from the weight of what lay ahead.

"I will go first," he said. "Let the forest hunger for me. When you follow, its gaze will already be drawn elsewhere."

Diamond's hand reached for his instinctively.

"Wait—just a moment longer," she whispered. "Let me stand beside you before the dark takes you from my sight."

Jade drew her into a final embrace, his voice soft but urgent.

"Fear not. You shall be safe. Walk straight—unyielding—until you see a grand tomb. That is her fortress. That is where your journey turns to fire."

And with that, he turned—vanishing into shadow.

The forest swallowed him.

It had no paths—only choices that led to ruin or revelation. The air shifted as though something ancient had just stirred.

Beneath the tangled roots of a dead tree, Topaz waited. Motionless. Silent. Mistaking Jade for Diamond, Topaz feigned death before him.

Yet Jade, versed in the craft and perils of the Forbidden, and mindful of its sinister enchantments that ensnare the unwary, paid no heed and strode resolutely past.

But Topaz rose like a serpent uncoiling from shadow, and with a motion too swift to follow, he hurled his blade. It struck Jade's leg with a sickening thud.

Jade cried out—not from pain, but in warning. The voice rang through the hollow glade.

Diamond heard it. She knew it. And without thinking, she ran—her heart pounding like a war drum, feet barely touching the earth.

Topaz turned. He saw her. And he understood.

With the precision of a hawk, he flung a second knife.

It whistled through the air and sliced a red kiss across her hand.

Then—three strides.

That was all it took.

He was upon them.

His movements were fluid, mechanical, merciless.

In seconds, they were disarmed.

In moments, they were bound.

No words. No mercy.

Only silence and steel.

15. Ash, Blade, Vow

In the upper chamber of the Fortress of Dread, beneath a ceiling scorched by soot and sorrow, Evil Basalt stood before a tarnished mirror. The firelight danced across the stone walls—but her reflection did not move. It stared back, cunning and still, as if it too had begun to think for itself.

She did not blink. She dared not.

Then the mirror began to shimmer.

A ripple coursed across its surface, and flames bloomed within the glass—first a flicker, then a torrent—until fire consumed it wholly. Yet the flames gave off no heat. From the heart of that blaze, an image unfurled: eyes like collapsed stars, a face neither man nor beast, cloaked in shadows more ancient than time itself.

A voice rose from the fire—low, vast, and dreadful.

"She has arrived. The Starborn walks the edge of destiny. The age of light ends now."

Basalt fell to one knee, breath snagged in her throat.

"Lord of the Forbidden Realms," she whispered, her voice no louder than ash on wind.

The fire flared.

"You will triumph, Basalt… or be devoured. I do not return to fail."

A chill crept through her bones.

"But I thought it was Amethyst," she stammered. "He was the one I prepared for—all the signs, all the omens—"

The voice cracked like thunder.

"You *thought*. And that was your mistake. Leave thinking to me. The girl—Diamond—is the final key. Her soul carries the last shard of my power. Through her, I shall return—not as shadow, but as fire made flesh. And when I rise... the war will drown in darkness."

Basalt's mouth was dry. Her gaze flicked back to the mirror, but already the fire was fading, smoldering down until her own face returned—pale, shaken, yet still cloaked in ambition.

A sound broke the silence.

Footsteps echoed in the stone corridor—measured, unhurried, certain.

She straightened.

Topaz never failed, as Topaz admired his shimmering wings.

The air inside the Fortress of Dread was colder than stone—colder even than the moment her hand was first struck. Diamond's wrists ached from the binding, the rough cords biting deeper with every motion. The halls she passed through whispered with windless voices. Shadows clung to the ceilings like cobwebs spun from fear.

Topaz said nothing as he led her onward. His grip was firm but not cruel. That, somehow, made it worse.

She did not ask where they were going. Diamond already knew.

As they descended into the bowels of the fortress, Diamond tried to summon courage—but her thoughts kept spiraling. Morganite. Jade. Even Amethyst. What would become of them now?

The chamber fell silent as Evil Basalt stepped forward, her cloak trailing like a living shadow across the stone. She had foreseen Diamond's arrival—dreamt of it, even—but still her eyes narrowed at the sight of **two** bound figures before her.

"Two?" she said, voice curling like smoke. "I expected one."

Topaz's chin lifted proudly, eyes gleaming like obsidian and his wings shone like stars and made him proud of his looks.

"I captured both. Yet which is the true Diamond... eludes me."

Basalt's gaze swept over them with predatory precision, until her eyes froze upon the glint of silver nestled against one woman's chest—a coiled **serpent encircling a pentacle**, ancient and unmistakable.

She inhaled slowly, reverently.

"Do you not see it?" she hissed. "The serpent-pentacle—borne only by the royal bloodline. It is a relic of old Emerland, forged in fire, steeped in oath. Even now, it hums with the magic of kings."

She moved to touch it—no, to seize it.

But as her hand neared, the pentacle **awoke**.

A radiant blast of light erupted from its center—white fire and silver lightning—hurling Basalt backwards with such force she struck the far wall. The air cracked with sound, and for a moment, time itself seemed to reel.

Basalt crumpled, then rose—slowly, deliberately—brushing ash from her robe with quiet fury. Her eyes blazed with new hunger.

"So," she breathed, regaining her poise. "The old power still protects you."

She stepped closer once more, though now she kept her distance.

"Impressive, girl. Very impressive."

Her gaze shifted to the second woman. Her voice dropped—low, dangerous.

"And *you*... who are you to walk beside the heir of Emerland? A shadow? A decoy? Or something else entirely?"

She circled them both now, cloak sweeping wide like wings unfurled.

"This one wears no crown... yet my lands are sealed. None enter without my leave."

She halted before Topaz and said, with icy command:

"Tell me, servant—have you brought me a queen and her ghost... or two storms yet unnamed?"

Without another word, Evil Basalt turned sharply—her cloak snapping like a storm wind—and faced the motionless figure in the shadows.

Spinel the Werewolf stood there, as he had for what felt like centuries. Silent. Watching. Enduring.

"Fetch Morganite," Basalt ordered coldly.

Spinel stirred at last.

Spinel was a werewolf.

In ancient times, such creatures roamed the world more freely—neither legend nor rarity, but woven into the tapestry of the wild. Now, they lived only in whispers, their kind exiled to the pages of forgotten lore. Spinel was perhaps the last, and his fate had been sealed long ago. He had been given to Evil Basalt by McVellian—an offering made in shadow after McVellian shattered her chains and set her free.

First, McVellian had slain the Wolf's parents—blood traded for freedom. Then he gave Spinel away: as a gift, a steed, or perhaps a fragment of memory. For McVellian had forfeited his present to walk into the past, to summon back the darkness he once served.

But Spinel remembered none of this.

The blood. The betrayal. The bond.

All of it lay buried beneath layers of silence.

And yet, something inside him ached. Not with rage, but with longing.

A hunger to remember.

To grieve something real.

Something once loved.

Something once lost.

Now, that ache twisted into cruelty.

Down the winding stone corridor, Spinel descended, his claws clicking with eerie precision. In a locked chamber of cold iron, **Morganite** sat hunched in silence.

His breath was slow. His eyes—older now—held the weight of unshed truths.

Spinel smiled, sharp and joyless.

"Your time as a guest ends, Morganite," he said, voice like gravel soaked in venom. "Now begins your torment... for the girl you cherish is here."

He paused, savoring Morganite's silence.

"Diamond... and another. A stranger. Two lambs at the altar."

Morganite's breath caught.

"So," he said quietly. "What I feared... has come to pass."

Spinel's grin widened.

"That is how it unfolds."

He seized the old steward with unnecessary force, dragging him through stone and smoke and echoing dread.

The chamber loomed wide and red-lit as Spinel thrust Morganite forward. Basalt stood waiting, twin swords at her side, eyes gleaming with cruel delight.

She did not waste breath on greetings.

"So, how shall we proceed?" she asked, tilting her head like a serpent watching prey. "Will you tell me where you've hidden my powerful tresses... or must I slaughter **Diamond** and this *vagabond* while you watch?"

Her tone was casual—almost amused—but the glint in her eye promised only death.

Morganite straightened, even in chains.

"You would do it regardless of what I say," he replied.

"Perhaps," she said sweetly. "But your pain tastes richer when you believe your silence matters."

She circled him now, slowly, dragging a clawed finger along his shoulder.

"Come, Master Steward. Where are my tresses? Where is the key you stole from me in the age before this one?"

Diamond gazed upon **Morganite**—her protector, her father, her Master Steward—and scarcely recognised the man before her. He stood shackled and bent, drained of all vigor, a remnant of the strength she once knew. His eyes, once warm with guidance, now flickered like dying embers.

Tears slid down her cheeks—quiet, unrelenting, hopeless.

Morganite met her gaze.

"I told you to stay away," he murmured, disbelief trembling in his voice. "I begged you not to follow this path..."

From the side of the dais, **Evil Basalt** stepped forward, her voice sharp and mocking.

"And yet she came. Of course she did. She is the one."

Her eyes locked on Morganite—cold, righteous, burning with wrath.

"I gave you time to reconsider. And what did you do with it? You clutched your secrets like a miser's coin. I remember the day you stole what was mine—my **tresses**, my power—and left me to rot in a forgotten fold of time."

Her voice dropped, venomous and slow.

"You looked upon me with indifference. And now you beg mercy?"

She laughed—low and cruel, the sound scraping against the chamber walls.

Morganite's voice was barely a breath, thin and frayed like parchment left too long in the wind.

"I beg of you, Basalt," he said, trembling. "If I give you the truth... if I reveal the secret of your lost tresses... will you grant my daughter her freedom?"

The word *daughter* echoed through the chamber like a forgotten prayer.

Basalt's eyes narrowed, and her expression twisted into something between amusement and contempt.

She raised her hand as if shooing away smoke.

"Enough," she said flatly. "Sentiment is a form of suffering I do not savor. Or is it the shadow of **McVellian** that darkens this moment?"

She chuckled, soft and sour, her voice curling like ink in cold water.

"You speak of bargains and love, Morganite, while I wield blades and names. You waste time. And time... is hungry."

Topaz, standing nearby, shifted. His gaze cut through the moment, offering her a silent look that said: *Now. End this game.*

Basalt smiled at him—and obeyed.

She stepped forward, placed the edge of her cursed blade against **Diamond's throat**, and let its chill draw the faintest line of red.

"Will you tell me," she said calmly, "or shall we start with her screams?"

Morganite broke.

"Onyx," he gasped. "It's Onyx."

Basalt tilted her head.

"Onyx?"

"Yes... the four tresses... your powers... I bound them to Onyx."

She paused.

"And who is this *Onyx*? Not another woman, I hope. Not a hidden queen disguised as a wanderer?"

She looked toward Diamond, her tone mocking and poisonous.

Diamond's lip trembled. Her breath hitched.

And then—too fast to stop—she spoke.

"Onyx is... my puppy."

The words hung in the air like a spell cast wrong.

For a heartbeat, the entire chamber froze.

Then Basalt's smile cracked—and fury bled through.

"You turned my tresses... into a *dog*?" she growled, voice low and rising.

Diamond's eyes widened. Realization flooded her.

Jade's warning echoed in her mind—*do not let emotion speak for you here... the Forbidden feeds on it.*

But it was too late. She had given the witch everything

"So..." Basalt seethed, her voice cracking like ice. "You turned my tresses... into a *dog*?"

The fury in her eyes became fire.

Without hesitation, she raised both cursed blades high—twin arcs of darkness, humming with stolen power—and **drove them through Morganite's chest**. The impact echoed like thunder in a tomb.

A gasp tore from Diamond's lips. Chains rattled. The world stopped.

Morganite fell to his knees, then to the stone, a tremor shaking his limbs. Blood spilled like spilled wine across the cold floor.

His gaze found Diamond's—weak but clear, full of love undimmed by pain.

"I love you, Diamond," he whispered, voice fading like a last wind. "Do not mourn me. *Save Emerland.* And when the day is won... *smile for me.*"

"Master Steward!" Diamond cried, her voice a raw wound torn open by grief. "Please—stay! Don't leave me. Not now."

But the light within him was already fading, dimming like the last star before dawn. His breath, once warm and steady, slipped into silence—vanishing into the unseen, as if the world had exhaled and forgotten to draw him back.

A hush fell, deeper than silence — the kind that settles only when the world holds its breath. Then came the cold.

It did not creep in like shadow or fall like night. It *arrived* — absolute and unyielding.

The flames in the Fortress of Dread gutters dimmed. Candles shuddered. The walls, living and breathing with soft enchantments, recoiled slightly, as though some great beast had drawn too near. Even Evil Basalt, steady as stone, gripped her dark sword a little tighter.

And then she came.

Death.

She did not enter. She *appeared*, as though the veil between life and what lies beyond had always held a door, and now—at last—it opened. She was cloaked in sable folds stitched with starlight, her eyes fathomless as the void, her presence neither cruel nor kind—only certain.

She was not bone. She was not specter. She was *form*—ageless, elegant, and terrible to behold. Around her, the air grew thin. Time rippled.

Evil Basalt bowed her head low, her voice a breath of scorn. "So... you come again."

Death said nothing.

With skeletal grace, **Death** bent over Morganite's body, beginning his claim—pulling something unseen from the shell that remained, and laughed as it said, "Immortals." As if in cruel mockery of the day Death had come to Emerland's gates and turned away empty-handed—for proud Baba Yaba had defied the Reaper, claiming his bloodline immortal beneath the throne's shadowed crown.

Then she turned—and vanished, as silently as she had come.

But the cold remained, like a hand upon the heart.

Diamond turned her head—yet her eyes refused to close. She saw, and wished not to see, and still she watched.

Jade stood across from her, his brow furrowed—not with horror, but with something deeper.

His gaze pierced through the smoke and sorrow and asked, without a word:

You came to save him. Then why do you still stand still?

Diamond lifted her head, slow as sunrise over ruins.

The tears still flowed, but they no longer spoke of weakness.

When she spoke, her voice struck the air like a bell tolling for war.

"Vengeance."
The word did not tremble. It rang.
A vow, a prophecy, a sword unsheathed in syllables.
And even Death paused to listen.
Jade's face shifted—just slightly.
Perhaps he remembered the **Baba Yaga's teaching**: *One must master the self before defeating evil.*
But it was too late for that.
The plan lay shattered. Hope was bleeding beside them.
And in the dark, a reckoning had begun.

16. Vessel of Power

In the hollow stillness that followed Morganite's fall, Diamond sank to her knees, alone in the dark. Chains bound her wrists, cold as betrayal, yet her hands lifted in prayer—not to Gods who had long abandoned the cries of mortals, but to the distant stars that still dared to shine through ruin. Her voice trembled like the last breath of a dying flame, soft as snow but threaded with defiance.

"Let not his sacrifice be swallowed by the void," she whispered. "Spare the boy. Light the way. And let me stand when all else falls."

The chamber gave no answer. Only the echo of her plea lingered in the stone, fragile as a memory.

Yet within her—deep beneath the weight of fear, deeper still than sorrow—a single ember stirred. It did not roar. It did not cry. But it glowed. Quiet. Unyielding. A flame that would not go out. She did not know how the world might be mended. She could not see the shape of victory. But she knew—utterly—that her story had not ended here.

The stars had not brought her through fire and shadow only to let her perish in chains.

They had placed her here for a reason. And she would rise.

Evil Basalt stepped forward, her boots striking the stone floor with the finality of hammers on a tomb. The echo

rolled like thunder in a crypt, sealing the moment with dread.

Her gaze narrowed, glinting like polished obsidian—predatory, precise.

"Then tell me," she murmured, voice soft as velvet drawn across broken glass, "who shall reveal the hiding place of Onyx? Shall it be you?"

She turned, slow and theatrical, to face Jade—still bound, still draped in the guise of a woman. Her movement was a dancer's—graceful, cruel.

Diamond's breath hitched. Her heart slammed against her ribs as she cried out, "No—she knows nothing of Onyx!"

Basalt stilled. Her brow lifted with cruel amusement, a serpent uncoiling its delight.

She stepped closer, the space between them vanishing with terrifying ease. Her smile was carved from mockery and menace.

"It seems your tongue knows more than it dares confess," she purred. "And still... I offer mercy. Still... I withhold the storm. But you, Diamond—you walk the blade's edge. One misstep, and I shall show you what ruin truly tastes like."

She turned to Jade once more, her voice dropping to a hush so sharp it could have sliced through bone.

"Tell me," she whispered, eyes fixed on his. "Will the truth spill from your lips before the blood pours from hers?"

A silence stretched—taut, trembling, endless.

Diamond, heart pounding like a drum in a hollow hall, felt that fragile hope flicker once more. She understood: the next breath, the next word, might damn them both... or turn the wheel of fate.

"Pray, act not in such manner," she pleaded, her voice cracking under the weight of urgency. "Onyx is but a small creature—my faithful dog, no more than a wisp of shadow and warmth. How could he bear the weight of your lost Tresses? Your severed Powers?"

"We shall see soon enough," replied Evil Basalt, a gleam like cut obsidian flashing in her gaze. "He will be summoned, and the veil shall lift. Now—tell me. Where is he hidden? Does he still dwell in that withered house you once called home?"

"Nay," said Diamond, lifting her chin though her breath trembled. "I entrusted him to Hematite—the matron of the old coffeehouse. He waits with her still."

Diamond believed, in the quiet cradle of her hope, that not even Basalt's wrath could breach the sanctity of that coffee-house. She did not know—could not know—that Hematite had glimpsed Onyx's end the very day he crossed the threshold. A fate written not in blood, but in silence.

"Hematite, you say?" Basalt's gaze sharpened, her eyes narrowing upon Topaz and Spinel as if weighing stones in her hand. A glint of intrigue lit the hollow beneath her brow. "Then tell me—which of you dares to face what lies beyond the veil?"

"I shall go," Spinel declared, his voice taut with urgency. He longed for the taste of air not steeped in stone and sorrow, as if the very walls of the fortress weighed upon his chest.

"So be it," murmured Basalt. "Venture swift and return swifter—for with each breath I wait, a heavier grief presses upon me."

Her voice trailed into the dark like smoke dissolving into night, and Spinel slipped away without another word.

"You two may speak as you wish," she said, rising with a weary grace. "My tongue has danced long enough for one day."

With a faint scoff and a shake of her head—half disbelief, half disdain—she turned and vanished into the shadows, seeking silence at last.

Alone in the dim-lit corridors of the Fortress of Dread, Topaz lingered in silence, his eyes drawn not to Diamond, but to the shimmer of his own wings. They glowed faintly in the gloom, radiant and flawless—a reminder that he was more than what the world had made him. He smiled, though no one watched. The wings were enough. He did not look at her.

Instead, his gaze settled upon the other prisoner—the quiet one, the wounded one. Jade. Though bound and beaten, Jade held himself with the solemn pride of a fallen knight. Blood streaked his brow, and grime clung to his skin, yet something noble, something unyielding, still clung to him. It was not strength of sword or voice, but of spirit. And that, more than anything, kept Topaz staring longer than he meant to.

For in Jade's quiet defiance, Topaz saw a mirror—not of his pain, but of that rare thing he secretly craved: dignity. The same dignity he pretended to feel when admiring his wings.

"You linger," Jade said, his voice raw but steady. "Do I strike a chord in that shadowed soul of yours? Or have you simply grown fond of watching me?"

Topaz shifted, as if roused from a trance.

"I do favor you, maiden," he said at last, the words slipping out with hesitant weight. "There is... something in you. Something I know, though I cannot name it."

Jade's heart tightened. The lie of his disguise clung to him like a second skin—uncomfortable, necessary. The moment for truth had not yet come.

"Is that all you seek?" he asked coldly. "To ensnare maidens beneath the cloak of night and call it conquest? To take captives in their weariness and boast of your courage? I pity such valor, for it gleams no brighter than fool's gold. There is no glory in casting nets over the broken."

With quiet defiance, he lifted his chin and tossed back the hair clinging to his bloodied brow. Though bruised and bound, his eyes sparked with smoldering fury—no longer pleading, but daring. The fire within him had not been extinguished; it burned low and fierce, like coals waiting for wind.

Topaz turned his face away, as if the truth might be softer if not seen head-on. "There is... a strange pull in your presence," he murmured, voice rough with restraint. "You stir something in me—echoes I can't place, memories I don't remember living. I wonder... had we met beneath open skies, far from these cursed halls, what might we have become?"

Jade stepped forward, his voice a quiet beckon in the gloom—still cloaked in mystery, but charged with something deeper.

"Then free me," he said, each word gentle but weighted. "Let us find out what that path could be. Why must we speak through chains, when wind and sky still wait to name us?"

Topaz's gaze flickered. His fingers slipped from his weapon, trembling as if caught between fire and mercy. He cast a glance toward the far end of the hall—where Basalt loomed like a monument to ruin, silent, still... but all-seeing.

"I would," he breathed, barely audible. "But she... she would burn the world to cinders, just to teach me the cost of defiance."

She had heard.

Without warning, she raised one hand—and from her fingers flew a shard of enchanted glass. It sliced through the air like moonlight turned to blade—silent, swift, and merciless. The sliver struck Jade across the cheek, tracing a crimson arc. He staggered back, gasping, half-falling.

But in that breathless instant—while all eyes turned to the witch's wrath—Jade moved. Like a falcon snapping its tether, he twisted, tore free the last of his bindings, and vanished into the gloom of the fortress, swift as shadow over stone.

A scream ripped from Basalt's throat, shrill and inhuman. Her eyes blazed, seething with fury as she turned on Topaz.

"Traitor!" she roared. "Was it you who let her slip through the cracks of fate? Shall I carve loyalty into your bones?"

Topaz fell to his knees, hands open in surrender. His heart thundered, unsure whether the blame was just or merely convenient—but the witch had found her scapegoat, and mercy was not in her nature.

But even fury fades before obsession.

At that very moment, Spinel emerged from the veil of mist, his fur glistening with dew and his breath shallow with haste. Curled within his trembling claws was a fragile bundle of life—Onyx, limp but breathing, his dark fur slick with shadow and rain.

Basalt's fury, which had once scorched the chamber like wildfire, now cooled into something far more dangerous—hunger. Her eyes locked onto the dog, and she stepped forward with the reverence of a queen presented with the crown she believed forever lost. Her lips parted, slow and trembling, not in horror—but in joy.

"Ahh..." she breathed, her voice laced with wonder and a twisted kind of triumph. "At last."

All else faded. Topaz vanished from her mind. The prisoner's escape meant nothing.

For Diamond stood helpless before her, and the dog—the hound who contained her powers—was here at last. The time of waiting had ended. The stars had shifted. The dark was ready to claim its price.

She lifted Onyx into the air, cradled between her clawed fingers like a relic long buried. The dog did not whimper. He did not struggle. He simply looked at Diamond—steady, solemn—like one who had always known this moment would come.

"This creature," Basalt thundered, her voice rising like a storm building on the sea, "is no mere hound."

She turned to her legion of cursed and craven followers. "Behold Onyx—the vessel of my stolen flame. It was Morganite who betrayed me, who spun from my severed tresses a soul and buried it within this quiet beast. A clever prison. A loyal mask. But not clever enough."

She turned in a slow, deliberate circle, her cloak sweeping behind her like the coils of a sleeping serpent roused to strike. Her voice dropped to a hush—more chilling than any scream.

"Fate demands balance," she said. "For my power to rise, the stolen fire must be reclaimed. The light must yield. The hound must fall. Pity has no place in prophecy."

Her fingers curled around Onyx like claws hungering for fate. Then she spoke—not in one voice, but in many, as if the echoes of forgotten centuries had found breath through her.

The chamber quivered. Whispers filled the air—ancient, cruel, incomprehensible.

The stones bled warmth. Shadows recoiled as if scorched by her breath.

From her mouth rose a black mist, thick and living, curling around Onyx like serpents spun of smoke and sorrow.

Behind iron bars, Diamond's scream rose like a wound torn open.

"No!"

She flung herself against the cold metal, her hands clawing for the unreachable. "He's innocent—only loyal—he followed me!" Her voice cracked, raw and desperate. "It was my folly. I called his name. I beckoned the dark. Punish me, not him!"

Her voice broke, and tears spilled freely now—unashamed, unrestrained.

"Forgive me, Onyx. Forgive my folly. Had I held my tongue... had I remembered the warning... this fate would not be yours."

The dog—small, weathered by hardship and shadow—lifted his head.

And in that moment, the silence shifted.

A stillness fell.

Deeper than quiet. Older than time.

Onyx's eyes met hers—not with fear, not with confusion, but with something ancient. Something final.

A knowing.

And slowly... solemnly... he nodded.

The witch's chant deepened.

Stone groaned.

The floor trembled.

From the shadows came sparks—tiny flares tracing the hound's limbs like threads of fire unraveling fate itself.

A wind stirred where no door stood open, as if the air had remembered what it once feared.

Diamond collapsed to her knees, arms outstretched.

"Not him," she begged. "Take me instead."

But Basalt did not speak.

She had already chosen.

Her eyes—those glistening orbs of ancient hunger—gleamed brighter than the storm she conjured.

With cruel delight, she lifted Onyx higher—toward the vortex that now whirled above her palms, a maelstrom of hunger and hate.

And in the heartbeat before horror...

Before cry or scream or flame...

The stars—hidden behind stone, behind magic, behind the veil—wept.

Unseen.

For what was about to begin.

17. Wings of Ruin

Slowly, with a deliberation forged in darkness, Evil Basalt raised her hands to her raven-black tresses. Before Diamond's stunned gaze, the strands began to writhe, serpentine and sentient—braids of shadow and smoke, alive with ancient malice. When she spoke, her voice rose not from her throat, but from the marrow of the earth itself—deep, terrible, and unyielding.

"The hour is come, Diamond," Basalt intoned. "At long last... my powers return."

From the veiled corners of the chamber, where darkness thickened like old blood, emerged three Wraiths. Cloaked in the mantle of eternal night, their eyes burned like distant stars glimpsed through a dying sky. Each bore a blade wrought from the ruins of broken ages—cold, humming with the memory of lost wars. Time clung to them like ash, and knowledge passed behind their hollow gazes like storms behind glass.

Then came The Power of Illusion: a figure without shape, shifting and insubstantial, made of dreams half-remembered and nightmares ful y formed. It flickered and twisted, distorting reality like heat over desert stone.

And last of all came the Clock of Darkness.

It hovered—no chains, no gears—only silence and dread. Its hands did not move, yet with each passing breath they seemed closer to midnight. Etched upon its face were runes no mortal tongue could name, and with its coming, the light dimmed as if the world itself remembered to fear.

These were the Harbingers.

They gathered behind Evil Basalt like a crown of doom, awaiting only a breath, a word, a flick of her will to bring unmaking.

"Hear me," said Basalt, her eyes locked upon Diamond who still knelt defiant in chains. "I am not your judge, nor your executioner. That honor belongs to the one you fear to name—the dark sovereign of the Forbidden."

Her voice lowered, thick with mockery.

"He shall claim your soul. Upon the rise of the eighth sun, your soul shall unravel... and the flickering light of your kind shall be snuffed."

She turned slowly, her arms raised like a priestess of ruin.

"So let the prophecy burn in your ears, Starborn," she whispered, voice soft as falling ash:
"But should the Starborn stumble, and their soul be lost,
Then within eight days shall darkness rise.
And Emerland's final hope be swallowed by night."
She laughed then—not loud, but terrible—a sound like cracking ice beneath doomed feet.

From the edge of that grim tableau, Diamond stood frozen, her hand hovering near the Pentacle, heart ablaze with the urge to strike. But time—cruel and swift—betrayed her. The relic pulsed faintly beneath her touch, as though testing her resolve, and she faltered. Her spirit longed to rise like a star from the deep, but the weight of doubt bound her limbs like chains. She was not ready. Not yet.

"The Pentacle shall find no rest in unworthy hands," the kings of Emerland once decreed, their voices echoing through the ages like wind through ruined halls. They had guarded the relic through epochs forgotten, knowing that only one of pure strength—and of fire born not just from power, but from pain—could ever wield it true.

Basalt's venomous gaze fell upon Topaz. "Take her to the cage," she hissed, her voice like rusted iron dragged across bone.

A storm of silent defiance stirred within him. He seized Diamond—not with cruelty, but with the urgency of one clinging to the last strand of mercy. Her breath came shallow, her body battered, but her spirit had not yet shattered.

He carried her down the corridor of ash and whispers, past pillars carved with the faces of the forgotten. Shadows clung to the walls like cobwebs spun from grief. At the threshold of the inner chamber, he faltered—but Basalt's eyes held him fast, and he obeyed.

Diamond was thrown into a cage wrought of bone and obsidian. Behind her, the shadows deepened. And Basalt, without a word, slipped away into the sanctum of her power.

There, in her private chamber, she approached the ancient mirror—the one veiled in velvet and sin. She drew back the cloth with reverent fingers. Its frame was forged from the spine of a fallen saint; its glass rippled like a pond disturbed by nightmares.

"She is ready," Basalt whispered, her voice trembling not with doubt—but with hunger.

But the mirror did not show her reflection.

It showed fire.

Wild, unbound, it surged within the glass like a dragon roused from slumber. Not a flame of warmth, but of wrath—pure, soul-eating fury. The kind of fire that remembers what was stolen.

Basalt's eyes narrowed. With both hands, she turned the mirror to face the cage.

Diamond stirred.

Her eyes fluttered open just as the flames erupted from the glass—not with heat, but with silence.

The fire did not burn her flesh. It reached inward, bypassing skin and bone, seeking the very thread of her being. It wrapped around her soul like a lover, then pulled.

And pulled.

And pulled.

Her scream never left her throat.

The light dimmed. The mirror went dark.

Diamond collapsed.

Not unconscious—empty.

Her body lay crumpled upon the cold stone floor, unmoving. Her eyes remained open, but vacant. The music of her spirit—the fierce, radiant melody that once echoed through every chamber of her heart—was gone.

Stolen.

Basalt stepped forward, silent and slow, like a mourner at her own wedding.

With a motion of almost sacred gentleness, she set the mirror back upon its altar—restoring it like a relic long missed.

And as she turned from the mirror's dark face, a cruel smile unfurled upon her lips.

The harvest was complete.

In that cruel hour, there was no time to think, no breath left to speak. The witch's spell had halted the very rhythm of the world—suspending wind, silencing birdsong, freezing even the pulse of time itself. In the span of a heartbeat, everything Diamond cherished was unmade, swept into a void beyond reason, devoured by the shadow of unraveling. And in the silence that followed, there was no sound—only absence, vast and hollow. Her spirit, too, seemed to flee her body, slipping away like smoke caught in a dying wind.

Emerland, once a haven of light and solace, now lay veiled beneath gathering darkness and the slow creep of shadow. In those final, fading moments, Diamond's heart cried out for courage—if only to deny the enemy the comfort of an easy triumph.

As the gloom thickened, Evil Basalt returned, her presence grim and imperious. With a regal sweep of her hand, she bade

Topaz stand guard over the captive Starborn. Then, wrapped in the chill of her own triumph, she ascended to her dread throne, eager to bask in the dread beauty of her newly awakened, fearsome tresses. This day had brought her victory—swift, bloodless, and rich beyond measure.

Yet Topaz, witnessing all this malice and cruelty, felt a thorned snare close around his thoughts. He could not look upon the agony without unease. The woman who had fled into the night haunted him still—like mist fleeing sunrise—and the witch's laughter, sharp and cruel, rang like cracked bells in his soul. The once-flickering joy he had known in Basalt's service now guttered, dim as a dying star swallowed by dusk.

He was caught—torn between waking and dream.

And in one dream, which returned to him with disturbing clarity, he saw his mother—gentle, radiant—tending to him and his brother beneath a sky untouched by darkness. They had been laughing, living quietly, peacefully. But then came the storm.

A storm like no other—howling with teeth of wind and drowning their joy beneath a tidal shadow. In the dream, they realized they lived not in Emerland, but across the Lake of Wonders... in the lands of the forsaken. And in that moment, his mother turned to him, her eyes filled not with fear but a strange resolve, and said:

"There must be a reason for it."

He always heard those words in the dream, and nothing more. Whether it was memory or illusion, he could never be sure. For when he awoke, there was no mother. No brother. Only shadow.

Only Basalt.

And he—Topaz—had chosen to serve her.

Because once, long ago, she had saved him from the storm. Though... perhaps it would have been better to die.

Who could say?

And yet, the voice of his mother always lingered—soft, stubborn, and inescapable:

"There must be a reason for it."

—

He blinked, and the vision dissolved.

His gaze shifted once more to Diamond, who now hovered at the brittle threshold between breath and silence. She was suspended—adrift in the hush between life and death—her light flickering like a candle lost in wind.

Soon, sorrow would devour her.

It would twist her mind like thorns around a rose, cloud her memories, drain her name of meaning, and sink her will into a pit from which none return whole.

And when the last of her resistance shattered...

...she would bow before a new and terrible master.

—

In mere hours, Diamond's world had collapsed. Fate had come like wildfire—ravenous, unreasoning—leaving only ash in its wake. The storm had torn through all she loved. Her grief had no voice, her burden no name.

Life offered no comfort.

Death, no peace.

Only one truth remained, heavy as iron and inescapable as dawn:

Emerland must endure.

Her thoughts flew to the three verdant leaves gifted by Baba Yaga—tokens of old magic: one to shield, one to flee, one to return. Like a secret heartbeat, the leaf of escape lay nestled deep within the seam of her weathered coat, hidden in Olivine's nest that Diamond kept close—a quiet relic of joy, untouched by the sorrow that followed. Though despair coiled tight around her soul, a whisper stirred within: it was not fury nor strength that awakened the leaf's magic—but the quiet defiance of the heart, the raw will to survive.

Diamond drew a breath as if pulling fire into her lungs. Her eyes flickered shut. Then, with a motion as soft as moonlight falling on water, she reached toward the left pocket of her coat.

Topaz's gaze sharpened, his instincts flaring like a falcon sighting prey. "What are you—"

But before his words could strike, before his hand could stop her, Diamond's fingertips brushed the leaf.

The runes ignited.

A surge of light exploded—not harsh or blinding, but beautiful and wild, like dawn ripping through a battlefield of night. Wind roared, though no wind blew. Magic, ancient and breathless, shimmered through the space between heartbeats.

And in that breath—she vanished.

Gone like a memory snatched from waking, Diamond slipped between worlds. Her form dissolved into radiant threads, faster than shadow, faster than Jade's own daring escape. Where she had stood, only a shimmer lingered, a trembling in the air—as if hope itself had exhaled.

Evil Basalt stood ensnared in a tempest of unraveling fate.

Around her, shadows fractured, mirrors bled light, and the air itself recoiled—as if the very world rejected her failure. Her thoughts clawed through the fog of disbelief, groping blindly for reason, but found only silence. Not the silence of stillness—but the suffocating quiet of a scream swallowed whole.

A low, inhuman sound coiled in her throat.

She spun.

Her eyes locked on Topaz.

He stood trembling beneath the dripping arches of her throne room, cloaked not in power but in disgrace. He would serve. A scapegoat. A broken coin cast to the feet of the Nameless Master.

For to falter now was to invite annihilation. And the Master's fury did not scold.

It devoured.

The mist within her chamber swirled, condensing into a crown of rage upon her brow. When at last she found her voice, it came not as speech, but as judgment.

"This cannot be!"

Her cry shattered glass and bone alike, echoing with such force that the walls seemed to bleed shadow. "You have squandered my most precious prize, Topaz! The soul... the Starborn... she was mine—mine to unravel, mine to offer! And now?"

She stepped forward, the floor cracking beneath her heel.

"There shall be **ruin** for such failure. You will pay—**with blood, or with soul.**"

"It happened in a breath," Topaz whispered, forcing steadiness into his voice. But his eyes betrayed him—darting to the wings that shimmered still with fading grace, as if they could hold back the storm gathering inside his chest. He kept his chin high, as though defiance alone could stop the grief from spilling. Yet behind the mask of courage, he was crumbling. His wings—his freedom, his pride—trembled with him.

"Then I shall still your breath," the witch replied, her voice like frost carving its name into glass. "Let time forsake your hours. Let all who gaze upon you know the price of disobedience. None defy me and walk away unscarred."

She moved with terrible beauty—graceful, unhurried, inevitable. Her blade slid from its sheath with a hiss that sounded like dying stars, its edge laced in ancient curses, honed by centuries of silence and vengeance.

And then—she struck.

The sound was not of metal meeting flesh, but of destiny torn apart.

Topaz gasped—not in pain, but in disbelief—as his wings were cleaved from him in a single arc of glowing steel. Feathers, kissed by skyfire, scattered like falling snow. His knees buckled as the remnants of heaven lay at his feet.

He fell to the earth—not because of the blow, but because there was no sky left to hold him.

In great haste, Topaz fled, unable to bear the sight of his broken wings. His sorrow clung to him like a shroud, heavy and suffocating. There was no joy left—only silence, and the bitter sting of what had been lost. His wings—his glory, his pride—were no more, and with them vanished the last spark of purpose. He ran, swift and shattered, seeking a place where no eye could follow, where even memory might fail to reach him.

At last, he found it: a withered tree, ancient and bare, its limbs stretched to the sky like the hands of a forsaken god. Beneath its twisted crown, he saw himself—ruined, hollow, forgotten. And there he collapsed, wordless and still, letting the earth cradle what remained. The wind did not speak his name. The stars did not mourn. Only the tree remained, witness to the quiet fall of a soul undone.

18. Before the Light

Topaz raised his voice to the unseen sky, sorrow etching every word. "When you give life, do you see the end? Or do you cast us adrift upon fate's tide?"

Childhood grief stirred in him, but his vow to the witch held fast—not for gain, but for truth.

"I shall honor the hand that gave me breath."

As his words echoed, the sky darkened. Wind tore through the silence like grief unspoken.

But Topaz did not flinch.

From the tempest, Rock the Hawk emerged—majestic, solemn, a sentinel borne of storm.

Topaz looked up, eyes wide with the quiet ache of not knowing. Rock the Hawk wrapped his wings around him like a cloak of dusk and said gently,

"Topaz, you are not what they made you believe. You were not born of malice—that is why your heart aches so. Your mother was Bulwark, the Brave Bird. She gave her life to save a soul beyond measure."

Topaz's voice broke as tears shimmered in his eyes.

"My mother was Bulwark," whispered Topaz, his voice low as embers fading in the wind. "The Enchanted Bird."

Rock the Hawk gave a solemn nod. "And you have a brother, Topaz."

Topaz lifted his gaze, the words striking something dormant in his soul.

"His name is Jade," Rock continued gently. "I saved him from the storm that scattered your nest. I searched for you too, but the winds had taken you far. He now walks the Forbidden Forest... in the guise of a woman."

A flicker passed through Topaz's eyes—recognition, aching and sudden. "I saw him," he breathed, and with that, the dam broke. Tears spilled, fierce and unbidden. "And my task... is to take his life."

Silence fell like snowfall.

"Why?" Topaz cried out, his grief raw, unguarded. "Why do you burden me with this now?"

"I do not speak to wound you," said Rock, his voice soft as dusk. "But so you may choose your path, not have it chosen for you."

The hawk's gaze, full of age-old sorrow, held him steady. "The storm stole your past, Topaz. I only wish to return your future."

"My loyalty is pledged to the witch," said Topaz, his voice low—each word heavy with a sorrow born of ancient, unspoken oath.

"Then I am proud you are of my blood," replied the Rock, his voice deep and unwavering. **"For you carry a rare virtue, Topaz—one that honors all debts, be they to the just or the damned. That is the mark of true nobility. You shall be remembered as a hero, not for whom you served, but for the strength to bear it."**

He paused, as if weighing his next words on the scale of fate. **"Live on with courage, my child. That is all I ask."**

And with that, the Rock vanished, swallowed by the wind.

Topaz stood alone.

His eyes fell to the space where wings once had been. Still gone.

Yet a faint smile curved his lips—soft, bitter, and full of ruin.

Even if wings returned, he thought, there would be no flight.

He was bound, not by spell or shackle, but by a deeper curse: Chains forged of choice.

Chains no blood could break, and no words could unbind.

In the shadowed heart of the Forbidden Forest, where thorns whispered secrets and moonlight feared to linger, a young man named Amethyst walked the twilight paths of longing. Son of Morganite—though the world, in its blindness, claimed King Alexandrite as his sire—he dwelled beneath the crooked roof of Jabba Doom Gabbro. Yet even within her shelter, he felt adrift. Love bound them, yes—but not the kind that soared. Jabba's love clung like ivy, winding tight, offering warmth that smothered more than it nurtured. And Amethyst, though loyal, felt like a flame caught in glass—seen, but never free to burn.

Jabba Gabbro dictated every detail of Amethyst's life—where to go, when to move, what to say, and what to withhold. It was not the kind of life he craved. Amethyst longed to explore the world on his own terms, to drift through the wild air of the Forbidden Forest like the wind itself, unclaimed and untethered. And yet, Jabba would always remind him: freedom was not the absence of rules, but obedience to the ones she laid down. "You are free," she would say, "so long as you do not wander from what I permit."

He hated those words. But he respected her. She was his mother—or so he believed—and that truth, however uncertain, was enough to bind him. So he folded his wings of longing and buried his hunger for more. For her sake.

His only solace was Agate—a sleek, Silver coated horse with the quiet gift of flight. In secret hours, Amethyst would ride him high above the treetops, soaring where no one dared follow. The sky, at least, made no rules.

And being Jabba's son came with certain... advantages. No one in the forest questioned him. No one challenged him. And in his pocket—ever ready, ever close—was the enchanted winning potion Jabba had slipped into his coat. A single drop, she had told him, could turn ruin into victory, despair into triumph. She called it her "final word," and made sure he never left home without it.

Not long ago, Toxico T—his uncle—had pledged allegiance to Evil Basalt. Amethyst had overheard a bitter quarrel between him and Jabba Doom Gabbro, a moment seared into memory. Toxico T had claimed him, declaring that Amethyst was heir to the throne. The words struck like thunder, leaving Amethyst adrift, uncertain of where he belonged. Since then, Jabba Gabbro had grown ever more protective, guarding him not just from danger, but from the truth.

And in the heart of this storm of clashing loyalties and half-spoken truths, Amethyst found himself ensnared—wrestling with the fragile threads of reality, caught between the shimmer of illusion and the weight of what might be real.

Then one twilight, Amethyst overheard Toxico T whispering of ending his life. That night, unable to bear the weight of his own thoughts, Amethyst wandered to his quiet refuge—a tree, vibrant and verdant, standing sentinel beside a lake so vast its edges blurred into the horizon, like the unanswered questions of his soul. He did not wish to return home. He lingered there, longer than he was ever meant to stay, as if the earth beneath him might offer the truth his blood could not.

The question—*"Who am I?"*—echoed within him like thunder trapped beneath skin. More haunting still was the silence that followed it. Why had he been abandoned? Why did every thread of affection now feel like rope—tightening, binding, false? Even Jabba's love, once his anchor, now felt like chains.

And so, with a heart heavy as stone and eyes blurred by unshed tears, he closed them at last, letting the wind cradle his face. There, beneath the tree that knew all his secrets, he whispered a single wish—desperate, trembling, and pure:

Let me be loved. Truly.

Let it be mine, and mine alone.

Not a lie. Not a shadow.

But something real. At last.

The hour had grown late, and though Jabba was not his true mother, Amethyst turned his path toward her home—for she had loved him like one. But just as he gathered his strength to rise from the moss-covered earth, a sudden wind tore through the grove, fierce and strange, as if the forest itself had drawn breath and now exhaled in warning. The gale wrapped around him like a whispered summons, blinding his vision with flying leaves and cold urgency. He shut his eyes tight.

When he opened them again, the world had changed.

Something had fallen like a star breaking through the firmament. A woman—her form cloaked in emerald leaves, as though the forest had cradled her descent. There she lay, half-curled in the grass, soaked not with dew but with blood and light. A hush fell over the trees, as if they, too, beheld a miracle.

Amethyst stood motionless, spellbound. For one impossible breath, he believed she could not be real. She was too luminous—her face aglow with a gentle radiance not born of moon or sun. Her lips were parted slightly, as though she had fallen mid-song, and her brow was furrowed in sleep or pain or both. She looked like the very image of longing—fragile, fierce, and unknowable.

He stepped closer, every heartbeat a thunderclap within his chest.

At first, he saw only her beauty, and the world dimmed around her. But then his gaze drifted downward—to the gashes across her arms, the dark stain spreading across her side, and the tremble in her fingers that clutched at nothing. She was hurt—deeply. Her suffering bled into the earth, a silent lament.

With trembling hands, he knelt beside her. His fingers brushed her cheek—warm, fevered, real.

And in that moment, something shifted in him.

It was not pity that bloomed in his chest.

It was not fear.

It was something far more dangerous.

It was love.

Tears welled in Amethyst's eyes. He did not ask who she was, nor from whence she came—for something in her face stirred an ancient recognition, as if his soul had known her across lifetimes. Yet one question rose above all others, fierce and aching: *How does one breathe life into one so near to death?*

Only one name came to him. One whose power and strange wisdom might yet hold back the veil—his mother, Jabba Doom Gabbro. If she willed it, she might save this fallen star. Without hesitation, Amethyst gathered the girl into his arms, mounted Agate, and rode hard into the wind—toward home, toward hope, with Diamond cradled close against his chest.

19. Flesh and Fire

Jabba Doom Gabbro sat hunched on the warped wooden porch, her gnarled fingers clenched around a chipped teacup that had long since surrendered its warmth. Amethyst was late—too late—and though the sky had folded into a velvet hush, it wasn't the hour that gnawed at her. It was the waiting. She had waited before—waited when all she'd had was Doom: in name, in fate, in breath. And the longer she waited, the more that name coiled around her like a noose, whispering she would never be free. Long ago, beneath this same tired sky, she had waited for a voice to break the silence. None came.

No one spoke to her. Not the wind that passed her crooked door. Not the trees whose roots wound round her home. Only a solitary rooster visited now and then, pecking at the crumbs she scattered outside her crooked hut. And so, Jabba Doom Gabbro would sit on the worn stone step, telling him all her woes—how the world had forgotten her, how even crows refused to land upon her roof. The rooster never replied, but tilted his head just so, as if listening. That was enough. At last, someone found her company worth keeping.

But then Death came—not with mercy, but with malice cloaked in generosity. She cast a gift like a net across Jabba's life: the

Deathly Chattel, and a cursed book so steeped in black magic it bled sorrow between its pages. With them came the unraveling. Her son died. His daughters vanished like dust in a storm. Jabba wept, but no one came. No voice answered her cries.

And so, in grief's ashes, she chose to rise. She took the curse Death had flung at her and turned it to her advantage. She read the dark book—every word, every wound—and taught herself the language of roosters. They became her only friends, and in time, her only family. She no longer needed the world.

Then came a knock. King Alexandrite, wrapped in sorrow, arrived to wield the Deathly Chattel. And in that bitter trade, Jabba gained something beyond spells—a child, Amethyst, heir to the throne. She read the forbidden tome until its secrets sang to her. No longer merely a mort, Jabba became something more—one of the most powerful witches alive. And in her grasp slept the future king.

But Amethyst had not returned. Midnight came, and the clock struck with a hollow chime that echoed through Jabba Gabbro's bones. For a breath, she considered venturing into the wild herself, to trace his steps through the haunted dark. But then—a whisper of movement. Footsteps. She felt them before she heard them.

Without waiting for a knock, she flung open the crooked door of her enchanting hut—a dwelling perched on rooster's feet, a tribute to both her arcane power and her peculiar fondness for the bird.

There stood Amethyst, shadowed and solemn, a limp woman cradled in his arms. Blood marred his tunic, dried like rust—evidence of suffering, of sacrifice... and something darker than mere defiance.

Jabba Doom Gabbro's fury blazed with each breath, her voice slicing the air like shattered stone. "Amethyst! You bring death to a place still clinging to life! Turn back the way you came—with the same reckless haste—and cast this cursed omen from my hearth before her shadow takes root!"

Amethyst stood firm, unmoved by the storm before him. His voice, quiet but unyielding, carried the weight of truth and hope. "Her breath still stirs—faint, but present. Please, Mother... save her."

Gabbro's reply came swift and cold, her voice sharp as winter glass. "I do not meddle in what lies between breath and burial," she said, each word falling like sleet. "Bear her back to whatever cursed realm she crawled from—let her fate be hers alone."

But Amethyst would not yield. He pleaded, again and again, his voice cracking with desperation. Yet Jabba Gabbro would not bend. Her eyes, dark and unmoved, flicked toward the shadowed woods beyond. "The Forbidden breeds illusions," she hissed. "It crafts ghosts from leaves and whispers. You bring me a stranger—and in these lands, shadows wear many skins. I will not risk my blood for a trick of the dark."

Then came the rooster—Jabba the Cluck—strutting boldly into the silence like a herald from some absurd dream. His feathers shimmered with strange iridescence, and he let out a single, sharp crow that shattered the stillness. He lifted one claw, pointed straight at the girl's throat.

There it gleamed—the Pentacle.

Jabba Doom Gabbro froze.

Her breath hitched as her eyes locked on the sacred symbol. She leaned closer, slowly, as though the very air had thickened around her. Her fingers twitched, half-raised—drawn toward it by instinct, memory, fear. Yet some unseen law halted her touch, as if the Pentacle itself repelled her.

Recognition dawned not like lightning, but like a fog creeping over ruined fields—slow, solemn, inevitable.

Her voice broke the hush in a whisper. "So it's true," she said, more to the past than to anyone present. "All these years... and the lie still burns."

Her eyes darkened. Her body swayed, trembling with fury barely caged. King Alexandrite. The betrayal. The secret she was never meant to know.

But she drew herself upright, forced stillness back into her limbs. Her voice, when it returned, was calm as winter frost—deadly and precise.

"She shall not perish—not while the Pentacle rests upon her neck," Jabba said, her voice steady as stone. "Set your worry aside."

She bent low over the wounded maiden, eyes narrowing at the torn flesh along her side where darkness had bitten deep. Without looking up, she gestured. "Go to the kitchen. Bring the eternal water. Then find the flesh that will mend what has been undone."

A hush lingered between them. Amethyst watched his mother, bewildered by the sudden shift—from fury to focus. The rage that had flared so hot was now tempered by something colder, older. Whatever force moved in her now, he welcomed it. At least she was tending to Diamond.

"Mother," he said, his voice low but urgent, "what kind of flesh is needed to restore her?"

Jabba did not answer right away. Her eyes flicked to the girl's broken frame, and something ancient stirred in her gaze.

"The kind you would see her robed in," she murmured, "or the flesh of something noble and fierce. For though she looks delicate, death will not yield to fragility."

Without a word, Amethyst turned and vanished into the starlit wood, driven by duty—and something softer, unnamed, pulling at the edges of his heart.

Beneath the silver boughs, he found Agate waiting, still and watchful.

He stepped close and placed a hand upon her mane. "Will you give of yourself, that another may live?"

the horse bowed his head, moonlight dancing along her flank. "Only if you promise me freedom beneath the open sky."

"I swear it," Amethyst said.

And so, Agate gave of himself—flesh torn freely, a gift offered without complaint. Amethyst caught it in trembling palms, cupping the bloodied piece like something sacred. With care, he anointed Agate's wound with the Eternal Water, watching as the glow of healing light swelled and shimmered.

But as the radiance faded, doubt crept in—cold, quiet, and cruel. Was it enough? Would this humble offering be sufficient to summon back the light in Diamond's fading form?

Then, from the hush of trees emerged a lioness, radiant and terrible in her beauty. Her golden mane shimmered like fire beneath the moon's solemn gaze, and each step she took stirred the earth with power. Her amber eyes met his—unyielding, wise, and old as song. Yet Amethyst did not falter.

The moon hung low, veiled in drifting clouds, casting a ghostly sheen across the clearing. Silver light shimmered against the lioness's fur, turning her into something mythic—half shadow, half flame.

He dropped to one knee, breath tight in his chest. "Queen of the wild," he said, voice soft but resolute, "I ask for a piece of your flesh—to save someone fading fast. She doesn't deserve this end. Let your gift keep her soul burning."

The lioness did not stir. Her golden eyes held him, seeing not the words he spoke but the shape of his soul beneath them. Silence stretched like a bowstring. Then she spoke—her voice deep, smooth, and resonant, like thunder wrapped in silk.

"I shall grant what you seek," she said. "But first, find the stag that dances in the shadowed grove. Bring it to my cubs. They have only ever known the ache of hunger and the bite of cold wind. Feed them, and I shall give you a part of myself—not my life, but enough."

Amethyst bowed low, reverence in every breath. "Gladly shall I fulfill thy bidding," he declared, his voice as sure as the mountain wind.

With unshaken resolve, he vanished into the forest's veiled heart. Twilight laced the branches like silver thread, and the hush of the grove welcomed him. There, beneath the breath of dusk, he found the deer, graceful and unafraid, and offered it to the lioness's young. When they were fed and stilled, the mother stepped forward, and with solemn grace, she parted her own flesh—not in pain, but as a gift freely given.

Returning beneath the velvet dome of night, Amethyst rode silently atop faithful Agate. his hooves made no sound on the moss-cloaked path, as if the forest itself held its breath. In Amethyst's arms, wrapped in quiet desperation, lay the final offering—the noble flesh, still warm with courage. He held it close like a final prayer, knowing it might be all that could save her.

At the threshold of the crooked hut, the air thickened with the scent of herbs, smoke, and sorrow. Jabba Doom Gabbro stood waiting, her shadow stretched long across the dirt floor, cast by firelight and fate. She moved to Diamond's side with a reverence not often granted by one the world had tried to forget. With trembling fingers, she dabbed the girl's wounds with the flesh, anointing them with the last drops of eternal water—an elixir older than stars, older than grief, older than song.

"She'll endure," Jabba murmured, her voice rough as wind through stone. "Let her sleep. Let her drift till the sun dares rise again."

Amethyst hesitated. "But what if she wakes? What if she needs—?"

"She won't need anything," Jabba interrupted, not unkindly. "Jabba the Cluck will stay by her side, faithful as always. And if the Gods have any mercy left, they'll let her sleep through till morning."

She turned back to the fire, her silhouette tall and strange against the shifting glow. Then, as if speaking to no one—or perhaps to something far beyond—she let out a bitter laugh, curling from her throat like smoke.

"What madness to think she needs anything at all," she muttered. "The girl's tasted the flesh of two noble beasts. Tell me... is that the act of a mortal? Or something else entirely—something cloaked in grief and hunger, wearing a girl's face?"

At dawn, the light did not come.

Dark clouds clung to the heavens, brooding and low, casting the world in a twilight hush. Amethyst rose without a word. The air smelled of damp earth and endings. With careful, reverent steps, he entered the small chamber where the woman slept.

Diamond lay still, her breath as faint as mist curling on a winter river. But her eyes were open. She had been waiting. Their gazes met—soft, silent, searching. No words passed between them, yet something unspoken lingered, fragile as morning frost.

Then the silence shattered.

Jabba Gabbro swept into the room, her steps striking the stone like hammers of judgment. Her robe flared behind her like a storm cloud caught in motion. Her eyes, dark as iron, fell upon Diamond with a fire that did not burn—it cauterized.

"You seem whole in spirit," she said at last, her voice a sharpened knife wrapped in velvet. "Then you must leave."

She did not sit. She did not soften. No bread was offered. No tea warmed the air. The hearth remained cold.

"When next you stand before your sire, King Alexandrite," she continued, "tell him his silence festers. That shadow rises, and the cost of his cowardice mounts like bones at a gate. Let him wear the weight of it. Let him carry what he chose to cast aside."

The room fell still again, but the words did not. They clung to the air like ash after fire—bitter, black, and unshakable.

"What do you mean by such words?" Amethyst asked, his brow knit with quiet thunder, his voice a blade honed by grief. The air between them thickened, stirred by a tremor neither wind nor time could quell—for his mother's bitterness struck not merely with scorn, but with an omen.

"You need not decipher riddles," Gabbro replied coolly, her smirk curving like a crooked blade. **"I did as you asked. I saved her. Now be gone."**

"Then I shall take her," Amethyst declared, his voice resolute, his stance unshaken. **"Wherever her path leads, I will walk beside her."**

But then Jabba Gabbro turned, her expression hollowing into something older than wrath—older than sorrow. Her voice dropped, low and sharp, as though spoken through the teeth of fate itself.

"But heed me well," she said. **"When twilight falls and the stars begin to burn, it will not be Diamond who returns from the edge of Emerland. It will be you. And you alone. Mark these words, my son—for night is coming, and not all who love are meant to stay."**

20. The Light Returns

Diamond said nothing. But in her silence, she understood. Jabba's words had carved her soul like a chisel to stone—sharp, irreversible. There was no path but forward now—no sanctuary left in yesterday. Her limbs moved like stone carved from sorrow. Yet still, she stepped toward the unknown.

Amethyst, ever her quiet sentinel, extended his hand. She took it—lightly, uncertainly—as though the gesture belonged to someone else, someone still whole. He helped her onto his horse, but the chill of her touch startled him. It was not the cold of wind or weather, but the cold of fading—like she was slipping from the world by degrees, and he could do nothing but bear witness.

"Emerland Woods, dear Diamond," murmured Amethyst, her voice gentle as falling ash. But Diamond did not stir. She sat motionless in the saddle, a ghost clothed in flesh. Two deaths in one day had carved her hollow. The world, once ablaze with marvels, now wore only a shroud of gray—the color of mourning and memory

"Naught but a trifle," Diamond replied, her voice brittle. "A mis-step upon a high bough. Nothing worth remembering." It was all she could offer.

"A fall from a tree?" Amethyst chuckled, his voice as soft as wind rustling through rain-soaked leaves. "I fell once too — more than once, in truth. But I climbed again. And again. Until the tree stopped shaking, and I stood."

Diamond's gaze softened, the edges of memory rounding into gentler shapes. She recalled the first time she fell, how Master Steward had caught her tears before they reached the earth and urged her to try again. "He believed in me," she whispered. "Always."

There was no boasting in Amethyst's voice—only quiet devotion, as steady and unshakable as the earth beneath their feet. Diamond held his gaze. And for a breathless instant, the world hushed.

Something passed between them—not spoken, not fully understood, but felt. A moment like mist in sunlight—vanishing, yet unforgettable.

"I nearly forgot," Amethyst said, his voice breaking through the hush like sunlight parting clouds, "to present our noble companion—Agate, my dearest steed. He carries not just my weight, but my moods, my silences, and my secrets. Now, he carries you too. When I call his name, he hears more than sound. He hears me.

And today... I offer that name to you as well."

And as she reached to stroke Agate's neck, the rain kissed her skin in soft droplets, like tears the sky wept on her behalf. A whisper stirred—not from the horse, but from memory.

"One day, your heart will thank me."

Hematite's voice, distant and delicate, drifted through the mist. Diamond had not understood her then. But now, beneath the gray hush of rain, the ache was softer than she feared.

Still, as Agate turned his head, something in her reminded Diamond of Onyx—his watchful eyes, his steady breath, his silent loyalty. The sorrow surged anew, curling inside her like smoke with no wind to carry it away.

Amethyst reached for her hand—not as a knight offering escort, but as a soul reaching out to another.

And she took it.

"Speak to me, Diamond," he said, voice hushed beneath the drizzle. "Why does your warmth fade so? The healing should be within you now. And yet... you seem to slip away."

She could not keep her brave face any longer. Tears broke from her eyes, unbidden and raw, and she spoke—not of healing—but of memory.

"Amethyst," Diamond began, her voice trembling like a leaf caught in the breath of autumn, "you are not the child of Jabba Gabbro. You are the true-born son of Morganite—Master Steward of Emerland."

She looked away for a moment, then met his gaze again, steady now. "And there is more. I must tell you all."

Then she spoke—of Morganite's death at the hands of Evil Basalt, of Onyx's brave end, of the moment her soul was stolen. She told him everything. Even the part where she would die in **eight** days. And two had already passed.

At first, Amethyst did not understand. The weight of it all pressed too heavily, too quickly. "You are to... what, in six days?" he repeated, as though the words were foreign, or his ears had betrayed him.

But Diamond did not flinch. She held his gaze, her voice no longer trembling.

"Whatever she did—whatever curse Basalt laid upon me—she took something from me. Stole it. And with every hour that passes, I feel... less. Less alive. Less whole. I feel a coldness in my bones. I feel death."

She did not cry. Not anymore. Her voice was distant, hollow—like someone speaking from the far side of sorrow, where tears no longer reached.

"I always knew Jabba wasn't my mother," Amethyst said quietly. "And my father... he left this world before I ever saw his face. I never even had the chance to mourn him."

He paused, his gaze unfocused, lost in some unreachable distance. "And now you tell me you'll die... in six days?"

His voice did not falter. No tears fell. He didn't shake or cry out. He simply held himself still—because he was a man holding a woman, and some ancient instinct whispered he must be strong.

Amethyst stepped forward. Without a word, he gathered her into his arms—not to comfort her, but to keep himself from breaking. In her silence, he found a steadiness he could not summon alone.

Then, Amethyst looked into her eyes—and something passed between them.

Their lips met—not with urgency or fire, but with a quiet vow. A kiss shaped by grief, and the fragile, flickering hope that perhaps... something beautiful might still survive the darkness.

"Evil Basalt," murmured Amethyst, as if speaking her name aloud might anchor the storm within him—to name the shadow was to face it. To face it, perhaps, was to defy it.

But names are not mere echoes. Names are chains, and spells, and summons. And somewhere beyond the veil—evil listened.

The witch's eyes snapped open, twin coals beneath a crown of dusk.

A shadow coiled around her spine like a serpent awakening from slumber, and her breath deepened—slow, deliberate, venomous.

"So... they dare speak my name," she hissed, rising from her throne woven of smoke and fused bone. "Let them try."

Wrath writhed in her chest, a nest of vipers biting inward, feeding on fury. "Six nights remain," she growled. "She must perish. Only then shall my master lift the stain of her escape."

Her fingers, pale as ash, drifted to her long, silken tresses—threads of power braided with forgotten curses. The moment she touched them, magic surged.

With a breath like a broken oath, Basalt called forth her sorcery. The Cloak of Darkness awakened—unfurling with a deafening crack, it surged behind her like a thunderstorm unchained, swallowing light, whispering death.

Far away, within the dim halls of Emerland Castle, Baba Yaga felt the shift. Her gaze met King Alexandrite's.

No words passed between them. None were needed.

The prophecy had begun to break.

"Evil wields the sword," Baba Yaga murmured.

"Evil holds the Starborn. And Evil has stolen her soul."

Once, this crown had burned with the fire of the Gods. Its light repelled demons, sealed ancient gates, and anointed kings with the strength to hold the line. But now it flickered—stripped of the blade that had once given it purpose. That sacred sword, forged before memory, was gone. Without it, the crown was neither shield nor beacon.

It was a relic.

And Emerland stood on the edge.

Baba Yaga, eldest of the forest's keepers, had foreseen such days. In dreams, she had watched thrones crumble, Gods weep, stars fall. She had buried hope before—but never like this. For the key to vanquishing Evil Basalt, the witch of fire and ruin, lay not in sword nor crown, but in a secret of evil's becoming.

And now the one meant to awaken it—the Starborn—was slipping into shadow.

Still, Baba Yaga did not yield.

She rose, spine straight as ashwood, and lifted her arms to the sky. "Then let the winds carry my call," she whispered.

With a cry like thunder, her ravens rose—wrought of storm and shadow, wings beating like war drums. They scattered into the twilight, bearing no parchment, only prophecy.

"To all who remember the light," she called, her voice ringing like silver across the trembling sky. "To all who dread the rise of night—come now. Rise now. Only six nights remain. Emerland shall not fall without a fight."

Far to the east, in her tower of twisted spires and poisoned stone, Evil Basalt stood before the Mirror of Shadows. Smoke writhed within the glass, and as ravens took flight across its surface, her laughter echoed through bone-carved walls—shrill, sharp, and unholy.

"Birds?" she hissed, her smile curling like fire catching in dry grass. "She sends birds against me?"

She turned to the cloak of darkness draped at her side and gave a nod. It understood.

And it departed.

What followed was not mere quiet—but a silence that devoured light, a stillness so vast that even time dared not move. It was the hush before extinction... the breath held before the world forgets itself.

Far beneath the golden hush of dawn, Diamond faltered.

Amethyst caught her—gently, like the fall of a petal—cradling her as though she were woven of light, fragile and fleeting.

A silence fell over the grove.

And though no voice had spoken them aloud, every soul that remembered the light heard them in their bones.

"When shadows lengthen and ancient malice stirs anew,

The Starborn shall rise—child of the fae, bearer of Emerland's crown-blood.

If the fire within their heart be kindled, and steadfast spirits hold true,

Then shall the light endure.

But should the Starborn falter, and their soul be lost,

Then within eight days the darkness shall devour all,

And Emerland's last hope be swallowed by night."

And already, the light recoiled—as if hope itself had been banished from the world.

At first, the change was slight: a pause between birdsong, the color of the trees losing their emerald sheen. But then came the darkness—not nightfall, but a power, a presence, cloaking the glade like a shroud drawn from some unseen hand.

It thickened like poisoned mist, curling in tendrils and then surging in waves, swallowing leaf and bark, sky and soil. It moved with intent, alive and malevolent. A wall of living shadow rose around them, coiling through roots and trunks, sealing every escape.

This was no storm. This was a curse—a veil spun by Evil Basalt herself.

And the glade, once bright with song, had become her snare.

"Agate!" Amethyst cried out, his voice a desperate blade slicing the dark.

But no hoofbeat came. No answering whinny, no stir of life. The forest had been swallowed whole.

Silence answered him—not silence born of peace, but the void of something stolen.

His voice echoed back, brittle and lifeless, like a question asked in a tomb.

There was no enemy to strike.

No blade to raise.

Only silence... and the soul he could not save.

He turned to Diamond, lying still as snow, her body curled in quiet repose. Not a flicker of fear touched her brow. Her face, serene. But the fire—the fierce, unyielding light that had once burned within her—was gone.

He gathered her into his arms, cradling her as one cradles a memory. Step by step, he carried her back to the stream's edge—the same place he had sat two nights before, whispering a wish into the wind.

And now, that wish had come true.

But at too high a cost.

"I asked for a soul to walk beside me," he murmured, his voice breaking as his tears fell upon her hair like rain upon scorched earth. "But if I had known the price... I would have chosen silence a thousand times. I would have lived alone in the dark—just to spare you this."

He knelt beside the stream, arms tightening around her as though he could will life back into her limbs.

"Take my strength," he whispered into the sky. "Take my joy. Let her live. Let her laugh again. Let me bear the shadow. Just... bring her back.

And in that hush, **Diamond stirred**. Her eyes fluttered open, and for a moment, he thought light had returned.

But her voice came soft and sad:

"No, Amethyst," she said.

She reached up, fingers brushing his cheek with the ghost of a touch.

"I failed **Emerland**," she whispered. "I failed before. Twice."

Her words pierced him deeper than any blade. But he held her close, unwilling to let go, even as the night crept closer

"No," he said. **"I will save you, Diamond. There must be something that can break this darkness. A key, a spark—anything!"**

Then his gaze fell — to the Pentacle of Emerland, resting against her heart, half-hidden beneath the folds of her cloak. The sacred sigil—cool, inert, as if it, too, had given up hope.

"What is this?" he murmured.

Diamond's lips barely moved. Her breath trembled through cracked silence.

"The Pentacle..." she whispered. **"I had forgotten... I have always been too weak to wield it."**

Her eyes shimmered with grief.

"It was never meant for me. I am no hero, Amethyst. Only a girl the world mistook for light."

Amethyst knelt beside her, his hand trembling as he took hers.

"Then let me bear it with you."

He lifted her hand and pressed it to the Pentacle with his own.

"You are not alone. Not anymore."

Their fingers curled over the sigil. For one heartbeat—nothing. Then—

The Pentacle erupted in brilliance—not a light to blind, but a light to heal. It poured through Diamond's veins like fire returning to the hearth, and through Amethyst's fingers like stars reborn.

It flared not from strength, nor lineage, nor prophecy fulfilled.

It flared from **love**—quiet, unshaken, real.

A brilliance burst forth—wild and pure—as if the very sky exhaled its first breath. The forest trembled. A **thunderclap split the heavens**. The shadows recoiled and shattered. The prison dissolved like ash in wind.

They were **free**.

Diamond collapsed into Amethyst's arms, her breath catching in awe. The Pentacle pulsed with radiant fire between them, no longer dormant—but awakened by a bond the darkness could not sever.

And Amethyst, cradling her, knew the truth.

He had bought them time.

Not enough to win.

But enough to **fight**.

Enough to **hope**.

And now, beneath the ancient tree where one wish had been answered, Amethyst made another:

The true battle for Diamond's soul had begun—and this time, he would not let her fall alone.

21. Battle Before Dawn

As soon as the darkness ebbed like a tide withdrawing from the shore, Amethyst rose—tall, silent, unshaken. He did not wait for dawn. The stars still clung faintly to the bruised sky, and yet he moved with purpose, for the moment Diamond's breath found rhythm in his arms, his own heart ignited. Thoughts surged like storm winds, scattering doubt—each one a flashing path that led to the same inevitable truth: her soul must be reclaimed before the sixth night fell, before the final grain slipped through the glass of doom and turned fate to ash.

Then the heavens stirred.

A shadow of wings swept across the sky—a thunderhead of ravens, blacker than midnight's grief, swarming above the ancient tree. They moved not like birds, but omens—swift as prophecy, precise as fate. One broke from the murder and dove like a streak of night, casting down a scroll sealed in deep-green wax, stamped with the symbol of forest flame.

Amethyst caught it with hands still trembling from all he had seen. The seal burned with Baba Yaga's mark—silver fire etched into a spiral of roots and stars. He cracked it open, and inside, scrawled in haste yet thunderous with meaning, were five words:

"A war—Light against Darkness."

No hesitation stirred his heart. He whistled, and Agate came galloping through the trees, swift as storm-wind, hooves barely touching earth. With Diamond wrapped gently in his cloak, Amethyst returned to the one place where she had never been welcomed: Jabba Doom Gabbro's hut.

Jabba narrowed her eyes as they arrived. She did not weep. She did not rise. But something in her face—tight as old rope—uncoiled. "She's fading," she muttered. "There's too much magic inside that girl. I warned her. But... I'll keep her alive. If I must."

"She's not just a girl," Amethyst said. "She's Emerland's last hope."

"And you?" Jabba asked, brushing dust from her palms. "Are you her sword—or her shadow?"

"I'm what she needs," Amethyst answered, voice low and steady. "And I ride to war."

Jabba's gaze shifted to Diamond's pale face—the barely-rising chest, the faded glow beneath her skin. Her mouth twitched.

"So it ends, then. Let the soul fall. And when it does, you'll be mine entirely."

Amethyst said nothing. Only bowed, placed Diamond gently in her mother's arms, and turned.

He did not look back.

He rode, and with him came the wild.

From the whispering woods, shadows stirred—not of fear, but of allies.

The lioness padded at his side, her golden eyes fierce with loyalty. Vampires rose from their hollowed glades, cloaked in dusk and bearing blades of frost. Even the whisper-trees, ancient and gnarled, leaned forward in silence as he passed.

By the time he reached the glade before Emerland Castle, he was no longer alone.

What had begun as a solitary rider on a weary horse had become a tide of life and purpose.

As Amethyst approached the castle, he remained mounted, bowing from the saddle to Baba Yaga, who stood waiting with quiet resolve.

Behind her, a meager band of warriors—no more than a dozen—stood scattered, weary, worn.

But then the earth began to thunder, and the trees gave way.

From behind Amethyst, the ground surged with kin and beast alike, a flood of faces drawn by courage, not command.

It was as though a sea had risen behind him.

He met Baba Yaga's gaze.

And just then, the sky answered.

From above came Rock the Hawk, wings wide with defiance, and beside him flew Jade—steadfast, wind-borne, and transformed.

They soared into the growing host, resolve burning like fire in their eyes.

In Emerland Castle, high above the banners dulled by years of regret, King Alexandrite opened the window he had once locked in grief. He drew in a deep breath as the march to the Fortress of Dread began—not a whisper of hope this time, but a storm of it.

In her obsidian stronghold, Evil Basalt froze. A tremor coursed through the black stone beneath her bare feet—not born of quake or storm, but of will. A force rising. The roots of the world stirred. The Fortress of Dread, forged in silence and sin, groaned like a slumbering beast disturbed. She turned to the Cursed Mirror, but it had already dimmed. Not with mist. With resistance.

They were coming. Not in days. In moments.

She had foreseen hesitation. Delay. Despair. But not this—**not an answer made of roaring hooves and burning hearts. Not the defiance of hope.** She had counted on their fear. She had misjudged the fire that still lived in their bones. *She clenched her fists until blood wept from her palms, but the pain did not quiet the truth: they were coming, and she had not stopped them.*

Gone was the mirror's certainty. Gone was her claim to mastery.

From the deepest vaults of shadow, where time curled in on itself like a dying star, the **Nameless Fear stirred.** He did not speak. He did not need to. His displeasure was thunder without sound—a pressure that bent the light and made walls weep blood. The fortress darkened at his awareness, like a sun eclipsed by something older than night.

His presence poured into her mind like smoke into glass. Thoughts not her own turned her spine to ice.

"You did not stop them."

Basalt fell to one knee—not in submission, but in self-preservation. She clutched the air, but it did not answer her.

"They march against us before the hour was ripe."

Basalt's breath caught. "The prophecy—"

"The prophecy was not theirs to wield."

There was no voice, and yet his meaning struck like a blade across the soul. **She was not the architect. She was the weapon. A vessel.**

Below the dread towers, the earth shuddered as if it, too, braced for war. From every corner of the realm they had come—warriors of Emerland clad in ancient armor, beasts of the old woods with antlers like spears, vampires with fire coursing through their veins, and the forgotten—those lost to time and tale—now risen to stand before the gates of shadow.

At the fore stood Baba Yaga, her staff held high, white hair unfurling like a banner of fate in the storm-swept wind. At her left, Amethyst reined in Agate, eyes burning with quiet purpose. At her right, Jade shimmered like a star loosed from the heavens.

Behind them, the lioness prowled, silent and regal, flanked by her vampire kin. Even the trees leaned in, ancient boughs bowed, as if listening for the cry that would ignite the end.

Evil Basalt emerged from the fortress gate, her silhouette cloaked in venomous shadow. Her eyes swept the field—cold, seething with malice. With trembling arms raised high, she summoned the last of her dying strength. The air trembled. Shadows convulsed. From the trembling dark rode three dread Wraiths upon steeds black as midnight, and behind them, phantoms slithered like smoke, formless and hungry.

"There is no more time," she hissed, her voice like iron dragged through ash. "Swear yourselves to the darkness now, and you shall stand beside me when the new age rises. The Lord awakens. The old light is dead."

Toxico T faltered, pale and uncertain, his trembling hands betraying the war within. But Spinel the Wolf stepped forward, snarling, eyes wild with fury—ready to kill or die. Then came Topaz, wings torn, soul shattered, yet heart still aflame. He took his place beside the witch—saying nothing, but pledging everything through pain.

The silence before the storm broke like glass.

Baba Yaga raised her staff. "Now."

The battlefield roared to life.

Lightning burst from Amethyst's blade as he charged. Vampires surged behind him, their hunger turned to vengeance. The lioness leapt forward with a thunderous cry, shielding her young and the man she loved from the rising dark. Rock the Hawk screamed from above, and Jade dove like a comet beside him.

Basalt unleashed her fury. The sky turned black as pitch. Gloom swallowed all light. Wraiths screamed through the dark. Shadows twisted into claw and fang. She struck with the power of ten dead ages—but Emerland's fire had been kindled anew.

Spinel, in wolf form, clashed with the lioness. Their roars split the night. Topaz faced Rock the Hawk in a bitter rematch, and fought with haunted fury, his wounds still open, not just upon his body—but across the soul he had tried to reclaim. No glory awaited him here. Only penance. Toxico T dared charge Amethyst, only to feel the lightning blade strike—once, twice— until he turned and ran like the coward he was.

Then, in the center of it all, Baba Yaga faced Evil Basalt.

Their duel was silent, grim, and terrible. Light against shadow. Memory against oblivion. Baba Yaga fought not with rage, but with resolve, every blow a prayer for all who yet lived. And Basalt, surprised by the force that met her, faltered—not defeated, but shaken.

The phantoms moved like drowned things—all eyes, all hunger, shrieking in voices that did not belong to them. But the vampires, starved for justice, tore through the mist with fangs like firebrands. Ghosts vanished like steam. The darkness recoiled, retreating inch by inch. But the lioness—brave and battered— collapsed beneath the weight of her wounds.

"Take her," Amethyst cried, lifting her into Rock the Hawk's talons. "Fly to my mother. Save her."

Then Amethyst rode—deep into the heart of the Fortress of Dread.

There, in a chamber choked with ruin and bone, he found the Cursed Mirror. Beside it, a small glass vial pulsed with pale light.

With trembling hands, he uncorked it—and in an instant, the bottle flared, blazing like a sun trapped in crystal. From within, like a breath returned to cold lips, Diamond's soul broke free.

Far away, in the quiet gloom of Jabba Gabbro's hut, Diamond stirred.

Light returned to her eyes.

And Evil Basalt, feeling that flicker of something ancient and defiant, screamed—a sound that split the sky. The shadows collapsed. The spell broke. And she—wounded not in flesh but in certainty—fled into the dark, her once-mighty army crumbling behind her like ash caught in wind.

When at last the echoes of battle faded into the bones of the earth, Baba Yaga turned to Amethyst. The storm had passed, but her gaze held the gravity of what still lingered. Her face, carved by time and wisdom, wore a rare and quiet softness.

"At first light," she said, her voice like twilight breaking, "take Diamond back to Emerland Castle. The respite will be brief. What comes next waits for no one."

Amethyst bowed his head in solemn assent, then cast a final glance across the field where courage had bloomed like wildfire in dry grass. Diamond slept—not in fear, but in the hush that follows victory hard-earned. Peace, at last, had found her—if only for a breath.

Nearby, Jade lingered beside Rock the Hawk, who had only just returned, having borne the wounded lioness to Gabbro's keeping the wind ruffling the bird's sleek dark feathers like whispers from the coming dusk.

"I think I'll stay a while longer," Jade murmured, eyes on the fading sky.

Rock gave a knowing caw of laughter. "Ah yes—because my cousin is visiting tonight."

At that, Jade's cheeks turned a delicate shade of rose. The others caught the glance that passed between them and burst into easy laughter, the sound rising like birdsong in a quiet glade.

And so, they parted with quiet joy. From his high tower, King Alexandrite gazed upon the returning stars—and for the first time in years, no tears touched his eyes. Though the war was far from over, the heavens no longer trembled. Laughter, cautious but true, found its way back to lips once sealed by sorrow. Smiles glimmered like lanterns caught in a gentle breeze. It was not triumph—not yet. The darkness still breathed, and the Nameless Fear had not spoken its final word. But for one fleeting night, beneath the weathered banners of Emerland, the wind carried no dread. Only the fragile hush of hope.

22. What Love Wakes

That night, as the moon spilled its silver hush across the floor like spilled dreams, Diamond turned to Amethyst beneath the quiet cloak of stars. Her gaze shimmered—not just with sorrow, but with something fiercer, something blooming. "You saved my life," she whispered, her fingers brushing his with the tremble of a vow. "And I would give mine to save yours. I swear it."

Amethyst's smile was soft, yet it held the weight of constellations—grief, longing, wonder. "I take my breaths in you, Diamond," he murmured. "You are the love I never dared to ask for... and the only wish I still believe in."

That same night, while all of Emerland slumbered beneath the hush of dreams and the slow turning of the moon, something else stirred. Evil does not sleep. It waits.

And beneath the black vault of the Fortress of Dread—where stars would not shine and the wind itself crept like a chained ghost—Evil Basalt stood at the shattered heart of her court, cloaked in the silence of rot and ruin—pillars cracked, banners scorched, the air heavy with old smoke and older shame. Around her, remnants of shadow crept like wounded beasts, silent and watchful, still trembling from the sting of their latest defeat.

"The time of the Lord's awakening is upon us," Basalt intoned, her voice forged in iron and ash. "If we slumber now, the hour shall pass us by—and who knows when such darkness shall rise again?"

Her gaze swept the circle of broken champions—hollow-eyed, armor rusted with dried blood, their lips sealed by silence and shame. But it halted on one: pale, sweating, trembling beneath her stare.

"Toxico T," she said, each syllable sharp as a dagger. "I want Diamond. And your sister guards her sleep."

He recoiled, hands twisting like reeds in a gale. "My sister... she does not guard Diamond. She guards Amethyst."

Basalt's eyes flared—twin shards of ice lit from within by cruel fire. "I asked for Amethyst long ago," she said, her voice low and glinting like the edge of a cursed blade. "And you gave me nothing but silence, wrapped in cowardice. Now I have failed before *Him*—before the One who watches from the void beyond light. The price of your hesitation is due."

She advanced a single step, and the shadows obeyed her motion, slithering forward like loyal hounds. The very air bent beneath her will, curdling with menace.

"You will bring Diamond to me before the stars extinguish," she hissed, her tone hard as obsidian struck upon stone, "or you shall offer your life to the darkness. One must be claimed before the dawn. Choose who it will be."

Toxico's heart fluttered like a dying moth against his ribs. His throat closed around the weight of dread. Even breath became a thing too costly.

"I go," he rasped at last, the words dry and brittle as scorched parchment. He did not believe them. Perhaps no one did.

"Spinel the Wolf will guide you," Basalt continued, her gaze falling to the massive, silver-flecked beast beside her—eyes glowing like coals in snow. "But heed me, both of you—return with empty hands, and only one of you shall crawl back. We shall learn which the darkness favors."

Spinel growled once—a low, primal sound—and without another word, the two vanished into the storm-veiled woods.

They did not knock.

They did not speak.

They came like breathless shadows to the edge of Jabba Doom Gabbro's crumbling hut, where two figures lay wrapped in the hush of healing sleep—Amethyst, his brow still furrowed in dream, and Diamond, motionless beneath the thin, trembling veil of the Pentacle's light.

Toxico crept toward her, each step weighted with dread. He reached out—

But could not touch.

The Pentacle flared, a silent warning. Its barrier shimmered like moonlight caught in frost, forbidding even his shadow from drawing near.

He stared, torn between fear and fury. The witch had warned him not to return empty-handed.

Then his gaze shifted to the other form—Amethyst.

A plan took root in his mind—dark, desperate, treacherous.

If I cannot take Diamond... I shall take the one she would die to protect.

Toxico's long-dormant power, once buried beneath cowardice, stirred at last. The fear of failure lent it shape. The fear of Basalt lent it fire.

And without a whisper, he cast the binding spell.

Chains of sleep coiled around Amethyst's limbs. Magic—jagged, black-veined, and bitter—sealed his voice and stilled his strength.

Toxico lifted him, heart racing.

And vanished into the night.

There awaited Basalt, veiled in stormlight and shadow.

When she glimpsed Toxico T and Spinel the Wolf returning so swiftly through the choking mist, a cruel smile curled across her lips—sharp, expectant.

But when her gaze fell upon what they carried—not Diamond, but Amethyst—the smile twisted, faltered, and broke into a snarl of molten rage.

"I asked for Diamond," she thundered, and the skies above the obsidian towers split with distant lightning.

Toxico dropped to one knee, holding Amethyst like a relic too fragile for the weight of his failure. "The Pentacle," he gasped. "It protected her. I couldn't reach her—not even the wind dared touch her. But... she will come. Diamond will come for him. My sister loves Amethyst. She would trade the world to bring him home. That is the only way he returns."

Basalt's eyes burned—twin coals sunk deep in a pit of night.

"Pentacle..." Basalt hissed, circling the unconscious Amethyst like a serpent poised to strike. Her eyes burned with a twisted hunger, as though studying a relic she had long sought to defile. "So now that cursed talisman shields her? The so-called Starborn—too weak to wield it, yet clutched by it like some sacred lamb. Hmph." She bared her teeth. "The Lord will be very pleased you retrieved that bloody charm—the same accursed thing that let the Elves triumph in The Hollow Star."

She turned to Toxico, her voice colder than black ice.

"She couldn't summon its light. Not even beneath my gaze. She collapsed into the dark. She pleaded with the shadows to claim her. And this..." Basalt's lips curled with disdain, her words like dripping venom, "this is the girl they dare call their hope? Emerland has gambled everything on a trembling ember—not a flame."

Basalt's voice curled with mockery. "I've seen them—the stolen kisses at twilight, the trembling hands clasped in fear. Let her prove herself now. Let her show she's more than a frightened child chasing shadows and dreams."

She turned her gaze upon Amethyst, a venomous smile blooming on her lips. "I want to see what love can do. I want to watch it unravel her."

She stepped closer, her voice a silken thread laced with poison.

"Tell your sister to strip the Pentacle from Diamond's neck. Tell her to speak Amethyst's name aloud. Then step aside and wait. She'll come—not for duty, but for desire. She'll come trembling, alone, not to save Emerland... but to save the one she loves. I want the world to witness the fall of their Starborn. Not as a warrior, but as a fool. I want her to walk into the Forbidden—unarmed, unguarded, and afraid. Let her see what festers beneath the world she thought worth saving. Let her learn the true price of being alive. Let her plead. Let her shatter."

With a single gesture, Basalt raised her hand.

From the scorched soil, chains of shadow slithered like serpents, writhing and hissing as they coiled around Amethyst's limbs. He did not stir as they dragged him into the depths—into a dungeon where no light dared follow, and even screams turned to stone.

Toxico T stood frozen, pale as moon-bone, as the iron door slammed shut with a thunderclap that echoed into silence.

Then Basalt turned her gaze upon him. Cold. Final.

"Go," she commanded.

And so he went—riding into the wind, his heart pounding like a war drum.

He had crossed battlefields awash with blood, ridden beneath skies torn open by lightning, yet nothing filled him with more dread than what awaited now.

He would have to wake his sister.

Jabba Doom Gabbro.

Though the truth now lay bare—that Amethyst was not the heir she once believed—still, she would not release him.

Not for Emerland. Not even for Diamond.

Toxico T slipped into her crooked hut beneath a moonless sky.

Gabbro sat waiting, already awake—seated in her ancient, creaking chair as if she had never once slept. Her eyes blazed—stormcloud and flame trapped behind glass.

"So," she said coldly, "you stole my precious… and thought I would never know?"

He had seen rage in her before—years ago, when everything she loved was taken.

But never like this.

"Basalt demands the Pentacle," he said swiftly. "She'll return Amethyst… if Diamond comes for him."

The silence that followed stretched like a drawn blade.

Then, at last, Gabbro spoke—her voice rough as cracked stone, thick with fury.

"I will bring ruin upon Basalt. She took you once. And now she dares take him?"

But Toxico T pressed on—desperate, cunning, his words laced with venom.

"You want vengeance, sister? Alexandrite lied to you. He gave you a false heir. This is your chance to punish him. Give the girl the truth—tell her where Amethyst is. Let her walk into the mouth of darkness. Let her choke on the lies that kept her alive."

A bitter flame caught in Gabbro's eyes. Decades of betrayal coiled within her chest, tightening with every word. Grief turned rancid. Rage became her breath.

And so, when morning broke, the sun refused to shine. Its golden fingers paused at the edges of the world, unwilling to touch the crooked panes of her hut. Shadows clung to the rafters like old regrets.

Diamond awoke, expecting warmth—expecting Amethyst's quiet smile, his voice a gentle balm recalling battles half-forgotten. But the room was hushed. Empty. The silence screamed. The morning pressed upon her like a shroud of mourning, thick and airless, and the cold whisper of absence coiled around her heart.

She turned—and there stood Jabba Doom Gabbro, framed by smoke and lamplight, her gaze neither cruel nor kind, but still. Terribly still. A stillness that clung to the air like the silence after thunder.

Diamond didn't need to speak. The chill in her bones, the ache in her chest—they already knew. Evil had come while hope lay sleeping.

"Where have they taken him?" Her voice broke like a reed in the wind.

"First," said Gabbro, her tone stripped of all softness, "the Pentacle."

Without a word, Diamond reached for the chain around her throat. Her fingers trembled as she unclasped the pendant, its familiar weight slipping from her grasp like the last ember of a dying fire. When Gabbro's hand closed over it, a hush fell— one that felt irreversible, as though a door had quietly locked behind them.

In silence, Gabbro led her to the back of the hut. There, hidden beneath dust and woven shadow, stood a cracked crystal ball, its fractured surface casting ghostlight across the walls.

"There," she murmured. "He sleeps in chains, beneath stone and scream."

"I must go," Diamond whispered, already turning. "I go now."

"You will die," said Gabbro—not unkindly, but with the quiet certainty of one forecasting rain.

"Then perhaps I do not deserve to live," Diamond replied, her voice steadier than stone. "But I am not dead yet."

She turned away and closed the door behind her, sealing off the weight of what had just passed. The room fell into a hush—a sacred stillness where even memory held its breath.

The girl who once sang lullabies to riverlight and danced beneath moon-silvered glades now moved like smoke—shattered, yes, but seething with fire. The world called her lost. Basalt hungered for her disgrace. And the Nameless Fear... waited in silence to claim what was left.

But Diamond no longer searched for hope.

She would become it.

Even if it burned her to ash.

23. Blood, Bark, Blade

In the hush of dawn, Diamond stood alone. The walls of Jabba Gabbro's hut—once a sanctuary of strange comforts and soft shadows—now pressed in around her like the ribs of a dying beast, too narrow to contain the weight of her purpose.

Diamond washed her face in a basin of cold water. The last of her tears fell silently, mingling with the ripples, then vanished.

"I must win. I am brave," she whispered to the mirror. "No more tears."

Only Amethyst's smile remained in her heart—and that was enough.

For a fleeting moment, she considered sending word to Baba Yaga. A message. A warning. A plea. But her hand faltered. *This is my path. My burden. My fight.* How long, she wondered, had she lived beneath others' shadows—shielded by sacrifice, guarded by grief? How many would fall so she might rise?

No more.

But across the realm, Baba Yaga already knew. She had told Amethyst to return at first light. His silence now was an omen clearer than any rune—evil had not waited. It had struck like a coward in the dark.

At the door, Diamond paused.

Jabba Gabbro stood there, hunched in the half-light, her hands trembling not from age, but from the weight of guilt. Her eyes met Diamond's—stormy, uncertain, fiercely human.

She did not speak at first.

Then, as though her voice had to claw its way through thorns, Gabbro spoke.

"Take these."

From beneath her cloak, she drew a long, slender sword—black-hilted, leaf-bladed, its edge faintly gleaming with a ghost-light not born of sun. A hunting knife followed, etched with runes too ancient for memory, wrapped in a sheath of scaled hide. Finally, she placed a folded bundle of warrior's garb—dark as forest shadow, stitched with thread that shimmered faintly when it caught the morning light.

"In the wild," she murmured, not quite meeting Diamond's eyes, "steel sings louder than sorrow. These might keep you one breath ahead of death."

Diamond took them without protest. The weight of the sword, the whisper of the blade—they meant little to her now. She wasn't thinking of weapons. She was thinking of Amethyst's smile, of the warmth she'd left behind. The gear in her hands was not hope. Not yet.

But she carried it anyway.

Because grief alone would not be enough to save him.

Jabba looked away. "They know you're coming. They watch the winds and whisper your name to every creeping root and branch. If you falter—even for a breath—they will take your life."

Diamond nodded.

Then Gabbro handed her a scroll—bound in cracked leather, sealed with red wax stamped in a sigil Diamond did not recognize.

"A map," the witch murmured. "The path it shows is forgotten by most, cloaked in old magics. Darkness dwells there—but not death. Not yet. It won't lead you straight to Amethyst, but it will lead you to someone who *can* break the spell upon him. Without that, you'll die before reaching the gate. And I know you don't care… but your death won't save him."

Diamond traced the brittle edge of the parchment with trembling fingers. The wax seal broke with a soft crack—like distant thunder echoing across a hollow sky.

"That will do," she whispered.

Without a glance behind her, she stepped into the gray hush of morning. The crooked door of Jabba Gabbro's hut creaked closed, sealing itself like a chapter ending. The air outside was cool, but not fresh—it was the breath of a world holding itself still.

Before her stretched the forest. Not yet the Forbidden, yet no longer the safety of Emerland.

She lingered at the edge.

The trees were familiar, but the silence was not. It wasn't peace—it was suspense. The hush of an audience before the play begins, or the stillness of prey sensing it's being hunted. The wind stirred, and the limbs above groaned like bones in restless sleep.

Something moved in the distance.

She unfolded the map.

Could she trust Gabbro? She did not know. But a path drawn, even by a foe, was better than no path at all. The map's ink shimmered faintly in the early light, as though the road it described remembered being walked once—long ago.

So Diamond took the first step.

And though she did not know where the road would lead, she knew this: she had to walk it.

Diamond walked on, guided only by the map and a resolve deeper than pain. Her boots moved soundlessly across moss-draped earth, leaving no trace behind. Above, the sky hung veiled in a colorless hush—not gray with weather, but with something older, as if the heavens themselves turned away from what was to come.

The map led her through a path nearly lost to time, once trod by the Greenblood Scouts in wars sung only in the fading songs of bards. Now, it was half-consumed by thorns and sleeping roots. As she pressed deeper, the forest shifted. The trees no longer stood like sentinels, but loomed like ribs of some great slumbering beast. Roots twisted like veins beneath her feet. The air grew still, thick with silence, as though even memory refused to follow.

She did not rest, though her limbs cried out and her breath grew thin. When the ache became too much, she cupped Olivine the Dove's nest—a small, fragile thing she kept in her pocket like a charm against despair—and curled beside a root as if within a mother's arms. Sleep would not come. The hush of the forest was too watchful.

In Amethyst's presence, she had once known softness—a quiet assurance that someone else bore part of the burden. But now, she walked alone, and in that absence, something fierce bloomed in her. A fire. A will. When her strength faltered, she would whisper into the hollow wind:

"I am strong. I am brave. I must save Amethyst."

The day waned, shaped by silent threats—creatures stirring beyond sight, branches clawing like hands, and trees that seemed to watch without eyes. Yet she endured.

At last, through a break in the ancient limbs, she stumbled upon a lake—vast and unmoving, a mirror of silver dreamlight cradled in the forest's embrace. Its surface bore no wind, no ripple—only the sky's pale ghost, and her own reflection, rising like a memory from the stillness. She knelt, parched, cupping the glacial water to her lips—but the moment she leaned closer, the image stared back with haunting clarity.

A girl stared up at her—a younger self, cloaked once in innocence and garlands of joy. But now, the petals of that childhood had wilted. Her flowered gown was torn and streaked with the grime of sorrow, her earrings dimmed like stars lost behind stormclouds. The headband she had once worn with pride now frayed at its seams, barely clinging to the strands of her wind-blown hair. Her eyes—those eyes—held no tears. Only the storm. The storm, and something deeper.

And then... a flicker.

A thread unspooled.

She remembered—though whether dream or memory, she could not say. A sunlit morning. Laughter echoing through the halls. Her feet chasing Onyx through meadows and rooms, around chairs, beneath beds, the sound of paws and giggles blending into one melody. And then a hand—warm, strong—enfolding hers. A voice, as soft as woven dusk, had whispered: *"That is the lake. Its waters are old as stars, and their magic is older still. And that, there... that is the Castle. Only wonders live there. But out beyond... beyond the veil lies darkness."*

She had looked up then—into a face she had not understood, but now remembered with a shiver. The crags of the voice. The sharpness in the smile. The sorrow veiled in the eyes. *Baba Yaga*, she now knew. It had been her.

She had been here before. Not in footsteps, but in spirit. Not with memory, but with dreams. And dreams, she now realized, were the first footprints of destiny.

She rose slowly, the reflection shifting with her like a second soul, but now it was hers to command. She glanced once more at the lake, at the trees, at the looming castle in the mist beyond.

Nothing looked familiar—and yet none of it was strange. It was frightening, yes. But it was the kind of fear she had met once before and survived.

Something inside her, long buried beneath layers of grief and hesitation, stirred.

Awakened.

"I am not a shade of weakness," she whispered, her voice low as embers murmuring beneath a bed of ash. "Not anymore. I am flame. I am fury. I will not break."

With hands that no longer trembled, she removed her earrings—tokens of gentler days, as delicate as dew-kissed petals—and cast them into the lake. Then came the headband, a circlet once blessed by the Fair Folk, now heavy with grief. At last, she shed the gown, a shimmering relic woven in dreams, now hanging upon her like funeral linen. One by one, her past fell away. The lake received each offering in silence, swallowing them whole as if erasing memory itself.

She donned the garments Jabba Gabbro had given her—the coarse wool of wanderers, the layered armor of those who endure. The fabric clung to her with purpose, its weight not a burden, but a vow. Her sword, now fastened at her hip, hummed like a storm held in restraint. Her knife, quiet at her side, gleamed with waiting resolve.

She recalled Baba Yaga's warning, etched into the marrow of her soul:

"If you look like defeat, the world will treat you so. Appear as the victor, and fate might bend."

And so, no longer robed in sorrow, but cloaked in defiance, Diamond turned from the still water. She did not walk—she emerged, as a warrior tempered in fire, as a daughter of battle and dusk.

Behind her, the lake rippled once, then stilled.

Before her, the forest waited.

The air grew colder. The path darker.

But Diamond did not look back.

Behind her came whispers—not wind, but breath. Flesh-eaters.

They lingered always just behind the trees, drawn to her scent, her silence, her soul. Pale things, born of hunger and ruin, slithered between root and fog. Waiting. Watching.

But she did not falter.

Her hand never left her hilt.

Her breath never broke its rhythm.

And her voice, soft but steady, murmured her vow:

"I am strong. I am brave. I will save Amethyst."

Not one creature dared test the fire that now walked the ancient woods.

Though fatigue gnawed at her bones and the night closed in like a vice, Diamond pressed forward—half walking, half stumbling—until the forest itself seemed to reject her. The path vanished beneath twisted roots. The map in her hand dissolved into unreadable lines, as if the world had turned its back on her purpose.

Lost. Or dead. Perhaps both.

Her steps faltered. Her limbs gave way.

Around her, the shadows thickened—living things with breath and hunger, curling just beyond the edges of vision. Beasts of bone and ash, drawn by the scent of despair, circled like vultures cloaked in mist. And Diamond, the last hope of a kingdom, sank to her knees upon a knotted patch of earth that pulsed faintly, like a dying heart.

She stared at the great black tree before her—its bark slick with cold, its branches clawing at the sky like pleading hands. Even the stars had turned away. The map had led her here, to this place beyond light and reason... and now it, too, failed her.

Tears welled, unbidden.

They fell.

Far across the land, within the Fortress of Dread, Evil Basalt waited. She hungered for any vision of Diamond's fear, any whisper of her faltering. But none came. No cries. No echoes. No sign at all. It was as if Diamond had vanished—or perhaps had never been.

Toxico T, standing beside her in uneasy silence, confirmed the truth: the girl had left Jabba Gabbro's hut. She had gone into the wild.

A search began. Spies crept through every crevice, slithering into shadow, vanishing into wind. Evil Basalt paced like a caged tempest, her fury sharp enough to splinter stone. That girl—so fragile, so unfinished—had slipped through her grasp. It was an insult she would not endure. She would find her. Break her. And this time, ensure she never rose again.

Yet far from the reach of darkness, Diamond faltered. Her breath came shallow, her body heavy with grief and strain. The forest seemed to tilt, and her knees gave way, lowering her to the roots of an ancient tree as though the earth itself mourned with her. Her tears fell freely, not in surrender, but in sorrow too vast to bear alone.

She pressed her forehead to the mossy ground, the hilt of Gabbro's dagger clasped tight—not as a weapon, but as a relic of hope. A tether to something still worth fighting for.

"I cannot... but I will," she breathed—defiant even in despair.

And then, at last, her eyes closed. Not in defeat, but in gathering strength. Sleep took her like a spell—deep, strange, and filled with the hush of waiting things.

And then—

Something shifted.

Time loosened its grip. The air trembled—humming not with wind, but with a song remembered only by the soul. Beneath her, the earth gave a quiet pulse, like a heartbeat long forgotten.

Diamond stirred. Her breath caught.

She opened her eyes—

And gasped.

The tree before her—once blackened and broken, a monument to despair—had changed.

It now rose tall and glorious, its bark laced with veins of silver, as though the moon had poured its light into the wood. Its leaves shimmered gold, each one flickering like a sun reborn. From its branches bloomed not flowers, but stars—jewels of light drifting slowly in the stillness, caught between the threads of time and memory.

Where once she had knelt in surrender, now she stood in reverent awe.

The forest was not silent.

It watched.

It remembered.

And Diamond, voice hushed and trembling, whispered—

"Am I dead? Is this heaven... or some beautiful corner of hell?"

24. Three Nights Broken

The tree spoke—its voice as old as starlight and as soft as autumn wind whispering through forgotten groves.

"What is it that you wish for?"

Diamond gazed up at the venerable tree, its silver-veined bark glowing faintly, as though pulsing with breath and ancient knowing. Her eyes shimmered, reflecting the starlight caught in the branches above.

Before she could answer, the tree continued, its leaves whispering like old memories in the wind.

"Be wise in what you wish for, child. If you ask for that which is not rightfully yours, you must also carry the weight of those to whom it belonged."

Diamond stepped closer, her voice trembling but sure.

"You are the One. Jabba Gabbro sent me to you," she said, and a faint smile touched her lips.

The great tree groaned softly, as though shifting in thought.

"Your face speaks what your lips do not. Now tell me—what is it your heart desires?"

Without hesitation, Diamond replied, **"I want Amethyst returned to me. Whole. Unharmed."**

A long silence followed. Then, with a creak of its ancient limbs, the tree smiled—not with lips, but with the gentle sway of its branches and the hush that fell upon the wood.

"It pleases me," the tree said at last, **"to see your longing lies not in vanity, but in love. Yet even love must pay a price. The laws of old are not broken lightly."**

Diamond lowered her head. **"What is it that you seek?"**

"What treasures do you bring?" the One-Wish Tree asked, though there was no greed in its voice—only custom, and the echo of old rituals.

Diamond lifted her palms, empty.

"Only myself. And the nest of Olivine the Dove, which I may not give—it was never mine."

A hush settled, and the tree's voice grew solemn.

"Then when your wish is fulfilled, bring Amethyst to me. Let him stand where you stand now. That shall be the price. Do you agree?"

Diamond nodded. **"I shall."**

The tree rustled, as though satisfied.

"Know this," it said, **"Amethyst lies beneath an enchantment—his body bound, his mind veiled. Each night, I shall grant you a single vision—a glimpse beyond the veil. In that moment, if you can stir his memory, if your voice can reach the part of him that still remembers... then the spell shall break, and he will be yours again."**

Diamond's breath caught.

"But beware," the tree whispered, and the leaves trembled like a warning. **"To awaken what has been sealed will bring him pain. The witch's curse cuts deep—and love alone may not be enough."**

Diamond stepped forward, her hands clenched at her sides.

"I yearn to behold him... to rescue him," she declared, her voice low but fierce. **"I cannot leave him in the clutches of that witch."**

The One-Wish Tree swayed gently, its boughs groaning with age and sorrow.

"Very well," it said at last, a mournful lilt in its tone. **"But mark this: if within three nights my enchantment does not break his spell, you must release him. I will not be able to help you again. There is a limit even to love's reach."**

Diamond nodded, a small flicker of hope trembling in her chest. **"I understand."**

That night, as Diamond lay beneath the sacred boughs of the One-Wish Tree, the forest held its breath. The leaves above her stilled, and even the wind seemed to wait for what might come.

The One-Wish Tree bowed its crown to the stars and whispered a spell older than the stones of Emerland. Silver light coiled around Diamond's form, and she was drawn into a vision—not of dream, but of veiled reality.

She stood in a chamber cold and hollow, carved from ancient stone. A single narrow window let in a thread of wind. There, on a low bed draped in black velvet, lay **Amethyst**.

His chest rose and fell, barely. His face was still and pale, as though time itself had forgotten him.

Diamond sank to her knees beside him, unable to look away. Memories surged—their shared laughter beneath starlit trees, the moment her fingers first brushed his in a hush of unspoken affection. Her heart ached with a love so strong it threatened to undo her.

"How could anyone wish you harm?" she whispered, her voice barely more than breath. But this was no time for longing. No time for sorrow.

She reached for him gently, calling his name like a prayer.

"Amethyst..."

He did not stir.

She shook him—once, twice—urgency rising like a storm tide.

"Wake up... please..."

But the spell held fast. Not sleep, not even silence—but something crueler. A magic of forgetting. A curse meant to peel away the soul by unraveling the memory.

And then, to her horror, faint lines appeared upon his cheek—red, hairline cracks, crawling like fire across porcelain. They spread to his throat, delicate and dreadful. Blood blossomed slowly, seeping from the fractures as though his body were breaking from within.

Two forces battled inside him—the gentle summons of the One-Wish Tree and the cruel venom of the witch's curse.

Diamond recoiled, her breath caught in her throat. She dared not touch him again.

Instead, she knelt beside him, her trembling fingers finding his hand, clutching it tightly as the stars beyond the window paled and disappeared.

She remained until the vision unraveled like mist beneath the morning sun.

When she returned to the clearing, the great tree awaited her—solemn, silent, as though it had never moved.

"I couldn't wake him," Diamond cried, falling to her knees beside the roots. "Amethyst began to bleed. I couldn't watch him suffer."

"I warned you," the tree replied, its voice low and ancient. "Two spells war within him. And neither will yield."

"It's breaking my heart," Diamond whispered, her grief tightening every word.

The leaves stirred—not from wind, but from something deeper, like sorrow swaying through their branches.

"Do not weep, child," the tree murmured.

A hush fell over the glade.

Then the boughs bent low, lowering themselves with quiet reverence. The voice that followed had changed—warmer now, laced with something Diamond could not yet name.

"Diamond... there is more you must know," the tree said softly. "I am not only the One-Wish Tree. I am the One-Wish Fairy—and I am your mother."

Diamond's breath caught. The world seemed to still.

The tree's branches unfurled like arms and wrapped around her—not in entrapment, but in an embrace. The bark shimmered, revealing hints of fairy light within, as if a slumbering soul had stirred beneath its skin.

"When King Alexandrite traveled through time," the tree whispered, **"we found each other. For a brief moment, joy bloomed. I regained my fairy form. And you... you were born of that love."**

"You're... my mother?" Diamond said, her voice a trembling thread.

She did not know whether to collapse in joy or sorrow. Tears came—of both. Of grief for the life never lived, of wonder at the truth newly born. Her eyes, red and raw, no longer knew how to tell joy from mourning. She had wept too long.

The One-Wish Tree cradled her beneath its luminous canopy.

"How I long to grant you peace," the tree whispered, its voice thick with sorrow. **"For all others I give freely... and yet my own daughter suffers."**

The leaves above shimmered—emerald and silver—each bearing a single tear-shaped fruit that glowed faintly, pulsing with memory and song.

They sang softly—not in words, but in tones of comfort, ancient and warm.

For one breathless moment, Diamond allowed herself to rest beneath them—not a warrior, not a wanderer, but a child held fast by love.

"I cannot live, nor fight, without Amethyst," she confessed, her voice trembling yet sure. "Even if I wished to, I feel lifeless."

Her eyes, dimmed by sleepless nights, now held the gleam of something brighter—love forged into resolve.

The One-Wish Tree, still and regal, listened as only a mother could. Her ancient limbs swayed like veils stirred by a wind long forgotten.

"Then fight for him, Diamond," the tree answered, her voice steady as stone and warm as fire.

"Fight with every breath in your body. Prove the truth of your love."

For love, when true, is stronger than any curse. You have given your Pentacle. You have crossed forbidden lands. You have returned night after night. Do not falter now. And remember—**truth** is mightier than fear. Let truth guide you."

Diamond bowed her head, as if beneath a crown she had not asked for.

Then the tree—mother and fairy both—gathered her sorrow and wrapped it in strength.

"Abandon not hope," she murmured one final time. "Let that be your lamp when all else fails."

The second night came and went like the first. Diamond returned empty-handed, weary and worn, her limbs trembling with grief and failure.

The third night descended like a shroud.

Within the vision chamber, she beheld Amethyst once more—but now he lay broken. Deep gashes marked his body. His breath came in shallow, shuddering gasps. The dark spells had grown crueler, more twisted. He was being undone.

Diamond did not dare reach for him. One more attempt might unmake him entirely.

She collapsed to the ground beside him, her soul fraying thread by thread.

"Tomorrow," she whispered into the shadows, "I shall go to the witch herself—to Basalt. I will give her my life, anything she asks. Only let him live. Let him breathe. Without him, the world holds no light. Without him, there is no path worth walking."

And there, in the witch's dark-breathing chamber, she wept.

She wept as she had never wept before—not even when Morganite died, not even when her soul was stolen, not even when her beloved Onyx was gone.

Time passed unnoticed. The night thinned. Her raw, reddened eyes bled tears so fierce they seared her cheeks.

And in one fina moment of surrender, she bent low and pressed her forehead to his chest.

One tear fell.

Just one.

But it was no ordinary tear—it was her vow, her heart, her flame. It carried all she could not say. It bore the weight of her sacrifice, her pain, her silent plea to the stars themselves:

"Return him... or take me too."

That tear, born from the deepest ache of love and loss, did what no spell, no blade, no fire could ever do.

It passed through enchantment. It slipped beyond curse.

It touched Amethyst's heart with the memory of her—not as a name, but as a soul.

His body shivered. Then stilled.

Then stirred.

His eyes openec—slow, like dawn breaking over a forgotten land. His gaze met hers.

"Diamond," he whispered—the name a spell of its own.

She reached for him. He pulled her close.

They clung to each other as the darkness receded, grief dissolving in the arms of love reclaimed.

The chamber began to crumble—the enchantment unraveling in the wake of true magic.

But they did not wait for ruin.

Drawn by the final spell of the One-Wish Tree, they fled that place of pain.

Together.

Swift and breathless, they ran—not as hunted souls, but as something reborn.

Not all was mended.

Not all was won.

But in each other's embrace, they found the courage to face what waited next.

And so they vanished into the thinning dark, not to escape, but to rise—born anew in the oldest magic: love, freely given.

When the morning came, Evil Basalt descended the cold steps to the chamber where Amethyst had been bound.

The door creaked open.

She stepped inside.

The bed was empty.

Chains, once taut with enchantment, now hung slack. The air was still, yet carried the faintest trace of warmth—the echo of presence. Not a single ward had been broken. No battle, no intrusion. Nothing disturbed... except that he was gone.

Basalt stood frozen.

Her mouth opened, but no sound came.

The walls did not shake. The mirrors did not scream. Even her shadow seemed to withdraw from her. For a long moment, the queen of dread—she who had scorched mountains and swallowed stars—could do nothing but **stare**.

It was not power that had taken him.

It was something older.

A magic that mocked her cruelty.

A spell stronger than hate: love remembered.

Finally, her breath returned.

With narrowed eyes and cold breath, she summoned her spies—the whispering ghosts, the beasts of ash, and those whose hearts still bore the stain of shadow.

"Find them," she commanded. "Search the grass. Search the rivers. Search the skies. Before the sun dares rise again, I will have their names... or your silence will be your end."

And in the hush that followed, even the wind—once so eager to obey her—dared not stir.

25. Where Wishes Bloom

As promised, Diamond and Amethyst returned first to the One-Wish Tree. At their approach, the ancient sentinel stirred—not with menace, but with joy. A breathless hush swept the clearing, as though the world itself leaned in to watch. The tree's bark shimmered with a soft, living light, like morning dew laced with memory. Then, as if delight had awakened in its very roots, the leaves began to glow—one by one—until the entire canopy glittered like starlight blooming through branches. Buds unfurled into radiant blossoms, casting the air into a swirl of fragrance and song, and the wind itself began to hum, as if it, too, remembered love.

From the skies above, Agate descended—not in haste, but in a regal, gliding arc. The winged horse soared in slow, widening spirals, his hooves skimming the air like stones over water, his mane unfurling behind him like a banner of silver flame. He had combed the heavens in search of Amethyst, and now, drawn by love, by memory, by some tether older than words, he had found him.

Amethyst laughed aloud—not the guarded smile of one who mistrusts happiness, but the full, unburdened laughter of a soul reborn. He ran to Agate and flung his arms around the great steed's neck, burying his face in the warmth of the creature who had once borne him beyond the edge of the known world. Agate neighed, low and soft, and folded his wings around them both like a silken cloak.

While they rejoiced beneath the golden branches, Diamond turned toward the tree—her mother.

"What is it you desire, Mother?" she asked, her voice hushed, laced with the quiet weight of obligation—as though she owed the tree more than words could ever repay.

The leaves stirred gently, like a memory waking from slumber.

"What does a mother wish for," came the reply, a voice like the rustle of old songs, "if not her child's happiness? I long to see you wed, my darling—to Amethyst. Not by fate alone, but by your own choosing, while love still lingers in this world."

Diamond smiled, soft and sorrowful.

"I wish it too," she said. "But how does one speak vows beneath a sky so clouded with war? When tomorrow may bring ruin, how can we pretend that today is safe?"

She turned to Amethyst then—just a glance, just a half-smile—but within it shimmered the ache of a thousand unspoken stories. In a world where wishes so often crumbled to ash, where hope drifted like dandelion seeds on a wind too cruel to carry them far, this moment felt like borrowed sunlight—fleeting, precious, unreal.

She thought of Morganite, who had died with a wish still echoing through her bones: that Amethyst would become more than a fading memory. Of King Alexandrite, who had blinded himself in the desperate hope of seeing his daughter once more. Of Baba Yaba, whose life had been a slow and silent offering. And of her mother—the One Wish Fairy—who had defied the impossible, only to place her child at the fragile center of a prophecy none could outrun.

So many had wished. So few had lived to see those wishes bloom.

Amethyst, though still young, had borne enough sorrow to recognize the ache hidden behind her smile. Without a word, he turned to Agate and whispered a single command.

At once, Agate unfurled her wings and rose into the burning sky, vanishing into the horizon like a flame swallowed by dusk.

By nightfall, in a quiet glade deep within the Emerald Woods, the call had been answered.

Rock the Hawk descended from the mountains, his feathers glinting like obsidian in the moonlight. Beside him strode Jade, son of Bulwark—fierce, bright-eyed, and resolute beneath the watching stars. Hematite came next, her cloak shimmering with twilight hues, every step measured and strange. And last, as if summoned from the folds of legend, came Baba Yaga—her gnarled staff striking softly against the earth, her face half-shrouded in shadow, half-creased in knowing mirth.

"We will give the world one night," Baba Yaga said. "Let Evil search the winds, the rivers, the flame—and find nothing but their own reflection. We will lie still and quiet. And in stillness, we shall glimpse their next move."

And so, by the grace of silence, a celebration bloomed.

Not one of feasting or fanfare—but a quiet moment of flickering love. A fire against the dark. A gathering of those who still believed.

In the golden hush of dusk, preparations unfolded like spring's first blush across the earth. Rock the Hawk, ever the sentinel of joy and wisdom, took it upon himself to orchestrate the affair. With wings tucked proudly at his sides and eyes sharp as the mountains of old, he adorned the sacred boughs of an ancient tree with garlands of wildflowers and ivy. Its limbs, outstretched like a guardian's arms, were cloaked in blossoms of pink and white, glowing softly beneath lanterns that danced like newborn stars.

At Rock the Hawk's call came his cousin—a gentle soul whose voice shimmered like morning light upon a mountain stream. In her eyes glowed the quiet truth of love, for it was her heart that cherished Jade deeply. And Jade, who had known silence more than safety and houses more than homes, reciprocated that love. Their love stood equal, steady, and real.

Beyond the glade, tucked beneath a veil of fragrant blossoms and birdsong, a crystal spring whispered to the roots of the world. There, the waters mirrored the sky, and the sky mirrored the hearts of those gathered. Flowers of every hue—crimson, gold, lilac, and moon-pale blue—danced in the breeze as if they, too, celebrated this rare hour of peace.

Diamond stood beneath the blooming canopy, where lanterns hung like captured stars and the air shimmered with unseen music. Her gown was simple yet radiant—not stitched from silk but from meaning, memory, and quiet defiance. In her hair, Hematite had woven strands of morning glory, clover, and lilies with star-shaped petals—each bloom a silent vow: to love without fear, to protect without faltering, to endure beyond despair. She did not glisten like a queen, nor blaze like a warrior. She glowed—softly, steadily, like the heart of a hearth that refuses to go out.

She turned to Amethyst, who wore a tunic of deep forest green, the color of healing and hidden strength. Upon his brow rested a circlet of silver fern, glinting with dew. His smile held no bravado, only truth, and in the calm of his eyes stood a man no longer running from his name, nor the weight it carried.

"You are perfect just as you are," Diamond said, her voice like a stream flowing over polished stone—clear, unwavering.

"And you," Amethyst replied, "are the wish I once whispered to the stars, not daring to be heard."

Above them, the wind stirred the lanterns, and their light quivered—like breath held at the edge of a miracle.

Then came the lioness—her golden coat catching the last threads of twilight, a living sun in motion. Her cubs danced behind her like flickers of starlight, their laughter rippling through the hush like a sacred bell. She did not speak, but bowed her great head to Diamond and Amethyst, and the stillness that followed felt as though the very earth was holding its breath.

Hematite and Baba Yaga stepped forward—not as witches of power, but as women of heart. No incantations, no crowns—only trembling smiles and the kind of tears that carry lifetimes. They wrapped the two in silence, offering blessings shaped by love, not ceremony.

"My daughter," Baba Yaga whispered, her fingers brushing Diamond's cheek like a falling leaf, "you have already chosen the harder path. Let this joy be yours, even if only for a night borrowed from the storm."

Then the cousin of Rock the Hawk lifted her wings toward the heavens. The birds above folded into stillness. The lanterns dimmed to a gentle hum, their light suspended in wonder.

"Before war returns to darken the sky," she said, her voice echoing like wind in high branches, "let this moment be held in golden time."

And so, beneath the soft fall of a thousand blossoms, with stars kindling above like ancient witnesses, Diamond and Amethyst clasped hands—not as prophecy or sacrifice, not as light or shadow—but simply as two hearts who had found one another on the trembling edge of the world.

No vows were spoken. The promise lived in their breath. And for that night, it was enough.

Clad in garments of shimmering grace, Diamond glimmered like a lone star against the celestial tapestry of a celebration spun from music and mirth. The wedding scene unfolded like a page torn from an ancient tale—each moment threaded with wonder, each breath gilded with joy. For what greater enchantment exists than to behold one's heart's desire made real before the eyes, if only for a fleeting hour?

Away from the laughter and the swirl of lantern light, Diamond and Amethyst slipped quietly into the hush beyond the clearing. Around them, songs floated like petals on the breeze, but their hearts sought no revelry—only stillness. The kind of stillness only love understands.

Though Baba Yaga had warned them to stay hidden beneath the valley's veil, Amethyst turned to Diamond and asked softly, "Would you dare it, if only for one last flight?"

Diamond smiled—brave, wistful, and full of light—and gave her answer without a single word.

Like wind reborn with wings of firelight, Agate rose from the glade, hooves skimming the dew-kissed earth before soaring skyward. The air split open around them as if the heavens themselves made way for their ascent. Beneath them, the forest blurred into shadow and song. They circled the sleeping land like a streak of starlight—wild, untamed, and fleeting. No words were needed, no oaths recalled. In that breathless flight, they were neither Starborn nor guardian—only a girl and a boy who loved the wind more than fear, more than fate.

Amethyst leaned low, his voice a thread against the wind's roar.

"To where I first found Diamond, Agate. The river. The tree."

Agate let out a cry—not of command, but of remembering—a wild, jubilant sound that broke the stillness of night. With the tempest's might and a star's descent, she turned and dove. The forest rose to meet them, yet parted like a veil of dreams, as if even the trees remembered. Down they flew, through mist and moonlight, until the world stilled once more—beneath the boughs of the ancient tree where destiny had first spoken their names aloud.

Beneath the hallowed canopy—where the branches arched like cathedral vaults and the air trembled with the breath of old magic—they sat close, faces lifted to a sky rich with stars and silence.

"The day I made my wish beneath this tree," Amethyst murmured, his voice catching on memory, "you appeared, Diamond. Let us wish again—tonight. Perhaps it's the last. Perhaps it's the end of wishing."

But Diamond felt no fear. Not anymore. In this sliver of forever, she had been given more than she had ever dared to dream. And still—if this was to be their final night—she would not let it slip by unlived, unloved, or unsaid.

"Let us wish for each other," she whispered.

So they did.

Diamond wished for Amethyst's life to be spared, and for Emerland to bloom with joy once more.

Amethyst wished for Diamond's happiness, and for the salvation that only she could bring.

In that quiet moment, they drifted into sleep—hand in hand beneath the hush of stars.

And within their dreams, they glimpsed a world beyond war:

A homestead cradled in green, alive with birdsong and gentle light.

Amethyst sat beneath a tree, a book titled *Emerland* resting on his lap, its pages whispering wonder.

Diamond stood in a sunlit kitchen, brewing coffee, her heart full and unburdened.

They awoke before dawn, the vision still clinging to their lashes.

Their eyes met, and in silence, asked: *Did you see it too?*

Amethyst reached for her hand.

"I long for it to come true," he said softly.

"It shall," she whispered, her voice barely rising above the hush. "And if this moment fades... we'll find it again, wherever the stars may carry us."

Then, in the quiet before dawn, as the world held its breath, she sang—soft and aching—a song of love.

And for a moment, time forgot to move.

26. When Darkness Spoke

Evil Basalt did not require ghostly whispers to track Amethyst and Diamond.

They had flown boldly through the sky—defiant, unhidden—as though the world beneath them held no more dominion over their fate.

And yet, the shadows had eyes. From barrows long forgotten and graves that never found peace, specters slithered toward the Fortress of Dread, carrying news like rot on the wind.

Basalt had no need of their murmurs. She had seen it with her own eyes—the shattered chamber, the sundered chain, the lingering scent of escape.

For one breathless moment, even her fury faltered. A silence, cold and blade-thin, filled her lungs.

Then came the scream.

A shriek, terrible and vast, erupted from her throat—so violent it cracked through the bones of the fortress. The stone trembled. The distant Hidden Valley flinched. And all who dwelled within its dreaming quiet understood:

The hour of pretending had ended.

The peace—fragile as frost—was broken.

The world must now return to dread.

The One-Wish Tree did not weep. She only smiled—solemn and brave—as she enfolded the young couple in her ancient limbs. A blessing passed in silence, leaf to heart, branch to soul. And with heads held high and fingers entwined, Diamond and Amethyst stepped beyond the glade, their feet turning once more toward the path of war.

Back in the Fortress of Dread, Basalt's fury echoed like thunder through corridors of bone. Windows shattered, columns split, and the very air thickened with dread.

She stormed through the labyrinthine halls with unnatural speed, her cloak trailing smoke, and burst into her private sanctum. There stood the ancient mirror—not for beauty nor vanity, but for dominion.

She did not gaze into it. Not yet. With a growl, she dragged it into the great hall where her court lay in uneasy wait.

Topaz stood at attention, pale and wordless, his loyalty battered but not broken. Spinel lingered near the edge of shadow, eyes twitching with unease. Around them loomed the assembled hosts of ruin—warlocks cloaked in smoke, beasts of ash, specters with hollow eyes, and the wicked who had long sworn allegiance to despair.

Basalt turned to the mirror.

She did not speak.

She stared.

And the mirror, slowly, began to burn.

From its heart rose a flame—blacker than void, brighter than death. It twisted and coiled, then split and reshaped itself into a face. No single face... and yet every face. It was shifting, ageless, a mask of all things lost to time—without pity, without name.

The Nameless Fear had awakened.

The Lord of the Forbidden.

And now, at last, he spoke.

His voice rumbled deeper than the roots of mountains, a sound not heard but felt—like the earth itself remembering pain.

"The day I opened my eyes, the Elves fled Emerland.

For ages, I lay buried beneath stone and story—

Sealed by Elven magic older than even the stars.

But spells are not eternal.

Concealment fades—

Especially when the heart that cast it forgets to remember.

The world grew careless.

Their guardianship... waned.

And the threads of concealment—once tight as iron—frayed like forgotten songs.

The ancient curses that veiled me had long begun to wither.

And then, Zelda came.

She stirred the stone.

And with her blood... I breathed.
With her life... she gave me mine.
The day I drew breath, Death herself came knocking.
Baba Yaba resisted—he always does.
But what is resistance to fate?
He delayed the end, but he did not undo it."
His shadow swelled, engulfing the hall in flickering dread.
The gathered dark hearts—Topaz, Spinel, the spectral lords and witches of decay—stood silent as the Nameless Fear continued.

"I had the plan.
And Death obeyed.
She held the Deathly Chattel—a perfect snare.
I sent her to end the Starborn.
And she would have succeeded...
But Alexandrite lied.
He deceived Jabba Doom Gabbro.
And in doing so, he rewrote the thread of fate with falsehood."
The flames within the mirror surged higher, twisting like serpents of black fire.

"Now that deceiver cowers in his palace—broken, blind, and spent.
Yet we, the true power, remain hidden.
Why?
Because of a tale...
A ruse whispered by Elves.
Let them whisper of stars and seals and saviors.
Let them speak of a child of fae and fire.
It was always a lullaby—not a truth.
And lullabies do not save kingdoms.
Their prophecy was meant to stall, to weaken, to buy them time.

But no more."
The Nameless Fear's gaze narrowed to a crimson slit.
"I do not need her soul.
I take lives now.
I shall consume her—not as prophecy foretold—but as one crushes a gnat: fragile, trembling, too late to run.
I will not wait.
I will not scheme."
His form loomed larger, eclipsing even the darkness.
"They struck while we slept.
We forgave.
They rejoiced while fire scorched Emerland.
Let them cheer beneath their hollow crowns.
For by nightfall... we gather.
And by morning... we march.
No more hiding.
No more patience.
Let every leaf and stone in Emerland know terror."
He turned sharply to Basalt.
"We spare none who look upon us with defiance.
Only those who kneel shall crawl away with breath."
Then came the final command—soft as snowfall, and twice as deadly:
"The sword?"
Basalt bowed her head.
"Master... it lies with you."
A smile—slow, poisonous—curled through the flames.
"Aye.
I placed it in the only place it cannot be touched—not by fool, not by kin.
I gave it to Death herself.
My sister watches over it...

and not even the wind dares steal from her lap."
He leaned forward, the mirror warping with heat.
"Fetch it, Basalt.
Let the sword return not to bear light—
but to crown darkness.
Let it rest in the shadowed throne where it belongs.
What light could not keep safe...
darkness shall claim."
And with that, the fire dimmed.
The mirror cracked.
Ash fell.

Basalt gasped. For a heartbeat, her face was bare of fury—only fear. Then it hardened, and the witch returned, stepping back as if waking from a long fever-dream. Her eyes gleamed with terror and awe. She turned, cloak whipping like smoke behind her.

Basalt turned first to Topaz.

"If only you had wings," she said, a sneer curling her lips. **"But no... your place is not in the skies."**

Her eyes slid to Toxico T, still clutching the Pentacle like a stolen prize.

"Not yet," she whispered, the words wrapped in silk and poison. **"But soon."**

And her smile lingered just long enough to make the air grow cold.

Then her gaze fell on Spinel—the Wolf—standing still as stone, his shadow stretched long behind him.

Her voice dropped to a whisper, low and cutting, heavy with command.

**"You. You know where the Forbidden Forest ends.
But beyond it lies the place where true darkness begins—
the edge of the world, where even light forgets to follow."**

Her voice dropped to a whisper, as though speaking its name aloud would summon something unspeakable.

"You must knock before you enter. And you must not speak while *she* speaks. Do not ask. You must *request*. And she must see the ashes."

Basalt handed Spinel a blackened velvet pouch—its contents still warm.

"The ashes of the mirror," she said. "She must see them before she will see *you*. If her gaze meets yours before the ashes touch the earth... you will not return."

Basalt turned away for a moment, then unrolled a piece of parchment—not inked with roads or rivers, but etched with threads of silver flame that writhed like veins. She passed it to Spinel.

"This is your guide," she said. "Not a map—*the* way. Without it, there is no path. And if you return empty-handed..." Her eyes glinted, and a cruel smile tugged at her lips. "I will not kill you. But I will kill you *every day*."

Spinel, the Wolf, bowed his head. He did not speak.

He ran.

Faster than wind, faster than dread. His cloak trailed behind him like smoke as he crossed the border into the Forbidden.

The trees thickened. The air congealed. Light fled.

Still he ran.

But as he went deeper, the darkness became a wall. No sound, no shape, no wind—just void.

His feet slowed. His breath caught. Not from fear—though fear pressed like ice behind his ribs—but because the path itself refused movement. His legs burned. His eyes, wide and unblinking, saw nothing.

And so he stopped.

Not to rest, but to listen.

Somewhere, far ahead in the dark, something was breathing. And it was not him.

But before Spinel could listen further, something brushed against his feet—soft, small, impossibly gentle. In the pitch of shadow, he could see nothing. Yet beneath him, a warmth stirred.

A seed.

It pulsed with a faint glow, then sprouted. Roots cracked the blackened soil. A stem reached upward. In moments—as if time had forgotten its rules—the seed became a sapling, then a tree, and then a bloom. From that blossom, a face emerged—ancient, wise, and crowned in light.

"You lived seeking a reason to grieve?" it asked, its voice neither male nor female, but resonant and kind. "Then I shall give you one... before your journey ends."

Spinel—the Wolf—stood frozen. All his life, he had longed for something to hold onto. A name. A memory. A truth. But not like this. Not at the edge of dread, with death watching.

He resisted.

"Whatever enchantment you are," he said, his voice steady, "I will not stray. I was born in darkness. Darkness trusts me. I have a task to complete."

"I won't stop you," the figure replied softly. "I am the One-Wish Tree. I thought your wish was to grieve. But if not, then another wish I shall grant. I only offer what your heart desires."

And that shattered something within him.

For the first time in his life, no one ordered him. No voice commanded. No shadow punished. No whip of cruelty lashed his back.

This one asked.

Gently. Kindly.

"What do *you* want?"

And Spinel—silent all his years—fell to his knees. Tears slipped down his face. A cracked, trembling smile appeared upon lips that had only known snarls. His voice, when it came, was scarcely a whisper.

"I want to know... who I am."

The One-Wish Tree reached out its glowing branches and touched his brow. "Then listen," it said.

And truth poured forth like a river long dammed.

"You were born in blood and enchantment. McVellian, the warlock who bent time to his will, wielded the Deathly Chattel to visit the past. To rescue Evil Basalt from ruin, he pierced the veil of present and past. But not even his magic could unbind her shackles—not until he spilled blood pure and potent, enchanted by love and lineage.

"That night, it was your mother's blood. And your father's. The spell was paid in full. And you, their child, were handed over to Basalt... as tribute. A living gift. A vessel. A wolf to serve the witch."

"A fleeting memory stirred in Spinel's mind—a scent of lavender, a lullaby hummed through trembling lips, a warm hand once cradling his cheek.

"It came and went like a dream forgotten on waking. But it was enough. Enough to feel that once, he had been loved."

Spinel's hands trembled.

"Now you know," the tree whispered. "And now you are free."

Spinel rose slowly. The ashes—the very ashes of the mirror that had summoned the Nameless Fear—slipped from his hand and fell to the forest floor. The map, too, he pressed into the bark of the One-Wish Tree.

"Then let me return your gift," he said. "This path may yet save a life—a life dear to you... and to the world."

The tree did not stop him.

With one last glance, Spinel turned.

He did not weep again. Nor did he speak.

Instead, the Wolf vanished—swallowed by the dark, borne on shadow.

Never again seen.

Never again found.

Yet somewhere, beneath moonlight and root, the earth remembered his steps—not as a servant of evil, but as one who chose the harder path... and walked it alone.

27. Chattel, Curse, Crown

But the moment Spinel veered from the path, Basalt felt it—a ripple in the deep.

Not just a suspicion. A knowing. A *seeing*.

Her eyes flashed with cruel clarity.

The ashes would never reach Death's throne.

The sword would not return to her waiting hand.

The plan had failed.

And yet—she did not waver.

She drank her fury like molten wine.

And in that fire, a darker design was born.

Why wait for the sword? Why strike them one by one?

She had power. Old power.

And today, she would *use it*.

"Walk them to Death," she hissed, voice low as a curse,

"And let them beg Death *from* Death."

Her gaze turned eastward, toward the veiled valley—the hidden path that once eluded her sight.

She could not see its entrance, but she did not need to.

She would smoke them out.

"Let them run," she whispered.

"Let the bastards *flee* to Death's door."

And then—she laughed.

A laugh like thunder cracking across the bones of the earth.

A stormborn shriek that scattered birds from blackened skies.

A sound to strip hope from the hearts of those who still dared love Emerland.

It began with a sound—subtle, strange—in the Hidden Valley, and it happened all at once.

Not a cry, nor a roar, but a rupture—deep and ancient. A sound like the spine of the world had cracked open, as though the old bones of time had shifted in their sleep.

Above the Hidden Valley, the wind held its breath. No bird sang. No leaf stirred. The hush was so complete it felt sacred—until the trembling came.

It began as a murmur beneath their feet, like the stirring of something vast beneath the earth's skin. Then it rose—growing, groaning—until the land itself convulsed like a heart in pain.

Baba Yaga, Hematite, Jade, Amethyst, and Diamond had only just crossed the valley's edge when the groan of earth grew into a scream. The ground split wide with a sound like thunder dragged through stone.

The sacred soil rent asunder, and from its depths came a howl not of wind, but of something older—something waking. Trees writhed and collapsed as if fleeing unseen terror. Rocks burst like shattered stars. The sky itself seemed to bend, light warping and twisting as if the heavens recoiled.

But it was not the world that broke.

It was the Hidden Valley.

The place that once held peace and prophecy now gave way to ruin—as if the land had fulfilled its final purpose, and let go.

Far away, in the charred heart of the Fortress of Dread, Evil Basalt rose from her throne. Shadows coiled at her feet like hounds made of smoke, eager to serve. Her hands trembled—not with fear, but with purpose—as she drew strength from the fraying threads of forgotten spells. Her lips moved, whispering incantations older than sin. And her eyes—two burning coals shaped by the first murder—pierced through time, distance, and concealment. She had seen the valley. She had found it—and now, she had broken it.

Nothing escaped her gaze.

She had seen the One-Wish Tree, glowing like a golden wound in the mist. And she had seen Spinel, kneeling like a penitent before it, offering the Deathly Map as though in prayer.

The tree had accepted.

Basalt did not scream.

She did not rage.

She smiled.

A slow, terrible smile cracked her face like lightning across an obsidian sky. She had woven this ending from the first thread—looped it, knotted it, and now pulled it tight. The collapse of the Hidden Valley was no failure. It was the opening note of her final symphony—a crescendo drawn from ruin.

The beginning of the end.

The land groaned one last time—low, long, and ancient—as if the earth itself remembered the curse.

And then, it shattered.

Baba Yaga and Hematite were hurled down one path, the earth splitting between them like a blade of fate. Jade and Amethyst rolled onto another slope, crying out, but unseen by the others. And Diamond—Starborn, soul-scarred, and silent—was thrown into a third chasm, utterly alone.

A hush followed.

The kind of hush that settles before a storm—tense, waiting, unbreathing.

And then, from the shadows of her broken throne, Basalt whispered:

"Alone. Let her stand alone. For how long shall she cling to others to feel strong? The Starborn must be severed. Only then will she break."

She turned toward the dark path where Amethyst had fallen.

"The deathly road… he does not need a map. I will walk him myself."

From her hands, she summoned illusions—phantoms spun from lies and grief, shaped like memories and sharpened like teeth—and sent them after Diamond like wolves in fog.

To Amethyst, she cast snaring darkness, coiling tight like smoke with fangs, soaked in sorrow, bound to loss.

Then she turned to her Wraiths—cloaked, fanged, patient as tombs.

"Stand guard," she hissed. "The moment has come. When the sun dies tonight, we rise. We leave no heart unbroken. No dream left breathing."

And the Fortress of Dread shuddered—deep beneath its bones—as if it, too, hungered.

Then Basalt looked toward Diamond—through vision, through distance—and a wicked hush fell across the world. Clutching her severed tresses like a relic of old power, she whispered into them, summoning the ancient arts of illusion and delusion. Shadows curled from her fingertips like ink in water, and with a flick of her wrist, she cast the spell toward the girl who defied her.

A smile, cruel and quiet, played across her lips.

She saw it clearly now—the curse slithering through the realms, unseen and unstoppable, coiling around Diamond's soul. Like roots wrapping a dwindling flame, it leeched the last light from her. Bit by bit, her strength bled away, not in a cry or struggle, but in quiet surrender.

And there stood Diamond—motionless.

Around her, the air had changed. The sky had turned a strange, bruised shade of ash. The wind did not move. The trees did not breathe. And the light that bathed her? It no longer belonged to the sun.

It was a hollow light.

A dying light.

A stolen light.

The Hidden Valley was gone. Swallowed. As if Emerland itself had been devoured by shadow, leaving only a memory of what once was.

She turned slowly in place, but all paths looked wrong. Twisted. Empty.

Then she saw him.

Amethyst—kneeling before Evil Basalt.

And smiling.

The witch placed a hand on his shoulder. Diamond gasped, her heart shattering.

"No... no," she whispered. "That's not... he wouldn't..."

But the image did not waver. The scene burned itself into her eyes. Amethyst's head bowed. Basalt laughed softly. Around them, the ruined land twisted, as if it welcomed the betrayal.

Diamond stumbled backward. Her breath grew thin. Her limbs trembled.

"What is this place?" she whispered. "What is real...?"

The world around her pulsed with silence.

She wanted to believe it was illusion, but how could one disbelieve the things she saw? Her soul—already splintered from days of torment—wavered.

She gave up.

She sank to her knees, unsure of where she was, or who she was anymore. Nothing felt real. Nothing made sense. And worst of all, she felt a hollow ache in her chest— Something vital was missing.

Then, through the mist, she saw a flicker.

A woman.

A rooster.

"Jabba Gabbro?" Diamond's voice cracked as she stared, unsure whether it was another vision conjured by Basalt or something real.

The woman marched up and grabbed her by the arm, rough and impatient.

"The Princess can't even tell real from false anymore," snapped Jabba Gabbro, eyes blazing. "And while she dithers, evl moves closer!"

Diamond blinked, still dazed. Jabba didn't wait.

"I told Amethyst to stay away from you—but he never listens. None of them listen. Eighteen years ago, I warned Baba Yaba not to enter the Deathly Chattel. Told him it was Death's trap, a door with no return. Did he listen? No. He stepped through, and look what it cost."

She dragged Diamond into her crooked little hut, the door slamming behind them. The air smelled of salt, smoke, and scorched herbs. Inside, a large cauldron boiled with an enchantment thick as memory. Jabba pointed toward it with a shaking hand.

"Look."

Diamond stepped closer—and saw.

Within the roiling vision, Baba Yaba stood before the threshold of the Deathly Chattel. Death herself waited on the other side. A figure cloaked in cold light. And then... he gave his life. Not in battle. Not in fire. But in silence. The price of passage had been his soul.

Diamond stared, unable to speak.

Jabba's voice softened—only for a moment. "He never listened to me. Then Amethyst listened. Then he stopped. Now my brother listens again. So now... I must listen to *him*."

She turned, fury returning to her face.

"You, Starborn. You brought this havoc. You want to save everyone? Then let *time* be your punishment. You'll live in the Deathly Chattel. I'll cast you back. And there will be *no* return!"

Before Diamond could protest—before she could even move—Jabba screamed a spell and shoved her forward. Light exploded around her. The floor vanished. The world spiraled.

Then arms caught Jabba from behind.

It was Toxico T. He wrapped his arms around her, trembling.

"I'll make sure Amethyst returns," he whispered, eyes full of fire.

"You'd *better*," hissed Jabba, not turning to look at him. "Or you know exactly what I'm capable of."

Toxico nodded once, kissed her hair with a cunning smile, and vanished into the mist, hand raised in farewell.

Back in the **Fortress of Dread**, Evil Basalt watched the scene unfold through the mirror of cinders—and smiled.

At last, Toxico T had done something worthwhile. Something more than sipping his poisonous tea and mumbling in riddles. He had delivered the Starborn.

To exile.

Forever.

"She is lost now," Basalt whispered, rising slowly from her throne. "Lost to the Deathly Chattel. How fitting."

A cruel gleam sparked in her eye as she turned toward the flames.

"Irony, isn't it?" she mused aloud. "Morganite once locked *me* in the Deathly Chattel. It took me years to claw my way back—and even then, only with help. But now... *his own kin* wanders there. No door. No guide. No return."

She laughed once—softly, savagely.

Diamond landed hard.

But it was not darkness that greeted her. It was a forest.

Still.

Quiet.

But not peaceful.

The trees leaned inward, tall and thin like grieving statues. The air smelled of time. And though nothing moved, Diamond *felt* it—something watching her. Breathing with her. Shadowing her.

She rose slowly to her feet. The illusions were gone. No more false smiles. No more whispered betrayals.

Only the echo of days that had already died.

Around her, the forest shimmered—and began to show her visions.

Her past.

She saw the moment of her birth, golden light cradling her cries. She saw Morganite—young and strong—holding her close beside a fire. She saw Onyx racing across the fields, wings slicing air like silk, and her own laughter chasing after.

Diamond smiled.

Just a little.

But then something stepped between the trees.

A figure.

Tall. Slender. Dressed in shadow like a second skin.

Not part of her past.

Not part of her story.

Not welcome.

"I am McVellian," the man said, smiling with lips that didn't match his eyes. "I entered the Deathly Chattel long ago. Gave up my present to save Wicked Basalt."

He tilted his head, voice dry and curling like smoke. "And now I live here. Since you forfeited your return... that means *you* must live here too."

Diamond didn't have time to respond.

McVellian seized her by the hair and hurled her deeper into the woods—into a thicket so dense the branches tore at her skin like claws. She rolled, breath knocked from her chest, the forest whispering now with voices that were not her own.

She scrambled to her feet, heart pounding.

Then she understood.

This place wasn't just memory. It was a prison built of past and pain. McVellian had become part of it—like mold in an old wound. And there were others here too. Other things. Dark things. Creatures that should never have had names.

Around her, the scenes kept playing. Her childhood. Her fears. Her failings. Morganite dying. Onyx shattering into sky.

And still McVellian walked toward her. Slowly. Deliberately.

Close enough now to kill her.

But then he paused—and looked at her.

There was something in his eyes. Pity, perhaps. Or mockery. Or... something darker.

Not cruelty, no—something worse.

A smile woven from lies.

And Diamond, in that moment, *saw* it. Not just the smile—but the memory it masked.

She saw the day Baba Yaba stepped into the Deathly Chattel.

The air had curdled. Death had already arrived.

And as Baba Yaba turned, unaware, McVellian struck—a blade laced with poison gifted by Death itself, plunged deep into the spine of trust.

There was no duel. No chance. Just a cold, calculated murder.

But what else would you expect from a man who bled ice and breathed deceit?

Today, though, the tide had turned.

Diamond no longer cared what McVellian saw in her—fear, defiance, madness, resolve.

She didn't care if she lived or died.

She would fight.

And that was all that mattered.

This was **not** the day her Steward died.

Not the day she screamed and could do nothing.

Today—she was still broken. Still alone.

But no longer helpless.

She had walked through death.

And returned.

So when McVellian leaned in, drunk on his own power—

Diamond moved.

Her fingers were already wrapped around the dagger Jabba Gabbro had placed in her palm.

Her grip—iron. Her will—unbreakable.

In one clean, breathless motion, she drove the blade into his chest.

Deep. True.

He gasped.

Not from pain—

But from *her*.

From the cold resolve in her eyes.

From the girl he thought he could shatter... who struck without hesitation.

Diamond didn't flinch.

She didn't weep.

She didn't look away.

She had killed a man.

The man who stole Baba Yaba's life.

Who silenced Emerland's laughter.

Her first kill.

And she felt... nothing.

Nothing but fire.

To live.

To save.

To rise.

28. The Second Death

Diamond turned—
Her gaze swept the gnarled trees, every branch like a claw poised to strike.

Her heart thudded to a strange new rhythm,
like war drums echoing from beneath the earth.

And then—

it appeared.

In the heart of the Deathly Chattel, the air began to shimmer.

Not with light—

But with memory.

A vision coiled into being like rising fog, silver and slow,
whispers forming shapes,
shapes forming truth.

The first vision.

Her gateway.

A haunted veil into the past.

Before her stood the **Cursed Cemetery**—black stones rising from ash-stained soil like the teeth of buried Gods.

Time seemed to twist around it, pulling at her limbs, her breath, her very will.

Was this the path to unravel the curse Basalt had bound to her soul?

Or merely the first step into another trap?

Another curse?
It didn't matter.
Diamond stepped forward—
and the vision opened like a wound in the world.
The air split.
The past took her.
And the forest held its breath.

What she beheld now tore the breath from her lungs—
swift and cruel as drowning.
Her knees buckled.
The world tilted.
It was as if all the darkness, cruelty, and ancient malice she had ever feared had gathered into *form*.
A figure. A presence.
Him.
He moved like a thunder made flesh.
Each step shattered the silence—
and something else.
A law. A promise. A piece of the world.
Broken beneath his tread.
Diamond stood frozen, a stone in a river of rot.
The air was thick with the stench of death— not just death, but **long-forgotten deaths**, unburied and unwept.
The walls oozed with filth. Bones lay where prayers had failed.
She knew this place without knowing it:
The Fortress of Dread.
And in the middle of that corpse-choked chamber,
he turned.
No face. No name.
Only a gaze—like the abyss opening its eyes.

Before that look could fall fully upon her—
before it could *end her*—
Diamond collapsed, scrambling with raw instinct behind a shattered relic of furniture,
its surface scorched and blackened by time.
She hid in the shadows, deep within the cursed entrails of the fortress, as if the stone itself might shield her from the weight of what she had seen.
Her hands shook.
Her breath came in broken fragments.
Her soul flinched with every echoing footstep.
And the strength she had once claimed—
the fire, the fury, the purpose—
felt like something far away,
a story someone else had lived.

It was not a past she remembered, but the past before memory. The past beneath the past—when the world still knelt beneath the reign of darkness, before even the rise of The Hollow Star. A time of forgotten terror. A time when the stars had looked away.

And before her loomed another figure veiled in consuming shadow—more Wraith than flesh, more curse than being. It did not walk; it hovered like despair. A ghost forged of ancient malice, crowned in hatred, with eyes that were not eyes at all—only black wells where starlight had gone to die.

Her arrival was a breath of frost upon the bones of the world. She did not walk. She drifted—tall, regal, draped in robes of mourning night. Her presence commanded silence. Her voice, when it came, was a thread of silk spun from the sorrow of the dead.

"Brother," she murmured, with a fondness too cold to be love. "You killed the elf."

"He trespassed," answered Him, his voice the grind of stone beneath the earth. "He dared to cross into the forbidden. My forbidden."

"He was lost," Death murmured, her voice like falling ash. **"But the Elves are not. They come now… for war."**

The shadow stepped forward—his form a shifting mirage of man, beast, and something far older. With a voice that cracked the silence like thunder over hollowed hills, he declared:

"Why should we tremble? We hold dominion over two great forces: the abyssal dark… and the Crown of Emerland."

Death's eyes flickered, dim coals beneath her hood. **"But the crown is treacherous,"** she whispered. **"It is not sworn to us. It follows strength. And strength… is ever changing."**

The shadow laughed then—a sound of crumbling stone and sp intering bone. **"You are Death, my sister. And I… I am neither born, nor breathing, nor blessed by ending. I am the Unshaped. I am the War Without Name."**

His form rippled, casting dread like a second skin.

"Ready the earth. Prepare the skies. The old war stirs anew."

Then he stopped.

His eyes narrowed—slits of molten black—and the air grew sti l, thick with the weight of unseen knowing.

"Who stirs in silence?" he snarled. "Step forth… or be devoured."

Diamond held her breath, eyes shut tight, her body still as stone.

But then—**crack**.

The groan of rotting wood buckled beneath her. A sharp gasp escaped her lips.

She had been found.

Instinct flared like lightning.

Her fingers shot to the leaf Baba Yaga had given her —

Three gifts in one: to escape, to hide, to return.

With trembling reverence, she pressed the *hiding leaf* to her chest,

as if it were a shield spun from sacred magic and whispered prayers.

And hoped — prayed — it would answer her call.

And just like that, the air shifted. The vision rolled forward.

And just like that, the air shifted. The vision stirred—ancient, immense—and rolled forward like the slow turn of fate.

She stood at the edge of the Lake of Wonders.

Its waters were dark glass, unbroken, mirroring neither moon nor star, only the weight of memory. And there—on the far shore—she saw herself.

Just as Baba Yaga had whispered: *"You have walked these lands before."*

It was true.

She had been here. But she had not been *Diamond* then. The figure by the water's edge was paler, almost luminous—strange in her own skin, clothed in silks and vanity. Beautiful, perhaps. Fragile, certainly. And for a fleeting moment, Diamond smiled at her own conceit. What was beauty to her now? Dust and shadow. All that mattered was life before death.

She crouched low behind the tall, whispering grasses, their blades slick with dew and blood. The air buzzed with the cursed drone of black-winged flies—death-scenting things, drawn to places where old magic had bled into the earth. They circled her like mourners.

Diamond watched in silence. Her former self moved with the ignorance of safety, the softness of a soul untouched by fire. She still wore the ornaments Diamond had since cast away— gilded things, trinkets of a world that no longer was.

Then the air cracked.

And all thoughts of gentler days were obliterated.

There She was.

Basalt.

She did not arrive. She *descended*. As if torn from a nightmare the world had tried to forget. Her presence fouled the vision—turning wind to poison, grass to ash, silence to dread. No word for what she felt could be found in any language. It was not fear. Not rage. It was the end of song, the stillness before the scream.

Diamond did not breathe.

It was the day Basalt was born. Or forged. Or summoned—none could say for certain.

The vision blurred and reformed. The air hung heavy with the reek of sacrifice, of seared earth and sky turned inward. It was here, on this blighted shore, that the Lord of the Forbidden Realms had claimed five souls—five lives offered like candles snuffed in a storm—to weave a vessel of dread and beauty.

And from their deaths, *she* rose.

Basalt.

Cloaked in wicked elegance, carved from sorrow and ruin, she stood like a queen of ashes. Her presence warped the light around her, a gravity of malice that drew even the flies into silence. Her voice was soft—a whisper laced with rot—as she knelt beside the Lake of Wonders and spoke.

But she was not alone.

Something answered.

The water trembled, not from wind, but from something *beneath*. A shadow moved across its surface—formless, ancient, *listening*. The same presence Diamond had seen before, in that fetid throne-room in the Fortress of Dread. That which called itself the Lord of the Forbidden Realms. He who had many names—none spoken now without fear—and some not spoken at all.

The Lake of Wonders did not reflect what stood before it. It revealed what *dwelt within*.

And now it revealed the truth.

Basalt was not merely flesh, nor simply soul. She was a vessel—an echo of the Lord's will, the shell of His return. She was *His shadow*, until such time that He could walk the world again, crowned in flesh and fire.

Diamond felt herself recoil, as if the truth itself was venom. Her hands trembled in the grass. This was no ordinary haunting, no memory left to fade. This was a beginning. A birth. A coronation of something too old and too terrible for the world to name.

And still, the whispering continued between them—lake and shadow, mother and maker—threading the past to the doom that crept closer with every breath.

Then Basalt turned. She saw her past self, the other Diamond, in the lake's reflection—and without hesitation, drew a dagger, aiming to kill her, and this Diamond closed her eyes.

But a cry shattered the silence.

Bulwark.

The enchanted bird with burning feathers, brave and fierce, dove between them. The blade struck him

He fell.

Diamond turned—but her other self was gone.

Vanished like mist before dawn.

Baba Yaga's words returned, chilling and precise: *"She cut the vision halfway to save the day. Had the other self died then, there would be no more visions. No more life. For what dies in the vision is taken from the world forever. So say the Elves."*

A silence fell—deep, ancestral—as if the earth itself held its breath.

And still, Diamond's heart wept.

For Bulwark, who had given his life to buy Emerland one final dawn. For Jade, who still wandered through the ashes of grief, never knowing how her mother had died. Perhaps it was mercy. Perhaps truth was a cruelty too sharp for the living.

Diamond longed to rise. To walk to the Lake of Wonders, to drink from its myth-laced waters. Her lips were cracked, her throat a raw wound. But her body had turned against her. She could not stand. Could barely crawl.

She dragged herself through the grass—fingers trembling, knees scraping stone and root—drawn by instinct more than hope. Each inch forward was agony, her breath a thin rasp in the windless air. Not for comfort. Not for relief. Just a drop. A single, sacred drop to touch her lips. To anchor her to the world. To *survive*.

The lake shimmered ahead—dark, unending—a black mirror trembling with secrets. And it whispered her name again, in the language of dreams and drowned stars.

She reached out.

But before a single drop could grace her lips—she *saw him again*.

Beneath the surface, veiled in the lake's obsidian depths, a shape emerged.

Him.

The one Death had called *brother*.

The one who whispered in corridors where even Gods feared to tread. He beckoned now, slow and smiling, his voice curling through the water like smoke through a grave. Feeding her rage.

Stirring it like coals long buried. His presence was a sickness made flesh, a hunger without end.

Then—Basalt turned.

As if the vision itself had shifted in the wind of fate. She sensed something at the lake's edge.

Diamond.

Basalt's eyes locked on her. Cold. Exact. Her hand moved to her dagger.

Diamond froze.

But just as the blade might have flown—

another Diamond appeared.

Stepping through the folds of time like a crack in glass. The past, reasserting itself. The distraction.

Basalt's gaze snapped to the new figure—momentarily confused, then calculating. The knife flew.

And again—Bulwark.

Like before. Like always. He threw himself into its path, the blade finding his heart as it had once before. Time curled inward. The vision spiraled. The old wound opened again, as if memory itself bled.

Diamond could not scream. Her breath caught. Her body stiffened. It was *her* death this time. The dagger had been meant for *her*—not the vision, not the memory, *her.*

And it was her other self—the one she had called delicate, distracted by beauty—who saved her.

She had judged that girl too quickly. That girl had been brave enough to die in her place.

Then, from the dark beyond vision, Baba Yaga's voice floated in:

"And the second time... the vision had to be cut halfway."

Even the witch did not know what had truly happened.

The past had risen to protect the present. And Diamond—trembling, breathless, alive—lay still beneath the whispering grass.

Her thirst was gone.

All she could taste now was blood in the air, the echo of Basalt's wrath still ringing like a curse through her bones—and the terrible knowing that somewhere, just beneath the veil of time, the Lord of the Forbidden Realms waited to be born.

And death, in the form of Basalt, stood before her—breathing, watching, *becoming*.

Diamond sat unmoving.

The silence around her was vast—ancient. Tears blurred her sight, and the world dimmed as if in mourning.

She pressed a trembling hand to her chest, to the place where the blade had nearly found her heart, and whispered into the hollow stillness:

"That is how I failed... twice. In the visions."

Time no longer held shape.

She drifted—weightless, undone—caught in a silence older than speech, older than sorrow. It was not sleep, nor waking, but some liminal space where ash floats through memory, and dreams decay into shadow. Her soul, threadbare and raw, clung to the edges of a vision that had tried to unravel her.

She hovered in the seam between breath and bone—where memory falters, and prophecy begins to burn.

And in that hush, the world waited.

Not for her to rise.

But for what would rise *through her*.

29. Crown and Coffin

Diamond remained—
    Trapped in the coils of the past,
Still as stone,
Blind to what had begun.

And so it seemed—as though the world itself, blind and unresisting, Bent to Evil Basalt's will. The stars watched in silence. The winds dared not speak. All was aligning—for Evil Basalt, for darkness unbound.

Basalt turned to her gathered legions—monsters sculpted from shadow, men whose souls had long since rotted into despair, witches carved from curse and scorched in fire. Her voice surged like thunder over a war-split earth, echoing through the void with the promise of ruin.

"By dawn," she thundered, "the banner of darkness shall rise once more above Emerland Castle! Let no tower greet the morning—only shadow. Let stone remember what time dared to forget!"

She threw her arms to the heavens or hell, and the sky cracked— ribbons of black fire tearing through the firmament. Beneath that unnatural glow, a smile curled her lips—terrible, triumphant, and final.

"We ride now!" her voice thundered like the crack of heavens torn asunder. **"For the Starborn fades—and the crown calls to its true master!"**

A cry rose from the host—terrible and glorious. It sounded not like men or beasts, but like the death of stars, the breaking of ancient mountains, the end of ages.

Far away, amid that storm of power, beneath a sky so barren not even the stars dared to blink, Amethyst walked a path not his own. Or perhaps he didn't walk at all—he was borne, like a fallen leaf down a river of shadow. The Darkness that held him had no shape, no edge, no echo. It was not absence, but hunger. Not silence, but the stillness before a scream breaks the air. Cold coiled around him, ancient and deliberate, like a serpent with no eyes, no heart—only purpose.

He could not tell if his eyes were closed or open. The dark was complete. He staggered at first, then stilled, for there was nowhere to go. His legs felt like water. Time was a blur. Thought, a fading thread.

And then—

A voice, cruel and sweet, like honey laced with poison.

"Oh, dear Amethyst," came the purr of **Evil Basalt**, echoing from everywhere and nowhere. "From beginning to end, all you see is nothing... and still, you walk."

Her laughter followed, a sound that scratched the soul like broken glass.

"Do not struggle. You are... fortunate. Death has come to many, but you—you are allowed to walk to her. Others must wait for her to find them. But you, lovely, trembling thing, are being sent straight into her embrace."

A sudden shift in the darkness—then the ground beneath his feet changed.

It glowed—softly, eerily. A pale, spectral trail coiled outward like a ghost's ribbon unraveling across the void. It shimmered with the hue of lost souls, weaving through the darkness like breath from a dying star.

"Behold," crooned Basalt, her voice like velvet soaked in venom. "The Deathly Path—where breath becomes silence, and hope decays into surrender. A bridge forged in the marrow of the fallen."

She laughed again—louder now, wilder, a sound that split the air like shattering glass.

"March, my precious gift," she sneered, her gaze fixed on Amethyst with cruel delight. "March to her gates. Let the bones of fate quake beneath your tread. Let even prophecy hold its breath."

But light is not so easily broken.
Even in death's devouring maw,
some embers remember the shape of flame—
and burn,
quietly,
until the dawn returns.

In the heart of Emerland Castle, where shuttered windows wept dust and every corridor whispered of yesterdays, King Alexandrite sat shrouded in silence.

Once, he had been a sovereign of light—his brow wreathed in gold, his voice carried in songs sung from tower to vale. Now, he wore regret like funeral robes. His chamber had soured into a mausoleum of memory, and his mind—once sharp as obsidian— lay tangled in cobwebs spun from sorrow. Diamond... Amethyst...

even the crown itself had become like ghosts to him—glimpsed only in the corners of fading dreams.

He unlatched the window—not in hope of light, but for the faintest trace of a scent, a memory, anything.

"Diamond," he murmured to the air, "Amethyst... Jade."

But no breeze stirred. The sky beyond hung in a breathless hush—the stillness that comes when even the clouds hold their breath before the heavens break.

He bowed his head, as if the very weight of time had bent his spine. His shoulders, once straight with the bearing of kings, now sagged beneath the quiet avalanche of years, of missteps, of things undone.

The crown—once ablaze with golden promise—lay forgotten in the dust, no brighter than a discarded trinket.

And then—

A shadow cut across the pale sky, descending like a falling star lit by flame and fate.

Rock the Hawk, wings ablaze with purpose, dove from the heavens—not to Baba Yaga, as all omens had once foretold—but to him.

With a sharp, rending cry, Rock tore through the castle's gloom and dropped from the shadows above—wings slick with blood, eyes burning with ancient purpose. At Alexandrite's feet fell a brittle scroll, its parchment yellowed like plague-flesh, its edges curled and crumbling, ink faded to ghost-smoke, bound in twine the color of old bone.

It was *the map.*

The one etched in sorrow and sealed in silence—the deathly path. The same Spinel had surrendered to the One-Wish Tree, and the Tree, in its mercy or madness, had given it to Rock... to deliver now, in a last desperate bid to save her daughter.

"It's your turn now, Alexandrite," said the Rock.

The king stared, blinking. His fingers, once strong, now trembled as they reached for the scroll.

"Amethyst walks the path of death," Rock continued. "He walks it for her. But he cannot walk it alone."

A shudder ran through Alexandrite's voice. "How can I help? I cannot even see."

But Rock only tilted his head, gaze sharp and unyielding as mountain stone.

"You don't need sight. You need purpose. That is the Deathly Map. It leads only one way—into Death's dominion. But how you walk it... that choice is yours."

Alexandrite rose with the slowness of stone long burdened by time. His knees ached, his breath was thin—but his heart no longer quivered. For the first time in many days, his hands did not shake. Not with fear. Not with sorrow. Only with resolve.

A wind stirred over Emerland—not the wind of weather, but the wind of fate. And the old king stirred with it.

He lifted the whistle to his lips. His fingers, cracked with age and worn by war, trembled at first. Twice he tried, and twice the sound failed. His breath caught in the hollow of grief, brittle as winter glass.

But on the third breath... a note rose. Low. Hollow. A sound not meant for men, but for myth. It soared into the sky like a question—one final plea cast into the waiting silence of the world.

And the world answered.

From the farthest edge of mist and memory, a shape emerged—winged, mighty, black as thundercloud and dream. A steed of the old blood. Not Agate, but kin. A brother of storm and star, born not for earth but for omen.

His mane flowed like fire through snow. His hooves struck sparks as he descended—stone shivering beneath the weight of prophecy.

Alexandrite stepped forward, eyes reflecting both shadow and sky. The hand he raised no longer trembled. It was steady now, like the dawn after mourning. He laid it upon the steed's flank, where warmth pulsed like a buried sun.

The beast bowed its head. He was his ride and his eyes.

It is time, the gesture said—wordless, sure.

And the old king, without looking back, mounted.

And the wind rose—howling, ancient, alive.

They did not gallop.

They soared.

Below them, Emerland Castle unraveled like a dream slipping into daylight. Its towers dwindled into mist, swallowed by the breath of sky.

The clouds parted not with grace, but with violence—as if the heavens themselves were being torn open.

Alexandrite gripped the Deathly Map. It pulsed in his hands like a second heart, fierce and urgent.

He opened it.

And the sky obeyed.

Not gently.

But with a shuddering, cosmic shift.

A gale rose from nowhere—no mere wind, but something older than stars, forged in the breath between worlds.

It seized them, mount and rider, not to guide but to claim.

They were no longer flying.

They were being carried.

Driven across the broken firmament by fate itself.

Below, the world became a smear of motion.

Mountains folded into themselves. Rivers twisted like serpents. Forests danced backward.

Overhead, the stars blurred—trails of fire streaming like tears across the cosmos.

And there, ahead of them—glowing like a thread of mourning light—was the path.

Not a road, but a ribbon of ghostlight.

A trail that writhed and shimmered like breath on glass.

The same path Amethyst had walked not long ago.

Now, it opened again.

Twisting through the void like memory made manifest.

Alexandrite gave no thought to turning back.

Not as a king.

But as a father chasing the grave.

No crown could shield him now. No throne could anchor him.

And so he flew toward death with open eyes—

not to conquer,

but to love

one final time.

King Alexandrite followed Amethyst through the skeletal remains of the old realm—his steps heavy with prophecy, his heart tethered to the fading sound of hooves. And Amethyst, noble and stricken, moved only forward, following the last path the world had left him.

Then—where once the trail had shimmered like a ribbon of moonlight upon frost—

Amethyst fell.

The ground beneath him shattered like illusion, collapsing into blackness. Amethyst plunged into waters black as oil and cold as the first night after the world's end. It was not water. It was memory drowned. A void that pulsed like something alive. There was no sky. No shore. No bottom. Only a silence so immense it pressed against the bones, stealing even the shape of thought.

And then—*the sound.*

Teeth.

Slicing through the water.

They came from the depths—

where no light had ever dwelled,

where even the stars had turned their gaze away.

Things not meant for waking eyes.

No flesh—only hunger.

No eyes—only the knowing.

They moved like the shadows of forgotten Gods,

coiling through the black like curses unspoken,

drawn by the scent of the living.

Nightmares born of drowned time.

And Amethyst—still falling—thrashed against the suffocating dark,

his hooves churning the void, defiant against the pull of death,

as the first *mouth* opened beneath him,

wide enough to swallow a star,

or a soul.

Then they rose.

Crocodiles—monstrous, primeval, blind with ancient hunger—

erupted from the abyss like blades of divine wrath.

Their jaws tore silence like paper.

Their scales, black as funeral stone, caught no light.

Their eyes—yellow, lidless, lifeless—burned with the cold gleam of hungers that had rotted in the dark since the world was young.
They did not breathe.
They did not pause.
They wanted **blood**.
And Amethyst—child of the wild moon, beast of the old flame—
fought.
He fought like a star falling from heaven's crown—
brilliant, furious, unwilling to vanish without fire.
He seized one beast by its gnarled snout,
wrenched its jaws apart with the rage of a dying god,
drove a fist into the dead-glow eye of another,
and tore loose a jagged fang—
a blade born of desperation.
With it, he slashed.
He kicked.
He screamed.
Not in fear—
but in fury.
The fury of one who remembers the sun.
The fury of one who will not go quietly into shadow.
The fury of one who bears a child's last hope in his heart.
But the darkness only deepened.
The water thickened, a blackness that crushed thought and light.
More came. More always came.
His limbs ached.
His breath faltered.
And hope—
hope slipped from his grasp like a name
forgotten in a dream.

This was no battle.
It was a devouring.
The sea writhed like a mouth unhinged,
and the end pressed in from every side.
But then—
A cry shattered the void.
High and raw, it split the air like lightning tearing open the vault of night. It was not the scream of a beast or a man—but something older. Something divine.
From above—not merely the sky, but from a realm beyond stars—came hooves of flame and wings cast in shadow.
Agate.
Amethyst did not remember him. Not fully.
His mind was fractured, fogged with loss.
The path, the fall, the world before—just fragments now, scattered in darkness.
But **Agate remembered.**
Agate had been with him in the Hidden Valley, before Evil Basalt shattered it—
before everything broke.
That was all Amethyst could still recall:
a valley of peace, and her beside him.
Then came the fall.
Basalt hurled him down the deathly path.
But Agate—
Agate followed.
Silent, relentless, chasing only his scent through shadow and ruin.
He fell like a burning comet, crashing into the waters with celestial force. His wings beat like war drums. His hooves struck like judgment. The beasts scattered. The tides recoiled.

And through the spray and chaos, Agate came for Amethyst—unstoppable, radiant, true.

Amethyst reached with the last of his strength.

Agate caught him.

Together, they rose.

Water tore past in silver sheets. Fangs snapped at shadows. But Agate soared, wing to wind, carrying him upward—toward something that felt like breath, like light, like the first whisper of hope reborn.

They flew through silence.

Above them, the sky stretched like black silk. Below, the world churned with death.

Amethyst said nothing. His body was numb. His memory, frayed.

But his spirit—his spirit burned.

Then he saw it.

A light.

Faint. Flickering.

30. What Death Keeps

Amethyst kept looking—eyes narrowed, breath held—until he saw it.

Perched upon a jagged spine of stone stood a mansion, ruined and silent, cradled in the dark. Its walls were pale as old bone, its windows hollow—

Except one.

From that single pane, a flame flickered—small, defiant.

And beside it... a figure.

Still as stone.

Too distant to name.

Too motionless to trust.

A watcher, or a memory?

A shadow, or a sign?

He did not know.

But it was waiting.

Agate descended gently, his hooves brushing the stone with reverence.

Amethyst slid down. The horse stood beside him, silent and waiting.

He looked again to the light. The figure had not moved.

He stepped forward.

His body ached. His lungs burned. But something in him whispered—

Go.

He placed a hand on Agate's neck—grateful.

Then he walked alone toward the dreadful mansion.

To find out whether the flame ahead

meant refuge...

or ruin.

Amethyst turned back briefly and laid a trembling hand upon Agate's mane.

"Wait here," he whispered.

The steed did not stir, only gazed at him with eyes that bore the weight of centuries—eyes as old as sorrow itself. His breath rose in slow, silvery plumes, curling into the frozen air like the fading sigh of a world on the brink of forgetting.

Amethyst moved forward, one cautious step at a time, his boots whispering against the stone as though afraid to wake the dead. He studied each step, every crack that split the path like old scars, every shadow that twisted with unnatural intent. The ground groaned beneath him, not in protest of his tread—but as if bearing the burden of countless sorrows long buried.

The air hung heavy—not with frost, but with the oppressive weight of unseen eyes. Each breath scraped his throat with the dry taste of dust and forgotten farewells. Even sound seemed distant here, swallowed by a hush so profound it felt as if the world itself had paused its heartbeat to watch him pass.

He moved like one wading through memory, each step slower than the last, searching for meaning in the silence.

What realm was this, where time frayed at the edges?

Was he still among the living—or had the dying already taken root in his bones?

At last, he reached the rim of the fire's glow—and halted.

There, within the hush of heat and shadow, sat Death.

Not cloaked in carnage.

Not armored in steel.

But still—undeniably Death.

Just sitting—calm, still—as if the world no longer mattered. Her face was veiled in shadow, but her presence cut through the room like the edge of time. She was not friend, nor foe. She was truth. She was finality.

The shape silence takes when the world runs out of breath.

And for all souls, her name meant the same.

Amethyst's breath caught.

His lungs forgot to move.

His heart forgot its rhythm.

He didn't know how long he had stood there—seconds, years. Time had no meaning in her presence. He felt her gaze upon him, though she never lifted her head. As if she had known he would come. As if she had been waiting since before time had a name.

And then—

a glint.

Something behind her, half-swallowed by the gloom.

His eyes shifted. Just past the hem of her stillness, something sharp caught the light.

Not gold.

Not steel.

But older.

Purer.

It shimmered like a fallen star—more precious than diamonds, more alluring than life itself. Within its glow pulsed a faint rhythm, as though it had once belonged to the world and still yearned to return.

Amethyst drew a breath, slow and reverent.

"What... is that?" he whispered to the silence.

But the darkness offered no reply.

And what, he thought, would Death protect so dearly?

Then he remembered.

Not clearly—like a dream slipping through fingers—but enough.

His mother's voice, low and reverent, speaking of a blade lost to time:

"They said it was forged in silence, when the stars first sang.

That the kings of old could hold back winter with a single strike.

That when it vanished, the world forgot how to bloom.

It vanished like death with life."

And in that instant, the pieces locked into place.

There was only one thing in all of Emerland that had vanished without trace—

Only one relic of such terrible worth.

The sword.

The Sword of the Crown of Emerland.

The blade that vanished when the light died.

The blade that bore the will of kings and the breath of stars.

Stolen in the last days of glory—

And with it, the hope of a realm.

Now he knew what Death guarded so fiercely.

This was the one place no soul could reach.

And those who tried—never returned.

The blade was more than a relic.

It was power. It was memory.

It was the key to everything they had lost.

And now it gleamed behind a single window,

alone in the dark.

it gleamed behind that window.

In Death's keeping.

If he could just reach it—

If he could bear the sword back to Emerland—
Perhaps even the light could return.
Amethyst clenched his fists.
He was trapped.
Marooned on the path of dying, a rider without escape.
And Amethyst shook his head, jaw clenched against the weight of helplessness.
Was there a way to fight Death?
Was there any path forward?
He didn't know.

The air had thinned, grown cold and sharp, as if time itself had drawn in a breath and dared not exhale. Shadows twisted at unnatural angles, recoiling from her presence. Stones long buried jutted from the broken path like ancient teeth, summoned to bear witness. Above, the sky held no sun—only a vast, unyielding pallor where light should have lived. And the silence... it rang in his ears like a funeral bell heard through layers of snow.

He remembered his mother's voice—Jabba Doom Gabbro, whispering through the fog of childhood, *"No one returns from Death's house. No one. Not unchanged. Not whole."*
A whisper touched the windowpane—
not wind, not voice,
but something older.
A warning, perhaps.
Or a memory trying to return.
And so he thought of Diamond.
"I just want her to be safe."
A sudden ache bloomed in his chest—sharp, hollow, terrifying.
As if some secret part of him, buried too deep for words, already knew: he might not see her again.

Diamond's face rose in his mind—not as a queen, not as prophecy's child, but laughing in the golden grasses, her hair wild in the wind, when she had first told him he made her feel brave.

And then, unbidden, came the coldest thought of all.

What if this is my last breath?

My last sight? My last moment in the world that holds her?

"I have nothing to give her," he murmured, his voice barely a breath. "Only my wishes."

His hands trembled. He wanted to send her something—a token, a safeguard, a farewell carved from love itself. But he had nothing. No sword. No charm. Only the fire in his chest and the fading sound of her name in his memory.

Then... his fingers brushed something.

In a hidden fold of his coat, wrapped in time and dust and memory, nestled a small glass vial—cold as moonlight, fragile as breath. The liquid within did not shine with any color, only with the shimmer of *possibility*.

Liquor of the Last Light.

The winning draught.

The same his mother had slipped into his hand when he was still a boy, her eyes fierce with love and fear.

"For when all else fails," she had whispered, as if even saying it too loud might summon fate too soon.

He could drink it now. Escape. Triumph. He could return to Diamond with victory in hand.

But he didn't move.

Instead, he gazed at the bottle, then at the pale sky, and then he knelt. Gently, he plucked a single leaf from a withered branch nearby—not green, not gold, but silver, rimmed with frost. The wind stirred as he wrapped the vial in the leaf, whispering an unspoken wish into the quiet.

"To Diamond," he said. "May this guide you… when I no longer can."

He placed it upon the wind.

And somehow, the wind obeyed.

It lifted the offering—slow, solemn, reverent—and carried it away, borne on a wind older than breath, toward a place far beyond sight.

Toward her.

Toward hope.

Toward the last light that might yet endure.

Amethyst stood, the weight of fate upon his shoulders, and turned to face the dark horizon, where Death awaited.

As the wind bore the vial through the veil of worlds, he watched it go—and though he spoke no word,

his gaze whispered:

If I cannot return,
let my love arrive in my place.
Let it burn in your blood,
when the world turns cold.
Let it be the hand you hold.

31. The Final Leaf

Diamond moved through a world that did not feel her own.

Not bound by time, but by something more ancient—an echo older than memory, stranger than dream.

She walked suspended between past and illusion, as if the thread of her life had been plucked from the loom and left to drift.

A heaviness clung to her—not just in the limbs or lungs, but in the soul.

She had survived death. Twice.

And now, survival itself felt like a curse still tightening its grip.

The air was suffocating, hot as a forge, though the sky wore its veil of clouds.

She was drenched in sweat, but the silence made her shiver.

No wind. No birdsong.

Only a path stretched thin and frail before her—like something not meant to be walked by the living.

Jabba Doom Gabbro had stolen her present—
and left her stranded in a time that no longer breathed.
Was she to wander the past forever?
To die there, alone and forgotten?
Or worse... to become something else?

A beast shaped by memory and grief?
She didn't know why that last thought came—
only that it chilled her more than death.

She no longer remembered how the thread began—only the ache of its unraveling.
She still did not know how to kill Evil Basalt.
Only that Basalt was no longer the end.
Behind him loomed a deeper shadow—one whose name even fear dared not speak.
The thought scoured her throat, dry as wind-blown sand.
She gasped—not just for breath, but for clarity, for water, for truth.
The vultures had gone, their hunger sated on Bulwark's broken body.
The ghosts had melted back into the trees.
Alone now, unseen, she dragged herself across blood-warmed earth,
toward the Lake of Wonders.

The waters shimmered like liquid starlight.
Diamond knelt at the edge, trembling—not to drink, but to gaze. This was the Lake of Wonders, the last great enchantment wrought by the elves. Born from the final breath of the stars, it was said to reveal what lies hidden: not the face, but the soul beneath it.
She leaned closer, bracing herself for reflection. Would she see herself as she was—or what she had become? Would the shadow still linger in the depths, coiled like a serpent around her spirit?
But the waters offered something else.

They shifted—not with wind, but with will. The surface, smooth as glass, rippled once... and changed. The reflection staring back was not her own. Not wholly.

A vision bloomed. Not of hope, but of horror.

Three lives. Three sacrifices.

Obsidian Swish—fallen so Basalt would live.

Jabba Doom Gabbro's son—surrendered, body and soul.

The Three Doomed Sisters—Their voices silenced, their blood spilled.

Each death had fed the making of Evil Basalt.

Each sealed beneath the stolen blade—the sword once hidden beneath the Crown of Emerland.

The lake trembled, as though stirred by breath not its own. And in the shivering light, a whisper rose. Not sound. Not language. But truth.

Strike her with the same blade.

Not once. Not twice. But three times.

Only then shall her curse be unmade.

Diamond drew back, breath caught in her throat.

The water stilled again. Starlight returned. But the knowledge remained—etched into her bones, sealed into her marrow. The elves had spoken. The lake had revealed.

The truth was hers now.

And the path ahead had only grown darker.

The blade—the lost sword—must return. Not to crown kings, but to unmake darkness.

She had the answers now—the lake had spoken, the truth had been unveiled. But knowing was not the same as returning.

Was there a path back from the clutches of the past? None that she could see.

Diamond lifted her eyes to the sky, as if the heavens might still remember her name. But this was not the present, where clouds were light and skies wore blue. This was the Deathly Chattel—a place where the sky sagged under the weight of forgotten time, cloaked in ash and silence. No stars. No sun. Only a hollow dusk that stretched in every direction like a wound that would not close.

In that endless dimness, Diamond sat down beneath a tree that had long since forgotten the memory of leaves. Its branches twisted like broken fingers, reaching for things long lost. Beside her, the Lake of Wonders murmured softly, as if still dreaming of starlight. She did not want to leave it—not yet. Here, at least, there had been clarity. Here, she had glimpsed the thread.

She pressed her back to the tree's bark, rough as old bone, and let her head fall against it. A part of her longed to be still—to stay in this strange cradle between knowing and doing, grief and motion.

And then... her fingers moved.

Without thought, she reached into her coat, searching. Hoping. Wanting.

Something cool and papery brushed her skin.

She closed her hand around it and drew it out.

The third leaf.

Dry, veined, and impossibly green—as though no time had passed at all. Baba Yaga's final gift. One to escape. One to hide. And one... to return.

How had she forgotten?

A breath left her lips—not quite laughter, not quite a sob. A smile unfurled, tremulous and wild, as if her soul had just remembered how to bloom.

The way was not gone.

Not yet.

And the past, for all its shadows, might still let her go.

Relief bloomed in her chest like a long-awaited spring. She could go back now—back to Emerland, back to the war, back to the fight that still waited for her. For the first time in what felt like lifetimes, a smile touched her lips, quiet and solemn.

But then—

The lake stirred again, as if it were not yet finished. As if it still had one more truth to show.

Diamond's gaze was drawn once more to the shimmering waters.

And there he was.

Amethyst.

Not in memory. Not in the past.

Now.

His image burned within the rippling surface—flickering like a flame behind storm-glass. He was reaching for something just beyond sight, his hand outstretched, his face taut with effort... and fear. Shadows coiled around him like smoke made flesh. He was trapped—fighting—failing. She could not hear him, could not hold him, but she felt the dread rising from the vision like heat from a dying fire.

He was losing.

She didn't think. She didn't hesitate.

Diamond lifted the leaf to her lips, breath trembling. "Please," she whispered, not sure if it was to the wind, the stars, or something older. "Let him live. Let him win."

She let the leaf go.

It caught the air like a spark on the wind, rising, turning, as if it already knew the way. The leaf vanished—caught by a breath of unseen current—spinning skyward like a promise cast to the stars.

No horn, no cry—just leaf in flame,
to guard the heart that bears her name.
Through night it drifts where shadows close,
a vow to shield what darkness knows.

A silence followed. One so deep, so strange, it seemed to bend the trees.

Diamond whispered, almost in apology, "Amethyst knows more than I do... and he will save Emerland more than I ever could."

She walked away from the shores—not seeking home, but shedding the idea of it.

The refuge behind her, once a cradle of calm, now felt hollow. She no longer sought safety. She longed to be unmoored—to vanish into the wilderness of what lay ahead, to dissolve into the unknown as if pain itself had become her compass.

She didn't walk far. Just far enough for the trees to fade, for the lake's glow to vanish behind twisted roots and stone.

And then—

The air changed.

The shadows ahead thickened, not like mist, but like something spilled and seething. They clung to each other, black and wet, until a shape emerged from the pitch—not a silhouette, not a figure, but a nightmare cast in flesh.

The Nameless Fear.

As if it had been waiting there all along. As if it had always known where she would come, and when.

Diamond did not flinch. She did not cry out.

She only stared, hollow and still—not with courage, but with a strange, aching calm. As if she had wandered here to find this end. As if ending it was the only truth left to grasp, because the beginning had become too monstrous to carry.

He held two swords, one in each hand. Both bled darkness, humming with stolen light.

His voice—ancient, amused, and utterly cruel—curled around her like smoke.

"Baba Yaga's enchantments saved you twice," he said. "But not this time."

Diamond stood still, her body frozen, her heart pounding like a war drum.

"You did not see how Basalt was made?" the Nameless Fear continued, circling her slowly. "I showed you. You did not see that Amethyst was in peril? I showed you that too. I made you look. I made you care."

He stepped closer, the blades gleaming with ash.

"I wanted you to spend your final leaf. And you did. So now... you die."

His grin stretched impossibly wide.

Diamond clenched her fists, nails biting into her palms. The world around her blurred—was this real? A vision? Some cruel echo cast by the past?

She no longer knew.

She had nothing left.

No leaf to call the wind.

No spell to part the dark.

No sword to raise against it.

Only herself—bare, breathless, burning with the weight of too many truths.

Diamond was not ready.

But readiness had never been the test.

The shadow loomed above her—immense, unearthly, its form cloaked in a darkness that seemed to drink the light. It was not merely a figure, but an eclipse made flesh, draped in the silence of forgotten tombs.

Twin swords hovered at either side of it, suspended like fallen stars that had refused to land—brimming with halted ruin, trembling with the hunger of unfinished fate.

But it was not the blades that gripped her.

It was the eyes.

Eyes without name, without mercy—blacker than any night she had known.

And within them, she saw a reflection.

Not of the creature.

But of herself.

A pale flicker—her own eyes staring back at her through the veil of that abyssal gaze. Wide, unblinking.

And filled with fear.

Not the shadow's fear.

Her own.

The fear of a child who had lost the road. The dread of one whose hope had slipped quietly through her fingers.

It was not a mirror of truth, but of surrender. The image of a soul already yielded to the dark.

Diamond's heart tightened, a cold ache blooming in her chest.

Is this how it ends?

She closed her eyes.

Not out of surrender—but out of stillness. To listen for one last truth. To brace for the end, not as a victim, but as herself.

She thought the blade would come first. Cold. Sharp. Unspoken.

Instead, something touched her.

Not metal.

Not pain.
But warmth.
Like a lullaby long forgotten. Like the hush of Morganite's voice, Onyx's cuddles or the way Amethyst once looked at her when words could not hold the love.
Diamond opened her eyes.
Then—
The stillness broke.
A wind stirred.
Subtle as a breath on dying coals, yet it moved through her like the memory of fire.
It curled gently through the dust, wrapping around her shoulders like a mantle. And from its current, a single leaf descended—slow, golden-edged, and glowing faintly.
It landed in her hand.
Trembling, she unfolded it.
Inside, nestled in the curve of the leaf, lay a small glass vial. Pale light shimmered within—not bright, not loud—but alive.
Scrawled upon the leaf, in hurried, crooked ink:
From Amethyst.
Diamond's breath caught in her throat.
The potion of victory.
He could have kept it—could have saved himself.
But instead... he had chosen her, and, Wind carried it—not wind of this world, but of magic stirred by longing.
She clutched it to her chest.
Then looked again at the shadow.
Still it loomed, waiting. Silent. Watching.
And again—her reflection.
But this time, something had changed.
She saw not fear.
But recognition.

The shadow saw her now not as prey—but as peril.

Diamond smiled—weary and fierce.

She raised the vial, and whispered, "Even if it's poison… better death by love than life stolen by fear."

And she drank.

The potion bloomed like fire in her chest.

A rush of light thundered through her veins—starlight, memory, music—as if the very soul of Emerland had been poured into her.

Her spine straightened.

Her breath steadied.

The darkness before her still held its swords.

But she… held herself.

Diamond took a step forward.

And the shadow—faltered.

Its blades flickered, its shape warped.

The illusion buckled.

Because Diamond had chosen to live.

And not just live—rise.

"I shall live," she said, her voice quiet as dawn—and just as unstoppable.

The shadow shattered.

It was not Death.

It was not the Nameless Fear.

It was the final enchantment of Evil Basalt—the last snare, meant to bend her spirit and steal her soul.

But Amethyst's love had reached her first.

She had not been saved by a spell.

She had been saved by choice.

As the echo of her words faded—"*I shall live*"—the world around her trembled.

Cracks spiderwebbed through the shadow's form, like fractures in ancient glass. Its twin swords, once poised to strike, turned brittle and shimmered with a dying light. A sound, thin and high like splintering ice, split the silence.

And then—it shattered.

The figure of dread broke apart into dust and smoke, its scream swallowed by the wind. Dark ash spiraled upward, not falling, but rising—as if fleeing the girl it had once tried to destroy.

All that remained was silence... and the shining leaf, now curled gently at her feet.

Diamond stood alone on the blackened shore of the Lake of Wonders. Behind her, the past lay broken. Before her, the veil between worlds shimmered faintly—a path unseen by eyes of doubt.

And she was ready to walk it.

32. Sword of Destiny

As the illusion shattered, so too did the past—dispersing like breath into cold air, vanishing into nothingness.

Diamond stood still, breathless.

It was day.

But not just any day—*her* day.

The day the tide could turn.

A day carved from prophecy and fire.

No longer a ghost adrift in memory, she had returned to the living world—right where fate had always waited.

The battlefield.

Before her, the darkness seethed.

A tide of ash-cloaked legions poured across the scarred earth.

At their helm stood Evil Basalt, terrible and tall, draped in razored shadows, her eyes twin pits of endless malice.

On her flanks loomed Topaz, cold and gleaming, and Toxico T, clutching the Pentacle like a prize defiled.

Above and between them, Wraiths coiled and howled—souls long unmoored, drawn to ruin like moths to flame.

And across from them, defiant though few, stood Emerland's last defense.

Baba Yaga, robed in starwoven cloth, held her staff like an unlit torch—ready to burn, waiting for the spark. Behind her stood Jade, face pale but firm, and Hematite, eyes steady, sword drawn. A scattering of thousands stood with them—a mere thread of gold against a storm of black. But their backs did not bend.

They had come to die, if need be, for light.

And Diamond... she had returned.

No one had seen her yet.

She crouched behind enemy lines, veiled in shadow beneath the twisted bough of a war-ravaged tree—the very tree she had once touched in another life, when time was kinder. Now it stood hollowed and blackened, its bark blistered with age and ash, yet still it clung to the soil like a sentinel defying ruin. The battlefield breathed around her, a slow, trembling exhale of broken earth and distant flame. It was as if the past had folded into the present—two ghosts meeting in a dream.

I'm here, she thought. *But where is he?*

Diamond's eyes, wide and burning, swept the scorched horizon in search of Amethyst. Every breath felt borrowed. Every heartbeat, too loud.

And then Basalt turned.

Not slowly. Not with ceremony. But with sharpness—like a predator scenting blood.

Basalt felt it.

The rupture of her illusion—not like a spell broken, but like a mirror shattered from within, shards slicing their way back through her chest. She staggered, not visibly, but inwardly.

Something had returned that she thought lost.

Diamond.

The name did not pass her lips, but it passed her heart. And it made her furious.

"She's here," Basalt hissed, her voice curling like smoke to the Wraiths. "She crossed back. Find her. End her. Before she even thinks of ending me."

Dark magic coiled around her wrists. Her gaze swept the field, teeth clenched, seeking a shadow within the light—but she did not see Diamond.

Not yet.

And Diamond... was not looking at her.

Her gaze raked the battlefield—not for Basalt, nor the Pentacle, nor even the silhouette of Baba Yaga.

She searched for Amethyst.

The last image burned into her mind was the Hidden Valley breaking like glass beneath a giant's heel—ash rising in spirals, the world crumbling, and his figure swallowed by the storm.

Had he made it out? Had the leaf reached him?

Her heart pounded louder than the war drums, a frantic rhythm echoing the ache of unanswered prayers. She scanned face after face—ghosts, warriors, strangers—but his was not among them.

Her hand twitched toward her cloak, instinctively reaching for magic that no longer answered her call. All that remained was the wild pulse in her blood—the potion, the flame, the parting gift of love still burning bright.

But still... no sign.

And now, Basalt moved—a shadow poised to strike.

Diamond crouched behind the shattered trunk of the tree, fingers sinking into the soil as if pleading with the earth for one more heartbeat of grace.

One more moment. One flicker. Amethyst, give me a sign.

She needed a glimpse—a thread in the wind, a heartbeat in the distance—anything to prove he still breathed beneath this dying sky.

Only then would she rise.

And when they rose, she would not rise alone—they would rise as the storm.

But, Amethyst was not on the battlefield.

He was still within Death's snare—and this was no illusion.

The world here held no sky, no earth, no air to breathe—only weightless silence and a lightless plain that stretched in every direction, like the hollow space between two heartbeats.

And yet... something pulsed.

Life.

His life.

He could feel it beating still, stubborn and raw. That was why he remained—and why Death had not yet struck.

But he could not wait.

He would not.

No more hiding.

No more delays.

The time for silence had drowned—

and now, he must rise.

Rise, and face the Dread.

Amethyst turned, breath ragged like torn silk,

steadying himself as though the abyss beneath his hooves

had grown fangs, eager to pull him under.

And there she stood—

Death, draped in shadow and certainty,

a grin carved from cruelty,

mocking his every tremble.

Not a specter,

but a mirror—

showing him everything he feared to become. The space around her bent, as if the world itself could not bear her stillness.

Death had found him first. This was her house—ancient, bone-quiet, absolute. Here, even silence dared not whisper, and nothing could hide from the eyes that saw beyond flesh, beyond time, beyond the veil of pretense.

She was not cloaked in rot nor shrouded in blackness. No—she was radiant, with a brilliance that did not comfort, but burned like truth. As radiant as fear itself. Her face bore no cruelty, no mercy. Only the unbearable stillness of eternity. She was vast. Final. Inevitable.

In her left hand, she held a knife fashioned from bone—dull in color, yet sharp enough to sever fate from flesh. In her right... a sword. But not just any sword.

It did not gleam with gold, nor blaze with fire. It shimmered with a quiet gravity, as if remembering every hand that had ever held it—and every life it had taken. A songless resonance hummed from its blade, and Amethyst knew it at once.

The sword once hidden beneath the Crown of Emerland.

The sword that had crowned kings and condemned innocents.

The blade that could sever darkness itself.

The sword of reckoning. The sword of fate.

"You thought," said Death, her voice echoing like bells beneath the sea, "that life could step into my realm unnoticed?"

She smiled—and the air cracked.

"How strange," she continued, drifting closer, her laughter like ice breaking, "that you, who lived like the Starborn... shall die in her place."

"I was not meant to take your life, dear boy. No. This was meant for Diamond. This whole path—the maps, the leaves, the mirror—all of it was to bring her to me. And now..."

She raised her knife—not the sword — but the one she always used. The bone one. The certain one. The one that took.

Amethyst did not flinch.

He stood unarmed, uncloaked by courage or cunning—only the raw instinct to survive.

No blade. No plan. No time.

Only the thundering drum of his heart, and the stillness that comes before the storm.

He braced himself, knowing it might be his final breath.

But then—like thunder cleaving the sky, a shadow of flame roared into the void.

A figure.

A king.

Alexandrite.

He struck Death with a blow that split the ground beneath them, sending her reeling—just for a breath, but a breath was enough. The radiant sword slipped from her grasp, falling with a sound like stars colliding. It clanged beside Amethyst, humming with power.

"**Amethyst—run!**" Alexandrite's voice rang like steel on steel.

Amethyst gasped. "King Alexandrite?"

But this was no broken ruler—not the man who had hidden in silence and grief. This was the Lion of Emerland, fierce and whole. His eyes burned not with fear, but with purpose.

"You must go!" Alexandrite shouted. "There's no more time!"

"There's no way out!" Amethyst shouted back. "We're trapped—!"

"Then try! For Diamond. For Emerland. If there's even a crack—find it."

Amethyst hesitated no longer.

He grabbed the sword, felt its weight sing in his palm, and turned—and there stood Agate, his steadfast horse, as if summoned by love alone.

He mounted with a leap, the blade flashing in his hand, and drove the beast forward. Wind screamed in his ears as hooves struck the broken air.

But there was no escape.

The snare of Death had no gate. No end.

All he could do was circle—round and round in an endless storm of silence.

Behind him, Death rose again.

She did not speak.

She did not hesitate.

With one swift movement, she pressed her knife to Alexandrite's chest—and the king did not resist.

He leaned forward and whispered into the ear of his horse, who stood **tall**, eyes wild.

"To my daughter," he said. "Live. With Diamond."

And then Death struck.

Alexandrite fell—proud, defiant, whole—and the void bowed in silence. The king had bought only moments.

But sometimes, moments were everything.

He had died long ago: the day he first read *The King Before the Darkness*, when its final lines etched a curse into his soul. He died again when he gave Amethyst to Gabbro instead of Diamond, and again when he sent Diamond into the Forbidden Forest. Since then, he had not left his chambers—not even to witness the union of Diamond and Amethyst—for death had clung to him like a shadow at every threshold of joy.

But today... today, he did not die.

Today, he gave life—to Amethyst. And in that act, he sought something more: forgiveness. From Morganite. From Emerland. And perhaps, in time, from the daughter he could never truly protect.

In that moment, Alexandrite did not fall to death—he rose into legend.
The man who once feared prophecy now embraced its flame.
The king who had hidden from fate now gave it form and breath.
No longer bound by the ink of *The King Before the Darkness*,
he rewrote his ending not with words—but with sacrifice.
And somewhere, in the great silence that follows sorrow,
a flicker of forgiveness stirred—
not only from Morganite,
but from Emerland itself.
For sometimes, a broken crown must crack the sky...
to let the light back in.

Amethyst's face twisted in pain—not for his own life, but for the man who had just given his.
He looked back once.
Death stood, untouched, watching.
Not smiling.
Not cruel.
Just... waiting.
As if to say: *Your turn, now.*
But then—something moved.
A wind.
A real wind.
It came from nowhere, sudden and fierce, blinding them both in a spiral of stardust and broken light.
And in it—a leaf.
Silver-edged. Familiar.
It struck Amethyst across the chest—soft as a kiss, sharp as memory.

He knew that leaf.

The leaf.

It was just like the one that had once carried Diamond to him—when she was half-dead, bleeding, fading—and he had saved her.

Or... had she saved him?

Was this the same leaf?

Or another?

He did not know. He did not care.

The leaf trembled in his hand.

And he understood.

Diamond had sent this.

For him.

It was not meant to carry him to victory—but to carry him to safety.

To the Emerland Castle.

To the place where his last light burned

I must go.

He held it tight—and the wind obeyed.

But something went wrong.

As soon as the wind swallowed him, he felt it—a jolt. A twist. The path had shifted.

Instead of light, there was shadow.

Instead of the castle, he was cast into a hollow place—the very ground where he had first begun this journey. The place where the Deathly **path** had revealed his doom.

Instead of light, there was shadow... he was not safe.

Not yet.

Not nearly.

Amethyst sank to one knee, breathing hard.

His fingers closed tighter around the sword—**but he** did not feel fear.

He felt resolved.

He rose.

There was nothing left around him.

No wind.

No sky.

No Death.

Only silence now—vast and strange, like the world had stopped to take a breath between one heartbeat and the next.

Amethyst stood alone where fate had once thundered, where kings had fallen, and time itself had nearly unraveled. The air was still, but heavy, as if the ground beneath him remembered every name spoken in grief and glory.

The earth was wounded—cracked and scorched, etched with the scars of sacrifice and the echoes of old magic undone. This was not just a place of battle, but of reckoning. And yet, he felt no fear.

He had trusted the magic of the leaf. And the magic, impossibly, had returned his trust.

As he stepped forward, something stirred in the corner of his vision—a flicker. A soft, sudden flash of light, faint but certain, like the last breath of a dying star. It pulsed once from the ground, drawing his gaze downward.

There, nestled in the fractured earth, lay something small.

A glass vial. Unbroken. Untouched. As if the world had burned around it and spared only this.

Inside—ashes

But not ordinary ash. These were fine as crushed stars, dark as eclipsed moons, and laced with faint glimmers of mirrorlight. They shimmered, softly, as though they still remembered fire, truth, and the voice of something ancient.

Without knowing why, he reached for it.

He didn't need a reason.
The light had called. The leaf had brought him.
And the ashes... the ashes were meant for him.

The moment his fingers touched the glass, a chill ran through him—not cold, but carved from memory itself.
These were no ordinary remains.
They were the ashes of the shattered mirror.
The mirror Spinel had left behind.
The mirror through which the Nameless Fear had once spoken—
once conjured, once commanded.
Ashes that still remembered.
"What are you still trying to show me?" Amethyst murmured, the air trembling around his voice. He saw everything—and yet understood nothing. The vision swirled with meaning, but its heart eluded him.
"What are you trying to tell me?" he asked the leaf.
There came no answer—only silence.
But it was not the silence of emptiness.
It was the silence of weight.
Not despair.
But potential.
A secret unfinished. A thread not yet tied.
A future that waited, holding its breath.
He pressed the vial to his chest, then slipped it into his pocket—alongside the sword that had once rested beneath the Crown of Emerland.
He did not know yet what the ashes would become.
But something inside him whispered:
They were not the end. They were the key.
He looked up.

Smoke curled in the distance. The battle had begun.

Emerland was calling.

Agate waited nearby, his mane caught in the hush, his wings half-spread—a question whispered to the wind.

"We ride," Amethyst said, his voice low but resolute. "Now... we ride."

And they did.

Agate surged into the air, hooves parting wind, feathers tearing shadow.

Above the trees.

Above the smoke.

Toward destiny.

Toward Diamond.

Toward the end.

And deep in his coat, the ashes stirred—

like prophecy reborn from ruin.

33. The Sky Remembers

Diamond waited—just for a breath.
One heartbeat. One hope.

She scoured the chaos for him—for Amethyst—her soul reaching through the smoke and ruin, yearning for his face to break the haze like dawn through storm clouds.

But before that miracle could come, Evil Basalt saw her.

A cunning smile unfurled across the witch's face like spilled ink across a sacred scroll. And then—she struck.

Out of the heavens she descended, astride a black-boned vulture whose wings beat like war-drums, vast as storm-sails billowing with thunder. Its talons trailed smoke, and each beat of its wings carved the sky in ribbons of shadow. Her cloak, stitched with razors and curses, bled darkness behind her like a falling night. In her hand she wielded a sickle-shaped blade, curved like a crescent moon soaked in ancient grief—a weapon meant not for battle, but for undoing.

Diamond stood on foot.

Alone.

But she did not run.

There was no more fleeing.

Not now. Not ever.

This was war—not the kind sung by bards, but the truest kind, where you lose or live, fall or rise. There is no turning back in war. Only the trembling courage to stand, to face the nightmare, and to meet fate with fire in your soul.

Diamond turned, her eyes ablaze—not with fear, but with fury, forged in the crucible of loss.

She stood alone amid ruin and smoke, the shattered bones of Emerland rising around her, ashes swirling like the ghosts of a dying dream. Above, the sky split open—not with light, but with grief and wrath—yet within her, a deeper storm stirred, fierce and unyielding, a fire that no shadow could ever quench.

She searched the heavens, her gaze defiant, for something—anything—to match the monstrous majesty of Evil Basalt.

And then, through the rift in flame and cloud, thunder answered.

A stallion erupted from the storm—a creature born of tempest and starlight. His mane shimmered like molten silver, his hooves struck fire with every stride, each spark shaped from the dying embers of fallen stars. He was King Alexandrite's steed—the last breath of the old world, the last blaze of the crown's hope.

Diamond faltered—but only for a heartbeat.

She had never mounted a horse alone—not in this life, not since the forgetting, not since the quiet unraveling of the soul she once carried in full. But in that single breath of stillness, something ancient stirred.

The air shifted—sharp and sudden—as though the world itself had paused, holding its breath. The wind curled around her like a familiar spirit, as if it had remembered her name long before she ever knew it. It rushed through her, clearing the dust of lives half-lived, stirring memories buried not just in mind, but in blood and bone.

She turned her gaze to Evil Basalt—a tower of ruin, crowned in shadow, forged from every sorrow Emerland had ever known.

Smoke rose in serpents from the broken ground. Blood stained the soil where hope once bloomed. The cries of the fallen still echoed in the stones. And Amethyst...

His absence was a blade lodged deep. It twisted with every breath. But sorrow did not consume her—it sharpened her. The ache gave way to fury, pure and rising, the kind that comes not from hate, but from love too long denied its peace.

This—*this*—was the evil she had been born to end. This was why the stars had whispered her name in their silence. Why the Elves had gifted her visions. Why the prophecy had echoed through time like a song no one remembered how to sing—until now.

They had called her Starborn. All believed it. All but her.

Until this moment.

Now she saw with terrifying clarity: the prophecy was never about lineage, never about destiny written in stone. It was about *choice*. The choice to stand when the world begs you to fall. To rise when your bones remember how many times you've broken. To fight when fear claws at your throat and the darkness has already begun to feast.

The Starborn was not a title. It was a becoming. A crucible.

And anyone could rise from its fire—if they dared to walk through it.

She had failed twice before. The Elves had known she would. Not because the Gods had lied, but because the truth is deeper than fate. Some lessons cannot be taught. They must be earned. In blood. In silence. In fire. And sometimes, one life is not enough—not to withstand a darkness that has slumbered for a thousand years, growing ever patient, like a poisonous seed buried deep, waiting for the last hope to fade.

Diamond had lost two lives to that darkness. Lost everyone she loved. Lost herself.

But not today.

Today, there was no next time. No second chance. This was it. The edge of the blade. The moment of becoming.

And she would not just face her fears—she would become the fear that *fear* remembered.

Her anger, once scattered and wild, now forged itself into something greater—a molten calm, volcanic and still. Power surged through her like lightning through the roots of the world, and with it, memory returned—not as fragments, but as fire.

She saw it all.

Riding through the wildwood under a moon that bled silver. Her blade a song of vengeance and vow. Her voice speaking words older than the mountains—oaths sworn beneath stars that remembered the first dawn.

Twice she had fought to save Emerland. Twice she had fallen.

But not this time.

Because now—she *remembered*.

One lesson had taught her to ride. The other had taught her *why* she must never fall.

Baba Yaga had been right. *"You do not need to be taught. You only need to remember."*

And now, she did.

Ahead of her, the storm-born stallion stepped from the smoke. He was made of cloud and starlight, forged in the breath of the old Gods. His silver mane rippled like moonlit silk, and his hooves sparked fire with every stride, a constellation galloping across the earth.

He moved toward her—not as beast to master, but as legend to legend.

And then, with solemn grace, he bent one mighty knee. His head lowered, his eyes full of stars and sorrow and knowing.

He did not bow to a warrior.

He did not kneel for a child.

He bowed to *her*.

To the flame.

To the force reborn.

To the Starborn—not foretold, but *forged* in failure, and fire, and unrelenting will.

The world had waited for her.

And now—she had come.

Diamond stepped forward, her fingers trembling as they brushed his star-dappled flank—The world held its breath.

As Diamond stepped forward, the stallion bowed—not to command, but to memory. And when her hand touched his silver mane, the stars flared.

A vision struck her like a blade of light.

She saw a battlefield wreathed in black flame. Her father—King Alexandrite—stood against Death itself, cloak torn, crown fallen, yet eyes unyielding. Behind him, Amethyst lay wounded, the boy barely breathing. Death raised its blade, cruel and soundless.

But Alexandrite did not beg. He gave.

With one last cry, the king struck a pact beyond time—his life for the boy's—and as his soul was claimed, he whispered to his steed, "Take her. When she is ready."

Then all was silence. And ash.

The vision broke. Diamond gasped, staggering.

But no tears fell.

Her eyes did not weep—they bled.

Her veins did not tremble—they burned.

This stallion was not just a mount.

He was the last breath of her father's love.

The final act of a fallen king.

And now, he was hers.

The world trembled.

Not from fear—but from awe.

The trees bent. The ruins sighed. The stars above shifted their ancient path. Even the Lake of Wonders shimmered, its waters whispering, **She remembers.**

The stallion knelt once more—flame in his hooves, moonlight in his mane.

And Diamond, no longer the girl who had faltered, mounted as the Starborn.

Not foretold.

Not chosen.

Forged.

In the next breath, they soared.

The wind shrieked like an ancient spirit, tearing past her ears as the stallion rose—hooves pounding air, wings of flame and starlight driving them skyward. Below, the world burned. Above, the heavens bowed. The sky itself seemed to part for her, folding open like a prophecy fulfilled.

Diamond, reborn in fire and memory, rode not to battle—but to destiny.

Through smoke and ash, through screams and ruin, she rose.

Not as a warrior.

Not even as a queen.

But as the *Starborn*—flame of the final hour, forged in the furnace of loss.

And from the roiling clouds ahead, Basalt came screaming.

Her vulture split the storm like a blade, feathers scorched black, talons trailing death. Basalt stood atop it, cloaked in shadow, eyes blazing with ancient hate. Her sword was jagged ruin. Her presence, a curse. She dove toward Diamond like nightfall descending.

Diamond met her—not with fear, but fire.

Their blades collided—steel against steel—and the world cracked.

Light exploded through the heavens.

The sky shattered like glass struck by thunder.

And for a heartbeat, the universe *paused*.

Even the flames below held still, frozen in awe.

Then the storm began.

They clashed again—and again—a blur of silver and smoke. Above fields drowned in ash and rivers that bled fire, they danced a war older than time: light against shadow, fate against oblivion.

Basalt fought like a god gone mad—raw, brutal, unchained.

But Diamond was no mere mortal either.

She was the fire that remembers.

The wind that returns.

The silence that sings before dawn.

Her blade was light made sharp.

Her rage was purpose, not chaos.

She did not falter. She did not flinch. She did not fall.

And when Basalt's vulture screamed and spiraled in fury, Alexandrite's stallion only soared higher—his hooves ringing with the echo of stars, his breath misting with the fire of worlds undone. He bore Diamond like he bore her father's final hope—swift, relentless, unbreakable.

And as they rose—as sword met sword and flame met shadow—the battle soared beyond sky and stone. But its stakes remained, always, on the ground below.

Emerland watched.

The dead remembered.

And the living dared hope once more.

Below, Emerland staggered on the edge of oblivion.

Its towers bled smoke. Its rivers wept ash. The once-golden fields were a graveyard of dreams, and the wind carried only the scent of ruin.

Basalt needed only a breath—a heartbeat's hesitation. One crack in Diamond's defense, and it would be enough.

A single falter, and the Starborn would fall.

And with her, the last hope of Emerland would be drowned in blood and silence.

But Diamond did not falter.

Not in the curve of her blade, nor in the fire behind her eyes.

Her soul did not flinch.

She moved like truth through shadow—swift, certain, inevitable.

She was the howl of wind through ancient trees.

She was frost refusing to melt beneath flame.

She was grief made light—and light made weapon.

She fought not for glory, nor for vengeance.

But for a promise etched in the bones of the world.

For the crown her father once bore like a flame held high against the night.

For the children huddled in ruined halls, praying to forgotten stars.

For the Elves who had waited.

For the fairies whose doors were shut. .

For the wounded earth of Emerland, pleading not to be abandoned again.

And still—she stood alone.

"Where is he?"

The thought came unbidden, slipping through her defenses like a ghost.

A whisper of longing across a field of screams.

One breath.
One flicker.
Then—the sky tore open.
Lightning screamed like it had been waiting.
Clouds split with a sound like Gods drawing breath.
And from the sundered heavens descended not a star, not a comet—but a sword made flesh.
Amethyst.
Not riding.
Not walking.
Falling—like judgment cast from on high.
Cloaked in stormlight, eyes afire with purpose, he was not the boy she had known—he was the reckoning that evil had forgotten to fear. His sword burned not with wrath, but with love sharpened to a perfect edge.
He struck the battlefield like thunder given form—into shadow, into flame,
into the heart of Basalt's legions.
The earth *screamed* with the impact, ringing with ancient power.
Flame recoiled.
Darkness cracked.
Where once Basalt grinned with certainty, now her lips curled in fury.
The tide had turned.
The stars had aligned.
The war had shifted.
Basalt reeled, fury twisting her face.
"It was meant to be one," she hissed. "*One Starborn!*"
But the skies had rewritten the tale.
Two stood before her—not rivals, but a reckoning.
Diamond and Amethyst.

Starborn and Stormbound.

Not chosen by fate—but forged by fire, by love, by loss.

They met in silence, eyes locking through ash and thunder.

No need for words. They remembered together. They burned together.

And the world answered.

The earth trembled.

The wind turned.

Even the stars leaned closer.

Then—together—they charged.

Twin lights, blazing toward the heart of shadow.

And Basalt, for the first time, knew fear.

What had once seemed certain—Emerland's defeat, Diamond's death, the crown crushed to ash—was no longer hers to claim.

Basalt snarled, teeth bared like a beast cornered.

Victory had been in her grasp.

Until the skies betrayed her.

Until two Starborn stood where there should have been only one.

Her wings trembled.

Her vulture shrieked.

And across the battlefield, firelight danced in Diamond's hair and stormlight blazed in Amethyst's eyes.

The prophecy had lied.

Or worse—it had kept its final line hidden.

With fury clawing up her throat, Basalt snapped her gaze to **Toxico T**, her shadow-bound general, the one she had trusted above all others.

He stood still in the smog, eyes wide, hands wrapped around the **Pentacle**—that terrible relic of flame and frost, stolen from time's cradle itself.

The last true power.

It pulsed in his grip like a living heart, casting fractured light onto his face—not sunlight, not firelight, but something older... colder... divine.

The Pentacle could pause time. Rewrite it. Twist the outcome like a thread between cruel fingers.

Basalt's voice did not rise.

But her will surged like a storm behind her eyes.

Use it. Now.

Strike him down. End the line of kings. Break the prophecy in two.

Toxico flinched.

Sweat beaded at his brow.

And then—

a whisper slid through the dark.

The voice of the shadow—old as rot, vast as winter—curled around them like smoke. It did not beg. It *promised*.

"Kill the boy. Unmake the girl. Shatter the light."

Toxico's fingers trembled around the Pentacle.

And yet... he hesitated.

He looked at Amethyst, still shining where he landed like a fallen star. He looked at Diamond, her soul aflame.

And something—

something—stirred in him.

Not mercy.

Not doubt.

Just a shadow of a memory.

A voice.

A face.

A whisper from long ago, buried beneath blood and ash.

"Bring Amethyst home safely,"

his sister had said—the last thing she ever spoke to him before the world fell apart.

It struck him not like comfort, but like a curse.

It splintered through his ribs and rattled the edge of his resolve.

From above, Basalt's scream tore through the smoke.

"You swore your oath to me!"

Toxico flinched.

His grip around the Pentacle tightened—veins bulging, glowing with raw power barely contained.

He lifted it higher, high enough for **all to see**.

A hush fell.

Even the wind drew back.

Across the battlefield, soldiers paused—shadow and light, bloodied and breathless—staring at him, the man holding the end of time like a sword at his throat.

Was this the fall of Emerland?

Or the rise of something far worse?

Toxico's jaw clenched.

His heart thundered in his ears.

But still...

he did not strike.

And the world hung in the balance.

34. Steel Against Shadow

Everyone had gathered on the battlefield.
Every soul still brave enough to defy the dark.
Every thread of fate pulled taut beneath the breaking sky.
All were there—
save one.
Far from the clash of blades and banners, in a forest long forgotten by maps,
Jabba Doom Gabbro sat alone.
Her hut—crooked, moss-cloaked, and swaying atop ancient chicken feet—watched the horizon like a living sentinel.
Inside, shadows danced across cracked walls. Herbs hung like sleeping spirits. And in the center, Jabba hovered before her crystal ball—its surface rippling like a frozen scream.
But her eyes, wide and dark as drowned moons, did not follow the war.
They searched the past.
They searched *him.*
"I will keep Amethyst safe."
Toxico's vow lingered in her mind like a knife left in the wound.
And now—through the smoke curling in her rafters—she smelled it.
Not hearth smoke.
Not incense.
Fire.

The land was burning again.
She could taste it on her tongue—the iron sting of betrayal.
Then came the whisper. A command.
Basalt, instructing her brother to strike.
To raise the Pentacle—that relic of ruin—and end the boy she had raised like her own.
A shriek tore through the air, not from outside—
but from the crystal ball as it shattered beneath her hand.
The future cracked open.
Fragments whirled:
Toxico's grin, stretched and wrong.
Diamond bound in shadow.
Amethyst falling—
vanishing.
Then—nothing.
Only silence.
Only ash.
Her breath came slow. Her fury, slower.
Toxico T.
The fool she once called brother.
The traitor she once forgave.
The coward who served the dark and cloaked it in charm.
"You were meant to save him," she whispered.
"You were meant to bring Amethyst back."
But this was no vision. No prophecy.
This was blood.
And she had felt it break.
Amethyst was still alive.
That was all she knew.
Not by vision, nor scrying, nor whispered omen.
But by the fierce truth in her bones.
He was in Emerland.
He was on the battlefield.

And no one would bring him home—
but her.

Gabbro turned, her robes swirling like a storm summoned from the roots of the earth.

The shadows in the room recoiled.

The years—so long hunched on her back like moss—peeled away in an instant.

Gone was the crone in exile, forgotten by courts and cursed by kings.

What stood in her place was something older than time, and harder than grief.

A mother sharpened into a weapon.

She looked up—

Past the moss-veiled rafters.

Past the chicken-footed hut that had carried her through the forgotten places of the world.

To the sky—

where smoke smeared the stars, and the heavens bled fire.

"You chose shadow," she said, voice low and bright as steel.

"I choose my son."

Outside, her companion stirred.

The crooked rooster—a creature of uncanny feathers, bone-white and oil-black—tilted its head. Its eyes, ageless and wrong, gleamed like obsidian.

It did not squawk. It did not flinch.

It **crowed**—once.

A deep, ancient sound—not of morning, but of reckoning.

Like thunder echoing through the bones of a dead god.

The hut groaned as if waking from a thousand-year sleep. Its chicken legs scraped against the mossy stone, restless beneath the weight of fate.

Jabba Doom Gabbro stood still, framed in the crooked doorway, eyes fixed on the smudged horizon. Smoke rose there—black plumes clawing at the stars—and somewhere beneath it, her son. Not by blood, but by bond. By promise. By love stronger than any curse.

"Hold on, child," she whispered, "your mother is coming."

Behind her, the rooster leapt from its perch.

Feathers tore free as it twisted mid-air, limbs contorting, beak splitting with a screech that bent the wind. Its wings snapped outward like thunderclaps, wide as sails, and its talons struck the ground—splitting stone with the weight of ancient magic.

But it was not wings she needed.

It was **feet**.

With another shriek, the rooster bent low, offering her its claws. The air shimmered. Fire licked the ground. The talons curled—and changed. Molten black and ember-red, they reshaped themselves into sandals. Sandals forged of obsidian, ash, and the soul of something forgotten.

Gabbro slid them on.

The instant they touched her skin, the earth beneath her **trembled**—as if the world recognized the return of a force it had buried too soon.

Outside, the sky howled.

She stepped into the wind, cloak snapping behind her like a banner of storm. Her hut groaned again, rising taller, its legs crouched to follow—but she raised a hand, stopping it.

"No. This I do alone."

And then—

she ran.

Not like a crone.

Not like the bitter outcast they had named witch.

But like a force undone.
Like fire released from a long-held breath.
Trees blurred. Rivers parted.
The night fled before her.
Each step cracked stone and summoned thunder. Crows scattered. Wolves bowed their heads. Old Gods in buried tombs stirred.
For Gabbro ran toward **Emerland**.
Toward **Amethyst**.
Toward the war that had stolen her brother, betrayed her vow, and now dared to claim her son.

And on the battlefield, beneath a sky stitched with lightning and scorched by war,
Toxico T clutched the Pentacle like a starving man hoarding bread.
His hands trembled.
He had never truly understood the relic—its origins, its limits, its price.
But he wanted it.
And for men like him, desire had always been reason enough.
All around him, Emerland burned.
Wraiths tore the air to shreds, shadows swarmed like smoke come alive.
Above, Basalt and Diamond clashed—flame against flame, fury against fate—Gods in mortal skins locked in a battle of becoming.
And yet, there on the broken earth, Toxico T stood alone.
Not frozen by fear...
But by something colder.
Doubt.

Then—out of the smoke, like a vision carved from vengeance—

He came.

Amethyst.

Cloaked in wind and blood,

Sword in hand,

Eyes alight with the fire of the undying.

He did not speak.

He did not threaten.

He walked.

One step.

Then another.

Until he stood before Toxico T—silent, still, unshaken.

A ghost.

A judgment.

The shadow of death shaped like the boy Jabba Doom Gabbro had once cradled and called son.

And for the first time, Toxico felt a chill that had nothing to do with wind or war.

"You…" Toxico rasped, voice brittle as frost, "You shouldn't be here."

His gaze flicked to the Pentacle, still pulsing with pale, reluctant light.

"You were supposed to be dead. No one returns from Death's domain. Not whole. Not real."

A pause. A breath.

"You cannot defeat what owns the end of all things…"

Toxico's voice faltered.

"…You must die."

But Amethyst did not move.

Did not blink.

Toxico T's throat bobbed as he swallowed hard.

His eyes locked on Amethyst—silent, waiting, inevitable.

With both hands now steady, he raised the Pentacle like a blade of final judgment.

He had made his choice.

And so, he spoke the words meant to end the light.

Ancient syllables, rusted with time, rolled off his tongue like poison from a dying god.

But then—

Crack.

A hand struck his face—open-palmed, furious, and forged from years of betrayed love.

Toxico staggered, reeling as if the blow had torn through more than bone.

As if it had struck his soul.

"You *fool*," spat a voice, raw and wrath-whetted. "You *absolute* fool."

He blinked through the sting and the tears—

And saw her.

Jabba Doom Gabbro, his sister..

But not as he remembered.

Not the broken hermit in a hut of bones.

Not the sister weeping for what was lost.

No—she stood crowned in stormlight, cloaked in ash, eyes lit with the fire of every mother who ever swore revenge.

She was fury made flesh.

"I told you to bring him *home*," she snarled, seizing his collar in both fists. "You swore, Toxico. *You swore to me.*"

"I—I tried," he stammered, voice cracking. "I wanted to—"

"*You wanted power*," she hissed, face inches from his. "But you were never strong enough to carry it. Never worthy enough to wield it."

Her eyes dropped to the Pentacle, still glowing faintly in his hand.

"Now give it to someone who is."
Before he could speak, she ripped it from his grip.
And the relic—so wild in his hands—went quiet.
Calm.
As if it had been waiting for her all along.
And above them, as if fate itself shifted...
Diamond faltered in her flight.
The wind stalled.
The fire paused.
Time held its breath.
She had clashed with Evil Basalt again and again—steel against shadow, light against ruin.
Each strike came harder. Each breath, shallower.
Her blade was chipped, her knuckles split, her limbs no longer obeyed strength—only memory.
And then—
Across the battlefield, through smoke and blood and the scream of sky, she saw it.
Gabbro.
And in her upraised hand—
The Pentacle.
Held not with fear, not with hesitation—
But with *purpose*.
The ancient relic caught the dying sun, and for a single, searing heartbeat, it flared—
Not with light,
But with meaning.
A signal to the heavens themselves:
Now.
Diamond gasped—
A breath deeper than the storm, sharper than fire.
It tasted of smoke.

Of ash.
Of memory.
Of **Amethyst.**
It tasted like home.
She didn't reach with her hand.
She reached with her *will.*
And the Pentacle answered.
Its five burning points split apart like shards of starlight—
Rays of gold and silver and something older than either—
Spiraled upward, then curved like destiny reborn...
Straight toward her.
Diamond's body flared. Her soul ignited.
She caught the five streams mid-air—fingers splayed, arms wide, heart wide open.
And for the first time—
She did not flinch.
She did not fear.
She did not ask.
She *commanded.*
"ENOUGH."
The word thundered through the sky like judgment cast in flame.
Wraiths froze mid-flight, wings rigid with sudden dread.
Vultures spiraled, shrieking, blind in the light.
Even Evil Basalt paused—blade inches from Diamond's throat—eyes narrowing.
The air thickened.
The ground held its breath.
The war paused.
Because light had not merely returned—
It had *risen.*
And Diamond Starborn no longer fought for Emerland.

She *was* Emerland.

The stillness that followed Diamond's command was not peace.

It was *pressure*—

A pause thick with breathless expectation.

But Diamond *felt* it.

Not just the power—but the price.

The Pentacle had given breath to the war...

And taken hers in return.

Her chest tightened.

Each heartbeat slowed, echoing like a distant drum in a deepening sea.

Air no longer filled her lungs—not fully. Not freely.

It was as if the world had paused to breathe through *her*,

and now... she was emptying.

She understood.

The Pentacle could pause a war.

It could still the The Hollow Star, silence the Wraiths, turn time to mercy —

but in doing so,

it borrowed breath from the one who held it.

How long could she last without air?

She didn't know.

Didn't care.

She would hold it—hold the stillness, the hush, the trembling peace—

for as long as it took.

And in that sacred silence,

where fire no longer screamed and swords no longer clashed,

Amethyst felt it.

Felt *her*.

Felt her slipping—breath by breath—into stillness.

And he moved.

Not with panic—

but with purpose.

With haste born of love, and fear, and the sharp clarity that only comes

when you know someone else is dying...

so others may live.

He turned, eyes cutting through the smoke, toward the one soul ancient enough to understand what must come next.

Baba Yaga.

Perched at the edge of war like a shadow that had seen empires fall.

Her bones older than any crown.

Her gaze met his.

She saw the sword in his hand—the Sword of the Crown of Emerland.

Forged in ages long buried, once wielded by the first true king.

It pulsed now like a living promise in Amethyst's grip.

Her eyes widened—just slightly—and she gave a single, solemn nod.

That was all.

The signal.

The seal.

The sanction of the old world.

Amethyst ran.

Across blood-soaked ground and shattered stone,

Through the hush of a war held in breath,

He surged toward Diamond—toward the Starborn—

The blade in his hand gleaming like a shard torn from a forgotten star.

And Basalt saw him.

She turned, slowly—like stone realizing it was no longer eternal.

Her eyes met his across the ruin.

And there—

There, Amethyst saw it:

A flicker.

Small.

Hidden.

But undeniable.

Not the fear of death.

No, Basalt had never feared dying.

This was worse.

This was **fear of destiny**.

She had tasted power, shaped illusions, bent worlds—but this...

This was prophecy.

And she was on the wrong end of it.

Amethyst did not waver.

He reached Diamond at last—breathless, bloodied, but whole—and pressed the sword into her hands.

No words passed between them.

There was no need.

In her eyes, he saw **understanding**.

In his, she saw **faith**.

Diamond turned.

The **Sword of the Crown** burned in one hand—a blade etched in sacrifice, tempered by time.

The **Pentacle** blazed in the other—five-pointed, eternal, humming with the will of the world.

Across from her, **Basalt hissed**, robes torn, crown cracked, shadows writhing like snakes at her heels.

The sky bled light and lightning. The Wraiths screamed, sensing the tide breaking.

They surged forward—

—but **Baba Yaga** raised her staff.

With a whisper and a storm, she struck the earth.

Thunder answered.

The Wraiths were flung back like ashes before a sacred wind.

Now.

Diamond stepped forward, cloak torn, fire in her lungs, death in her shadow.

The Pentacle flared. The Sword sang.

Basalt screamed—arms raised, curses on her tongue, venom in her breath—

But her spell came **too late**.

The blade fell.

Once—and Diamond saw **Obsidian Swish**, the first to fall.

fear—nameless, ancient—had torn the flesh from her bones, stripping her soul and story until only silence remained.

Now, Evil Basalt stood as she once stood—

a creature of bones without breath,

a shell where hunger had once lived.

Twice—and she saw **Jabba Gabbro's son**, the innocent wagered.

His soul, once whole, had been split—

half cast into the void, the other scattered like ash in wind.

No name. No laughter. No return.

Now, Evil Basalt bore that fracture—

empty as a husk, splintered like shattered glass,

each shard whispering a name it could no longer remember.

Basalt turned to Topaz, her eyes wide—not with power, but with a flicker of something far older. Desperation.

A silent plea passed between them, unspoken but clear: *Stop her. Stop Diamond's hand.*

But **Topaz did not meet her gaze.**

Instead, he looked down—

to the shattered remnants of his wings, strewn like fallen stars across the stone.

His hands trembled at his sides, empty.

And his silence answered her.

Only if I could fly,

it seemed to say.

Only if I were still whole.

But no wings rose. No salvation came.

And in that breath between silence and storm, **Diamond struck.**

Once.

Twice.

Thrice.

Each blow rang like thunder over a ruined sea—

and in the wake of the third, the veil of shadow tore.

She saw them.

The Three Doomed Sisters—

those who once stood beside Evil Basalt, cloaked in dread and darkness.

One by one, they abandoned her:

First, the gift of deception faded like smoke.

Then, the veil of shadow unraveled from her shoulders.

And finally—the Wraiths, her loyal terrors—

vanished into nothing, as if even ghosts would no longer serve her.

And with the third strike—

Basalt shattered.

Not into flame.

Not into shadow.
But into *nothing*.
As if she had never been born...
Only *summoned*.
As if all her rage, all her ruin, all her horror
had only ever been the nightmare of something too hollow
to be real.
The darkness **reeled**.
The Wraiths howled one last time—and vanished.
The Pentacle dimmed, then stilled.
The battlefield fell silent.
No cheer.
No cry.
Just a breath.

35. Ashes and Stone

As Evil Basalt fell—unmade not only by blade, but by truth—the world did not rejoice.

It paused.

Somewhere far from the battlefield, where sunlight had never kissed the ground, the earth stirred.

Not in mourning.

In *remembrance*.

Beneath the roots of mountains long abandoned, where even the Gods no longer looked, the stone of a cursed tomb cracked.

It had been sealed by ancient Elves. Forgotten by kings. Feared by time.

But it had never been empty.

And now, as Basalt's final breath slipped into silence, something beneath that tomb inhaled.

Not a roar.

Not a scream.

A *breath*—drawn deep, cold, and ancient, as if it had been waiting seventeen centuries to rise.

Because Basalt's death...was *Lord of Darkness's* life.He had worn her life as a mask, but when her breath ceased, the mask broke—and what lay beneath rose unbound: the Nameless Fear. The curse upon the grave shattered like glass beneath thunder.

The runes burned and turned to ash. And from the deepest vault beneath the world, the **Lord of Darkness** rose. He rose *not alone*.

Around him, the dust of the dead began to stir. Bones remembered their names. Eyes once empty flickered with terrible light.

Those who had died long ago in his silence now rose again at his command.

Warriors. Warlords. Witch-priests.

All bound to the dirge of his song.

All who had once served the darkness opened their eyes, and the earth groaned beneath the weight of the rising dead.

The sky turned black—not with night, but with *reckoning*.

A wind screamed across the plains, and somewhere, the trees wept.

From his ruined cradle of stone and bone, the **First Shadow** opened his eyes—no light, only void—and spoke the words that split the world:

"The hour has come."

Across the realms, torches went out.

In temples, statues cracked.

And beneath the crown of Emerland, Diamond's fingers tightened on the Pentacle.

She felt it.

So did Amethyst.

So did the sky.

The shadow behind the shadow had awakened—not in vengeance, but in **answer**.

Evil Basalt's death was never an end.

It was a *summoning*.

And now, with the veil torn and the true darkness unsealed, the final war would no longer be waged in dreams or whispers.

It would burn in daylight.

It would stain the skies.

And when it ended—only one would remain.

Diamond had not seen it coming.

Amethyst could not have guessed.

The darkness had not been destroyed.

It had waited—

Not in the skies,

Not in the ruins,

But folded quietly in the corner of a cloak, close as breath.

Still.

Patient.

Very much alive.

The darkness had crafted its perfect plan.

The cursed mirror—once the eye of all that was twisted—had been shattered, its cruel truths reduced to a fine, pale ash. That ash was more than remains. It was a memory. A will. The breath of the darkness itself. It could not be destroyed. But it could be hidden—locked beyond reach, where no hope dared follow.

To Death's dominion.

There, in that place without time, the Lord of Darkness meant to bury its soul—just as the Sword of the Crown had once been hidden in fire and silence. If no one could find it, then no one could destroy it. And so Evil Basalt, ever cunning, handed the ashes to her last willing shadow: Spinel.

His task was simple.

Carry the ashes across the threshold.

Hide them.

Return with the Sword.

But Spinel faltered.

And he chose not to carry the darkness forward.

He cast the vial away—into the abyss—not with rage, but with reverence.

As though casting off a sin too terrible to speak aloud.

And there—

By fate, or folly, or the strange grace of the world—

It did not fall into the void.

It fell into a hand.

Amethyst's hand.

He did not know what it was. Only that it was cold. Light.

Weightless as breath, yet heavy with something unspoken.

The vial pulsed in his grip—not with power, but with something older.

Something he could almost remember.

Grief.

Or was it guilt?

He held it without knowing why.

Without a word, Amethyst had slipped the vial into his pocket—thinking he would ask later, thinking there would be time to understand.

But darkness does not wait.

The ashes had never reached Death, their destined keeper.

They had not been buried.

Not purified.

Not laid to rest.

They had only waited.

Not asleep—but watching.

Listening.

Wanting.

And in that waiting, something stirred.

The Dark Lord—who called Death his sister, and hunted Time like a beast in the dark—felt the moment strike like a heartbeat beneath the earth.

The ashes were no longer lost.

The sword obeys the power.

And the Starborn walked the world once more.

All the pieces were in place.

All within his reach.

Now came the moment he had waited for across centuries folded like maps—

The moment to return.

And with him, extinguish Emerland's final light.

From the cursed cemetery—where the ground had long since curdled and the wind spoke in broken tongues—a storm began to rise.

It came not as weather, but as a warning unheeded.

Dark as dried blood, vast as the night before time, it did not roll across the sky—it surged, alive with purpose.

A million winged things, small as ash flakes and blacker than pitch, moved as one—an unholy swarm of shadow, a single mind with countless wings.

They rose like smoke, but flew like thought—deliberate, intelligent, cruel.

As they passed, they turned everything beneath them to darkness. Leaves withered. Stone cracked. Light bent away. And the air, once filled with wind, grew still and choking, as if the world itself recoiled from what had come.

This was not a storm.

This was ruin set loose.

The Nameless Fear had returned—not to conquer, but to erase.

Diamond turned slowly.

In her hand, the sword still glistened with sorrow—heavy not with steel, but with stories. It pulled at her like gravity, as if it, too, felt the hour darkening.

Her gaze lifted to the west.

There, once, light had broken. Songs had soared. Hope had found breath.

But now, only the shadow moved.

The sky was not clouded—it was infected.

The winged swarm coiled upward in vast spirals, threading the heavens with veins of sentient dusk. A single darkness, moving with purpose. Alive. Unstoppable.

Beside her, Amethyst stood as if carved from time, his breath caught between memory and fate.

He saw it too.

The Nameless Fear had awakened.

And it was coming.

Jade turned to Rock the Hawk, eyes wide with a silent question—*Was there still a way?*

The great bird met his gaze, solemn and steady. No words— just a nod, and the firm grip of talons curling gently around Jade's hand.

Rock the Hawk leaned in, his voice no louder than the wind slipping through leaves. Whatever he whispered—only Jade heard it. But it was enough.

Jade broke into a run.

He crossed the ruined field where magic still shimmered faint and broken, and reached Amethyst—breathless, urgent, burning with resolve. He spoke only once.

Amethyst listened. His jaw tightened. His eyes clouded—not with fear, but with the weight of inevitability. He did not nod. He did not speak.

He simply reached for Diamond's hand and clasped it with fierce, unyielding tenderness.

"Run, Diamond," he said—not as a command, but as a vow.

His voice held no fear.

Only the quiet, sacred finality of a prayer already answered.

Diamond hesitated. Her gaze flicked to Jade—her brother in bond if not in blood.

Jade stood tall amidst the brokenness, his back to the dark horizon, eyes bright as drawn steel.

A warrior now. The last shield of Emerland.

He gave her a nod, not of farewell—but of faith.

He would be there.

When she returned.

He would hold the line.

He would make King Alexandrite proud.

"Go," Amethyst urged again.

Not louder—but firmer.

It was not desperation.

It was destiny—spoken from the lips of one who had already paid the price.

And so, **Diamond and Amethyst ran**, hand in hand, hearts pounding like war drums in the hush before storm.

Not away from the war—

but toward the flame she alone was born to bear.

And the world—ancient, wounded, watching—**seemed to rise with them.**

The trees leaned forward, their branches outstretched like old hands offering blessing.

The ground beneath her boots throbbed with power, as if remembering her steps from lifetimes past.

Even the wind, sharp with the scent of rain and ruin, brushed her cheek like a mother's parting kiss.

She didn't question him.

There was no time for doubt. No space for fear.

Only forward.

Only fire.

Behind them, the sky had begun to darken—not with cloud, but with something deeper.

A shadow older than stars, patient as stone, rising to claim what it had long been denied.

But Diamond did not look back.

She ran—

and the earth ran with her.

Because somewhere deep in her bones—older than memory, older than fear—**Diamond knew.**

They were not ready.

Not yet.

The thing that stirred behind the veil of shadow was more than vengeance, more than darkness.

It was **ancient unmaking.**

And it would not be faced by courage alone.

But there was hope—fragile as frost, buried like a seed in winter.

Rock the Hawk's words rang in Amethyst's mind like prophecy sealed in feather and wind:

"Follow the breath of the kingdom. It will take you where the light still remembers. Where Sword Belongs."

The sword...

Once, it had lain beneath the **Crown of Emerland**, in the heart of the old palace where kings once dreamed and queens once wept.

There it had slumbered for generations—**not dead, but dreaming**—wrapped in the memory of justice, waiting for the world to remember what it once stood for.

If it could return—if it could wake—then maybe, just maybe, **the land would remember too.**

And now, **Amethyst and Diamond carried that sword.**

Amethyst had gone to Death's home—where no breath dares linger—and emerged with what was once theirs.

The price for such a gift was steep, carved not in coin, but in blood.

King Alexandrite's life was the toll.

A soul given so a weapon might return.

A father lost so a future could be held.

And so— **They ran.**

Ran not just with their feet, but with **the will of Emerland** itself surging behind her.

Not to escape—but to awaken.

To return what had been lost.

Not away from the darkness—

but **toward something older than it.**

Toward the **Throne of Emerland.**

Diamond's fingers locked with Amethyst's, her grip fierce, as though letting go might shatter the world itself.

Behind them, Jade followed—his stride steady, his eyes bright with fire, even as the breath trembled in Diamond's chest.

Above, **Rock the Hawk** soared in wide, furious arcs—a sentinel of feather and thunder—his cry a blade that tore through shadow-choked skies.

And at the broken threshold of Emerland, beneath a sky churning with storm and ruin, **stood Baba Yaga.**

She did not speak.

She did not turn.

She simply raised her staff high—

and slammed it into the earth.

The world flinched.

The storm parted—for one breath, one heartbeat.

Enough.

Through that sliver of fury and cloud, Diamond and the others ran—

not as fugitives, but as flame.

They slipped past the closing dark like light between slammed doors.

And behind them, the gate sealed shut with the groan of finality.

At her chest, the sword pulsed.

Heavy not with steel, but with legacy.

Ahead loomed the **Emerald Castle**—its spires crooked with time, its gates gaping like the open jaw of a forgotten god.

Diamond did not think of prophecy, or war, or even survival.

Only this:

Return the blade.

Return it to the place it had once been cradled, beneath the **Crown of Emerland**, where kings had once dared to hope.

And pray—fiercely, silently—that something good still lingered in the stone.

Behind them, **Baba Yaga, Hematite, and Jade** stood at the kingdom's last edge, watching as a sea of shadow surged across the hills, swallowing sky and soil like a tide of oblivion.

The wind had stilled—

as though the earth itself held its breath.

Then came the sound.

Not a scream. Not a howl.

But silence—fracturing.

Like ice cracking beneath unbearable weight.

The sound of something vast, ancient, and wrong awakening beneath the world.

Diamond and Amethyst reached the tower—

Emerland's highest, where the crown had slept through fire and famine, untouched by time.

A crown not made for conquest—
but for remembrance.
Without hesitation, **Diamond knelt.**
And laid the sword beneath it.
The castle trembled—
Not in terror, but in **recognition.**
Stone groaned like a long-silent heart beginning to beat.
Stained-glass windows flickered with sun that had not shone in years.
And the air itself shimmered, as if the kingdom remembered its name.
Something had awakened.
Not just in the tower—
but in **Emerland itself.**
Not just the light—
but the will to stand.
The runes on the walls stirred first—lines of old speech glowing faintly, like veins remembering the pulse of life. Then the Pentacle trembled in Diamond's hand. A breath. A heartbeat. And then—light.

It burst from the Crown of Emerland in a flare of green, gold, and white, rushing through the halls like dawn chasing night. The stones drank it in. The banners were lifted. The throne room exhaled a breath it had held for centuries.

But it was not enough.
Because with the light came the truth.
Not dreams. Not visions.
Memories.
The crown. The sword. The war.
A voice rose—not from the walls, but from the bloodline of the crown itself. It did not speak. It declared:
"The crown does not serve good. It serves power."

And now—power belonged to the shadow.

The crown, once a beacon of hope, bent its grace toward that rising dark. The Pentacle dimmed. The light faltered. The castle itself seemed to draw back, uncertain of its allegiance.

Diamond stood still, as if the very stones beneath her feet had claimed her. The sword was gone now—returned to its resting place beneath the Crown of Emerland. It no longer weighed in her hand, but in her chest.

Across the chamber, Amethyst watched her. His eyes held no fire, only depth—deep as old rivers, carved by the current of knowing too much, too soon.

They did not speak.

But silence passed between them like a thread drawn taut across centuries.

We are not them.

Not the Elves who had earned the Crown's favor through sacrifice and song. Not the First Guardians who had bound the darkness in chains of light and buried it in the world's oldest grave.

They were not chosen.

They were only here.

We are all that's left.

The thought settled heavy between them—heavier than any blade. The Elves had fought for power and earned it; Diamond had returned it, not knowing whether it would answer her call. The light had flared—but it had faltered. The Crown no longer stood guard. It waited to see who would rise... and who would fall.

And now, with the Dark Lord rising and the sky unraveling, the truth became plain:

They could not fight. Not and live.

Not and stop what was coming.

If they were to stand, it would not be as heroes—but as the last hope of a kingdom that no longer knew how to hope. And then— beyond the battered gates of Emerland—the earth groaned.

Not like a tremor or quake, but like the slow, solemn thud of a giant's heartbeat: heavy, ancient, and inevitable. A sound older than language. The soil itself seemed to flinch, its roots recoiling from what now marched to claim it. The very bones of the world remembered this dread—and shuddered.

At the threshold, Baba Yaga raised her staff.

Not from frailty. But from intention.

As if drawing a final boundary between all that must remain and all that threatened to end.

Her spine did not bend. Her fingers did not tremble.

She was not defying death—she had walked beside it for centuries.

She was defying **oblivion**.

The darkness poured forward—not as flame or beast, but as a tide of pure undoing. Smoke, scream, shadow—all fused into one advancing truth. And yet Baba Yaga did not retreat. She stood rooted, a figure carved of storm and memory, unmoved before the unraveling tide. Her presence was the last tower before the sea.

And then she spoke—her voice low, but vast. A voice that had once called stars down from the sky.

"Go back," she said, not pleading, but commanding.

"You are not yet welcome here."

For one breathless moment, the darkness paused.

Not in fear—but in recognition.

As if even it had to consider the weight of her will... before it swept forward again.

The Nameless Fear had no face.

No name.

No voice.

And yet it stood at the castle gates.

Not like an enemy come to fight.

But like a truth finally told.

It didn't move. It pressed.

Its weight pushed against the stones, not with fists or fire, but with the quiet pressure of something inevitable.

The air grew colder, thinner—as if it had forgotten how to be air at all.

The wind no longer blew.

The ground no longer shook.

Everything just... waited.

Inside the castle, the walls creaked—not from impact, but from memory.

Like they knew what was coming.

Like they had always known.

No screams. No shouts.

Just a steady, unbearable silence.

The kind that comes before a door opens that should never open.

36. Light Without Omen

Then Amethyst stirred. Not in fear—but in recognition.

The darkness outside had thickened. He could feel it pressing closer—a suffocating presence like the pause before a scream. It would breach the gates soon, not by shattering stone, but by ending Baba Yaga's life... or her will. Time was no longer a thing they had.

He looked at Diamond. She stood utterly still—not in surrender, but in silence. Not defeated. Not yet. There was no way to win. She knew it. But she also hadn't stopped searching. And that was why he moved.

As though a quiet wind passed between them, Amethyst reached for her hand. Not in desperation, but in shared defiance—a final vow between two who had already given everything they could, except their hope.

Together, they stepped forward and bowed before the Crown. Not to seek power. Not to ask for salvation. But to ask—for guidance, not glory.

The Crown did not glow. It did not sing. But it pulsed—once—a heartbeat carved into emerald, soft and solemn. It had never answered to kings. Never bent to wrath or pride. It listened only to those who bore power as burden, and wielded it in service of love, not dominion. It answered those who knelt not because they were weak—but because they chose to be small before something greater.

And so it guided. Not with commands. But with memory.

The stone beneath their feet vibrated. A line of ancient runes shimmered to life, crawling along the floor like veins of starlight—leading not forward, but down. Down into the roots of Emerland. Where truth slept. Where the war had begun. And where, perhaps, it could finally end.

A whisper. A flicker. A knowing. It slipped through the air—not as sound, but as a memory too old for language.

Diamond stood frozen, but not in fear. Amethyst turned toward her, and in the brief touch of their eyes, something passed—not hope, not light... but understanding.

"I have this," he said, his voice hollow with something deeper than dread.

From beneath his cloak, he drew the vial. The ashes within stirred. Not with life. Not with light. But with hunger—the soft, curling hunger of something that had waited too long in the dark. They pulsed like a second heartbeat. They churned like a tide rising beneath still water. They burned—not like fire, but like rot: slow, inevitable, absolute.

Outside, the Nameless Fear stirred. It felt the vial. Felt the ashes awaken. And with a sound like thunder tearing through bone, it entered the castle.

Baba Yaga stood no longer. Her knees struck stone, her staff split in two. Yet even in defeat, she did not fall. She offered herself—as the gate, as the final delay.

The shadow surged past her. It moved not like a beast but like a verdict—inevitable, cold, ancient. It poured through the halls of Emerland, consuming the light, drawing breath from stone, and turning memory to dust.

And then once more—through ash and ruin—the steed returned to Diamond.

Its hooves struck the ground like falling stars, its mane braided with threads of salt and shadow, as if it had galloped straight out of memory and mourning.

Amethyst saw it first. His voice broke into a whisper, almost a prayer.

"Your father sent it… born of his final sacrifice."

Diamond froze, her breath stolen. Her heart thudded with a grief too vast for words. The horse—this radiant creature—had come for her once before, when all seemed lost. And now again.

Her father. Alexandrite.

Even from death's dominion, he had found a way to reach her.

To guide her.

To love her still.

Tears burned her eyes, not from sorrow alone, but from the fierce, unyielding truth: she was not abandoned. She was never alone.

The steed's wings cleaved the storm clouds, catching the wind like forgotten banners of a once-glorious realm. He did not gallop. He descended—through shattered roof and sky, through magic and ruin. He landed before them with a low, solemn bow of his head. Not in fear. In duty.

As if Alexandrite himself had spoken one final command from beyond the veil: Go.

Diamond placed her hand on the steed's flank—warm, solid, real. The legacy was not a crown. It was a path. She mounted— not as a girl, not even as the Starborn—but as a daughter answering a call.

The sky broke open. The final hour had come.

They both rode on the steed's back , The vial in Amethyst's hand pulsed with the ache of memory. And they flew.

Through smoke. Through screams. Through the unraveling of all they had known—they flew. Not to escape. But to become the storm the darkness had not foreseen.

Below them, the darkness did not flow—it crawled. It coiled. A legion of writhing silhouettes—not shadow, but shape. Tendrils of night stretched across the land, threading through root and ruin, wrapping fields in silence, turning every leaf, every breath, into ash. Where it passed, life obeyed—by vanishing.

But the horse—King Alexandrite's blood made flesh and flight— flew faster. Not by speed alone, but by will. By memory. By love carried forward on the back of loss.

They reached it. The cursed cemetery. That place where time held its breath and never exhaled. Where light dared not speak its name.

The sealing stone still stood—but cracked. Not broken, not shattered—cracked, as if it had heard the ancient name whispered once more and shuddered in recognition.

Diamond dismounted first—like a spark breaking through smoke. Amethyst followed, his feet touching the ground as if answering a call written in his blood.

Before them lay the grave. The grave. Not of a man, nor monster—but of a memory so terrible the world itself had tried to forget. And now it groaned. Not in grief—but in anticipation.

"The ashes," Diamond whispered.

Amethyst opened the vial.

Amethyst had not spilled the ashes.

He had only loosened the seal—just enough for the breath within to stir.

What escaped was not air.

It was corruption.

A whisper that had waited ten thousand years to be heard.

It slid into the wind like poison, and the wind recoiled—shuddering low, as though some ancient wound had been torn open again.

But before that breath could spread—

before the ashes could be set free—

the dark came.

Not night, but the thing that devours night.

A presence older than stars, patient as stone, hungering as fire.

It did not fall like rain, but like a curtain of blindfolded stars—veiling not sight, but truth.

The storm rose without thunder, without howl.

It moved in whispers.

It remembered.

Graves unsealed. Names unspoken. Bloodlines betrayed.

And from the heart of that impossible hush, he stepped forth—

the Nameless Lord, no longer buried, no longer bound—

as if the world itself had drawn him out of the bottle.

The ashes were his life—his marrow, his breath. So long as they endured, he would never fall. And now, in triumph, he would bear them to his sister, Death, to place within her most guarded vault. There they would be kept, safe for eternity, while he strode the world as its conqueror. In his keeping, the light would not merely serve—it would kneel. Forever.

The Lord of the Forbidden—the Nameless Fear - The Lord of Darkness.

He did not walk—he arrived. As if the earth had made space for him. As if the cemetery had drawn him back with its final, failing breath.

And when he rose, it was not with fury, nor with triumph—
but with a stillness steeped in rot.
A silence sovereign.
It was the hush of graves refusing their sleep,
the pause of breath before a scream.
The air curdled and bent around him.
Stone cracked beneath his shadow.
Trees withered as though their roots had forgotten the taste of water.
And the world—once more—forgot how to breathe.

Nothing moved without his will. The Dark Lord stood above the world like the silence before a storm—absolute, immovable. Not a breeze dared stir. Not a leaf dared fall. The air was thick with his dominion.

It was too late for the Pentacle. He had seen it—the vial in Amethyst's hand, its ghostly glow betraying everything. His eyes, blacker than starless night, locked onto the boy.

And then The Lord of the Darkness moved—not walked, but arrived, like the hunger that follows famine. A shadowed tempest, a promise of unmaking, he surged forward to end the game and claim the soul meant for him since the beginning.

Amethyst turned—not to flee, but to shield her, to trade his breath for hers if fate would allow. Just once more he let his gaze drink her in, as though he could carry the memory of her face into whatever void awaited him.

But Diamond did not wait.

She was already moving. Not with haste. Not with fear. But with knowing. With a silence that thundered louder than war drums. With the stillness of one who had already died once—and chosen to rise again.

"Then shall the Starborn rise—
Child of the fae, blood-bound to fair Emerland.
If fire within be kindled bright,
And steadfast hearts endure the storm,
Then shall the light prevail, and hope not fade.
But if the Starborn falters, if the flame is lost,
Then night shall fall eternal,
And Emerland's last hope be swallowed by the dark."

And in that moment, Diamond felt the prophecy burn within her bones. If death awaited, she would take it with pride. But the fire in her breast was not for herself—it was for Emerland. For the kingdom that had suffered, for the people who had believed, for the crown that had been bought with so much blood.

Her courage was no longer the courage of a child. It was the courage of a land that refused to bow. The fire was not for her life, but for its life.

And her heart—though scarred by sorrow—had never burned so brave.

She rose into the prophecy not as a captive of fate, but as its fulfillment.

The Starborn had come.

And with her, the dawn.

She mounted the steed in a single breath, as if the heavens themselves had drawn her upward. No command touched her lips. No cry split the air. Only motion—pure, unstoppable, fated.

From her sides the twin blades leapt free, silver arcs catching what little light dared linger. Like moons torn from their orbits, they blazed against the night, and bent themselves toward shadow.

And Diamond rode.

Not as a fugitive.

Not as a child of prophecy.

But as fire incarnate—straight into the heart of darkness.

The Lord of Darkness had not foreseen her defiance. Her fury struck him like a fire too pure to belong to mortals—not chaos, but consequence. Not wrath, but judgment long deferred. He staggered, and for the first time in an age, the unshaken one tasted surprise.

And in that fracture—Amethyst moved.

He turned to the grave and loosed the vial.

It fell from his hand like a final breath, a soul exhaled into ruin.

The ashes stirred, not gently, but as if roused by hunger. They rose screaming in silence, whirling like **embers torn from hell's own forge**—glowing, rising, remembering.

Each mote carried voices long buried: shards of the mirror, fragments of the curse, names once damned to silence and now clawing back into the air.

The wind did not bear them; it recoiled. Even the air knew better than to touch what had been awakened.

The grave—forgotten by all but stone and time—listened.

The Dark Lord roared. Not rage. Something older. A cry of a thousand broken thrones, of unfinished wars. He hurled

Diamond aside like a broken thought—and she flew, her blades scattering like meteors.

Then—silence. Not the calm kind. The holy kind. The kind that cracks mountains. The kind that comes just before the Gods weep.

The Nameless Fear leapt—not into battle, but into the grave. It dove after the ashes like a serpent chasing its own heart. It moved without wind or weight, a presence wrapped in absence, a hunger shaped like a scream.

The skies recoiled. Stars blinked out. Even time flinched. Light bent backward. As if the world itself tried to flee what now stirred.

But it was too late.

The ashes—falling like sorrow made visible—touched the grave. And the shadow followed.

Stone groaned. Runes pulsed. Earth remembered. And something older than memory—something bound in the marrow of the world—opened its eyes.

A scream tore through the air—not heard, but felt. In marrow. In memory. In the blood of the world.

"I shall return... and bring your doom," the The Lord of Darkness hissed—not in speech, but in heartbeat, in trembling leaf, in every creature that had ever dared to hope.

Diamond and Amethyst, their souls joined in defiance, pressed their shoulders to the sealing stone. It did not move.

Then—the horse neighed. It rose, not in fear, but as if lifted by unseen hands. The spirits of Alexandrite and Morganite moved through it—unseen, yet undeniable.

The ground groaned, old as mountains, and the stone shifted—slow, immense.

And then—it sealed.

A tremor passed through the earth. Not violent, but a sigh—centuries of sorrow released in a single breath.

Then—silence.

And then... collapse.

The darkness caved inward—not in fury, but in surrender. It folded upon itself. It withdrew. Ashes to ash. Sin to soil. Not shattered, but undone.

And so it ended—completely, utterly.

For now.

Clouds peeled from the sky like torn cloth. Smoke melted into strands of gold. The wind turned soft—sweet with jasmine, moss, and rain-soaked earth.

Diamond stood, trembling in the hush of a world redeemed.

She turned to Amethyst and folded herself into his arms—not to cling, but to anchor. Eyes closed, brow pressed to his shoulder, she listened... for the silence of peace.

When she opened her eyes—the world had changed.

The sky was blue. Deep, like a newborn hope. Trees shimmered with morning, not magic. The cursed cemetery slept—still, sacred. No longer a place of dread, but of rest.

And far across the hills, the bells of Emerland began to ring. Not for mourning. But for peace. For the first time in living memory.

Birdsong rose like a hymn. Rivers, once still with fear, danced again. The grass breathed—glistening, green, alive.

Diamond and Amethyst stood side by side, bathed in the quiet of a world made whole.

"We won," she whispered—voice shaking, soft as a prayer.

Tears traced her cheeks, not in grief,but as a blessing.

Amethyst smiled—not wide, but deep. A smile born of pain weathered. Of love proven true. Of hope fulfilled.

Above them, the sky whispered no more omens.

Only light.

And the shadow—at last—was sealed.

Then came Baba Yaga, quiet as dusk. Her hands lifted, her eyes full of endings. With one final incantation, she cast the last enchantment:

A veil of forgetting.

A curse of concealment.

The cemetery would be hidden.

Untouched by time.

Undiscovered.

Forever.

37. The Light Remains

Diamond and Amethyst returned to Emerland not with swords drawn, but with hope held high—not as warriors seeking glory, but as quiet heralds of a dawn long yearned for.

The kingdom rose to greet them, arms outstretched, hearts unguarded. Tears flowed freely—not of grief, but of release, as though the land itself had exhaled at last. From the hidden glades and forgotten hollows, the fairies returned, wings aglimmer, their laughter spilling like sunlight through emerald leaves.

For eight nights and eight radiant dawns, the palace blazed with joy. Music danced along the marble halls, and golden light poured from the windows, as if the very stones had remembered how to sing. Flowers burst from the blackened earth, blooming defiantly where fire had once scorched the soil—lilies from ash, roses from ruin. Laughter—tentative at first, then rising like a river breaking its banks—swept through the land, washing away the silence that had long lodged in every corner of the heart.

And Baba Yaga remained—no longer merely the keeper of forgotten paths and forest shadows, but a revered presence at the heart of all things. She stood watchful and wise, her eyes deep as dusk, her smile soft with pride. Once a legend whispered in fear, she now shone—quiet, steadfast, and utterly beloved.

Beneath the One-Wish Tree, whose branches shimmered with blossoms reborn in peace, Jade wed Rock the Hawk's cousin. Their vows were humble, spoken not before kings but before the wind, the sky, and the leaves that danced like snow.

In time, Diamond and Amethyst brought forth twin stars into the world—a boy and a girl, whom they named *Sapphire* and *Chrysolite*. The children were laughter made flesh, light in the cradle of twilight, a new beginning carved from the ashes of sorrow.

Jade too had a son—wild-hearted and untamed, always climbing what was forbidden, chasing winds as if they were dreams.

Topaz chose the wandering path. With only a flute slung over his shoulder, he vanished into the whispering wilds, forsaking palace and title to dwell among birds and trees, where no crown could follow.

At the edge of Emerland, in a crooked little cottage tangled in ivy, Jabba Doom Gabbro and Toxico T made their peace with life. By day she scolded him with fire in her voice, and by night they laughed—hers louder than thunder, his tea still as dangerous as ever.

And so, with time and tenderness, the realm began to heal.

Hematite's coffeehouse glowed even brighter now, as though joy itself had kindled every lantern and corner. The scent of fresh cakes, warm bread, golden scones, and sweet pancakes wafted through the air, wrapping the space in a gentle, nourishing warmth.

No one had seen Spinel the Wolf again, but whispers traveled on the wind—that he had found a new pack in a land far beyond Emerland's reach. There, it is said, he lives in quiet peace, never looking back—for not a single happy memory remained for him in the land he left behind.

At long last, Olivine the Dove returned.

She came not in haste, but in grace—her pale wings gliding through the quiet skies like whispers across a dream. The wind carried her gently, and the setting sun painted her feathers in hues of soft gold and rose. She circled once above the palace, a glimmer against the amber light, before descending to the place she had always known as home.

Diamond stood waiting, her laughter like windchimes in spring. She held out her hands, scattering dried petals and honeyed sweets into the hollowed nest—the very one she had kept safe through every trial. It was a nest that, no matter where she wandered, had always made her feel at home.

Olivine cooed with delight, her wings folding as she nestled in, her eyes bright and wise with distant joy.

"I have found him," she said in the secret language of wind and wings—a murmur only Diamond could understand. "My soul's twin—and we have been rejoicing ever since."

Diamond's smile deepened, her heart swelling with quiet gladness. No fanfare marked the reunion, no trumpets, no songs—only the soft rustle of feathers, the scent of wildflowers, and the shared warmth of peace found and peace returned.

Peace had returned—not the stillness of sorrow, but the quiet breath of a life reclaimed.

That evening, atop the palace where once the winds had howled with omen and dread, Diamond stood beneath the constellations. Amethyst stood beside her, watching the stars drift like ancient ships across the velvet dark.

"It's quiet," she whispered.

"For now," he replied, his voice a gentle tether.

She smiled,not with triumph, but with a calm born of survival.

"That's enough," she said.

Below them, Emerland slumbered in the hush of safety, wrapped in moonlight and dreams, while the past folded itself away like an old song—soft, distant, half-remembered.

And the future... the future waited, trembling on the edge of time, still unwritten, still listening.

For those who leap with heart laid bare,
The wind may catch them unaware.
Yet stars must fall before they rise,
To blaze anew in midnight skies.

38 The Song Beyond Fire

The war was over.

The stars—long shrouded in smoke and sorrow—shone again over the plains of Emerland.

The silence that followed was vast, like the breath of the world itself returning after centuries of storm.

Diamond sat by the high window of the Emerald Tower, quill in hand, ink faintly smudged across her fingers.

The wind slipped through the broken arches, carrying the scent of rain, charred stone, and the first breath of spring.

Before her lay a single sheet of parchment.

Not a command, not a prophecy—

but a song.

One she had carried through fire and forest, through battle and birthright.

And now, at last, she gave it voice.

The Song Beyond Fire
(by Diamond)

When I first beheld your light,
I could scarcely believe—
You were the dream the stars had whispered,
The one fate had woven for me.
The magic in your eyes,
It saw through shadow and flame.
From the day you looked at me,
Nothing in Emerland was the same.

From the day you looked at me,
My heart forgot to breathe.
You are the song the heavens wrote,
The soul the stars conceived.

Your voice, like rivers under moon,
Moves through my every vein.
Your smile, a spell of silver fire,
That burns away my pain.
Even your wrath is holy,
A storm I long to see.
For the warmth of you can set ablaze,
All that's left of me.

From the day you looked at me,
My heart forgot to breathe.
You are the dream the dawn foretold,
The light I still believe.

It feels like morning, seeing you—
Though the night may never fade.
With every breath, I call your name,
Through darkness unafraid.

Through tide and flame and prophecy,
Through loss and memory,
I'm grateful to have found my truth—
In the way you looked at me.
From the day you looked at me,

My heart forgot to breathe.
You are the dream the stars foretold,
The love that set me free.

When the final line fell silent, Diamond laid her quill aside.

For the first time since fate had named her Starborn, she smiled—not as ruler nor redeemer, but as one who had fulfilled what the heavens had once written in light.

The stars outside shimmered brighter, as if echoing her song.

It was no mere love—

it was remembrance.

Of all who had fallen, of all who had risen, and of the light that endures beyond war and shadow.

Below, in the garden of new bloom, Amethyst paused as the wind carried the tune past him.

He lifted his gaze toward the tower, understanding.

It was not meant for him alone.

It was for Emerland.

For every soul that had dared to dream of dawn.

And so, under a sky reborn, the song of the Starborn Queen
drifted into eternity—
    a hymn to light after darkness,
    to love after loss,
    to life after fire.